SLEEPING WITH A KILLER

KATHY WINSLOWER

DEDICATION

To all those who have loved and been betrayed.

CONTENTS

Prologue: A Night to Remember 11

Chapter 1: The Revelation 23

Chapter 2: A Task Force Assembles 35

Chapter 3: The Hunt Begins 51

Chapter 4: Tensions in Florence 68

Chapter 5: The First Close Call 86

Chapter 6: A Web of Deception 100

Chapter 7: A Trap in Tuscany 113

Chapter 8: Flashbacks and Doubts 124

Chapter 9: The Roman Marketplace 135

Chapter 10: Fractures and Revelations 150

Chapter 11: Face-to-Face 165

Chapter 12: The Extradition Attempt 180

Chapter 13: The Trial Begins 196

Chapter 14: A Jury Divided 213

Chapter 15: Marco's Offer 221

Chapter 16: The Final Showdown 237

Chapter 17: Bella's Breaking Point 253

Chapter 18: Public Sentiment Shifts 265

Chapter 19: A World Turned Upside Down 275

Chapter 20: The Seduction of Darkness 284

Chapter 21: A New Beginning 297

Chapter 22: The First Mission 307

Chapter 23: The Bond Deepens 324

Chapter 24: The Target in Berlin 333

Chapter 25: A New Identity 342

Chapter 26: The Monaco Job 354

Chapter 27: Cracks in the Foundation 366

Chapter 28: The Ultimate Target 378

Chapter 29: Doubts and Decisions 391

Chapter 30: Into the Shadows 403

Epilogue: The Shadowed Path 417

ABOUT THE AUTHOR 422

PROLOGUE: A NIGHT TO REMEMBER

The ballroom shimmered like a dream spun from gold and crystal. Chandeliers dangled from the vaulted ceiling, their light cascading down in waves of soft brilliance. Gilded sconces cast delicate shadows along the marbled walls, each intricately carved panel telling a story of wealth and decadence. The air smelled of extravagance: a heady cocktail of expensive perfume, polished wood, and chilled champagne that seemed to cling to the skin. Isabella "Bella" Rossi adjusted the strap of her midnight-blue gown, the sequins brushing against her fingertips like tiny shards of glass—beautiful but sharp, much like herself. The gown had been a gift from Marco, who had insisted on dressing her "properly" for the occasion.

"You'll stand out, amore mio," he'd said with a smirk, his dimple flashing. She'd protested but ultimately gave in. Tonight was supposed to be her night off, after all—a rare and precious thing for an FBI cybercrime agent.

Yet, as Bella glanced around, her heels too high and her police instincts too sharp, she couldn't shake the unease thrumming under her skin.

Her boyfriend, Marco DeLuca, seemed to embody the room's opulence. Tall and effortlessly charismatic, he floated through the crowd with the ease of a man born to navigate power. His tailored suit hugged him perfectly, the fabric whispering against his movements like an intimate secret. His Italian accent softened as he introduced her to tech titans and socialites who looked at her like she was some intriguing anomaly.

"This is Isabella," he would say, letting her name roll off his tongue like a lover's secret. "My brilliant and beautiful girlfriend."

Bella's polite smile never faltered, though her gaze was anything but passive. She cataloged faces, noted the subtle shifts in body language, the micro-expressions people didn't realize they gave away. It was second nature to her—a habit honed through years of sifting through digital footprints and following trails only she could see. It was the part of her job she loved: uncovering secrets, making connections no one else could. Even when she'd been burned out by endless hours staring at screens, Bella had never doubted her calling.

When she'd first met Marco, she'd hesitated to tell

him what she did. Most men didn't appreciate dating someone who could crack into their phone—legally, of course. But Marco had been different. On their first date, mini golfing of all things, he'd surprised her. Watching her line up a shot, he'd leaned close and murmured, "I'm guessing you're not just another tech nerd. Your eyes…they're always scanning. Like you're reading the world in ones and zeros."

He'd been right, and she'd told him the truth that same evening. To her shock, he hadn't run. Instead, he'd grinned and said, "Remind me never to lie to you."

Tonight, though, Marco wasn't himself. Usually so self-assured, he seemed jittery. His hand hovered over his watch as if it were a lifeline, and his dark eyes scanned the room far too often.

"Everything okay?" Bella asked when he leaned in close, his cologne brushing her senses like a stolen kiss.

"Of course, cara. Just business," he replied with a smile, but it didn't reach his eyes.

Bella sipped her sparkling water, her senses attuned to the undercurrents of her boyfriend. Something felt… off.

He had been edgy all evening, a stark contrast to his usual suave demeanor. Checking his watch. Scanning the crowd. Laughing a beat too late at a joke from one of his equally polished associates.

She told herself it was nothing. Maybe he was nervous about the ring she suspected was burning a hole in his pocket. He'd been secretive the past few days, dodging her questions with teasing evasions and the kind of smiles that melted her resolve. She loved him, even when he was infuriating. So, when he finally asked, what would she say?

"Are you alright, my love?" she'd asked earlier, placing a hand on his arm. His smile had come quickly, but his eyes betrayed him.

"Perfect," he'd said, kissing her forehead. "Tonight is… important. For us."

Her heart had swelled, hope blooming in her chest. He was going to propose. It explained his secretive phone calls, the hushed conversations she'd overheard in Italian, too rapid for her limited fluency. Bella had felt a rush of certainty then: when the moment came, her answer would be yes.

Their table was a microcosm of the evening's excess. Fine china gleamed under the soft glow of candlelight, while crystal glasses reflected a kaleidoscope of colors from the ballroom's dazzling decor. The food was a symphony of indulgence: foie gras garnished with edible gold, seared scallops nestled on beds of truffle risotto, and desserts that looked more like works of art than food. The guests at their table—a mix of venture capitalists and politicians—spoke in low, measured tones about things Bella had no interest in. But she listened anyway, her sharp mind parsing their words for anything unusual.

Beside her, Marco engaged in an animated conversation with a tech mogul about the future of Advanced-System. His laughter was easy, his charm magnetic, but Bella couldn't shake the feeling that his attention was split—like he was waiting for something. Or someone.

As the night wore on, the unease in her chest grew. The laughter and clinking glasses seemed too loud, the air too thick with perfume and champagne. Even the chandeliers, with their delicate crystal drops, seemed to glimmer with a kind of ominous intensity. Bella's hand found Marco's under the table, squeezing it gently.

"Hey," she murmured, her voice low and steady. "You'd tell me if something was wrong, right?"

His fingers tightened around hers. "Always," he said, his voice soft but firm. Yet, the look in his eyes told a different story. And for the first time that evening, Bella wondered if her instincts weren't just overreacting.

Because something was wrong.

She just didn't know what.

Her fingers brushed over the sequins of her gown, tiny shards of elegance and discomfort, as Marco leaned in, his hand resting on her thigh. The heat of his touch sent a flicker of reassurance through her.

"Amore." His voice was low, intimate, his Italian accent curling around the words like a lover's caress.

Bella nodded, though unease coiled tight in her chest. "Yes, my love."

Marco's dark eyes searched hers, his thumb brushing a circle over her knee. "I'll be right back," he murmured before kissing her deeply, a promise in the press of his lips. He stood, his broad shoulders cutting a confident path through the crowd.

"Don't go far," she called softly, her gaze trailing after him until he vanished into the throng.

Across the room, the applause swelled as Marcus Kane, Dusker Corporation's celebrated CEO, ascended the stage. He was an imposing figure, his presence magnetic. Kane's angular face, framed by meticulously groomed silver-threaded hair, exuded a predatory charm. His tailored charcoal suit, sharp enough to draw blood, reflected his reputation as a man who thrived on power and precision.

Since his appointment as CEO, Dusker Corporation had raked in billions, dominating the global tech market with innovations that blurred the line between surveillance and convenience. Tonight, the audience hung on his every word as he spoke, his baritone voice weaving a narrative of progress and safety.

"Ladies and gentlemen," Kane began, his tone smooth and commanding, "in a world where threats evolve faster than we can anticipate, security must be absolute. Dusker Corporation is proud to lead the charge, creating technologies that protect not just nations but the individuals within them."

Bella's lips tightened as she half-listened, her focus snagging on snippets of conversation around her. At her table, a woman in an emerald gown leaned toward her companion, her voice a sharp whisper.

"He talks about protection, but all he's protecting is his offshore accounts," she said, her diamond necklace catching the light as she shook her head.

The man beside her snorted. "Kane's a snake. Word is he's blackmailed half his competitors into folding. The other half? They're just waiting for him to slip up."

Bella's eyes flicked back to Kane, who now gestured expansively, his words polished to perfection.

"Our newest Advanced-System model will redefine global security," he declared, his gaze sweeping the room as though daring anyone to challenge him. "Imagine a system that anticipates danger before it strikes. A world where safety isn't just a possibility but a guarantee."

The applause was deafening, yet Bella felt a chill snake down her spine. The words were designed to inspire confidence, but to her, they rang with the ominous promise of control. Surveillance. Manipulation. Beneath the veneer of progress, she sensed something far darker. Marco hadn't returned.

Kane's speech was a symphony of ambition and bravado. Words like "revolutionary" and "unprecedented" peppered his address, his tone laced with the certainty of a man who knew the world was watching. Yet, beneath the applause, Bella caught murmurs—low, cautious, edged with doubt.

"Spying programs."

"Data manipulation."

"Corporate espionage dressed as progress."

The hair on Bella's neck prickled. She turned, scanning the room. Too many eyes darting nervously, too many conversations cut short when her gaze passed over them.

As the applause subsided, Kane's gaze met hers briefly, and Bella's breath hitched. There was a flicker of recognition—a moment too brief to be certain but unsettling nonetheless. She glanced away, her pulse quickening.

The murmurs at her table grew louder, fueled by hushed outrage and the clink of champagne glasses.

"He's got everyone eating out of his hand," the woman in emerald muttered. "But the whispers about those missing engineers…"

"Careful," her companion warned, his tone dropping. "You know what happened to the last guy who started digging. Disappeared without a trace."

Bella's instincts sharpened, the fragments of conversation fueling her growing suspicion. She scanned the room, her senses on high alert. Whatever business Marco was involved in, it was clear Kane's influence ran deep—and dangerously close to home.

She tightened her grip on her glass, the chill of the crystal grounding her for a moment. For the first time that evening, her unease crystallized into something sharper.

Something was definitely wrong.

And she wasn't sure she was ready to find out what.

Then, the lights flickered.

The ballroom's opulence dimmed for a fraction of a second, a breath held by the universe, before a masked figure stepped from the shadows at the edge of the stage.

Then came the gunshot.

It was muffled but unmistakable, but its aftermath roared through the room.

One second, Kane was at the podium, his hands gesturing emphatically. The next, there was blood blooming across the pristine white of his dress shirt.

Marcus Kane's body jerked violently before crumpling to the polished floor, his microphone hitting the ground with a hollow thud.

For a moment, there was nothing but silence—a fragile, stunned quiet that shattered under the weight of collective screams. Chaos erupted like a tidal wave. Guests in their glittering finery stumbled and pushed toward the exits, their desperation turning elegant heels into weapons and tuxedos into shields.

Bella's hand instinctively went to her thigh, where her service weapon was holstered beneath the flowing fabric of her gown. The smooth grip of the gun grounded her, even as her pulse hammered in her ears. She scanned the room, her sharp gaze slicing through the pandemonium. She searched for the shooter, but her line of sight was blocked by panicked bodies rushing for the exits.

"Bella!"

A hand grabbed her arm, the grip unyielding and urgent.

"We have to go!" a voice hissed in her ear, close enough to send a shiver down her spine. She turned sharply, her weapon half-drawn, to find Marco. His face was pale, his usual confidence replaced by a raw, almost feral urgency.

"No! I need to..."

"Come with me," he hissed, yanking her toward a side door.

"Wait!" She tried to dig her heels in, her eyes darting back to the stage. "Someone's been shot. I need to..."

"There's no time!" he snapped, his dark eyes blazing with an intensity that rooted her momentarily in place. His fingers dug into her arm, pulling her toward the nearest exit. Around them, the crowd surged like a living beast, bodies pressing and shoving in blind panic.

Bella resisted, her instincts warring with the trust she'd carefully placed in him. "Trust me, Bella!" he shouted, his voice cutting through the cacophony like a lifeline.

Her breath hitched, and for a fleeting moment, she let him guide her. But the nagging voice of her instincts grew louder, clawing at her resolve. Something was wrong. She wrenched herself free, spinning to face him—but Marco was already gone, swallowed by the chaos.

Bella stood frozen for a heartbeat, her mind a storm of suspicion and dread. The masked shooter, the silenced gunshot, Marco's pale face and inexplicable urgency—the pieces didn't fit, and yet they painted a chilling picture.

She tightened her grip on her weapon and forced

herself to move. The opulence of the ballroom was now a battlefield, littered with abandoned shoes, overturned chairs, and the echoes of fear. She pushed against the tide of panicked bodies, her eyes locked on the stage where Marcus Kane's lifeless form lay crumpled under the harsh spotlight.

Bella's heart pounded as she climbed the steps, her heels clicking against the polished wood. The sharp tang of blood hit her nose, mingling with the acrid scent of fear and adrenaline. Kneeling beside Kane, she scanned his body, her training overriding the shock. A single bullet wound marred his chest, precise and fatal. Whoever the shooter was, they'd known exactly what they were doing.

She glanced up, her eyes darting to the shadows beyond the stage. The shooter could still be here. Her grip on her gun tightened as she rose, every muscle coiled like a spring.

"Bella!" a voice called from behind her. She turned sharply to see Agent Carter, her FBI colleague, pushing through the crowd. His face was a mask of grim determination.

"What the hell happened?" he demanded, his gaze flicking to Kane's body.

"Shooter's still at large," she replied tersely. "And Marco… he was here, Carter. He pulled me out, but then he…" Her voice faltered, the weight of her realization pressing down on her chest.

Carter's expression darkened. "We'll find him. Right now, we need to lock this place down."

Bella nodded, swallowing hard as she stepped off the stage. The grandeur of the ballroom now felt suffocating, its gilded edges mocking the stark reality of what had just happened. With every step, her unease grew, the nagging voice in her head echoing louder.

Something was very, very wrong.

CHAPTER 1: THE REVELATION

The apartment was too quiet. The kind of quiet that pressed against Bella's ears like cotton, suffocating her thoughts and magnifying every beat of her heart. She stood in the doorway of the living room, her fingers digging into the edge of the doorframe as if it could anchor her to something solid. Something real.

The living room had once felt like their sanctuary. Now, it felt foreign, hollow—like a stage set, where the actors had vanished, leaving behind only remnants of their lives. Marco's shoes were neatly lined by the front door, the polished leather gleaming under the faint morning light that slanted through the blinds. His favorite jacket, the one she always teased him about because it looked far too expensive for the gritty New York streets, hung perfectly on the coat rack.

Everything was in place, every object where it should be—except for him.

Bella stood frozen, still in the same gown she had worn to the gala the night before. The fine fabric clung to her body, wrinkled and disheveled from hours of sleepless turmoil. The once-glamorous evening dress now felt like a shroud, a reminder of how everything she thought she knew had unraveled in the span of a single gunshot. The cool silk brushed against her skin as she shifted her weight, her limbs heavy with exhaustion.

She forced herself to step forward, her heels clicking softly against the hardwood floor as she moved toward the couch. The throw blanket they'd fought about—Marco had hated the color, thought it looked too childish—lay in a rumpled heap. She had loved it. Now, it was just another discarded thing, a casualty of a life that had gone from predictable to unrecognizable in the blink of an eye.

Her knees buckled as she reached the cushions, and she sank into them, her body folding in on itself. The weight of the last twelve hours pressed down on her chest, suffocating her, and for the first time in a long while, she let herself crumble. She squeezed her eyes shut, but the images wouldn't fade.

The memory played in an endless loop: the flickering lights, the sharp crack of the silenced gun, the screams and the shuffling feet as chaos tore through the ballroom. And then there was Marco. His face pale, his grip on her arm bruising, his voice cracking as he insisted, "We have to go. Now."

The scent of his cologne still clung to her, faint and bitter, like a ghost she couldn't shake. His breath had been too quick, too shallow. His eyes too hollow when they locked onto hers. Trust me, Bella, please, he had pleaded, urgency threading through his words. But the moment they were out of the ballroom, something shifted. He had pushed her forward, urging her toward the exit. She hadn't been able to shake the feeling that something was wrong, but she couldn't pinpoint what.

Bella's palms pressed into her temples, her fingers digging into her scalp as she tried to will the images from her mind. But the more she fought, the sharper they became—Marco's hand on her arm, too firm, too insistent. His eyes darting around the room like a man caught between two worlds. His breath catching in his chest when the gunshot rang out.

And then, there were the small moments from the gala that now seemed so much bigger in the context of what had happened. Marco had been distracted, his smile tight when he introduced her to some of the more powerful figures in the room. He hadn't been himself—hadn't been her Marco.

He was nervous. But why?

Bella's mind stalled, grappling with a truth she wasn't ready to face. The little things she had brushed off, the pieces of a puzzle that hadn't seemed to fit, now loomed large in her mind. She thought back to the way he'd checked his watch repeatedly, how his gaze had flitted nervously over the crowd, never resting. She remembered how he'd excused himself just after the speech, his voice too strained when he said he needed to go to the restroom. And then there was the way he'd been in a hurry when they left, as though he couldn't wait to get out of the gala, to leave everything behind.

But she had dismissed it all. Nerves. Maybe even a proposal. The thought had crossed her mind—a romantic gesture she had dreamt about for so long. She had convinced herself that whatever unease she felt was just her own anxiety, her own fears about the future. But now, the pieces were rearranging themselves, clicking into place with an icy clarity she couldn't ignore.

Her stomach churned. What the hell had Marco been involved in?

The weight of it all threatened to crush her, but Bella didn't let herself linger in the soft, dangerous space of doubt for long. She had been a cop too long to let emotional turmoil cloud her judgment. She couldn't afford to fall apart—not now, not when there were so many unanswered questions.

But how was she supposed to face this? How was she supposed to reconcile the man she thought she loved with the man who had left her last night without so much as a glance back? The more she thought about Marco, the more she realized she was no longer sure who he was. And that truth? It hurt.

Forcing herself to stand, Bella wiped the tears she hadn't realized had slipped down her cheeks. She couldn't—wouldn't—break down like this. She had a job to do.

And Marco, wherever he was, was the key to it all.

The FBI had scoured the wreckage of the gala's shattered opulence with clinical precision. Like surgeons with their scalpels, they'd dusted every surface for fingerprints, analyzed every shard of glass, and tracked down every potential lead in the cascade of interviews that followed. Yet Marco remained a ghost, slipping through their grasp like smoke, vanishing without a trace. His absence hung in the air, suffocating her, louder than any scream. Bella's mind couldn't reconcile the two images of him—the man she had known and the man who had just disappeared into the night.

And the place she once called home now felt more like a crime scene, violated and cold. Under orders, she'd returned here, only to be greeted by the kind of silence that made her skin crawl. It was the silence that follows a storm, when the damage is done, and everything that was once familiar becomes alien. She'd paced the apartment for hours, the rhythmic sound of her footsteps the only thing that filled the empty space, her eyes darting to every corner, expecting him to step out from the shadows with a sheepish grin and some ridiculous excuse. But he didn't.

Bella's mind went into autopilot as she used the one skill that had kept her grounded through all the chaos: disassociation. She peeled herself from the frayed edges of reality, putting on the mask of control that had always gotten her through the hardest days.

Her training had taught her to function, to separate emotion from action. She made her way to the bathroom, stripping off the gown Marco had insisted she wear—wrinkled and crumpled now, a casualty of the night's events. She turned the faucet on, the cold water splashing against her skin, washing away the remnants of what was once a night full of promise.

The dress hit the floor in a heap, and she stood before the mirror, her hands braced on the counter, trying to steady herself. Her reflection was a stranger now—bloodshot eyes, dark circles beneath them, and the weight of something unspoken pressing down on her. She splashed water on her face, the cold bite of it sharpening her senses. But even as the water cleared the haze in her mind, there was no escaping the suffocating weight of the question: Where the hell was Marco?

She dried her face with a towel, staring into the mirror, her thoughts swirling like the water that had just drained from the sink.

The faintest indent on the bed—his pillow, slightly sunken where his head had once rested— pulled her gaze back to the bedroom. She crossed the room slowly, as if afraid the movement would shatter the fragile shell she'd built around herself. She sat on the edge of the bed, her fingers brushing the pillow where he'd lain, as if she could read the truth there, as if it could tell her what had happened. But it remained silent, its soft fabric offering no answers.

The events of the night before played on a loop in

her mind, each detail, each fleeting moment magnified in the harsh light of the aftermath. Marco's hand had rested on her thigh beneath the table, a touch meant to reassure, to ground her. She had thought it sweet, even romantic—a subtle promise. But now, in the brutal clarity of hindsight, that touch felt like it had been calculated. His whispered words, his constant presence at her side—she'd believed he was about to propose, to finally make all the future they had talked about real. The way his eyes lingered on hers, the way he'd drawn her close on the dance floor, it had all felt like a prelude to the forever she had allowed herself to imagine.

But instead of a ring, there had been a gunshot. Instead of promises, there had been nothing but silence. Marco had vanished, leaving her with nothing but questions and the hollow ache in her chest that refused to dissipate.

Her phone buzzed, snapping her from the fog of memories, the harsh vibration against the glass coffee table echoing in the stillness of the room. She picked it up without hesitation, knowing exactly who it was before she even looked.

"Rossi, we need you in the briefing room," Lawson's voice barked through the phone, gravelly and urgent. "Now."

Bella didn't respond. She didn't need to. She hung up and grabbed her jacket, the fabric cold against her skin as she slid it on. She stepped into the hallway, her senses alert, but the lingering scent of Marco's cologne made her pause. It hung in the air like a ghost, a reminder of everything that had slipped through her fingers.

Her world was unraveling, thread by thread, and the more she pulled, the more she realized that every single thread would eventually lead back to Marco.

With a deep breath, Bella tried to steady herself. She couldn't lose focus—not now. Not when she knew she was on the edge of uncovering something far darker than she could ever have imagined.

As she reached for the door to leave, she glanced at her phone, the screen lighting up with dozens of missed calls and text messages from Marco. The sight of it made her stomach twist painfully. She had called him over and over again, the calls going straight to voicemail each time. But now, for the first time, when she dialed his number, it didn't go to voicemail.

The call failed.

Instead, a cold, mechanical voice on the other end told her that the number had been disabled.

A chill ran down Bella's spine. Marco had erased himself, severed every connection between them as if he had never existed.

The weight of that realization hit her with all the force of a wrecking ball.

Minutes later, Bella found herself facing the cold, sterile walls of FBI headquarters, a far cry from the glittering nightmare of the gala just twenty-four hours ago. The building loomed like an ominous sentinel, its steel and glass exterior mirroring the dull gray of the overcast sky, as if the world itself had succumbed to the weight of the tragedy.

∞

Inside, the briefing room was suffocating—tightly packed, lit by the harsh, unforgiving glow of fluorescent lights. The air reeked of stale coffee, sweat, and the faint tang of disinfectant, mixing in a nauseating cocktail that made Bella's stomach churn. Agents filled the seats, their low murmurs a backdrop to the mounting tension, their faces grim as they tried to swallow the bitterness of the situation. But it was Lawson who commanded the room. He strode to the front with military precision, his presence swallowing the space, his hard gaze silencing the room in an instant.

"Let's get to it," Lawson said, his voice clipped, his words cutting through the suffocating air like a scalpel. His tone was a perfect match for the oppressive atmosphere, sharp and unyielding.

Bella slid into a chair near the back, her hands clenched tight in her lap as her stomach twisted into knots. She couldn't escape the feeling that everything—every small decision, every gesture, every word from the night before—was now under a microscope. The fluorescent lights above hummed faintly, casting harsh shadows that made her feel like she was being watched, even as she tried to focus on the task at hand.

Her breath caught in her chest when Lawson tapped a button on the remote. The room darkened, the hum of the projector filling the air like a prelude to disaster. The grainy surveillance footage flickered to life on the screen, illuminating the collective unease that had settled over the room. Bella felt the weight of every agent's gaze, their silent judgment pressing down on her.

"This," Lawson said, his voice harder than steel, "is Marco DeLuca. Now officially the prime suspect in the assassination of CEO Marcus Kane."

The words hit Bella like a slap to the face. Her heart slammed painfully against her ribs, and the world seemed to tilt as the footage played out, each frame an unwelcome revelation. She hadn't braced herself for this. Not for this.

A masked figure entered the frame. The camera shook, the action chaotic, but then there was the unmistakable flash of the gun. Bella felt the air leave her lungs. The eruption of chaos was palpable—screaming guests, security guards scrambling, glass shattering—but through it all, there was Marco.

His face was unmasked. Calm. Composed.

The room held its breath as he moved with deadly precision, his every step deliberate, measured, like a man executing a plan he'd rehearsed a hundred times. There was no panic in his movements, no signs of fear or confusion. He moved through the chaos as if it was nothing more than a scripted performance, a role he had long been prepared to play.

The camera caught his faint, disarming smile—one that Bella had once believed to be full of warmth, affection, even love. But now, in the stark light of truth, it felt like a weapon, a mask that had shattered in front of her eyes. He had been playing her.

She could hardly breathe as the footage froze on his face, that smile frozen in time. She wanted to scream, to hurl the truth back at the screen, but all she could do was sit there, paralyzed by the realization. Marco wasn't running for safety. Marco wasn't even running for cover.

Marco was running away.

Her breath hitched, and her mind reeled, scrambling for something—anything—to hold on to. But there was nothing.

She had thought she knew him. She had believed in the promises he had made to her, the whispered words in the dark, the way he had looked at her with such certainty, as if nothing could tear them apart.

And then, like a drowning woman gasping for air, Bella's thoughts drifted back to that day—the day Marco had first told her he loved her.

It was the kind of moment that belonged in a fairytale, one that had felt so real at the time, but now seemed like a cruel joke.

They had been sitting on the balcony of her apartment, the city lights twinkling below them like a thousand distant stars. Marco had looked at her then, his eyes soft, full of unspoken promises. The scent of his cologne—warm, rich, familiar—had mingled with the crisp night air. He had reached for her hand, his fingers brushing hers with that tenderness she had believed was reserved only for her.

"I'll always be here for you, Bella," he had whispered, his voice thick with emotion. "No matter what happens, I'll always protect you. I love you."

At the time, she had believed him. She had believed that, no matter the obstacles they faced, Marco would stand by her, would always choose her. But now… now, the weight of his words felt like a lie. A betrayal.

The footage on the screen flickered, drawing Bella's attention back to the present. Lawson's voice cut through the tension, thick with professional resolve.

"So, we've got a name and a face," Lawson continued, his gaze sharp. "And we're not letting him slip away."

But Bella's mind was elsewhere, stuck in that moment on the balcony, when Marco had promised her forever.

It felt like a dream now. One that had unraveled before her eyes.

Her chest tightened. She had known love. She had known betrayal. But she had never known this.

She didn't know who Marco was anymore.

And that realization… it was colder than any of the bodies they'd found. It was a wound that wouldn't heal.

She had to move past it. She had no choice.

But how do you hunt someone you love?

CHAPTER 2: A TASK FORCE ASSEMBLES

The hum of the FBI briefing room seemed to press against Bella's skull, a soundless buzz that matched the pounding of her heart. Every agent, every set of eyes seemed to be watching her, dissecting her every breath, every flinch.

Lawson's voice cut through the static in her mind, clear and commanding, as though pulling her back to reality. "Agent Rossi."

She snapped her gaze to him, her pulse roaring in her ears, drowning out everything else in the room. Her hands clenched into fists on the edge of the table, her knuckles white against the smooth wood. She didn't know how to breathe, how to think, with the crushing weight of the moment pressing down on her.

"Anything you want to share about your boyfriend?" The words were like a sharp blade, slicing through the tension in the air with brutal precision. His gaze, cold and unflinching, pinned her to her seat, stripping away any pretense of calm.

The word "boyfriend" hung in the air, distorting it, warping it into something dark, something she hadn't been prepared for. Bella's breath hitched, her throat constricting as her mind scrambled for words.

"I…" She faltered, her voice barely more than a whisper, barely audible. The weight of every pair of eyes in the room crushed her chest like a vice. "I don't know what to say. I didn't know he…"

"Didn't know he was capable of this?" Lawson interrupted, his tone sharp, but not unkind. His gaze softened just enough to acknowledge the war waging behind her eyes, the betrayal that gnawed at her insides. But there was no softness in his words, no room for empathy in the weight of what he was asking.

"No one's saying you did," Lawson continued, his voice low but steady. "But you've been closest to him. That makes you valuable to this investigation. But that also makes you a liability."

Bella's jaw tightened, a bitter taste flooding her mouth as the words settled into her bones. The room was closing in on her. The walls, once neutral, now felt like an interrogation chamber. It wasn't a briefing anymore—it was a trial. She couldn't let them see her crack. Not here. Not now.

Her pulse quickened, and a fire sparked in her chest, rising up through the fear and the confusion. The words spilled out before she could stop them, sharp and defiant.

"Is this a briefing room, or an interrogation, Lawson?" she demanded, her voice steady despite the chaos in her mind. She leaned forward, her eyes narrowing. "Because if you want to question me, I can take a polygraph right now. I've got nothing to hide."

For a moment, Lawson said nothing. His gaze locked with hers, calculating, probing. The air thickened, charged with the silent electricity of unspoken tension. Then, he gave a slight nod, and a chill ran down Bella's spine.

"Clear the room," Lawson ordered, his voice low, cold as ice.

A ripple of movement swept through the agents, their faces unreadable as they filed out, leaving Bella alone with Lawson and the quiet hum of the fluorescent lights. The door clicked shut behind them with a finality that seemed to echo in the pit of her stomach.

Moments later, the door behind her creaked open again, and Bella turned just as the polygraph examiner stepped into the room, his expression professional but detached. He set up the machine with mechanical precision, the soft whirring of the machine filling the room, making the tension in the air feel even heavier, more suffocating.

"Time to take the test," Lawson said, his voice gruff, a command disguised as a suggestion. "It's not going to be easy, Rossi. But I need to know you're with us. And you need to know you're not above suspicion."

Bella didn't flinch. Her resolve was steel, and her voice was a quiet promise as she stood to face the examiner. But Bella saw the flicker of something—something unreadable—in his eyes.

"I'm ready," she said.

The machine hummed to life, and for the first time since this nightmare began, Bella knew—truly knew—that there would be no going back.

Lawson turned his gaze back to Bella, his expression unreadable, but the weight of his expectations was palpable. "Well," he said, his voice cold and professional. "Let's see how well your answers hold up."

Bella's throat was tight, but she forced herself to remain calm. She settled into the chair opposite the polygraph machine, her back straight, her eyes never leaving Lawson's. She was all too aware of how every movement, every breath, every flicker of her gaze would be scrutinized. But she couldn't afford to show weakness—not now. Not when everything she had believed in had been turned upside down.

"Start with something simple," Lawson said, his voice steady but heavy with the weight of his responsibility. "Is Marco DeLuca your boyfriend?"

"Yes," Bella answered without hesitation. The truth stung, even as the word left her lips. It had always been so simple, so clear. Now it felt like a betrayal.

The polygraph machine clicked, whirred, the needle flickering as it measured the smallest shifts in her pulse, her breathing. Bella forced herself to stay still, even as the air grew heavier, more suffocating. The room seemed to close in around her, the walls pressing in on her chest as she braced for the next question.

"Did you know he was involved in the murder of Marcus Kane?"

Bella's heart stopped in her chest, and for the briefest moment, she forgot how to breathe. The question was a hammer, a sharp blow to everything she thought she knew. She could feel her pulse racing, the blood rushing to her head as she fought to keep her composure.

"No," she said, her voice firm, though her hands trembled slightly as she gripped the edges of the chair. The polygraph machine hummed, and the needle quivered.

Lawson didn't flinch. He didn't look away. He just stared at her, his gaze hard as granite.

"You sure about that?" he pressed, his voice laced with something darker now—doubt, suspicion. "You don't think you might have missed something? Something... small? Something important?"

Bella felt a bitter laugh rise in her throat, but she swallowed it down. She could feel the walls closing in again, her throat tightening, the weight of the question almost suffocating.

"I know him," she said, her voice low but unwavering. "I know the man I loved. And this... this..." She couldn't finish the sentence. The words wouldn't come, not when the reality of what he'd done was still unraveling in her mind. "I don't know the man in that footage. But I swear to you, I didn't know about any of this."

A beat of silence stretched between them, thick and heavy, before Lawson nodded once, curtly. The room felt colder. His gaze never wavered, though there was a flicker of something—perhaps regret—deep in his eyes. But he wasn't about to give her any quarter.

"Good," Lawson said finally, his voice steady, but there was a hardness beneath the calm. "But remember this, Rossi: you're playing a dangerous game. Marco DeLuca is no ordinary man. You think you know him, but if you slip up—if you let your emotions get in the way—you're out. Got it?"

Bella's jaw tightened, her resolve hardening like steel. "I'm in," she said, her voice fierce, unwavering. "And I won't back down."

Lawson studied her for a moment longer, before he finally nodded. "Fine. You're on the task force. But one misstep, and you're gone. You understand?"

"I understand," Bella said, her voice steady, her hands no longer trembling.

Her world had been shattered, and the man she had loved was now a stranger. But she wasn't going to stop. Not until she found the truth.

And when she did, Marco would pay.

Even after Lawson and the Polygraph examiner had left, Bella lingered at the table, staring at the freeze-frame of Marco's face on the screen. Bella sat in the stark, fluorescent-lit briefing room, the hum of the overhead lights echoing in the silence that enveloped her. Her fingers hovered over the keyboard, but she couldn't bring herself to press the keys. The freeze-frame of Marco's face filled the screen in front of her—cold, impassive, the eyes that once seemed full of promise now a chilling reminder of the storm she found herself in. A storm she hadn't asked for, yet here she was, trapped in its fury.

"Hey." Sam Grayson's voice cut through the fog of her thoughts, gentle yet knowing. He was leaning against the doorframe, arms crossed, eyes scanning her face with that all-too-familiar concern. The same concern that had softened when he'd watched her struggle through the pain of Marco's absence, of the strange tension that had hung in the air between them.

"Define 'okay,'" Bella replied, her voice a hollow echo of its usual strength. She tried to smile, but it felt brittle, like glass under pressure.

Sam pushed off the door, his boots making a soft scuff on the concrete floor as he crossed to her. His presence—steady, like a rock—was a relief she didn't know she needed. She had worked with him long enough to understand the weight of the job and the burden it placed on the soul, but even Sam's calm couldn't quiet the storm inside her.

"No one would blame you for sitting this one out, you know," Sam said, his voice low, the words measured. He lowered himself into the chair across from her, leaning forward, elbows on his knees, trying to make himself as small as possible. He didn't want to add to her stress, but she knew him too well. He was calculating, always careful with his words.

"Would you?" Bella asked, locking eyes with him. The challenge in her gaze was unmistakable, and Sam faltered for just a moment, his lips pressed into a thin line.

"No," he finally admitted, and his voice softened. "But I'd understand if you did. This is personal, Bella. And personal gets messy."

Her spine straightened, tension rippling through her shoulders like a live wire. "Messy or not, I'm seeing this through," she said, her voice firm, laced with the steel of determination. "Marco owes me answers. And if he's guilty..." Her throat tightened, and she swallowed hard, the words lodging like broken glass in her chest. "If he's guilty, then I'll put the cuffs on him myself."

A flicker of something—concern, maybe fear—crossed Sam's features. His jaw tightened as if to hold back the words that threatened to spill out. "I always thought there was something off about him," he said, his voice tight with restraint, each word a confession of suspicion long buried.

Bella's eyes narrowed, her heart pounding in her chest as a rush of heat flooded her veins. "Don't," she snapped, her tone biting, cutting through the air like a knife. "Don't stand there and act like you knew."

Sam's gaze hardened, but he didn't back down. "I didn't know," he said, his voice a low rumble, controlled but unwavering. "But I had my suspicions. He was too polished, too... calculated. Like he was playing a role."

"Or maybe you just didn't like him because he wasn't you," Bella shot back, the words sharp and jagged as they left her mouth. She regretted them immediately, the weight of the accusation heavier than she could bear.

Sam didn't flinch. His face remained a mask of neutrality, but there was something darker in his eyes— a flicker of hurt, or perhaps something even deeper. "I'm on your side, Bella," he said, his voice softer now, almost pleading. "Always have been. Don't forget that."

A lump formed in her throat, but she refused to let it show. She couldn't afford weakness—not now. Not with everything at stake. "I know," she murmured, the words quieter now, the tension between them palpable. "I'm sorry. I just... I need to figure this out."

Sam stood, his shoulders heavy with the weight of their past, the unspoken history between them lingering like smoke in the air. He squeezed her shoulder—brief, firm, and filled with unspoken understanding—before he turned and walked out of the room, leaving her alone with the cold, hard image of Marco staring back at her from the screen.

Bella's gaze never wavered from his face, the man who had once made her feel invincible now reduced to a series of pixels and suspicion. She leaned forward, elbows on the table, eyes burning into the screen as if willing it to reveal the truth.

Who are you, Marco DeLuca?

The question echoed in her mind, a drumbeat of uncertainty and fear. She had believed in him once—believed in the love they had shared, in the life they had built. But now, with every passing second, the man she thought she knew slipped further into the shadows. And as the truth loomed, she realized with growing horror that the answers she sought might not be the ones she wanted to hear.

Sam's voice, low and measured, sliced through the room like a lifeline. "Come with me, Rossi." His eyes met hers briefly, an unreadable expression crossing his face.

Bella didn't hesitate. She followed Sam as he led her out of the suffocating room and down the narrow hallway, the silence between them thick and heavy. Her heart pounded in her chest, each step feeling like a drumbeat of impending decisions.

They entered a larger room, the cold, sterile air here a welcome contrast to the heat of the conference room. A few agents stood near a table littered with evidence bags, crime scene photos, and notes. But Bella barely registered them. She was too focused on the man who had led her here, Sam's face unreadable, his every movement purposeful.

He didn't speak immediately, but when he finally did, his voice was low, almost conspiratorial. "You're not alone in this, Bella. You don't have to carry this weight by yourself."

Her chest tightened, and for the first time in a long while, she allowed herself to feel the weight of the burden. Marco, the man who had once held her heart, was now the very person she might be tasked with bringing down. The man she loved had become her greatest challenge.

Sam's gaze softened as he continued, his voice a quiet anchor. "I don't care what anyone says. I'm with you. I always have been. Let's get to the truth together."

Bella looked up at him, her heart pounding, but it was no longer from fear. It was the start of something new—a bond forged in the fire of this investigation. The kind of bond that would see them through whatever lay ahead.

"I'm with you too," she said quietly, her voice steady now, the storm inside her beginning to settle. But Bella knew one thing for sure—she was about to uncover a truth that would change everything.

∞

The conference room was stifling, the kind of heat that made the air feel thick and heavy, clinging to her skin like a second layer. Bella Rossi shifted in her seat, the plastic chair creaking beneath her as if it, too, felt the weight of the tension in the room. The hum of the air conditioning was a feeble attempt to cut through the stifling atmosphere, but it only added to the sense of discomfort. The room smelled of burnt coffee, stale takeout boxes, and the sour scent of too many hours spent chasing leads that never seemed to pay off.

She sat at the end of the long table, her back rigid,

jaw clenched so tightly that it ached. She was acutely aware of the way the team's eyes darted to her, some with barely concealed judgment, others with suspicion. The real spectacle in the room wasn't the projected image of Marco DeLuca, the polished facade of the man she had once trusted. No, the spectacle was her—the woman who had once shared his bed, his life, and now, with every passing minute, wondered if she had been living a lie.

Lawson's voice cut through the oppressive silence, his words cold and methodical, as if he were reciting facts rather than revelations. "Marco DeLuca," he began, pointing at the projected photo of Marco. The screen flickered, the image sharp in its clarity—his warm brown eyes, his easy smile, the very face that had once lit up her world now staring back at her like a cruel, taunting stranger. "Born in Naples, Italy. Raised in a family with deep ties to the art world."

Bella felt her stomach twist, the weight of those words crushing her chest. That smile had been hers. She had memorized every detail of it—the way it would soften when he whispered something sweet, the way it would deepen when he teased her in the quiet of their shared moments. Now, that smile was alien, a mask that hid the man she thought she knew.

Lawson continued, his voice unwavering. "DeLuca's family is widely suspected of smuggling valuable artifacts out of Europe. They've dodged charges for decades, thanks to clever laundering schemes and their proximity to legitimate art circles.

No convictions, but plenty of whispers. DeLuca himself has no prior arrests. Clean record. At least, on paper."

The words hit Bella like a punch to the gut. Marco had woven himself into her life so seamlessly that she hadn't questioned the little things—the phone calls, the secrecy, the way he always seemed to be just one step ahead. The image of him, clean-cut and charming, now seemed like a mask—a mask that had concealed a man she couldn't fully understand.

"Convenient, don't you think?" Agent David Park's voice sliced through the air, sharp and dismissive. He leaned back in his chair, arms crossed over his chest, his eyes glinting with a dangerous edge. "He cozies up to an FBI agent, gains intel, and then uses her to cover his tracks. Classic."

The words hit Bella like a slap, the sting of them igniting a flash of anger. She shot him a glare, her voice low and controlled, but the heat of her anger bled through. "You don't know what you're talking about."

"Oh, don't I?" Park smirked, leaning forward, his gaze turning venomous. "You can't deny you're compromised, Rossi. Your apartment's practically a honeymoon suite for a suspect."

The room seemed to close in around her as the eyes of the team turned toward her, the weight of their scrutiny unbearable. She felt the heat rise in her cheeks, but she refused to let it show. She could handle this. She had to.

"That's enough," Lawson snapped, his voice

cutting through the tension like a blade. The murmurs in the room died instantly, the air thick with the unspoken command to stay in line. He turned to Bella, his tone softer now but no less firm. "Rossi, we need to stay focused. What can you tell us about his recent behavior?"

Bella inhaled sharply, forcing herself to calm the churning turmoil inside. She couldn't afford to break—not now, not when the walls were closing in. She had been trained for this moment, for the pressure, for the chaos. But it didn't make it any easier. "He… he changed in the weeks leading up to the gala," she said, her voice tight with the effort of holding herself together. "Late-night phone calls he brushed off as work. Packages he wouldn't let me open. And he insisted on attending the gala, even though he doesn't have direct ties to Dusker Corporation."

The words tasted bitter in her mouth, each one a reminder of how blind she had been. How had she not seen the signs? How had she let herself believe in a lie?

"And you didn't find that suspicious?" Park pressed, his voice cutting through the air like a blade, eyes narrowing in judgment. His words were as cold as ice, but there was something deeper in them, something darker that made Bella bristle.

"Enough, Park," Lawson barked, his tone sharp and final, shutting him down. The rest of the room remained silent, but the tension between Bella and Park simmered beneath the surface.

Bella kept her gaze fixed ahead, her hands

clenched into fists beneath the table, trying to force her mind to focus, to push past the knot of emotion that threatened to break through. She wasn't going to let them see her crack. She wasn't going to let them see the doubt gnawing at her insides.

But Lawson's voice cut through the air like a judge's gavel.

"Agent Rossi," Lawson called out, his tone no-nonsense. "You're leading the manhunt."

The words hit her like a jolt of electricity, her heart leaping in her chest. She stopped breathing, turning around to face him. Her mouth went dry, her mind suddenly spinning.

"Excuse me?" Bella asked, her voice sharp with disbelief.

"You're the one who knows DeLuca best," Lawson said, his gaze unwavering. "You're the one who can think like him. You're leading this investigation."

Bella stared at him for a beat, but the fire inside her ignited. This was it. This was what she wanted. She wasn't going to let anyone else take control of this hunt—not when it had already taken everything from her.

But not everyone agreed.

The room erupted in protests. Sam's jaw clenched, his lips pressing into a tight line, but he remained silent. Agent Park scoffed under his breath, clearly displeased.

"Are you fucking serious?" Park barked, his voice laced with scorn. "Rossi's too close to this case. She's compromised."

"She's not compromised," Lawson shot back, his voice sharp with authority. "She's the right person for this job."

Bella felt the weight of the room's judgment, the harsh eyes of her colleagues boring into her back, but she stood tall. This wasn't about their doubts. This was about justice. And she wasn't going to let them take this from her.

"I'll find him," she said, her voice low but resolute. "I'll find Marco."

And with that, the path ahead of her was clear—if not the one she wanted, at least the one she would walk.

CHAPTER 3: THE HUNT BEGINS

The meeting had ended in a silence so thick it could suffocate. The room, dimly lit by the harsh overhead fluorescents, was heavy with the aftermath of the damning footage that had played on a loop. Bella Rossi stood motionless, staring at the screen in front of her, her mind a tangled web of disbelief and fury.

Marco.

The image of him—his broad shoulders cutting through the chaos of the gala—was seared into her memory. No mask. No hesitation. Just that haunting smile, as cold and calculated as the business deals he'd never once mentioned to her. She could hear her pulse in her ears as the footage froze on his face, that smile flickering like a ghost in her chest. The man she thought she knew—trusted, loved—was a stranger. An assassin.

The room seemed to close in on her, the hum of the air conditioning a hollow drone, as if even the walls were whispering secrets she wasn't ready to hear. She'd spent months peeling back the layers of Marco DeLuca, convinced there was more to him than the polished exterior, the suave charm. Now, in the stark fluorescent glow of the conference room, the truth hit her like a sledgehammer.

"Staring at it won't change anything, Bella." Sam's voice cut through the thick fog of her thoughts, his steps deliberate as he moved beside her.

He looked at the screen with something that resembled pity—something Bella didn't want or need.

"I'm fine," she muttered, though the lie stuck in her throat. She wasn't fine. How could she be?

If Sam noticed the tremor in her hands as they hovered over the controls, he didn't say anything. Instead, he cleared his throat and leaned in closer, his voice dropping to a near-whisper. "Bella, if you need to step back—"

Her laugh was short, bitter, like a knife in her gut. "Step back? Sam, my boyfriend—no, our suspect—just assassinated one of the most powerful men in the country."

There it was. The words she'd been avoiding, the reality she couldn't deny. Her voice cracked, and she hated herself for it.

Sam's jaw tightened, a faint line appearing between his brows. "And that's exactly why you shouldn't be leading this investigation."

His words were sharp, cutting through her like a blade. Bella felt her pulse quicken, a swell of anger rising to meet the hollow pit in her stomach.

"You're too close," he finished, his tone not unkind but firm.

Bella's eyes flicked to him, dark and resolute. The words hung between them, heavy with unspoken truths. She didn't need Sam's sympathy. What she needed was closure.

"I'm not stepping back," she bit out, her voice low and filled with a resolve that she didn't quite feel. "I'm going to find him. And when I do, he's going to tell me why."

Sam opened his mouth, but she turned away before he could say anything else. Her mind was set. This wasn't just about justice anymore. It was personal. Marco DeLuca hadn't just betrayed her trust—he'd shattered everything they had, everything she'd believed. And she was going to make him pay for it.

But the task force wasn't about to let her slip back into that world of personal vendetta so easily.

As she stepped into the hallway, Bella's thoughts spiraled, unable to stop the waves of anger and confusion that swirled inside her.

She hadn't gotten far when Agent Anna Vasquez appeared, her face flushed and tense, her movements quick but uncertain, as though she were walking on eggshells.

"Agent Rossi," Vasquez said, her voice tight, like she was measuring every word. "There's something you need to know."

Bella turned toward her, irritation already building. "What is it?"

Vasquez hesitated, her eyes flicking to the ground before meeting Bella's gaze. "They... they're searching your apartment."

Bella froze, the words like a slap. "What?" Her voice came out as a hiss, sharp and disbelieving. She didn't know if she was angrier at the intrusion or the betrayal of trust that had followed. "Why?"

"It's protocol," Vasquez explained, her voice softer now, tinged with something Bella couldn't place. "DeLuca's your boyfriend—"

"Suspect," Bella interrupted, her voice cutting through the air like ice. "And don't you forget it."

Vasquez paused, as if calculating her next words carefully. "Right. Suspect. But the team's already on-site. They're taking everything."

The weight of it hit Bella like a freight train. The walls were closing in, her space shrinking with each breath she took. Her apartment—the one place she thought was still hers—had just been violated. And worse, the truth of Marco's deception was now laid bare for everyone to see.

Without waiting for another word, Bella's body moved on its own. She grabbed her keys, ignoring the dull thud of her pulse in her throat, and stormed down the hallway. The heat from the overhead lights above felt suffocating, like the walls were closing in on her, trapping her in a labyrinth she couldn't escape.

Every footstep was a countdown.

"Bella, wait," Sam called from behind her, but she didn't stop.

"Stay out of my way, Sam," she said, the words bitter in her mouth. She didn't have time for him to tell her to step back again. The door to her world had just opened, and she was stepping through it, ready or not.

She was going to find Marco. And when she did, she'd make him tell her why—because the answers she was getting from this nightmare were never going to be enough.

But the sight of her apartment stopped her cold.

The door was wide open, the lock dangling uselessly from the frame. Yellow crime scene tape fluttered in the hallway's stale draft like a macabre banner. Beyond the threshold, agents swarmed like locusts, their gloved hands dismantling every piece of the life she had built with Marco.

The throw blanket on the couch had been tossed aside, a colorful casualty in a sea of chaos. Kitchen drawers were upended, their contents spilling onto the counter like disemboweled secrets. A forensic tech knelt by the nightstand, carefully bagging Marco's cufflinks, his movements clinical and detached. The click of his camera's shutter punctuated the room like a judge's gavel.

Bella's heart clenched as she stepped inside. The air felt heavier here, thick with the weight of betrayal and the sting of invaded privacy.

"Agent Rossi, you shouldn't..." a young agent

started, his hand raised in protest.

"Spare me," she snapped, brushing past him with a sharpness that belied the tremor in her hands.

Her eyes scanned the living room, but it was the coffee table that held her attention. A folder lay open, its contents like an autopsy report for her life. Photographs of Marco at the gala stared back at her, damning evidence framed by notes scrawled in angry red ink. Beside them sat a single bagged item: two train ticket stubs for a departure the morning after the gala.

Her knees threatened to buckle. Every detail screamed of a life she'd shared, now dissected by strangers.

"Agent Rossi, we're just doing our job," one of the techs offered hesitantly, his tone devoid of comfort.

Bella didn't answer. She couldn't. Her throat tightened as she turned toward the hallway leading to the bedroom and bathroom, seeking refuge or perhaps a final shred of truth.

The bathroom was untouched, a pristine tableau in stark contrast to the destruction outside. Her gown from the gala still hung where she'd left it, a shimmering reminder of the night Marco had insisted she wear it. Her fingers trembled as she reached for it, the silk cool and deceptively innocent beneath her touch. A sudden thought struck her, sharp and insistent. She flipped the gown inside out, her fingers searching the seams with methodical precision.

And there it was. Behind the label, faint writing etched in black ink, unmistakably Marco's handwriting.

Bella barely registered the footsteps behind her until Lawson's voice cut through the silence. "Agent Rossi."

She turned sharply, the gown still clutched in her hands. Lawson stood in the doorway, his broad frame blocking her escape. His face was unreadable, a mask of professional detachment.

"This is a crime scene now," he said firmly. "I need you to step back."

Her laugh was bitter, a sharp contrast to the tears burning the corners of her eyes. "Step back? From my own life?"

"From his life," Lawson corrected, his voice low but steady. "We need to be thorough, Bella. You know that."

"Did you have to destroy everything?" she demanded, her voice cracking as her gaze flicked to the remnants of the vase Marco had brought back from Venice.

Lawson's silence was answer enough.

Bella swallowed hard, her hands tightening around the gown. "Fine," she muttered, her voice barely above a whisper. She turned, but as she moved past Lawson, she yanked the label from the gown with a quick, practiced motion, slipping it into her jacket pocket before he could notice.

The ride down in the elevator was agonizingly slow. The walls felt closer with every floor, their mirrored surface reflecting the anguish etched on her face. With shaking hands, she pulled the scrap of fabric from her pocket and unfolded it. Her breath caught as she read the words written there:

"Addio, amore mio."

Bella's chest tightened, a sharp ache spreading as the words sank in. Marco's handwriting, so familiar, so deliberate. The finality of it hit her like a punch to the gut. Was it really a goodbye? A warning? Or something darker? The questions swirled, their weight suffocating.

Tears welled in her eyes, but she blinked them back, refusing to let them fall. Her emotions warred within her—grief, anger, and a faint, desperate hope that there was more to the story than what lay on the surface.

As the elevator dinged, signaling the ground floor, Bella straightened her spine, shoving the label back into her pocket. Whatever Marco had done, whatever secrets he'd kept, she would find the answers. And she would decide what justice meant when she had the truth in her hands.

For now, she stepped into the cold night air, leaving behind the ruins of her past and a man who had turned her world into a crime scene.

But the stale air inside Bella's apartment felt thicker as Lawson stood in the middle of the chaos, his phone pressed tightly to his ear. The remnants of a life shared with Marco surrounded him, but his attention was elsewhere, his sharp gaze flicking between the forensic team and the shattered remains of trust scattered across the room.

"Grayson," Lawson said when the line connected,

his voice clipped and authoritative.

"Chief," Sam replied, his tone laced with caution. "What's this about?"

"I need you to tail Bella," Lawson said, stepping aside as a tech passed with a bagged item. "She's in a precarious place right now—volatile. And frankly, that might work to our advantage."

Sam's silence stretched, weighted with unspoken disapproval. "You're using her."

"She's not a suspect," Lawson countered. "Not yet. But Marco's gone dark, and if anyone can lead us to him, it's Bella. You've worked with her before. She trusts you."

"And you think that gives me the right to betray her trust?" Sam's voice was low, barely restrained.

Lawson leaned against the doorframe, his gaze hard. "Don't get righteous on me, Grayson. If she's innocent, this surveillance will prove it. If not..."

Sam sighed heavily. "If not, she's still my friend."

"And you'll handle it," Lawson replied coldly. "Keep me updated."

The call ended, but the weight of the decision lingered in the room, as oppressive as the yellow tape fluttering in the hallway.

∞

The faint morning sunlight spilled through the sheer white curtains, pooling golden warmth on the bedspread. Bella stirred, her body tangled in soft sheets that smelled faintly of lavender and something else—

Marco's cologne. The faint, woodsy aroma wrapped around her like a second skin, pulling her deeper into the dream.

Her head rested on his chest, the steady rhythm of his heartbeat beneath her ear grounding her, even in this surreal haze. Marco's fingers trailed lightly down her arm, tracing invisible paths that sent shivers across her skin.

"Italy," he murmured, his voice a rich timbre that made her insides melt. "Picture it, amore mio. A villa on the Amalfi Coast. The sea stretching out like an endless sapphire."

She tilted her head up, meeting his gaze. His dark eyes sparkled with that familiar mixture of mischief and warmth.

"A villa, huh?" she teased, her lips quirking into a smile.

He grinned. "Not just any villa. Ours. With a garden for tomatoes and basil. You'd love it, Bella. Sunsets that turn the water gold. Evenings spent with wine and the kind of pasta that makes you cry because it's so good."

She laughed softly, her hand resting on his chest. "You make it sound like heaven."

He shifted, propping himself up on one elbow so he could look at her fully. His fingers brushed a stray lock of hair from her face. "Because it would be. You and me, away from all this madness. No badges, no suspects, no threats. Just us."

His words sank deep, their sweetness an ache in

her chest. She reached for him, her hand resting on his cheek. "It sounds perfect."

Marco's expression softened, and he leaned down to press a kiss to her forehead. "One day, Bella. I'll take you there. I promise."

The warmth of his promise wrapped around her like a cocoon, the dream bleeding into reality as her heart twisted. In that moment, she let herself believe it, her mind refusing to acknowledge the betrayal waiting on the other side of her consciousness.

The Amalfi Coast wasn't waiting. Only the cold truth of Marco's betrayal lay ahead.

Bella jolted awake, the remnants of her dream dissolving into the oppressive silence of the hotel room. Her chest heaved, her heart slamming against her ribs as she sat upright, her mind struggling to separate the dream from reality. For a fleeting second, she reached instinctively toward the empty side of the bed, expecting Marco's warmth, his steady breathing. But her fingers brushed only cold sheets, a stark reminder of the void he'd left behind.

But as the sunlight grew brighter, reality began to claw its way back. The soft murmur of his voice faded, replaced by the faint hum of a hotel air conditioner. Bella stirred, the emptiness of the bed beside her a stark contrast to the dream she'd clung to.

The dream clung to her like cobwebs, sticky and suffocating. She could still hear his voice, rich with that soft Italian lilt, painting pictures of the Amalfi Coast, of a life they'd never have. It wasn't just a memory; it was a cruel mirage—a ghost of what she'd thought was real.

Swinging her legs over the side of the bed, she pressed her bare feet to the cool wood floor. The sensation grounded her, but only just. She rubbed her face with trembling hands, her fingers catching on the stray tears that had escaped while she slept.

"Get it together," she whispered, her voice rough and bitter.

The weak light of early morning seeped through the half-drawn blinds, casting long shadows across the room. The hotel felt like a cage—walls too close, air too stale. She stood, wrapping her arms around herself, and paced toward the window. The city below was waking, but she felt like she hadn't slept in weeks.

Her thoughts swirled, the fragments of the dream refusing to fade. Italy. Marco's voice had been so vivid, so insistent. The villa, the sunsets, the escape—it had been more than romantic musings. She could see it now, in hindsight: it had been a plan. A getaway disguised as a dream.

Her pulse quickened.

If Marco had gone to Italy, he wouldn't be sipping wine on the Amalfi Coast. He'd be hidden in the shadows, slipping through alleyways and using the kind of connections that had kept him one step ahead of her. She'd been chasing his ghost for days, but now she had a thread to pull—a thread he hadn't intended her to find.

Her eyes darted to the bedside table where her

laptop sat, its screen dark. She grabbed it, flipping it open with shaking hands. She didn't need a plan yet—just an idea, a direction.

She typed quickly, pulling up databases she shouldn't have access to without proper clearance. But her badge still carried weight, even if her trust in the system had crumbled.

Fake passports. International flights. Border crossings. The screen filled with information, a flood of data that was both overwhelming and exhilarating. Her fingers hovered over the keyboard, the possibilities spinning out in her mind.

A knock at the door shattered her focus.

"Rossi, open up." Sam's voice was muffled but firm.

Bella froze, the tension in her body snapping taut. She shut the laptop with a snap, her breath catching.

"Give me a second," she called, her voice steady despite the storm inside her.

She crossed the room, unlocking the door but leaving the chain latched. It opened a crack, just enough for her to see his expression—calm, unreadable, and laced with authority.

"Do we really need the theatrics?" Sam asked dryly.

Bella didn't move. "Are you stalking me?"

His jaw tightened. "We need to talk."

"And I need sleep." She started to close the door, but his hand shot out, stopping it.

"Bella, don't make this harder than it has to be."

His tone was softer now, almost pleading, but his eyes told another story.

She stared at him for a long moment, then relented, unhooking the chain and stepping aside.

The tension in the room sharpened the moment Sam stepped inside. His presence carried a gravity that seemed to pull the walls closer, making the small hotel room feel claustrophobic. His gaze swept over the space, cataloging every detail—her hastily shut laptop on the bedside table, the untouched cup of coffee on the dresser, and the disheveled sheets that told of a restless night.

"Still trying to play the rogue agent?" he asked, his voice calm but laced with an edge that cut straight to her defenses.

Bella's lips quirked into a humorless smile, one that didn't reach her eyes. "You'd know all about that."

Sam's expression didn't change, but the air between them thickened, a heavy weight of shared history and unresolved tension.

Bella folded her arms and leaned against the desk, her stance casual but her eyes sharp. "So, tell me, Sam, did Lawson send you to babysit me? Or is this your way of making sure I'm not about to run off and do something reckless?"

The corner of his mouth twitched, but it wasn't amusement. "Lawson's worried about you. Hell, I'm worried about you. And if keeping an eye on you keeps you from spiraling, then yeah, I guess I am babysitting."

Her jaw tightened. "I don't need a damn chaperone, least of all you."

Sam stepped closer, his voice dropping to a low, measured tone. "This isn't a game, Bella. Marco's not the man you thought he was. You need to stop chasing ghosts before you destroy your career—or yourself."

Bella straightened, her arms crossing tighter over her chest as if to fortify herself against his words. "I don't need you to save me, Sam. And I sure as hell don't need you to tell me what Marco is or isn't."

Sam's gaze softened, a flicker of something—regret, maybe—breaking through the hard lines of his face. "I'm not your enemy, Bella."

Her voice dropped to a whisper, but her words hit like a hammer. "No? Then stop treating me like one."

The space between them sizzled with unspoken words, the air crackling with a volatile mix of frustration and something deeper, something neither of them wanted to name.

Sam's eyes flicked downward, almost imperceptibly, and Bella caught the briefest hesitation. Her bathrobe. She was standing in front of him in nothing but the soft, terrycloth wrap, loosely tied at the waist. His gaze snapped back to her face, but not quickly enough to hide the way his pupils dilated, or the tightening of his jaw.

The realization hit her like a jolt. He still saw her—not just as the sharp-edged, battle-worn agent she'd become, but as the woman he'd once known, the woman who had let her guard down with him in rare, fleeting moments.

A faint blush rose to her cheeks, but she masked it with a wry smile. "Enjoying the view, Sam?" she said, her tone sharp enough to cut.

He didn't rise to the bait, but there was no mistaking the heat in his eyes, even as he tried to temper it. "Just noticing you haven't changed," he replied, his voice rougher than before. "You still know how to get under my skin."

Bella felt a twinge of vulnerability and wrapped her arms around herself, her fingers tightening on the robe as if to shield herself from the weight of his stare. Her pulse quickened, not with anger, but with the undeniable awareness that lingered between them.

"You always did have a thing for complicated women," she said softly, almost to herself.

"Only one," he murmured, the words slipping out before he could stop them.

Their eyes locked, the moment stretching into something raw and intimate. For a fleeting second, the years of tension and heartbreak seemed to fade, leaving behind only the echoes of what might have been.

But Bella wasn't ready to dwell on it. Not now. Not when the ground beneath her feet was already crumbling. She cleared her throat and turned away, breaking the spell.

Sam let out a quiet sigh, the sound heavy with things unsaid. He reached into his jacket and pulled out a slim folder, setting it on the table with deliberate care.

"These are the latest updates on Marco's case," he

said, his tone back to business. "Take a look. Maybe it'll help you see what we're up against."

He headed for the door, pausing with his hand on the handle. When he turned back to her, his eyes were guarded but earnest.

"You're a damn good agent, Bella. Don't let him ruin that."

And just like that, he was gone, leaving Bella alone in the too-quiet room with the folder—and the weight of every choice she'd ever made.

CHAPTER 4: TENSIONS IN FLORENCE

The FBI's task force office was dimly lit, the glow of monitors casting ghostly blue shadows on the walls. A mix of muted voices, clacking keyboards, and the hum of air-conditioning filled the space, but Bella barely registered it. Her focus was pinned to the grainy footage playing on the central screen, the scene frozen in a perpetual loop of Marco's calculated movements.

She stood at the head of the room, her posture rigid, her arms folded like a barrier against the rising tide of emotions clawing at her. The air reeked of stale coffee and tension, mingling with the faint scent of sweat and frustration.

"Here," she said, her voice clipped as she jabbed a finger toward the figure in the frame. The man in the dark overcoat and flat cap moved with unsettling ease through the crowded terminal at JFK Airport, his posture casual, almost bored.

Agent Park stepped closer, a thick file clutched in his hands. "Facial recognition tagged him three times," he said, his tone efficient but laced with a hint of admiration. "Once at check-in, once at security, and again at the gate. No flags on his alias, Enrico Bernini. He had a damn near perfect passport and swapped boarding passes just before boarding. He's meticulous."

Bella's jaw tightened as she studied the screen, her chest constricting with every frame. She knew that face intimately—every line, every shadow. And yet, watching Marco now, she felt like she was seeing a stranger. The man she had loved was a ghost, leaving behind only this cold, calculated version of himself.

"He's going to Italy," she said, her voice flat but certain.

Lawson, standing beside her with his arms crossed, didn't look away from the screen. "Interpol has sightings in Rome. He landed at Leonardo da Vinci Airport, cleared customs without a hitch, and disappeared into the crowd. He's good, Bella. Damn good."

A bitter smile tugged at her lips. "Tell me something I don't know."

Lawson turned to her, his expression unreadable. "We've got the green light. You and Sam are on the next flight to Florence. Interpol's set up a task force there. You'll be liaising directly with them."

Bella stiffened, her stomach twisting at the mention of Sam. She opened her mouth to argue, to insist that she didn't need a partner, let alone him, but Lawson cut her off with a sharp look.

"I don't care about your history with Sam," he said, his voice low but firm. "You're both professionals. You'll act like it."

Agent Park cleared his throat awkwardly, handing Bella the file. "Here's everything we have so far. Fake IDs, travel patterns, known associates. The Italians will have more when you land."

She nodded curtly, taking the file and flipping it open. Her eyes scanned the pages, but her mind was already racing ahead, picturing Marco slipping through the cobblestone streets of Florence, blending into the throngs of tourists and locals.

The jet roared to life as Bella fastened her seatbelt, her eyes fixed on the tarmac outside the window. The cabin lights dimmed, and the hum of engines filled the air. Sam slid into the seat beside her, his presence as inescapable as the mission ahead.

"You could at least pretend to be excited about working with me," he said, his voice laced with dry humor.

She didn't look at him, her fingers tightening around the file in her lap. "I don't have the energy for games, Sam."

He leaned back in his seat, his gaze studying her profile. "It's not a game, Bella. And you know damn well why Lawson paired us up."

She finally turned to him, her eyes sharp. "Because he doesn't trust me to keep it professional?"

Sam smirked, but there was no humor in it. "Because he knows I'll have your back when this gets messy. And it will get messy."

Her chest tightened, the truth of his words cutting deeper than she wanted to admit. She turned away, focusing on the file in her lap. The neatly organized reports and grainy photos felt like a lifeline in the chaos of her emotions.

Sam's voice softened, a rare note of vulnerability slipping through. "This isn't just about Marco, is it? It's about proving something—to yourself, to Lawson, hell, maybe even to me."

Her hands stilled on the file, but she didn't respond. The words hung between them, heavy and unspoken, as the plane taxied down the runway and lifted into the night.

The hunt was on. And as Bella stared out into the darkness, she knew the next steps would test her in ways she hadn't dared to imagine.

∞

Rome greeted them with chaos and charm. The city bustled beneath a slate-gray sky, its narrow streets alive with the sound of Vespa engines, snippets of rapid Italian, and the occasional bark of a street vendor hawking roasted chestnuts. Bella gazed out of the window of their car as it wove through the labyrinth of traffic, her thoughts dark and tangled.

"Not quite the romantic getaway you imagined, huh?" Sam's voice broke through her reverie.

She turned to look at him. The shadows under his eyes were darker than usual, a testament to the long hours and jet lag pressing down on both of them. His tie was askew, and he hadn't bothered to shave, leaving a rough edge to his otherwise composed appearance.

"You look like hell," she said flatly, though a faint smirk tugged at her lips.

Sam leaned back in the seat, his eyes narrowing in mock offense. "And here I thought jet lag gave me that rugged, devil-may-care charm."

"More like the devil who forgot to care," she shot back.

For a moment, the tension between them softened, giving way to the easy banter that used to come so naturally. But then Sam's gaze lingered on her a beat too long, the corners of his mouth lifting in a way that sent heat rushing to her cheeks.

"Still sharp-tongued," he said, his voice low. "I missed that about you."

Bella's stomach tightened, her pulse skittering as she forced herself to look away. "Don't," she said firmly, folding her arms across her chest like armor. "We're here for work, Sam. Focus on that."

His smile faded, but not completely. "As you wish, Agent Rossi," he said, his tone tinged with amusement.

The driver pulled up in front of a nondescript building, its stone façade weathered by time and pollution. The headquarters of the Polizia di Stato wasn't flashy, but it exuded the air of a place where hard decisions were made, and justice was pursued at any cost.

Inside, the scent of old paper, coffee, and faint cigarette smoke clung to the air. Bella and Sam were led through a maze of hallways until they reached a sparsely furnished office. Behind a battered wooden desk stood Inspector Luca Moretti.

Luca was tall and wiry, his sharp cheekbones and perpetual five o'clock shadow giving him a distinctly wolfish appearance. His suit was rumpled, and his tie was loose, but his eyes—dark and penetrating—spoke of someone who missed nothing.

"Agent Rossi," he said, his accent precise as he extended a hand. "And Agent Grayson. Welcome to Rome."

Bella shook his hand, noting the calluses on his palm, a detail that hinted at a man who wasn't afraid to get his hands dirty.

"I'll be blunt," Luca continued, his tone as unpolished as his appearance. "I don't like working with outsiders. Especially Americans."

Bella arched an eyebrow. "Good. Neither do I."

A flicker of surprise crossed his face before he let out a short, humorless laugh. "This will be interesting."

Sam stepped forward, his tone smooth. "We're not here to step on your toes, Inspector. Just to help you catch a killer."

"Can we skip the pleasantries and get to work?" she asked, her voice sharp. Luca's smile faded, replaced by the seriousness of a man who had spent years chasing ghosts.

His eyes flicked between them, assessing, before he nodded. "Fair enough. Let's get to it."

He gestured toward a table in the corner, where a map of Italy was spread out alongside a stack of photographs and reports. Bella leaned over the map, her eyes scanning the markings as Luca spoke.

"We've tracked Marco to Florence," he said, his voice grim. "Two days after the assassination, he met with an art dealer there. Enzo Bianchi. Known connections to smuggling networks and forgery rings."

Bella's breath caught at the mention of Florence. The city wasn't just a location; it was a memory. Marco had always spoken of it with reverence, describing its art, its hidden beauty. She'd once imagined walking its cobblestone streets with him. Now, it felt like another betrayal, another piece of the puzzle that didn't fit.

"Then we go to Florence," she said, her tone firm.

Luca's gaze lingered on her, his expression unreadable. "Just remember, Rossi," he said quietly, his voice softening. "This isn't just about catching him. It's about making sure we don't lose him to bad police work."

Bella straightened, her jaw tightening. "I'll be fine," she said, though the words felt hollow.

Luca didn't press the point, turning instead to the stack of files on the table. But Sam, standing a few feet away, watched her closely.

Because Luca was wrong. Bella had already lost

him the moment Marco walked away.

Now, all that was left was the hunt—and the truth, no matter how much it cost her.

∞

The drive to Florence was tense, a journey where silence competed with the hum of tires against asphalt. Luca insisted on driving, and his skill behind the wheel was as sharp as his wit. The sleek, dark sedan cut through the Italian countryside like a knife, the golden glow of vineyards and ancient stone houses blurring into a haze outside the windows.

Sam leaned his head against the window, his exhaustion palpable. He'd barely spoken since they left Rome, and Bella couldn't decide if his silence was deliberate or simply the byproduct of too many sleepless nights.

"You okay over there?" Bella asked, keeping her voice low.

Sam turned his head slightly, a crooked smile playing on his lips. "Define okay. If you mean being crammed in a car with two perfectionists and a case that could implode at any moment, then yeah, I'm just peachy."

Bella rolled her eyes, though her lips twitched. "At least you're self-aware."

"Can't say the same for you," he teased, his voice softer now, the edges tinged with something unspoken.

She opened her mouth to respond, but Luca interrupted, his eyes never leaving the road. "Save the flirting for later. We're almost there."

The comment hit its mark, the tension snapping back into place. Bella crossed her arms, staring resolutely ahead as the outskirts of Florence gave way to the city's heart.

When they arrived, Florence was waking up to a morning cloaked in gray. The drizzle had stopped, leaving the cobblestones gleaming like wet onyx. Bella couldn't deny the city's beauty—the domes and spires rising like whispers of history—but today, it felt suffocating. Every street seemed to echo with the ghosts of Marco's footsteps, his presence as vivid as the Renaissance art that adorned the walls of the galleries.

Luca parked the car in a narrow alley near a café that looked like it had been untouched by time. Its faded awning drooped over the entrance, and a neon espresso sign buzzed faintly against the morning quiet.

Inside, the café was dimly lit, the air heavy with the mingling scents of espresso, stale cigarettes, and something faintly metallic that Bella couldn't quite place. Luca gestured toward the counter.

"Stand down," he murmured to Bella. "Let me handle this."

Her jaw tightened, but she gave him a curt nod. Sam, already picking up on the dynamics, drifted toward the counter, ordering espresso and a croissant. He lingered at a small table, his casual demeanor masking the sharp glances he cast toward the back corner.

There sat Enzo Bianchi, a wiry man whose presence dominated the space despite his unassuming frame. His face was lined with age and secrets, his eyes sharp and calculating. A half-finished espresso sat in front of him, the tiny spoon resting at an angle that suggested he hadn't touched it in a while.

Luca approached with deliberate steps, Bella trailing a few paces behind. She hated this part—the games, the posturing—but it was necessary.

"You must be Inspector Moretti," Enzo said, his accented English smooth, almost musical. His gaze slid to Bella, and his lips curved into a smirk. "And you… Marco's firebrand."

The words hit her like a slap, but she refused to let it show. "If you know who I am, you know I'm not here to waste time."

Enzo chuckled, leaning back in his chair with an infuriatingly casual air. "Marco always did have a taste for the fiery ones."

"Enough," Luca snapped, his voice cutting through the tension. "You know why we're here."

Enzo gestured to the empty chairs. "Sit. Let's not make a scene."

Luca took the seat opposite him, his movements controlled, every detail calculated. Bella stayed standing, her arms crossed as she glared at the man.

"We're looking for Marco DeLuca," Luca began, his tone sharp but even. "He was here two days ago. Don't waste my time by denying it."

Enzo's smirk didn't waver as he lit a cigarette,

exhaling a plume of smoke that curled toward the low ceiling. "I haven't seen Marco in years."

"Bullshit," Bella snapped, her voice loud enough to draw a glance from the barista behind the counter.

Luca shot her a warning look but didn't contradict her. Instead, he leaned forward, his elbows on the table. "You have two options, Bianchi. You can cooperate, and we'll leave you to your charming life. Or…" He let the implication linger, heavy and menacing.

Enzo's smile faltered, his eyes narrowing. "You don't scare me, Moretti. But her?" He nodded toward Bella. "She looks like she'd shoot first and ask questions later."

Bella stepped closer, her voice dropping to a cold, deadly calm. "Try me."

The café seemed to hold its breath, the air thick with unspoken threats. For the first time, Enzo looked unsettled. He crushed his cigarette into the ashtray, leaning forward as his smile faded.

"All right," he said quietly, his tone losing its smug edge. "Marco was here. But if you think you'll catch him, you're already too late."

Bella's stomach twisted, but she didn't let it show. She leaned in, her voice barely above a whisper. "Tell me where he's going, or I swear to God, I'll make you regret every lie you've ever told."

The words hung between them, sharp and brittle, as the truth edged closer to the surface.

Bella could feel the tension, pressing against her

chest, her pulse thrumming in time with the faint drip of a leaky faucet behind the counter. For a moment, Enzo remained silent, his dark eyes flitting between them, calculating. Then he exhaled sharply, as though surrendering to a battle he never wanted to fight.

"Fine," he muttered, his voice a low growl. He stubbed out his cigarette with a deliberate twist. "Marco was here. He bought forged passports. Paid well, too."

Bella raised an eyebrow, folding her arms across her chest. "Forged passports? From an art dealer? Forgive me if I'm skeptical, Enzo. Where does 'counterfeit Michelangelo' intersect with international forgery?"

Enzo smirked, the lines on his face deepening. "Bills don't pay themselves, signorina," he said in clipped, sarcastic English. "When the paintings don't sell, one must diversify." He glanced at Luca with a hint of mockery. "Even you should understand that, Moretti."

Luca's jaw clenched, his voice cutting through the air like steel. "Why did he need them?"

Enzo hesitated, his fingers tapping an erratic rhythm on the table. Bella's sharp eyes followed the movement, noting the slight twitch in his jaw, the way his gaze flicked to the left. A subtle tell, but a tell nonetheless.

"He said something about Dusker Corporation's European operations," Enzo finally admitted, the words tumbling out reluctantly. "Didn't give details, just hinted that big things were happening. Told me to stay out of it, 'Il Fantasma."

The name hit Bella like a gut punch. Dusker Corporation—an enigmatic tech conglomerate whose fingerprints were on everything from Advanced-System to high-stakes security contracts. Marco's connection to them was deeper than she'd anticipated, and forged passports meant he wasn't just running. He was preparing for something calculated, dangerous.

Bella stepped closer, her voice sharp and unyielding. "You're lying."

Enzo flinched, but she pressed on, her words razor-edged. "You said Marco paid well. Men like him don't overpay unless they want something extra. What else did he want, Enzo?"

The café seemed to shrink around them, the dim light casting long shadows across the worn wooden floors. Sam, still lingering at his table, abandoned his pretense of casual disinterest. He rose, approaching with an easy, unthreatening stride that masked the tension in his shoulders.

"She's right," Sam said, his tone softer but no less insistent. "What's the angle here, Enzo? If Marco trusted you enough to buy fake passports, he trusted you with more than you're letting on."

Enzo looked between them, his composure cracking. His lips pressed into a thin line as he leaned forward, his voice dropping to a near-whisper. "All right, all right. There was one more thing. He wanted intel on someone. A name."

Luca's expression darkened, his voice dropping to a menacing growl. "What name?"

Enzo hesitated, his fingers curling into fists on the table. "Yours."

The single word detonated in Bella's mind, scattering her thoughts like shrapnel. Her breath caught, and for a moment, the only sound in the room was the faint hum of the espresso machine.

"Mine?" she demanded, her voice breaking on the word.

Enzo nodded, his gaze flicking to Luca, then back to her. "He said he needed to know everything. Where you go. Who you talk to. Your weaknesses."

Bella felt her knees threaten to buckle, but she forced herself to remain upright, her mind racing. Marco had been one step ahead of them this entire time, and she'd never even realized it.

Sam stepped closer, his presence grounding her as he addressed Enzo with a cold edge in his voice. "And you gave it to him?"

Enzo didn't answer, but the silence was answer enough.

Enzo opened his mouth to speak, but before a single syllable could escape, Luca's sharp voice cut through the haze.

"That's enough, Rossi."

Bella spun toward Luca, her frustration surging like a tidal wave. Her eyes burned with anger, and her voice lashed out, cold and precise.

"Enough? He's holding back, and you're letting

him!" Her tone turned sharper, more personal. "Don't stand there and act like this is some routine interrogation. Marco isn't just a suspect—he's dangerous."

Luca stepped forward, his imposing frame casting a shadow across the table. His voice, rising above hers, carried a warning edge. "And you're too close to see clearly. You're letting your emotions cloud your judgment, and it's going to cost us!"

The clash of their words silenced the café. Every patron turned to watch, their curiosity mingling with unease. Bella's cheeks flushed, but her determination didn't falter. She met Luca's glare head-on, her pulse a fierce rhythm beneath her skin.

"You think I can't be objective?" she shot back, her words laced with ice. "Then explain why I'm the one who caught his slip. 'Il Fantasma.'"

Luca's brow furrowed, his confusion momentarily disarming his ire. "What are you talking about?"

Bella pivoted toward Enzo, her movements quick, precise, and loaded with purpose. "You said Marco told you to stay out of it. That wasn't just a warning. That's Marco's way of claiming control. He's used that nickname before—back in New York. Il Fantasma. The Ghost."

Luca's gaze flicked to Enzo, who had gone pale beneath his olive complexion. "Is that true?"

The man hesitated, his bravado crumbling under Bella's unrelenting stare. She watched the cracks spread across his carefully crafted mask.

"It's a codename," Enzo said at last, his voice quieter, almost reluctant. "A shadow network. People who handle… delicate matters."

Bella's breath hitched, the weight of his words sinking into her. Her mind spun with the implications, but she pressed on. "And Marco? He's part of it?"

Enzo swallowed, his Adam's apple bobbing visibly. "He's not just part of it. He is their ghost. Their best. The one they send when things need to disappear—quietly."

The revelation hit like a thunderclap, a deafening boom in her mind that drowned out everything else. Bella's pulse raced, her chest tight as the pieces of Marco's double life locked into place.

"Where did he go?" she demanded, her voice fierce and unyielding.

Enzo shook his head quickly, hands raised as if warding off her intensity. "I don't know. And even if I did, I wouldn't tell you."

Luca shot to his feet, the sudden motion rattling the table and drawing startled glances. "Then we're done here," he said curtly, his voice slicing through the tension like a blade.

Enzo smirked, his confidence returning now that the encounter was nearing its end. "Always a pleasure doing business."

Luca stood close, towering over the smaller man, his voice low and dangerous. "You've just made yourself very useful, Enzo. I suggest you remember that. Because if we find out you're holding anything else back…"

Bella didn't wait for him to finish. She turned on her heel and strode toward the door, the weight of Marco's betrayal pressing heavily on her chest. Sam caught up to her just as she pushed through into the damp morning air, his hand brushing against her arm.

"Bella," he said softly.

She turned to him, her composure fracturing just enough for him to see the hurt beneath her icy exterior. "He's been watching me, Sam. I didn't even see it."

Sam's gaze was steady, his voice quiet but firm. "We'll figure this out. But you have to let us help you."

Behind them, Luca emerged from the café, his expression stormy. "Enzo gave us a lead," he said grimly. "But we're running out of time."

Bella's hands trembled, whether from anger, adrenaline, or the sheer enormity of what they'd uncovered, she couldn't tell.

"You shouldn't have pushed him like that," Luca said, his tone low and controlled, but the accusation was clear.

Bella spun on her heel to face him, her eyes blazing. "And you shouldn't have underestimated me," she snapped.

For a moment, the two of them stood locked in an unspoken battle of wills, their breaths visible in the cold air. The narrow street, hemmed in by tall stone buildings, felt suffocating. The city that once enchanted her with its old-world charm now seemed to conspire against her, the shadows stretching long and dark.

Luca sighed, the sound heavy with frustration. He raked a hand through his hair, his usual polish cracking just enough to reveal his vulnerability. "You were right," he admitted grudgingly. "About the nickname. Good catch."

The acknowledgment should have felt like a victory, but it didn't. Bella turned away from him, her gaze fixed on the cobblestones beneath her boots. "Marco's slipping further into the shadows," she said, more to herself than to Luca or Sam. "And we're running out of time to stop him."

Luca stepped closer, his presence a steadying force. "Then let's make the next move count," he said quietly, his voice softened with something close to reassurance.

Bella squared her shoulders, forcing the doubt and fear into the far corners of her mind. She didn't have the luxury of breaking down—not yet.

"Let's move," she said, her voice hardening with determination.

Bella nodded, though the weight in her chest didn't lessen. Marco wasn't just a ghost—he was her ghost, and she wasn't sure if she could catch him before he disappeared entirely.

CHAPTER 5: THE FIRST CLOSE CALL

The warehouse stood like a relic of forgotten dreams, its rusted corrugated metal exterior bruised by time and neglect. The sharp angles of its roof jutted against the violet-and-amber twilight, casting long, jagged shadows that sliced across the cracked asphalt like the marks of an unseen blade. Bella sat in the passenger seat of the unmarked sedan, her nails biting into the armrest as her gaze locked onto the warehouse's steel doors. Each groan of wind against the structure seemed to echo inside her chest, a low, haunting sound that prickled her nerves.

"This place screams cliché," Luca muttered from the driver's seat, breaking the suffocating silence. His tone was dry, but the edge in his voice was unmistakable. "Criminals really need to get more imaginative."

"Maybe they like clichés," Bella replied absently, her attention fixed on the figures slipping in and out of the shadows near the entrance. They moved with eerie fluidity, their identities obscured by the dim light and the grime-streaked windows of the warehouse.

Luca leaned back, his fingers tapping a rhythm on the steering wheel. "If we had any sense, we'd call for backup and wait this one out. But I know you're not going to do that."

Bella didn't respond. Her focus was on the possibility that he could be there. Marco. The thought of his name sent a shiver through her, sharp and electric. Her grip on the armrest tightened. Was he inside, hiding in the shadows, slipping through her fingers yet again?

Luca sighed. "Rossi, you're doing it again."

She turned toward him, her brow furrowed. "Doing what?"

"Thinking with your heart instead of your head," Luca said, his dark eyes cutting toward her. There was no malice in his tone, just a blunt honesty she hated and needed in equal measure. "Don't let him mess with your focus."

She bristled but couldn't muster a retort. He wasn't wrong. Marco had a way of burrowing into her thoughts, twisting the past until she questioned everything. Their moments together had felt real—until they didn't.

Before she could respond, Luca's phone vibrated on the console. He glanced at the screen, muttered a curse under his breath, and shoved the door open.

"Stay here," he said, stepping out into the crisp evening air.

The door slammed shut, leaving Bella alone with Sam in the backseat.

Sam leaned forward, his voice low. "Do you trust him?"

Bella glanced at the young officer in the rearview mirror. His wide, searching eyes betrayed more than curiosity—they were riddled with doubt.

"Luca?" she said with a wry smile, letting her gaze flick to where Luca stood a few feet away, phone pressed to his ear. His shoulders were broad beneath his leather jacket, the setting sun casting an almost golden halo around him. "If you're asking if he's good at his job, the answer is yes. If you're asking if he's trustworthy…" She let the sentence hang, teasingly.

Sam frowned, his jaw tightening. "That's not an answer."

Bella turned her attention back to Luca, her lips curving upward. "You've got to admit, though, he makes for one hell of a distraction. Italians do have that whole tall, dark, and brooding thing down to an art form."

Sam's frown deepened, his boyish features darkening with something close to jealousy. "If you're saying that's why you trust him, then I'm definitely worried."

Bella chuckled, the sound soft but dry. "Relax, Sam. Luca's complicated, but he's not the enemy.

Marco is."

The door opened abruptly, and Luca slid back into the driver's seat. His expression was unreadable, but his energy had shifted, coiled tighter.

"There's a lead," he said, his voice clipped. "Someone reported a trespasser here a few nights ago. Filed a police report but no follow-up. Matches Marco's description."

Bella straightened, adrenaline sparking through her veins. "You think it's him?"

Luca nodded, his jaw tight. "I think it's the closest we've been in weeks."

The words hung heavy in the car as Luca started the engine, the faint hum doing nothing to cut the tension. Bella's mind raced, the promise of proximity to Marco bringing equal parts dread and determination.

As they pulled into the lot, the warehouse loomed larger, its walls rising like the steel ribs of a beast waiting to devour them whole. Bella's chest tightened, and for a moment, doubt whispered in her ear.

But then she glanced at Luca. His steady grip on the wheel, the set of his jaw, and the glint of resolve in his dark eyes reminded her of why they were here. Whatever lay beyond those doors, they'd face it together—even if it meant confronting ghosts, both literal and metaphorical.

The air outside the car was sharp with the scent of oil and damp concrete, and the occasional gust of wind made the warped metal doors groan as if protesting their vigil. Bella sat motionless in the passenger seat, her gaze locked on the shadows slithering along the building's edges.

"This place screams cliché," Luca muttered from the driver's seat, his voice a low rumble of irritation. His hands gripped the steering wheel, the leather creaking faintly under the pressure. "It's like they've been watching too many bad gangster movies."

Bella didn't acknowledge the comment. Her attention was on the figures darting between the flickering industrial lights and the shadows, their movements fluid and deliberate, like predators stalking prey. Her pulse quickened, a steady thrum in her ears. The question that gnawed at her relentlessly surfaced again: Is Marco here?

Sam shifted in the backseat, leaning forward slightly. "Bella," he said softly, his voice cutting through the tense silence. "You're doing it again."

Her brows furrowed, and she turned just enough to glance at him over her shoulder. "Doing what?"

"Thinking with your heart instead of your head," he replied, his boyish face tinged with concern. "You can't let him mess with your focus."

Bella stiffened, a wave of defensiveness rolling through her, but the truth in his words stung. Sam might have been younger, less experienced, but his insight had a way of cutting through her armor. She turned back to the warehouse, refusing to meet his gaze.

"You don't understand," she said, her voice tight.

"No, I don't," Sam admitted, his tone softening.

"But I see what it's doing to you."

The words hung in the air, heavy and undeniable. Bella's chest tightened, her breath hitching as an image from her past forced its way to the surface.

Marco, standing in the kitchen of their Manhattan apartment, a soft smile playing on his lips as he rolled dough on the marble countertop. His sleeves were rolled up, revealing strong forearms dusted with flour, and the rich aroma of tomatoes, garlic, and basil filled the air. "You've never had real pasta until you've had it handmade," he'd said, his voice smooth and warm like the wine they'd shared that night. She'd laughed as he pressed her hands into the dough, guiding her movements. For a moment, she'd believed that this— this warmth, this intimacy—was real. That he was real.

The memory hit her like a punch to the gut. Her throat tightened, and she blinked rapidly, forcing herself back to the present.

"Bella," Luca's voice cut through the fog, sharp and commanding.

She nodded, exhaling slowly as she dragged herself back to the grim reality in front of her. The warehouse wasn't just a building; it was a stage for the lies Marco had spun, a place where truth and deceit blurred until they were indistinguishable.

Luca glanced at her, his dark eyes unreadable. "If you're not ready for this, say so now."

"I'm ready," Bella said, her voice steadier than she felt.

The tension in the car was palpable, a silent

acknowledgment of the storm they were about to step into. As Luca reached for the door handle, Bella tightened her grip on her weapon, the cold metal grounding her.

Whatever waited for them inside that warehouse—Marco, or just more shadows of his lies—she would face it. And this time, she wouldn't let her heart get in the way.

∞

Movement near the warehouse doors drew Bella's sharp gaze. A man emerged from the shadows, tall and broad-shouldered, his gait unhurried, deliberate. The dim light caught the edge of his profile—sharp jawline, the faint gleam of a smirk playing at his lips. Bella's breath hitched, and her fingers tightened around the door handle.

"It's him," she whispered, her voice barely audible but laced with certainty.

Luca grabbed a pair of binoculars from the console, lifting them to his eyes. "Could be," he muttered, his tone carefully neutral. "Hard to tell from this distance."

Bella didn't need the confirmation. Marco's presence hit her like a phantom punch, visceral and undeniable. She knew the slope of his shoulders, the effortless arrogance in the way he carried himself—like a king surveying his kingdom, even if that kingdom was built on lies and blood.

"Wait for my signal," Luca ordered, his voice a

steadying anchor in the storm of her thoughts.

The minutes crawled by, each one dragging on her nerves like a taut wire ready to snap. Figures moved in and out of the building, their shapes distorted by the interplay of light and shadow. Each time the warehouse doors creaked open, a sliver of yellow light spilled out, momentarily illuminating stacked crates, industrial machinery, and the faint glint of metal surfaces inside.

Sam fidgeted in the backseat, the glow from his phone casting eerie shadows on his face. Bella noticed his thumb swiping across the screen with unusual urgency, and he quickly pocketed the device when he caught her watching.

"Something you want to share, Sam?" she asked, her tone deceptively light.

He hesitated, his boyish features tightening for a fraction of a second before he forced a grin. "Just checking in with a contact. Routine."

Her eyes narrowed, but she let it drop—for now. The nagging suspicion in her gut would have to wait until Marco was no longer the immediate threat.

Finally, Luca's voice broke the silence, low and decisive. "Team Alpha, move in."

The unmarked car came alive with movement as they prepared for the raid. Bella slid her gun into place, her heart hammering as adrenaline surged through her veins.

The assault on the warehouse was swift, a well-rehearsed symphony of controlled chaos. Gravel crunched under boots as agents stormed the entrance, their movements precise and silent save for the muted clang of steel doors being wrenched open. Bella followed close behind Luca, her flashlight slicing through the darkness as she scanned the interior for signs of Marco—or anything that might lead to him.

The space inside was oppressive, a labyrinth of rusting machinery and forgotten crates that loomed like tombstones in the dim light. The air was thick and heavy, saturated with the acrid stench of oil, mildew, and something faintly metallic. It clung to her skin, worming its way into her lungs as she advanced, gun drawn, each step a calculated risk.

"Clear!" a voice called from the far corner, echoing off the steel walls.

"Empty," another agent shouted, frustration tinging the word.

Bella's stomach twisted. Every darkened corner, every untouched crate seemed to mock her. She moved deeper into the maze, her flashlight catching glimpses of old tools, scattered bolts, and remnants of lives long abandoned.

"Bella, don't lose focus," Luca warned, his voice sharp as he gestured her back toward the main group.

"I'm fine," she snapped, though her pulse told a different story. She wasn't fine. Not with Marco so close and yet maddeningly out of reach.

Behind her, Sam was on his phone again, his voice low and urgent. Bella spun on her heel, her flashlight catching his startled expression.

"Who the hell are you calling?" she demanded, her voice slicing through the tense air.

"It's nothing," Sam said quickly, stuffing the phone into his pocket. "Just keeping tabs on another lead."

Her eyes searched his face, but before she could press further, a shout rang out from the far side of the warehouse.

"Boss! Over here!"

Bella was already moving, her flashlight bouncing against the shadows as she raced toward the sound. The agent stood near a crate partially pried open, his gloved hands holding up a small vial. The liquid inside glimmered faintly under the harsh beam of his flashlight.

"What is it?" Bella asked, breathless.

"Not sure," the agent replied grimly, handing the vial to her. "But it was locked up tight. Feels important."

Bella turned it over in her hand, her mind racing. Whatever this was, it felt like a breadcrumb leading directly to Marco—or worse, to something even darker.

"This isn't over," she muttered, the weight of the vial heavy in her palm.

And deep down, she knew it was just the beginning.

Bella moved around, her flashlight skimming over the room's debris—a graveyard of forgotten tools, splintered crates, and machinery long rendered obsolete. The suffocating air of decay was punctuated by the faint hum of electricity, so faint it could've been a figment of her overstimulated imagination. But then she saw it.

A laptop.

It sat incongruously on a battered metal desk at the center of the room, its faint glow stark against the grime and shadows. The sight was jarring, as if the sterile glow had no right to exist amidst the wreckage. Bella's pulse quickened as she approached, her fingers itching to uncover whatever it might hold.

"Bella, wait," Luca's voice cut through the silence, sharp but not loud. He moved in closer, his tall frame casting a shadow over the desk. "Could be a trap."

She hesitated only for a second before holstering her weapon, the weight of it suddenly a hindrance to what she needed to do. Her hands hovered above the laptop, her breath catching.

"What is it?" Luca's tone was cautious, measured.

Her voice came out low, tight with tension. "Marco. This is his signature."

Luca stepped closer, his sharp gaze narrowing. "Or it's bait."

"I know it is," she said, her tone sharper than she intended. She opened the laptop with a flick of her wrist, its hinges creaking faintly. The screen flared to life, casting pale light on her face.

There was a single file waiting, its name too nondescript to be accidental. She clicked it, her breath stilled as though her lungs refused to cooperate.

The message stared back at her, taunting in its simplicity:

You're closer than you think. Do you really know who the enemy is?

Her heart stuttered. For a moment, the words blurred, their meaning obscured by the flood of anger and unease surging through her.

"Damn it," she muttered under her breath, her voice trembling just enough to betray the firestorm inside her.

Luca leaned over her shoulder, his breath warm against her neck. His jaw clenched as he read the message aloud, each word laced with disdain. "He's taunting you. Trying to get inside your head."

"Well, it's working!" Bella snapped, slamming the laptop shut with a sharp clap that echoed in the hollow space. She turned to Luca, her chest heaving, her eyes blazing with frustration. "This isn't just a game to him. He's not just taunting me. He's making me doubt everything—everything and everyone."

"Everyone?"

Sam's voice broke the tension, its timing too convenient. Bella whirled around to find him leaning casually against the doorway, his arms crossed, the faint glow of his phone screen reflecting in his eyes. The look he gave her wasn't concern—it was something harder to define.

"Don't you mean someone?" he added, his voice dripping with implication.

Bella froze, the accusation in his words hitting too

close to home. "What the hell are you talking about, Sam?"

"You've been chasing Marco for weeks, Rossi. Long enough for it to mess with your instincts. Maybe you're so focused on him, you're missing the bigger picture."

Luca shot him a sharp look. "Enough, Sam. This isn't the time."

Bella stepped closer to Sam, her anger boiling over. "You're hiding something. Those calls, the texts—what aren't you telling me?"

Sam's expression flickered, a crack in his otherwise smug façade. "I'm doing my job. Maybe you should focus on yours."

Before Bella could retort, Luca intervened, stepping between them. His hand found her shoulder, grounding her with a firm grip. "Focus, both of you. We've got the laptop. That's our lead. Let's stick to it."

Bella pulled away from his touch, her body rigid with tension. She watched as the tech team carefully packed the laptop into a secure case, their movements efficient but somehow detached. The room began to clear, the once-tense atmosphere dissolving into the mundane shuffle of gear being packed away.

But Bella lingered. She couldn't shake the feeling that Marco's presence still clung to the air like smoke— tangible, choking, inescapable. The message he'd left was more than a taunt. It was a seed, planted deep in her psyche, designed to grow roots of doubt.

Her gaze swept the empty space one last time.

Why had Marco left the laptop behind? The answer felt just out of reach, a half-formed shadow lurking in her periphery.

As the echoes of footsteps faded, Bella felt the silence press in, heavy and suffocating. The question that gnawed at her wasn't just where Marco had gone.

It was why he'd let her get this close.

CHAPTER 6: A WEB OF DECEPTION

Bella paced the polished marble floor of her hotel room, her mind churning with the weight of the case and the tangled emotions she thought she'd buried.

Across the hall, Sam sat in the hotel bar nursing a whiskey, his gaze fixed on the melting ice in his glass. He hadn't seen Bella since they checked in, though he knew exactly which room was hers. She'd been distant—too distant—and it grated on him more than he cared to admit.

The bar was dimly lit, with warm amber tones and sleek modern furniture that whispered of understated luxury. Luca joined him without a word, sliding onto the stool beside him and ordering a beer. For a moment, the only sounds were the low hum of conversation and the faint clink of glasses being cleared.

"You've got that look," Luca said finally, taking a sip of his drink.

"What look?" Sam asked, his tone sharp.

"The one that says you're about to do something stupid," Luca replied evenly. "Like bang on her door and demand answers you're not ready to hear."

Sam's grip tightened around his glass. "Don't pretend you know what's going on between us."

Luca smirked, leaning back against the bar. "I don't have to pretend. It's written all over your face."

Sam turned to face him, his jaw tight. "And what about you? Always hovering around her like some damn guard dog. What's your angle, huh?"

Luca's expression darkened, the easy humor evaporating. "My angle is the job. The sooner we find Marco, the sooner Bella can get her head straight."

Sam snorted, his laugh bitter. "You think it's just the case that's messing with her? You don't know her like I do."

"And you think you know her better than she knows herself?" Luca shot back, his voice low but sharp. "She's a professional. She doesn't need you—or anyone else—deciding what's best for her."

Sam's retort was cut short as Bella entered the bar, her stride purposeful, her expression guarded. Her hair was pulled back in a no-nonsense ponytail, and she wore a simple black blouse with jeans that hugged her curves just enough to remind both men of the tension simmering between them.

"I hope you two are enjoying yourselves," she said dryly, crossing her arms.

Luca glanced at her with his usual calm, but Sam couldn't help the flicker of irritation that crossed his face.

"We were just discussing the case," Luca said smoothly, rising from his stool.

"Sure you were," Bella replied, her tone clipped. She turned her gaze to Sam, her eyes narrowing slightly. "And you? Have you been discussing the case or sulking because I didn't invite you to dinner?"

Sam bristled, his jaw tightening. "I'm not sulking. I'm just..."

"Drinking and waiting for me to come find you," she finished for him, her voice softening slightly. "We don't have time for this, Sam. Marco's trail is getting colder by the minute."

Sam sighed, running a hand through his hair. "You're right. But you can't keep shutting me out, Bella. Not about this."

"I'm not shutting you out," she said, her voice firm but tinged with weariness. "I'm keeping us focused. And right now, that means Sophia Ricci."

Luca cleared his throat, stepping between them. "Then let's focus. We've got a long day tomorrow, and I don't think Sophia Ricci is the type to appreciate sleep-deprived agents questioning her."

Bella nodded, her gaze lingering on Sam for a moment longer than necessary before turning and heading toward the elevator.

Sam watched her go, his chest tight with unspoken words.

Luca clapped him on the shoulder as he passed, his voice low but pointed. "She's not your battle to win, Sam. She's hers."

The elevator doors closed behind Bella with a soft ding, leaving Sam standing alone in the bar, the weight of Luca's words settling over him like a lead blanket.

∞

Naples was a paradox wrapped in sunlit chaos. Its streets pulsed with life—the staccato rhythm of Vespas weaving through the gridlock, the aroma of espresso wafting from corner cafes, and the lively banter of street vendors hawking everything from antiques to counterfeit designer bags. Yet beneath its colorful vibrancy lay a darker, unspoken layer—a city that had thrived for centuries on secrets, shadows, and sins.

Bella leaned her head against the cool window of the car as they navigated the serpentine roads leading to their destination. Her mind raced, piecing together fragments of a past conversation with Marco that now seemed to carry far more weight.

"My family's business isn't much different from mine," Marco had said, his tone casual as he poured them each a glass of wine on their last trip to Venice. He'd smirked, the kind of grin that danced the line between charm and provocation. "Art is about knowing how to see what others miss. That's the trick to everything."

At the time, it had felt like just another of Marco's

enigmatic quips, a flirtatious tease. Now, it was a lead.

Their next stop was the Sophia Ricci Gallery, a name pulled from an encrypted file on Marco's laptop—a name that reeked of exclusivity and the kind of wealth that thrived on whispers and backroom deals.

The gallery stood out like a modern jewel in the heart of Naples' historic district. Its facade was sharp and geometric, all reflective glass and brushed steel, daring to exist among weathered stone buildings that had withstood centuries. Bella stepped out of the car, her heels clicking against the uneven cobblestones. The air smelled of salt and lemon trees, but there was a faint undercurrent of something metallic, something off.

"Subtle," Luca remarked as they approached, his dry humor masking the same tension Bella felt.

Inside, the gallery was a temple to elegance. Soft, recessed lighting seemed to caress the artwork—an intimate, deliberate touch that made the gilded Renaissance masterpieces appear almost alive. The room was eerily silent, the kind of silence that demanded reverence and promised danger.

At the far end of the gallery, Sophia Ricci stood before a painting, her silhouette poised and commanding. Her emerald-green suit caught the light, its deep hue a stark contrast against the muted tones of the gallery. Her every movement was deliberate, exuding the kind of confidence that could either disarm or destroy.

"Detective Rossi," Sophia greeted, turning with a smile that was all polished charm and no warmth. Her espresso-dark eyes fixed on Bella first, then shifted to Luca with a flicker of recognition. "And Inspector Moretti. Naples is fortunate to host such esteemed guests."

Her voice carried an undercurrent of steel, every word calculated and deliberate.

"Ms. Ricci," Bella replied, her tone polite but firm. "We appreciate you seeing us on short notice."

Sophia's gaze lingered on Bella, her lips curling slightly as if she could sense the weight of the moral tightrope Bella was walking. "When the FBI and Interpol call, one doesn't refuse." She gestured toward a seating area—a semicircle of cream leather chairs that seemed more suitable for whispered conspiracies than casual conversation. "Please, let's sit. How can I be of assistance?"

Luca declined the invitation with a curt shake of his head, his stance deliberate and unyielding. "We're looking for Marco DeLuca," he said. "We believe you've had recent contact with him."

Sophia's smile widened, her perfectly manicured nails tracing the arm of the chair she lowered herself into. "Marco," she mused, her tone laced with a familiarity that made Bella's stomach tighten. "Such a complicated man."

Bella crossed her arms, refusing to take a seat. "Complicated doesn't begin to cover it."

Sophia's gaze shifted to Bella, sharp and assessing. "You knew him well, didn't you?" she said, her voice a velvet blade. "You're not just here because of duty,

Detective Rossi. There's something... personal in your pursuit."

Bella felt her pulse quicken, but her face betrayed nothing. "Marco's crimes are personal to every life he's ruined," she said evenly, though the words felt rehearsed.

From behind her, Luca shifted. His presence was a steadying weight, but Bella could sense the tension emanating from him—an unspoken wariness that mirrored her own.

Sophia's gaze flicked to Bella, her expression softening. "Ah, you're the one he spoke of."

Bella's pulse quickened, but she kept her face impassive. "And what exactly did he say?"

Sophia leaned back, crossing her legs. "That you were exceptional. Stubborn, determined. And that you had a sense of justice that bordered on obsession."

Luca cut in, his voice hard. "We're not here to discuss Bella's personality, Ms. Ricci. We need answers."

Sophia shrugged, her gaze drifting back to the painting on the wall. "I haven't seen Marco in years. But if I had, I imagine he'd have much to say about your little investigation."

"That's convenient," Bella said sharply. "But we both know you're lying."

Sophia's gaze snapped back to her, and for the first time, Bella saw a glimmer of something raw beneath her polished exterior—anger, maybe, or respect.

"You're bold," Sophia said softly. "I see why he was drawn to you."

Bella took a step closer, her eyes narrowing. "If you think you can distract me with cryptic compliments, you're mistaken. You know where he is, or at least where he's going."

Sophia smiled again, but this time it was cold, calculated. "Marco doesn't trust easily, Detective, but when he does, it's absolute. Can you say the same?"

The question struck like a slap. Bella's throat tightened, but she refused to falter. "My loyalty is to the truth. Not to him. Not to anyone."

"Truth," Sophia murmured, as though testing the word. "That's a dangerous thing to chase. Especially with Marco. He has a way of making you question it."

"Enough riddles," Luca snapped, his patience clearly wearing thin. "Tell us what you know about Dusker Corporation's European operations."

Sophia's expression turned coy. "If Marco wanted you to find me, it wasn't to get answers. He's smarter than that. He wanted to see how far you'd go, how much you'd risk."

"And what is that supposed to mean?" Bella demanded.

Sophia rose, smoothing the hem of her suit jacket. "It means you're playing his game, Detective. And he always plays to win."

She turned toward the painting she'd been admiring when they arrived—a Madonna and Child, the gold leaf shimmering under the lights. "Marco loved this piece," she said, her tone almost wistful. "He said it reminded him of home."

Bella clenched her fists, her frustration threatening to boil over. But before she could press further, Sophia turned back, her eyes sharp again.

"Be careful, Detective," she said, her voice low. "Marco may be the ghost you're chasing, but the real threat is much closer than you think."

Sophia laughed softly, the sound low and rich, like the first sip of good whiskey. "You're good, Detective. But you're also predictable. Marco always did know how to find the cracks."

"Maybe you'd like to tell us where those cracks have taken him," Luca interjected, his voice cutting through the room like a whip.

Sophia tilted her head, her amusement deepening. "If I knew where Marco was, do you think I'd be here talking to you?"

Before Bella could respond, a gallery assistant appeared, her heels clicking nervously against the polished floor. "Ms. Ricci, your next appointment is waiting."

Sophia waved her off without breaking eye contact with Bella. "Duty calls," she said with mock regret. Rising to her feet, she added, "I do hope you find Marco. He's far too interesting a man to be caged. But then again," she said with a glint of something predatory in her eyes, "you already know that, don't you?"

The silence that followed her exit felt suffocating.

"She's lying," Bella said finally, her voice sharp.

"Of course she is," Luca agreed. "The question is, about what?"

As they stood at the gallery, Bella's mind churned. Sophia Ricci knew more than she let on—but how much of it would lead them to Marco, and how much would drag them deeper into his web?

∞

The streets buzzed with life, but Bella barely registered the sounds of the city as she stepped out of Sophia Ricci's gallery. Her heels echoed against the uneven cobblestones, each step precise and controlled, masking the turmoil roiling beneath her calm exterior.

Luca walked beside her, his usual swagger muted, his gaze scanning the narrow streets with a practiced intensity. He lit a cigarette with a flick of his wrist, the tiny flame momentarily illuminating his angular features. The tension between them was as tangible as the heavy Mediterranean air.

"She's hiding something," Luca said, taking a long drag and exhaling smoke that curled like a ghost in the cooling air.

"Of course she is," Bella snapped, her voice tight as she glanced back at the gallery, its sleek modern facade a sharp contrast to the centuries-old buildings around it. "But she's not the one we're after. Marco's the mastermind here. He's leading us exactly where he wants us."

Luca's eyes narrowed as he studied her, the

cigarette dangling loosely between his fingers. "You think she's a pawn?"

Bella shook her head, her gaze fixed on the Naples skyline where the sea met the fading light. "No. She's more like the queen. And Marco's letting her make the first move."

Luca let out a low whistle, his tone laced with grim amusement. "Let's hope we're not already in checkmate."

The words hung in the air, heavy with implication. Bella didn't answer. She couldn't. Her mind was a battlefield of possibilities, each one more dangerous than the last. Sophia's cryptic words echoed in her thoughts.

Can you say the same?

The question twisted in her gut like a knife. For all her training, all her instincts, she couldn't shake the gnawing doubt. Did she really know who the enemy was?

Later that night, Sam found himself at the hotel bar, nursing a drink he didn't want. The low hum of conversation around him was a dull backdrop to the storm raging in his head. He glanced at the elevator, half-hoping Bella would appear, her sharp wit and fiery determination cutting through his conflicted thoughts.

Instead, Luca slid onto the stool beside him, his presence as unwelcome as it was inevitable.

"Rough day?" Luca asked, signaling to the bartender for a drink.

Sam didn't respond, his gaze fixed on the amber

liquid swirling in his glass.

"Let me guess," Luca continued, his tone edged with sarcasm. "You're torn between loyalty and… whatever it is you feel…"

Sam shot him a glare, but Luca just smirked, leaning back against the bar.

"You're not the first guy to fall for a woman who doesn't need saving," Luca said, his voice quieter now, almost contemplative. "But you'd better figure out where you stand before this gets messy."

"It's already messy," Sam muttered, more to himself than to Luca.

Luca took a sip of his drink, studying Sam with a knowing look. "Then you'd better hope you're not the one who gets burned."

The words lingered long after Luca walked away, leaving Sam alone with his thoughts and the heavy burden of a decision he wasn't ready to make. Upstairs, Bella sat by her window, staring out at the city lights, unaware of the storm brewing just a few floors below.

Inside his hotel room, Sam shut the door behind him, locking out the vibrant chaos of Naples. The room was spartan, its only adornment a single abstract painting that did little to distract from the oppressive beige walls. He pulled out a secure phone from his jacket, his fingers hesitating for a moment before dialing.

The line clicked, and Lawson's voice came through, cold and efficient. "Update."

Sam ran a hand through his hair, pacing the small

space. "She's unraveling," he said, keeping his voice low. "Sophia Ricci rattled her. And this case? It's personal for her now—too personal."

There was a long pause, the silence stretching like a taut wire. "We can't afford personal," Lawson said finally, his tone devoid of sympathy. "You know the protocol, Sam. If she becomes a liability..."

"She's not a liability," Sam cut in, his voice sharper than he intended.

"Yet," Lawson countered. "But if it comes to that, you're authorized to neutralize her. Make it clean."

The words hit Sam like a blow, the weight of them settling heavily on his shoulders. "You're asking me to..."

"I'm not asking," Lawson interrupted. "I'm giving you an order. Marco's too dangerous, and if Bella's emotions get in the way, the FBI can't risk the fallout. You know what's at stake."

The line went dead, leaving Sam staring at the phone in his hand, his chest tight with a mix of anger and dread.

CHAPTER 7: A TRAP IN TUSCANY

The phone sat heavy in Sophia Ricci's hand, the gold trim gleaming under the gallery's low lights. Her manicured nails tapped against the screen, the rhythmic sound betraying the nerves she kept hidden behind a practiced facade. When Marco DeLuca's voice finally came through, smooth and controlled, it was like slipping into a well-worn mask.

"She was here," Sophia said, keeping her voice low. "Your girlfriend. Asking questions about you."

A beat of silence. Then Marco's laugh, quiet and without humor. "Girlfriend is generous. Bella's predictable, isn't she?"

"She's not predictable; she's dangerous," Sophia snapped. "She had someone with her. That cop. Luca."

"I'll take care of Bella," Marco said, his tone hardening. "You just keep doing what you're told.

Don't make me regret trusting you, Sophia."

The line went dead before she could respond. Sophia lowered the phone, her lips pressed into a thin line. Marco always had a way of making threats sound like promises.

The encrypted text came through Bella's phone just past midnight. She was alone in her hotel room, the faint hum of Naples nightlife filtering through the cracked window.

We need to talk. You know where to find me.

An address followed: a remote villa outside Florence.

Bella stared at the screen, her chest tightening. Marco had never been one to beg, but this message carried a different weight—desperation laced with danger. She debated deleting it but hesitated. There was too much history between them, too many unanswered questions.

But now she'd brought Luca and Sam into the fold. The cavalry, as Marco would no doubt call them. And she wasn't sure whether she regretted it or welcomed the backup.

The villa perched on a hill just outside Florence, its terracotta walls glowing faintly under the rising moon. It was a postcard-perfect image, but to Bella, it felt anything but serene. The olive trees swayed in the light wind, their shadows dancing across the gravel driveway like skeletal fingers. A faint scent of lavender clung to the air, almost mocking in its peacefulness.

From their vantage point in the brush, Bella, Sam,

and Luca surveyed the scene. The villa's darkened windows offered no clues, but the faint glow of a security camera above the front door didn't go unnoticed.

"We approach methodically," Luca said, his voice clipped as he adjusted his earpiece. His movements were precise, almost ritualistic, as he secured his weapon. "I don't want anyone rushing in there blind."

Bella's jaw tightened. "If Marco's inside, we don't have time to play this safe. He's not the kind to linger."

"And if he's not?" Luca shot back, his tone sharp. "If this is a setup, you want to walk straight into his trap?"

The tension between them thickened, pressing against the cool night air. Bella tore her gaze away from Luca and back to the villa. Her fingers brushed the grip of her Glock, the familiar weight grounding her.

Sam broke the silence, his voice even but laced with an undercurrent of unease. "Marco sent her the address. He wants her alone." His gaze shifted to Bella, unreadable in the dim light. "What are you not telling us?"

Bella's stomach churned. She'd kept Marco's text to herself until they were en route, a decision that now felt like a betrayal—not of her team, but of the fragile balance she was trying to maintain.

"I don't trust him," she said finally, her voice low. "But if there's even a chance he's inside, I have to see this through."

Luca cursed under his breath, the sound harsh in

the stillness. "Then we do it my way. Slow and methodical. I don't care if he's your ex or the devil himself—you're not going in there without backup."

Bella nodded, her lips pressed into a thin line. She hated Luca's caution, hated how it mirrored the doubts gnawing at her. But she couldn't afford to let emotions cloud her judgment—not now.

∞

The villa, perched atop the Tuscan hill, bore witness to the past like a mausoleum for forgotten sins. Bella's gaze trailed over its facade, weathered by years of abandonment and neglect. Ivy clung to its walls like secrets desperate to stay hidden, and the stillness surrounding it felt oppressive—a suffocating weight pressing against her chest.

Every crunch of gravel underfoot felt like a betrayal, the sound carrying far too loudly in the night. She cast a glance at Luca, his jaw set in a way that betrayed his nerves, though his eyes remained locked ahead, scanning for movement.

"Stay sharp," he muttered, his voice barely audible over the faint whistle of wind cutting through the olive trees.

Bella's pulse quickened as she followed his directive, breaking off to skirt the villa's perimeter. The flashlight in her hand felt like a lifeline, its beam slicing through shadows that seemed eager to swallow her whole.

She paused near a cracked stone pillar, her instincts bristling. Something was wrong—off. The air carried an unnatural tension, like the world itself was holding its breath.

The first shot shattered the stillness, followed by the hiss of bullets carving through the air.

"Ambush!" Luca's voice barked through the earpiece, sharp and controlled.

Bella dove behind the pillar, plaster dust exploding around her as bullets chewed into the stone. Her breath came in shallow gasps as she pressed her back against the rough surface, her Glock drawn and steady.

From her vantage point, she saw the source of the chaos—three figures emerging from the treeline, their silhouettes dark against the faint glow of the villa's security lights. Mercenaries. Well-trained and precise.

She returned fire, the recoil jolting up her arm as her shots forced the figures to scatter.

"Sam, status!" she called, her voice strained.

A grunt came through the comms, followed by Sam's clipped response. "Took a hit—just a graze."

But Bella caught sight of him near the front steps, clutching his side where blood seeped through his fingers.

"Damn it," she muttered, her grip tightening on her weapon. "Hang in there."

The fight raged on, each second an eternity of chaos and violence. Bella moved like a shadow, her body low as she weaved through the villa's uneven terrain. She was hyper-aware of every sound, every shift of the air around her.

One of the mercenaries broke from the group,

flanking her position. She heard his approach before she saw him, the crunch of gravel betraying his intent. As his shadow stretched across the stone wall, Bella braced herself.

When he rounded the corner, she didn't hesitate. Her elbow struck his jaw with a sickening crack, and as he staggered, she fired. The shot was deafening, and the man dropped to the ground in a heap.

The fight felt endless, the villa's tranquil setting now a warzone of splintered wood and shattered stone. But eventually, the gunfire ceased, replaced by a silence so profound it pressed against her ears.

Bella rose from her cover, her chest heaving as she scanned the scene. The mercenaries lay sprawled in the gravel, their dark uniforms blending with the shadows.

"Clear?" Luca's voice came through, weary but resolute.

"Clear," Bella confirmed, though her hands still trembled around her Glock. She moved toward Sam, dropping to her knees beside him.

He waved her off, his face pale but determined. "It's just a scratch," he said, though his wince betrayed the lie.

"You're lucky it's just a scratch," she muttered, her voice tight with barely concealed worry.

He was sitting against the villa's crumbling wall, his hand pressed to his side. The wound wasn't fatal, but his face was pale, and his breathing was labored.

"I'm fine," he insisted through gritted teeth.

"You're bleeding out, and you call that fine?"

Bella's voice cracked, betraying the edge of panic she tried to suppress. She tore a strip from her shirt with trembling hands, pressing it against the wound on his side.

His smirk was faint but infuriating. "Takes more than this to take me down."

Bella muttered a curse, her hands trembling as she worked.

Luca appeared beside them, crouching down and rolling up the sleeve of his own jacket. A thin, angry gash ran along his forearm, shallow but bloody.

"See?" he said, flashing Bella a grin that didn't quite reach his eyes. "This is a scratch."

Bella spared him a sharp glance. "Don't start with me, Luca."

"I wasn't planning to," he shot back, his tone deliberately light. "But you're making that face like the world's ending, and one of us has to stay optimistic."

"Optimistic?" Bella hissed. "The man's bleeding out on my lap, and you think optimism is the answer?"

"It's worked for me so far." He tugged a bandana from his pocket and tied it around his arm with a practiced ease that only heightened Bella's irritation.

Sam groaned softly, drawing her attention back to him. "Can you two quit bickering?" His voice was barely a whisper. "You're giving me a headache."

Bella bit back the lump rising in her throat and forced a tight smile. "Shut up, Sam. You're not dying on me tonight."

Luca tried to ease the tension, his expression grim

as he surveyed the aftermath. "This wasn't random. Marco knew we'd come."

Bella didn't answer. Her mind was already racing, piecing together Marco's intentions, his endgame.

Once Sam was stable enough to stand, they moved inside. The villa was eerily empty, its rooms stripped of all but the barest furnishings. Bare walls bore the faded outlines of where paintings had hung, and the stripped floors echoed their every step. Bella felt the weight of its emptiness pressing down on her. This wasn't a home—it was a staging ground, meant for fleeting shadows and whispered plans.

And somewhere inside, she knew, Marco was waiting.

The question was no longer if she could face him. It was whether she could survive what came next.

In the main room, Bella's flashlight swept across the floor, catching a glint that made her freeze. She crouched, her fingers brushing against something cool and familiar.

A bracelet.

Her bracelet.

She stared at it, the tiny charms still intact, their edges polished smooth by time and wear. She'd given it to Marco months ago, slipping it into his pocket as a playful gesture, never imagining it would find its way back to her like this.

It wasn't just a token. It was a message.

"He knew we'd set a trap," Bella whispered, her voice trembling with a mix of anger and anguish.

Luca leaned against the doorframe, his bandaged arm hanging at his side. "Yeah, and he's loving every second of this. He's playing you, Bella."

She clenched the bracelet in her fist, the cold metal biting into her palm. "Or he's leaving breadcrumbs," she said. "He wants me to follow."

"Follow him where? Into another ambush?" His frustration was palpable, but Bella's mind was already spinning, threading together Marco's intentions with the precision of a surgeon piecing together a shattered bone.

But before she could respond, a strangled gasp from behind drew her attention.

"Sam!" Bella turned, just in time to see him collapse against the wall.

Blood seeped through his shirt in a deep crimson stain, and his legs buckled. Bella and Luca rushed to him, lowering him gently to the floor. His eyes fluttered open, but the fight was gone from them.

"No, no, no," Bella murmured, her hands frantically pressing against his wound. "Stay with me, Sam!"

Luca was already on his radio, barking for an emergency evac, but Bella knew the truth before the words left his mouth. The wound had been worse than Sam let on. The bullet had caused internal damage, and his fading breaths were confirmation of how dire it was.

"No," Sam croaked, his hand feebly reaching for Bella's. "Leave me."

"Not a chance," Bella snapped, pressing harder against the wound. "You don't get to give up, Sam. Not here. Not now."

His lips twitched in a ghost of a smile. "Stubborn as ever."

Luca knelt beside her, his expression grim. "We need to move him. Now."

Sam's hand weakly grasped hers. "Bella..." His voice was barely audible, a shadow of its usual strength. "Find him...finish this..."

Tears blurred her vision as his hand went limp in hers.

And then his eyes slipped shut.

The medics' rushed efforts had been in vain. Sam was gone.

Bella stood frozen as they carried him away, her hands smeared with his blood. The world felt cold, hollow, and infinitely quieter.

Her chest felt hollow as she watched them load Sam into the evac vehicle.

Later, when the villa was cleared and the silence returned, Bella sat alone, her fingers trembling as she sifted through Sam's belongings. Among the standard-issue items, one object stood out: an encrypted phone.

Her stomach churned as she scrolled through the recent call log. The last number dialed sent a chill through her.

Lawson.

She pressed the call button, her breath tight in her chest. The line clicked, and a familiar voice came through, deep and steady. "You're not supposed to be calling me on this line."

Bella dropped the phone as if it had burned her. It clattered onto the table, the sound echoing through the empty room.

Lawson and Sam, communicating through an encrypted phone? Not the agency-issued lines?

Her mind raced with questions, each one darker than the last. What the hell had they been hiding? And why did she feel like the truth was about to shatter everything she thought she knew?

As Luca entered the room, his gaze heavy with concern, Bella looked up.

"It's just us now," she said quietly, the weight of her words sinking in.

"And Marco?" Luca asked.

Bella's eyes hardened. "Marco isn't the only one with secrets. And I'm going to uncover every single one of them."

Bella's instincts screamed that the truth would be far worse than any betrayal Marco could devise. Because it wasn't just Marco's web she was trapped in—it was the agency's.

And the deeper she went, the more she feared the truth might destroy her. But she wasn't sure if she was ready for it.

CHAPTER 8: FLASHBACKS AND DOUBTS

The safehouse in Rome was a coffin of muted sounds and dim, oppressive light. The walls were a sickly beige, scuffed and scarred with years of neglect. The air reeked faintly of mildew and stale cigarette smoke, suffocating and dense, making every breath feel like an effort.

Bella sat cross-legged on the threadbare rug in the corner of the cramped living room, a half-empty cup of tepid coffee on the floor beside her. Her fingers toyed with the bracelet Marco had left behind—a cruel breadcrumb on the twisted path he'd laid out for her. The charms clinked softly as she rolled it in her palm, their faint metallic notes eerily discordant in the silence.

On the sagging couch, Luca sprawled in a restless attempt to get comfortable. The bandage on his arm had already begun to darken, though he claimed the injury was nothing. His sharp, assessing eyes never left Bella, tracking every twitch of her hand, every tightening of her jaw.

"You're torturing yourself," he said finally, breaking the thick silence. His voice was roughened by exhaustion but carried a gentle undercurrent of concern.

Bella didn't respond at first, her gaze glued to the bracelet. The tiny elephant charm caught the light, throwing a flicker onto the grimy wall.

"I can't shut it off," she murmured, her voice low, almost a confession. "Not when it's him."

"Especially because it's him," Luca countered. He swung his legs over the side of the couch, wincing as he sat upright. His free hand pressed against his side, but the grimace on his face vanished quickly, replaced by the steady determination she knew too well. "You've got to stop seeing him as the man he pretended to be, Bella. That man doesn't exist anymore. Ma è pazzo!"

Her knuckles whitened as she gripped the bracelet tighter, the cool metal biting into her skin. "That's the thing, Luca. I don't know if I ever saw the real him at all."

She looked up then, her eyes meeting his. They glistened, but no tears fell. Bella didn't cry—not anymore.

"I keep going back to the beginning," she said, her voice trembling but steady enough to cut through the room's thick air. "To how perfect it all was. Too perfect, maybe. But when you grow up the way I did…"

Her words faltered, and she shook her head, exhaling sharply as if to rid herself of the memories clawing at the edges of her mind.

Luca's brows knit together, the lines on his face deepening. "Bella…" he began, his tone wary, but she held up a hand, cutting him off.

"No, I need to say this." Her voice cracked slightly, but she pressed on. "I didn't have family. No one. Not really. Foster homes, group homes, social workers who barely remembered my name unless it was in their files. And then Marco…" She laughed bitterly, a harsh sound that echoed off the peeling walls. "Marco felt like a miracle. Like someone had written him into my life just to prove that I wasn't completely unlovable."

The memory rose unbidden, as vivid as if she were living it all over again.

It had been late, the streets of New York bathed in the amber glow of streetlights as Marco led her through a side door of the art gallery. The space was empty, save for them, the only sound the faint echo of their footsteps on the polished floors.

"How did you manage this?" Bella had asked, her voice tinged with awe.

Marco had grinned, that boyish, disarming grin that always made her heart skip. "I have my ways," he said, slipping his arm around her waist.

They strolled through the exhibits, Marco pausing now and then to comment on a piece with a passion that took her breath away. He spoke about justice and morality, about how art could expose the truths people wanted to hide.

"This," he said, gesturing to a dark, haunting painting of a lone figure walking a tightrope over a fiery abyss, "is the world we live in. Every decision is a balancing act. One wrong step, and you're done."

She'd looked up at him, struck by the intensity in his eyes. "That's a bleak way to see things."

Marco had turned to her then, his expression softening. "It's not bleak. It's honest. And sometimes, the only way to survive is to understand the rules of the game better than anyone else."

At the time, she'd thought his words were profound, a reflection of the moral complexities she grappled with daily as a detective. Now, they felt like a warning she'd ignored.

Bella dragged herself back to the present, her heart pounding as if she'd just run a marathon. She set the bracelet on the table, the clink of metal on wood unnaturally loud in the stillness.

"He played me," she said quietly, the words tasting bitter on her tongue.

Luca leaned forward, his elbows resting on his knees. "He's still playing you, Bella. That bracelet? The messages he leaves? It's all part of his game."

"I should've seen it coming," she said, shaking her head. "There were signs. The late-night calls. The way he'd change the subject whenever I brought up Dusker Corporation. Hell, even that gallery night… He wasn't just showing me art. He was planting seeds."

Luca's expression softened, a rare flicker of empathy breaking through his usual gruff exterior. "People like Marco? They know how to weave a story, Bella. They tell you exactly what you want to hear until it feels like the truth."

She swallowed hard, her throat tight. "He made me believe it all, Luca. That I could have something good. That I could be someone who mattered to someone else."

Luca leaned forward, resting his elbows on his knees. "And now you think it was all a lie?"

Bella's laugh this time was quieter, hollow. "I don't know what to think. Maybe he loved me, in his own twisted way. Or maybe I was just another pawn, a means to an end."

She tilted her head, studying the bracelet like it held the answers she couldn't find. "But it doesn't change the fact that I let him in. All the way in. I gave him every piece of me, and now he's using it against me."

The silence that followed was thick, heavy with unspoken truths. Luca shifted, his injured arm held protectively against his chest.

"Bella," he said finally, his voice low and steady, "whatever he was to you, whoever he pretended to be—you're not that person anymore. You're stronger than that."

She looked at him, her expression unreadable. "You don't get it, Luca. He wasn't just some guy. He was everything I didn't even know I wanted. He was my family, my home… and now he's my nightmare."

Luca's jaw tightened, his eyes dark with something she couldn't name. "Then it's time to wake up," he said softly. "And take him down."

The words hung between them, sharp and unyielding. Bella looked away, her gaze drifting back to the bracelet.

Another memory surfaced, this one gentler but no less painful.

She'd come home late after a grueling day—a hostage negotiation that had gone sideways. She'd been exhausted, covered in grime, her hands still shaking from the adrenaline crash.

Marco had been waiting, his face shadowed with concern as he took her coat and pulled her into his arms.

"You're freezing," he'd murmured, his voice warm against her hair.

She'd let him lead her to the couch, where he'd wrapped her in a blanket and brought her a steaming cup of tea. He hadn't asked about her day, hadn't pressed for details. Instead, he'd just sat with her, his presence a balm she hadn't known she needed.

"You don't always have to carry it alone," he'd said softly, his hand resting over hers.

In that moment, she'd believed him. She'd let herself lean on him, convinced he was her safe harbor in the storm.

Bella pressed her hands to her face, the weight of the memories crushing. "How do you reconcile that?" she asked, her voice breaking. "The man who held me when I thought I'd fall apart… and the man who's tearing everything apart now?"

Luca didn't answer right away. When he did, his tone was low, steady. "You don't. You accept that both versions exist. And then you focus on the version you're chasing—the one who's making the choices that endanger lives."

Bella met his gaze, her vulnerability stark against her usual steely exterior. "What if I can't do it, Luca? What if, when the time comes, I can't pull the trigger?"

Luca held her stare, his expression unreadable. "Then he's already won."

The words landed like a blow, but Bella didn't argue. Deep down, she knew he was right.

"I just hope," she whispered, so quietly he almost didn't hear, "that when this is over, I can live with the choices I've made."

Luca didn't answer, but his silence spoke volumes. Outside, the city buzzed faintly, a muffled sound that felt a world away. Inside the safehouse, the tension was a living, breathing thing, coiling tighter around them with every passing moment.

As the safehouse settled into uneasy silence, Bella stared at the bracelet once more, its delicate charms glinting like tiny pieces of a puzzle she couldn't solve.

Did you love me, Marco? she thought bitterly. Or

was I just another move in your game?

The question would haunt her, but she pushed it aside. Marco might have played her once, but she wouldn't let him do it again. Not from a distance. Not ever.

And somewhere out there, Marco was waiting.

But Bella's whispered confession hung in the air, echoing in Luca's mind as he sat on the edge of the couch, his bandaged arm cradled against his chest.

Bella glanced at him, her sharp gaze flicking to the blood seeping through the gauze. "You need to change that before it gets infected," she said, her voice brisk, cutting through the thick silence.

Luca opened his mouth to argue, but her raised brow silenced him. "Fine," he muttered, reaching for the makeshift first aid kit on the coffee table.

"Let me." Her words stopped him mid-motion.

He hesitated. "Bella, I can..."

"Don't argue," she snapped, already kneeling beside him. Her fingers brushed his good hand as she took the bandages from him, her touch light but sure.

Her nearness unsettled him more than he cared to admit. The faint scent of her—jasmine and a hint of something sharper, like gun oil—filled his senses, making it hard to focus on the pain in his arm.

"This is going to sting," she murmured, her voice softer now, almost tender.

She worked with practiced efficiency, dabbing antiseptic onto the gash. The cool liquid burned, but Luca barely flinched, too distracted by the brush of her fingers against his skin. He watched her, the way her lashes lowered as she concentrated, the slight furrow of her brow.

"You've done this before," he said, more to fill the silence than anything else.

Her lips curved into a humorless smile. "When you grow up in the system, you learn to patch yourself up. No one else is going to do it for you."

The words were light, but the undertone hit him like a punch. He didn't reply, unsure what he could say that wouldn't sound trite.

When she finished, she smoothed the bandage into place with a gentle press of her palm. The touch lingered just a second too long, and their eyes met.

The air between them shifted, heavy with something unspoken. For a moment, neither moved, the weight of her hand on his arm a tether neither of them wanted to break.

"Thanks," he said finally, his voice rough. He stood abruptly, taking a step back as if to put distance between them—and the crackling tension in the room.

"I'm going to pick up some food," he announced, grabbing his jacket.

Bella frowned. "I'll come with you."

"No," he said quickly, too quickly. "You're safer here. I'll blend in better." He tried for a smirk. "Italian, remember?"

She didn't look convinced. "Luca..."

"Stay put, Bella." His tone brooked no argument. "I'll be back soon."

Before she could protest further, he was out the door.

∞

The cool night air hit him like a slap, a sharp contrast to the stifling confines of the safehouse. Luca tugged his collar higher, keeping his head down as he navigated the narrow streets. The city pulsed around him, vibrant and alive, yet he felt like a ghost slipping through its veins, unseen and unnoticed.

He avoided the crowded piazzas and well-lit avenues, sticking to shadowed alleyways where he could move without drawing attention. The sharp smell of roasted chestnuts wafted from a nearby vendor, mingling with the tang of exhaust fumes and the faint saltiness of the Tiber.

As he walked, his thoughts drifted back to Bella. Her touch. The way her eyes had softened, just for a moment, as she'd tended to him.

She was a puzzle he couldn't solve, her sharp edges and hidden vulnerabilities tangling his thoughts. Could she really be innocent?

He wanted to believe her, wanted to trust the woman who had risked everything to bring down Marco. But every instinct in him, honed by years of undercover work and too many betrayals, screamed caution.

Her whispered confession echoed in his mind: Did you love me, Marco? Or was I just another move in your game? The question wasn't just hers. It was his too, though the name might change.

Did you know, Bella? Or were you just another pawn?

Luca stopped at the edge of a bridge, leaning against the cold stone railing. The river flowed beneath him, dark and unyielding, its surface rippling like the doubts swirling in his mind.

He couldn't afford distractions—not now. Yet, as he stared into the inky water, he couldn't shake the memory of her touch, the way it had ignited something in him he thought he'd buried long ago. Shaking his head, he straightened. There was no room for this. Not here, not now.

He shoved his hands into his pockets and turned away from the river, his jaw set. Somewhere out there, Marco was waiting, and Bella was either his greatest ally—or his deadliest trap.

And Luca intended to find out which before it was too late.

CHAPTER 9: THE ROMAN MARKETPLACE

T he Campo de' Fiori buzzed with life, a kaleidoscope of sounds, colors, and motion that made it the perfect cover for someone who didn't want to be found. Morning sunlight spilled across the cobblestones, turning the vibrant produce stands and rustic flower carts into bursts of color. Vendors barked out their prices, their voices competing with the hum of tourists and locals alike. The air carried the layered scents of ripe fruit, fresh bread, and the faint tang of motor oil drifting from a nearby Vespa.

Bella lingered by a stall bursting with tomatoes so red they seemed almost surreal, her fingers brushing one absently as her gaze swept the crowd. Her scarf, carefully chosen to blend in with the locals, framed her face in soft folds. She tugged it higher, more for something to do than against the chill, her tension humming just beneath the surface.

"Anything yet?" Luca's voice came through the earpiece, low and gravelly, punctuated by a faint crackle of static.

"Not yet," Bella murmured. Her lips barely moved, but her eyes flicked to a group of men unloading crates of artichokes a few stalls away.

"Don't look suspicious," Luca warned. "You're not exactly fluent in Italian."

Bella smirked, her tone light to mask her nerves. "Posso parlare un po' di italiano."

Luca's silence was heavy, then, "Impressive. But let's not test how far 'a little' will take you, principessa."

The nickname, tinged with a mix of irritation and humor, was a callback to their earlier arguments. It drew a faint smile from her, despite herself.

"They'll buy it," she said, picking up a tomato and inspecting it like a seasoned shopper. Her hand was steady, but her pulse betrayed her, a steady drumbeat in her ears. "What's our timeframe?"

"Short," Luca replied. "Marco was spotted here three days ago, blending into the crowd. If he's here, we'll see him. If not..."

If not, it was back to square one, chasing the faintest threads of a ghost through the labyrinth of Rome.

Bella put the tomato back on the pile, her eyes scanning beyond the stalls, lingering on faces. A man in a tailored coat arguing over the price of cheese. A woman juggling an armful of flowers and a squirming toddler. Another man, casually flipping through wallets at a leather goods stand.

And then she saw him.

The world seemed to sharpen, the chaos of the market narrowing to a single point. Marco stood at the edge of the crowd, his dark jacket blending into the patchwork of shadows and sunlight. A baseball cap shielded most of his face, but it wasn't enough to hide him.

Their eyes met, and Bella's breath caught.

His lips curved into a faint smile—not warmth, but something colder, sharper. A predator's smile.

"Luca," she said sharply, her voice steady despite the adrenaline surging through her veins. "I've got him."

"Where?" Luca's tone changed instantly, all business.

"He's heading west," Bella said, already moving. Her feet carried her forward before her mind could catch up.

"Don't lose him," Luca ordered.

"I won't." Her eyes locked onto Marco's retreating figure as he weaved through the crowd with a casual ease that belied his purpose.

But as she followed, her gut twisted with doubt. This wasn't just about catching Marco. This was about confronting the man who'd once held her heart, the man she'd trusted with everything, only to find herself betrayed.

The chase was a blur of sound and motion. And this time, Bella promised herself, she wouldn't let him get away.

Bella wove through the teeming throngs of the marketplace, her senses locked on Marco's retreating form. The cap he wore was an unassuming black, blending into the sea of bobbing heads, but she knew his stride, the almost languid confidence that dared anyone to follow.

Her boots struck the cobblestones with precision, dodging strollers and street performers, the chaos of the Campo de' Fiori folding into background noise. A juggler stumbled into her path, his pins scattering like fallen soldiers. Bella barely registered his curse as she surged forward.

"Marco!" she called, her voice cutting through the din like the crack of a whip.

He didn't look back.

Her heart pounded against her ribs, each beat reminding her of the stakes. The weight of her Glock at her hip was both a comfort and a warning. If this ended in blood, she wasn't sure whose it would be.

He veered into a narrow alley, and she followed, the space claustrophobic, the air heavy with the smell of damp stone and something acrid, like spilled wine. Her pulse quickened as she turned the corner into a quiet courtyard, the marketplace's cacophony reduced to a distant murmur.

Marco stood in the center, his back to her. The sunlight caught the edges of his frame, gilding him in gold and shadow.

Bella drew her weapon, leveling it with precision honed through years of training. Her breath came in sharp bursts, her voice steely. "Don't move."

Slowly, deliberately, he turned. His hands rose in mock surrender, the movement fluid, like he'd rehearsed it a thousand times. His face, achingly familiar, was etched with a quiet amusement that ignited her anger.

"Bella," he said, her name falling from his lips like a caress.

"Hands where I can see them," she snapped. The slight tremor in her voice betrayed her resolve, but she steadied herself, tightening her grip on the Glock.

He complied, his dark eyes never leaving hers. "You found me," he murmured, his lips curving into that maddening, faintly amused smile.

"Don't flatter yourself," she said, her voice cold, but her pulse roared in her ears. "What's the endgame, Marco? Why are you here?"

He tilted his head, studying her as if she were the puzzle he'd been trying to solve. "The endgame?" His voice was quiet, almost tender. "You're looking at the wrong board, bella mia. The real killers, the ones pulling the strings—they're in your own backyard."

She scoffed, her finger hovering near the trigger. "You expect me to believe that? After everything you've done?"

"Everything I've done?" He stepped closer, his voice rising, not with anger, but with something raw.

"I've been trying to protect you. To stop them. Dusker Corporation, the agency—they're not what you think they are."

"Dusker Corporation?" Her laugh was bitter. "By assassinating Marcus Kane? By killing a man in cold blood?"

His jaw tightened, and for a fleeting moment, his composure cracked, revealing something more vulnerable. "Kane was a pawn. His death was a message, one that needed to be sent. But they didn't stop, did they? They'll keep going until the world is theirs to control."

She narrowed her eyes, the weight of his words pressing against the wall she'd built between them. "And what about the villa in Tuscany? Was I just collateral damage?"

His expression softened, and when he spoke, his voice was low, pleading. "That wasn't me, Bella. That was Sam."

She flinched at the name, her mask slipping for just a moment.

"You knew," he pressed, his voice slipping into his Italian lilt, warm and persuasive. "Deep down, you knew he wasn't who he said he was. You felt it, didn't you?"

"I don't believe you," she whispered, but the words felt hollow.

Marco took a step closer, his hands still raised, his gaze boring into hers. "Sam was a double agent, working for the FBI. He had orders to take you out,

Bella. Orders from your own people."

Her heart twisted, a war waging between her instincts and the truth she didn't want to face. "Stop."

"Why would I lie to you about this?" His voice softened further, and he took another cautious step forward. "Why would I try to protect someone who's holding a gun to my chest if I didn't care about them?"

"Marco…" Her voice broke, the years of betrayal, doubt, and longing converging into a single word.

"I missed you, bella mia," he said, his voice dipping to that dangerous murmur that always unraveled her. "Every day, every hour."

Her grip faltered, but she willed herself to hold steady. "You missed me? Is that why you played me? Why you…"

"I never played you." His voice was sharp, cutting through her accusation. "I never lied about you. Not once."

The silence stretched between them, heavy and taut.

Finally, she spoke, her voice cold and determined. "Then prove it."

Marco smiled, a ghost of the man she once knew, and took a deliberate step close. "I will, Bella. But you're going to have to trust me first."

Bella could smell him, the subtle mix of aftershave and musk that always seemed to follow him, clinging to her clothes, her hair, her skin. The memory of it, the warmth and intimacy and promise, flooded her with longing.

She lowered her gun.

Marco didn't waste the chance, his hands reaching up to cup her cheeks, his thumb grazing her lips as his dark eyes held hers. He buried his face in her neck, his lips trailing along the hollow of her throat, and for a moment, she let herself sink into him, his warmth and strength and scent overwhelming her.

He whispered into her ears, "Come with me."

Bella tensed, reality crashing through the haze of emotion. She pulled away, her eyes searching his, the Glock heavy in her hand. "I can't do that."

Marco smiled, and the tenderness of it pierced her, a knife to the heart. "I know."

His words clung to Bella's mind like the acrid smoke that had yet to fully dissipate. They were a toxic cocktail of truths and half-lies, designed to worm their way under her skin, and damn it, they were working.

"I'm done listening to your excuses," she said, her voice razor-sharp, cutting through the tension between them. "You're coming in."

Marco sighed, a rueful smile ghosting over his lips. It was infuriating, that calm, unshakeable confidence of his. The kind that had once charmed her and now set her teeth on edge.

"You've always been so quick to judge, bella mia," he said softly, the endearment sliding off his tongue like silk. "But ask yourself this—if I'm the monster, why did I leave you the bracelet? Why did I let you get this close?"

The bracelet. She hated how the mention of it

made her chest tighten.

Her jaw clenched, and her finger tightened on the trigger. She didn't have time to answer—not that she had an answer to give.

With a sudden hiss, smoke erupted from the ground. Thick and acrid, it swallowed the courtyard in an instant, stinging her eyes and clawing at her throat. Bella coughed violently, stumbling forward as she raised her gun into the dense haze.

"Marco!" she shouted, her voice raw and desperate.

No response. Only the muffled echo of retreating footsteps, faint and infuriatingly distant.

When the smoke finally began to dissipate, the courtyard was a barren, mocking reminder of her failure. Marco was gone.

∞

Bella slammed her fist into her other palm, the sting a poor substitute for the sharp, burning edge of frustration that coursed through her veins.

"He was right there," she said, her voice trembling, anger lacing every syllable. "I had him."

A familiar voice answered her from the edge of the courtyard. "And he wanted you to."

She spun, startled by Luca's sudden presence. He stood at the archway, his sharp suit now slightly disheveled, his expression carved from stone.

"What the hell is that supposed to mean?" Bella snapped, her frustration spilling over.

Luca stepped closer, his movements measured, careful. The faint scent of his aftershave—something crisp and citrusy—cut through the lingering smoke, grounding her for a fleeting moment.

"What the hell was that back there?" he demanded, his voice sharp enough to cut through the hum of her thoughts.

Bella faced him, her eyes flashing with anger. "I had him, Luca. I was this close to bringing him in, and he slipped away—again. Don't you think I'm as furious as you are?"

"That's not what I'm talking about," Luca snapped, pointing at her. "You hesitated."

Her heart stuttered, but she covered it with a glare. "I didn't hesitate. I was calculating my move..."

"Bullshit!" Luca's voice rose, and for a moment, Bella saw the strain of the past few days etched into every line of his face. "You didn't pull the trigger because you wanted answers. You're not chasing him to bring him to justice, Bella. You're chasing him because you need to understand why he betrayed you."

The words hit her like a physical blow.

"That's not true," she shot back, but her voice lacked conviction.

"Isn't it?" Luca stepped closer, his dark eyes unrelenting. "Marco knows exactly how to play you. That stunt in the courtyard? It wasn't about escaping. It was about planting more doubt in your head. And it's working."

Bella's chest tightened, anger and guilt warring

inside her. "You think I don't know what he's doing?" she hissed. "You think I haven't been questioning every choice I've made since this started? Marco betrayed me, Luca. He lied to me, used me. I won't let him do it again."

"Then prove it," Luca said coldly. "Start acting like the detective you are, not the woman who's still in love with a ghost."

The words hung in the air like a guillotine, and for a moment, Bella couldn't breathe.

She turned away, her fists clenched at her sides. "Fine, you caught me," she said tightly. "If you want to lecture me, save it for later. Right now, we have work to do."

"This wasn't about getting caught, Bella," he said evenly, his dark eyes scanning the empty courtyard as if Marco's shadow might still linger. "It was about him sending a message. He wanted you to see him."

Bella's fists tightened, her nails biting into her palms. "What message, Luca? That he's always one step ahead? That he can walk away whenever he damn well pleases?"

Luca tilted his head, studying her with a blend of patience and pity she didn't want to see. "Or that he's more in control of this game than you think."

His words landed like a punch to her gut, and for a moment, the world seemed to tilt. Marco's voice echoed in her head, slippery and insidious. *The real killers are the ones you work for.*

"Damn it," she muttered under her breath, her

gaze dropping to the uneven cobblestones beneath her feet. Her mind replayed every detail of their encounter, every word, every flicker of emotion on his face. Was he lying? Twisting the truth to manipulate her, to pull her closer into his web? Or was there a kernel of something real buried beneath the layers of deception?

"You're doubting yourself," Luca said, his voice softer now. He stepped closer, his tone holding a rare note of concern. "Don't let him do that to you, Bella. Marco's a master manipulator. If you're not careful, he'll make you question everything—even yourself."

She raised her eyes to meet his, her jaw set, her voice quiet but resolute. "I have to know, Luca. I have to know if he's lying—or if I've been chasing the wrong enemy all along."

For a moment, Luca said nothing, his expression inscrutable. Then he sighed, his hand brushing over his short-cropped hair. "You're walking a dangerous line, Bella."

"I know," she said simply, the weight of her words hanging in the smoke-filled air like a storm cloud.

∞

The quiet after Marco's escape felt oppressive, as if the narrow alleyways around her were closing in, mocking her failure.

Luca paced near the fountain, his sharp profile illuminated by the faint glow of the afternoon sun. He had his phone pressed to his ear, his free hand resting on his hip in a gesture of barely contained irritation.

Bella didn't need to hear the other side of the conversation to know that something had shifted. She caught fragments—names, locations, a clipped confirmation in Italian—but the rest was a blur.

She focused on the fountain, the gentle trickle of water a stark contrast to the storm raging inside her. Marco's words played on a loop in her mind, a poison she couldn't purge. The real killers are the ones you work for.

Luca ended the call with a sharp grazie before turning to her. His expression was all business, but there was an edge of something else—urgency, maybe.

"We've been called back to the Interpol office," he said, his voice steady but low, as if the courtyard itself might betray them.

Bella frowned, her brow furrowing in irritation. "What's so urgent that they're pulling us off this?" She gestured toward the now-empty space where Marco had stood just moments ago.

Luca hesitated, his jaw tightening. "They didn't say. Just that we're needed immediately."

Bella's eyes narrowed, her instincts flaring. "You don't believe that any more than I do."

He didn't answer right away, which was answer enough. Instead, he gestured for her to follow him, his stride purposeful as they navigated back through the labyrinth of alleys.

The marketplace was a different world now, its earlier chaos subdued as vendors began packing up their stalls. The vibrant colors of the day—ripe oranges, handwoven scarves, and gleaming trinkets—seemed muted in the dying light.

"What aren't they telling us, Luca?" Bella asked, breaking the tense silence between them.

He glanced at her, his expression unreadable. "Maybe it's nothing. Or maybe it's something big enough to warrant us abandoning the lead we've been chasing for months."

Her stomach tightened. She hated the way his calm delivery made her feel unmoored, like the ground beneath her feet was shifting. "You think they're trying to pull us off Marco for a reason?"

"It wouldn't be the first time," he said quietly, his voice tinged with bitterness.

They reached the edge of the marketplace, where their car was parked. Luca opened the door for her, his eyes scanning the crowd with the practiced ease of a man who never stopped calculating threats.

As they drove through the winding Roman streets, Bella's mind raced. The Interpol office loomed ahead, its sterile, unyielding walls a far cry from the chaotic beauty of the marketplace.

Luca broke the silence as they approached. "Whatever this is, we need to play it smart."

"Smart," Bella repeated, her voice laced with skepticism. "Right now, smart feels a lot like letting them dictate the game."

He glanced at her, a faint smirk softening his otherwise hard expression. "You've always been bad at playing by the rules."

She met his gaze, her lips curving into a wry smile. "And you've always been too good at pretending to."

They parked in silence, the weight of what awaited them inside the Interpol office settling over them like a shroud. Bella stepped out of the car, her pulse quickening as she squared her shoulders.

Whatever was waiting for them, she wasn't sure if it was an opportunity or another roadblock. But one thing was certain: the truth, slippery and elusive as it was, would demand a higher price than she'd ever imagined.

The truth—whatever it was—might just destroy her.

CHAPTER 10: FRACTURES AND REVELATIONS

The Interpol headquarters loomed against the dusky Roman skyline, its cold, modern façade a glaring dissonance to the ancient city that cradled it. Inside, the atmosphere was sterile, humming with unyielding efficiency. The sharp click of heels on polished tile echoed in the corridors as Bella pushed forward, her thoughts as turbulent as the storm brewing in her chest.

Marco's words still haunted her. The real killers are the ones you work for.

Luca walked a half-step behind her, silent but ever-watchful, his body language as taut as a wire stretched to its breaking point. The weight of their unspoken tensions shadowed them like a predator.

When they entered the conference room, Bella was struck by the stark contrast between the high-tech environment and the smell of stale coffee, old paper, and faint traces of sweat that clung to the air. A wall of glowing monitors threw eerie, bluish light onto the weary faces of the analysts huddled over their workstations. At the center of the room, Matteo Di Carlo stood like a conductor orchestrating chaos.

Matteo was a wiry man with sharp, angular features and a mouth permanently twisted in what seemed like disdain. His salt-and-pepper hair was slicked back, revealing a high forehead that creased every time he glanced at Bella. He wore his Italian roots like armor—a proud Roman who tolerated outsiders only when he absolutely had to. And as far as Matteo was concerned, he didn't have to tolerate Bella Rossi.

"Agent Rossi," Matteo greeted, his voice dripping with a barely concealed disdain. His eyes darted briefly to her FBI credentials hanging from her neck, then back to her face. "You're just in time for the revelation of the century."

Bella arched an eyebrow, refusing to rise to his bait. "Don't let me interrupt your show," she said, her tone cool and professional.

Matteo's lips curled into something that could barely be called a smile. "Oh, I wouldn't dream of it."

Luca cleared his throat, stepping forward slightly as if to diffuse the tension. "Let's hear what you've found, Matteo."

The analyst clicked a few keys, and the main monitor filled with cascading documents. Charts, diagrams, and cryptic memos flashed across the screen, each stamped with the sleek logo of Dusker Corporation. Matteo's expression darkened as he stopped on a specific file—a web of lines connecting names and faces to corporate branches and government offices.

"This," Matteo began, his voice low and heavy, "is one of their secret projects. Codename Sentinel. It's an Advanced-System designed for something far beyond traditional surveillance. It's meant for 'population management.'" He spat the words like poison. "Espionage, psychological warfare, suppression of dissent. Journalists, whistleblowers, activists… they're identified, tracked, and neutralized—permanently."

The air thickened with unease. Bella's gaze locked onto the screen, her fists clenching at her sides.

"Neutralized," she repeated, her voice like a blade slicing through the tension. "You mean murdered."

Matteo shrugged, his face impassive. "If you want to call it that, sì." He turned to Luca, ignoring Bella entirely. "This isn't just a corporate game. It's government-backed. A partnership between Dusker Corporation and at least three global intelligence agencies." His dark eyes flicked to Bella briefly. "Though I'm sure the American agencies would deny it."

The subtle jab wasn't lost on her. Matteo, she'd learned quickly, had no love for Americans. He viewed her as an interloper—an outsider stomping through his beloved homeland with arrogance and entitlement. He despised her cool confidence, her refusal to defer to him, and most of all, her badge. To him, it was a symbol of every time the Americans had overstepped in international affairs, a reminder of what he saw as their chronic disregard for other nations' sovereignty.

Bella, for her part, had no patience for Matteo's posturing. But she knew better than to let him see it rattle her. "What about the names on that web?" she asked, pointing to the screen. "Are they targets or collaborators?"

Matteo's eyes narrowed. He hated that she went straight for the jugular, cutting through his carefully constructed narrative with the precision of a scalpel. "Both," he admitted grudgingly. "Some are Dusker Corporation insiders. Others are high-profile dissenters. Journalists, political activists, NGO leaders… even a few of your own people, Rossi."

She didn't flinch. Instead, she crossed her arms and leaned forward, her voice steady and sharp. "What's your take on Marco's connection to all this?"

Matteo's nostrils flared, his dislike of her question almost palpable. "Marco is a symptom, not the disease. He was their operative, yes, but he's gone rogue. Now he's a liability they need eliminated before he talks. And if you ask me, you're wasting your time chasing him when the real danger is staring us in the face."

"And what exactly do you suggest?" Bella shot back, her tone laced with challenge.

"Stay out of the way," Matteo said flatly. "Let those of us who understand the stakes handle it."

Luca stepped in, his voice calm but firm.

"Enough, Matteo. Rossi's here because she's earned her place. Let's focus on the intel, not the politics."

The analyst muttered something under his breath in Italian, but he relented, turning back to his monitors. Bella didn't miss the flicker of respect in Luca's eyes as he stood beside her, a subtle but important show of support.

As Matteo continued the briefing, Bella found herself grappling with a new wave of doubt. Marco wasn't just a criminal—he was a key to unraveling a conspiracy far larger than she'd imagined. But trusting anything he said felt like playing Russian roulette with the truth.

"They're not just selling security," Luca said, his voice low. "They're selling control."

"This… this goes far beyond corporate espionage, Inspector," Matteo said, his voice a low tremor in the oppressive silence. "This is a weaponized Advanced-System, designed to control populations, to eliminate dissent. They're building a digital guillotine."

Bella felt a wave of nausea wash over her. "Eliminate? How?" she whispered, her voice hoarse.

"They identify targets, track their movements, manipulate their environments… ultimately, they disappear. No trace, no evidence." Matteo's gaze lingered on the screen, the chilling implications of his words hanging heavy in the air.

Marco, his face a mask of grim resolve, stepped forward. "We need to find a way to shut them down. We need to find the victims."

"But how?" Bella demanded, her voice rising. "The system is designed to be invisible. We're chasing shadows."

Matteo shook his head. "We have to find the cracks, the vulnerabilities. It's a race against time, Bella. They're already out there, hunting."

A chilling silence descended upon the room, broken only by the rhythmic ticking of the clock, each second a hammer blow against their dwindling hope. Bella felt a surge of adrenaline, a desperate need to act, to fight back against this invisible enemy. This wasn't just a case; it was a war, and they were the first line of defense.

"But it gets worse," Matteo said, his tone as sharp as the click of the keys beneath his fingers.

Another screen illuminated the darkened conference room, the stark glow washing over their faces. A list of names appeared, each one a heavy, invisible weight pressing on Bella's chest. The heading above them read: Liabilities.

Marco's name was near the top, bold and unmistakable. Every detail of his life was chronicled in cold, unfeeling precision—birth date, known aliases, associates, recent movements. The dossier was a chilling testament to the system's reach, the way it reduced lives to data points on a screen.

But it wasn't Marco's name that struck Bella like a gut punch.

"Alessandro DeLuca," she read aloud, her voice barely more than a whisper.

Beside her, Marco's name hung like a phantom in the air, but it was Alessandro's that shattered the room's brittle calm. Bella's eyes snapped to Luca, who had gone still, his broad shoulders taut with unspoken tension.

"That's his brother," Matteo confirmed grimly. "Flagged two years ago as a potential dissenter. They burned him alive in what they called an 'accidental fire.'"

The room went deathly silent, the hum of the servers now a faint roar in Bella's ears. Her stomach clenched as she read the details: dates, times, and strategies buried in sanitized corporate jargon. But the meaning was unmistakable. Murder, dressed up as coincidence.

Bella's gaze flicked to Marco, her pulse racing. She hadn't wanted to feel sympathy for him—he was supposed to be her target, a criminal. But now, as she imagined the agony of losing a brother to such cold precision, she found herself shaken by the raw humanity of it. Marco wasn't just running from Dusker Corporation; he was running toward something— justice, revenge, closure. And he was running alone.

"He'll never stop," Luca said suddenly, his voice low and deliberate, cutting through her thoughts.

She turned toward him, startled. His face was unreadable, but his eyes betrayed something darker— disapproval, perhaps even frustration.

"You saw it back at the marketplace," he continued. "You hesitated."

Bella bristled, heat rising in her cheeks. "I didn't."

"You did," Luca interrupted, his tone clipped. "You had a clean shot, Bella. And you let him go."

Her jaw tightened, but she didn't respond. He wasn't wrong.

The scene in the marketplace flashed through her mind like an unforgiving reel of film. The smell of spices and sweat, the press of bodies, the way Marco's eyes had locked on hers. She had him in her sights, her finger curled around the trigger. But in that split second, something in his gaze had stopped her—pain, anger, desperation.

And then he was gone.

"You think I don't know what's at stake here?" Bella shot back, her voice low but laced with steel. "You think I don't see what he's capable of?"

"I think," Luca said evenly, "you're letting this get personal. And personal gets people killed."

The words stung more than she wanted to admit. She turned away, her eyes drawn back to the screen where Alessandro's name glowed like an accusation.

Matteo, who had been watching the exchange with thinly veiled amusement, cleared his throat. "If I may," he said, his voice as smooth as oil on water, "your target isn't just a grieving brother. He's a man with nothing to lose. That makes him dangerous. Unpredictable. And if you don't handle him properly..." Matteo let the sentence hang, his meaning clear.

Bella squared her shoulders, forcing herself to

meet Matteo's condescending gaze. "I'll handle it," she said firmly.

Matteo smirked, clearly unconvinced.

"Let's not forget," she added, her tone icy, "that you were the one who lost him in the first place."

The smirk vanished, replaced by a flicker of irritation.

Luca stepped in before the tension could escalate further. "Enough. We don't have time for this. Marco's not going to sit still, and every minute we waste, he's getting farther ahead."

Bella nodded, though her mind was still racing. Matteo's revelation had changed everything. This wasn't just a manhunt anymore—it was a race against a system that had already proven its capacity for violence. And if Marco was as reckless as Luca believed, then stopping him might mean doing the unthinkable.

"I want everything you have on Alessandro," she said to Matteo. "Emails, surveillance, whatever you've got. If Marco's following a pattern, we need to figure it out."

Matteo hesitated, his disdain momentarily eclipsed by curiosity. Then he nodded, turning back to his keyboard. "Fine," he said. "But don't say I didn't warn you. This ends badly for everyone involved."

Bella glanced at Luca, who was watching her with a mixture of concern and something else she couldn't quite read. She thought about the marketplace again, about the moment her finger had faltered on the trigger.

Maybe Luca was right. Maybe she was letting this get too personal. But as she stared at Alessandro's name on the screen, she couldn't bring herself to regret it.

Luca stood a few feet away, his hands braced on the edge of the long metal table, his eyes drilling into her with quiet insistence.

"Bella?" His voice was a low rumble, threaded with concern, yet sharp enough to pull her back from the edge of her spiraling thoughts.

She blinked, forcing herself to focus, even as the ghost of Marco's face—haunted, angry—lingered in her mind. She straightened her spine and schooled her features into calm professionalism.

"I'm fine," she said, her tone clipped, betraying just enough irritation to push him away without inviting more questions.

Luca wasn't buying it. His jaw tightened, his sharp blue eyes narrowing slightly, but he let it drop—for now. Instead, he turned his attention back to Matteo, whose fingers danced over the keyboard with practiced precision. Lines of code scrolled across the screen, interspersed with damning files, timestamped memos, and surveillance records that painted a picture too horrifyingly precise to ignore.

"We need to escalate this to Lawson," Luca said, his tone resolute. "If there's a link between Marco's brother and Dusker Corporation's cover-ups..."

"It's more than a link," Matteo interrupted, his

voice flat, his gaze still glued to the screen. "It's a goddamn highway. And if we blow the whistle too early, Dusker Corporation will bury every trace of this before we can act." He leaned back in his chair, running a hand through his dark hair. "We're already playing catch-up."

Bella exhaled slowly, the weight of the conversation settling in her chest like a stone. Luca was right—protocol demanded that they report what they'd found to their superior. But Matteo wasn't wrong either. Every step they took was a calculated risk, and Dusker Corporation had proven time and again that they were always one step ahead.

The tension between them was palpable, a silent war of pragmatism versus procedure. Bella's mind raced, cataloging possibilities, weighing risks. The brutal reality of their position pressed down on her.

"Marco DeLuca is still our primary target," she said finally, her voice measured but firm. "We can't lose sight of that."

"Capturing him won't mean a damn thing if we don't understand the bigger picture," Matteo shot back, his tone laced with frustration.

"That's why we need him alive," Luca said, his voice cutting through the argument like a blade. "If Dusker Corporation's behind this, he's the only one who can lead us to the truth. Killing him accomplishes nothing."

Matteo snorted. "Tell that to the FBI."

Bella frowned. "What are you talking about?"

Matteo turned his monitor slightly, the glow illuminating his grim expression. "This just came through."

Her eyes darted to the screen, where an official memo from the FBI filled the frame. The words at the center of the document made her stomach drop: Capture or Kill Order – Marco DeLuca.

For a moment, the room was silent, the weight of the directive settling over them like a dark cloud. Bella's pulse quickened, her mind racing to process the implications.

"This changes everything," Luca muttered, his tone laced with disbelief.

"No, it doesn't," Bella said, though her voice wavered slightly. She cleared her throat and tried again, firmer this time. "Our job hasn't changed. Marco's still the key to unraveling this mess, and if we're going to take down Dusker Corporation, we need him alive."

"You think the FBI cares about that?" Matteo countered. "They've decided he's expendable. A loose end to be tied up."

"And they're wrong," Bella snapped, her frustration bubbling to the surface. "Marco's not just some fugitive. He's..." She caught herself, the words hanging on the tip of her tongue. He's the victim of something much bigger. But she couldn't say that— not here, not now.

Luca's gaze flicked to her, sharp and searching, but he didn't press her. Instead, he turned to Matteo. "We need to move fast. If the FBI's involved, they'll be sending in teams to hunt him down, and they won't be as concerned about collateral damage."

Matteo nodded reluctantly, his usual smirk absent. "I'll start scrubbing the feeds for his last known location. But if we don't find him before they do…" He let the sentence hang, the implication clear.

Bella turned away from the screen, her hands clenched at her sides. The weight of the FBI's directive, combined with the chilling revelations about Alessandro's death, threatened to crush her resolve. But she couldn't afford to falter. Marco might be reckless, dangerous even, but he wasn't the enemy. Not the real one.

She forced herself to meet Luca's gaze. "We find him first," she said, her voice steady despite the storm raging inside her. "Alive."

Luca nodded, a faint flicker of approval in his eyes. "Alive," he agreed.

As Matteo began pulling up maps and surveillance footage, Bella stepped toward the door, her mind already racing ahead. The conference room's sterile walls seemed to close in on her, the air heavy with unspoken fears and unanswered questions.

The hunt for Marco DeLuca had just become a race against time—a race that would force her to confront not only the monsters lurking in Dusker Corporation's shadow but also the growing shadow of doubt in her own heart.

As the meeting ended, Luca pulled her aside, his expression grave.

"Whatever you're thinking, Bella," he said quietly, his voice a low growl, "don't let it cloud your judgment. We're after Marco because he's dangerous. We can't let our personal feelings interfere."

Bella met his gaze, her own eyes hardening. "I haven't lost sight of anything, Luca," she retorted, her voice steady despite the storm brewing within her. "But maybe we need to start asking ourselves what's more dangerous – Marco, or the people he's trying to stop."

Luca's jaw clenched, his eyes narrowing. He didn't reply, the unspoken accusations hanging heavy in the air. As Bella walked away, the sterile white corridors seemed to close in around her, the decrypted files replaying in her mind like a haunting symphony.

Marco's words from the courtyard echoed louder now, laced with a chilling truth she couldn't ignore. "The real killers are the ones you work for."

And for the first time, a chilling doubt pierced through her certainty. Was Marco the enemy, or was he a desperate man fighting a battle against a system so corrupt, so insidious, that it had devoured his family whole? Was she, in her pursuit of justice, simply another cog in the machine, blindly serving the very forces that were destroying the world?

The questions gnawed at her, leaving a bitter taste in her mouth. As she navigated the maze of corridors, the sterile environment began to feel claustrophobic, the sterile white walls mirroring the growing uncertainty within her.

Meanwhile, a few miles away, Marco, his face

grim, navigated the winding mountain roads, the stolen car a silent accomplice in his next mission. The FBI and Interpol were closing in, their net tightening, but he had one advantage –someone he could manipulate.

He glanced at his phone, a flicker of a smile playing on his lips as he read the encrypted message. A simple word, a silent acknowledgment, a lifeline in the storm.

A wave of memories washed over him, memories of her – her fiery spirit, her intelligence, the way her eyes sparkled when she debated a point, the way her laughter filled a room. He remembered the feel of her skin beneath his, the taste of her on his lips, the intoxicating scent of her perfume that still lingered in his memory. He remembered the way she looked at him, a mixture of admiration and a simmering, unspoken desire that had ignited a fire within him.

But those memories were bittersweet, a constant reminder of what he had lost, of the life they could have had, shattered by the ruthless hand of fate. Now, all that remained was a desperate hope, a fragile thread connecting him to the woman who held the key to his freedom, the woman who, he secretly believed, understood him better than anyone else.

CHAPTER 11: FACE-TO-FACE

The Colosseum loomed like a wounded giant, its crumbling walls a testament to centuries of violence and survival. Shadows stretched long and deep under the pale glow of the moon, giving the ancient arena a spectral, foreboding air. Bella's breath formed faint clouds in the chilled Roman night as she moved cautiously, her steps muffled by the uneven ground. The silence was unnatural, oppressive, as if the Colosseum itself was holding its breath for what was about to unfold.

Her phone buzzed in her jacket pocket. She hesitated, glancing down at the screen.

You're close. No weapons. Just answers.

The message was short, direct—exactly like the man who had sent it. Marco DeLuca.

Bella's jaw tightened, the weight of what she was about to do pressing against her ribs. She knew she shouldn't be here alone. Luca's warnings played on a loop in her head: "You don't go into the lion's den unarmed. Not with someone like him." But Luca didn't understand. This wasn't about protocol or the case. This was personal.

The faintest scuff of leather against stone broke the suffocating silence. Bella froze, her hand instinctively reaching for the weapon that wasn't there. She had locked her Glock in her hotel safe, knowing Marco's terms wouldn't allow it. Her flashlight beam cut through the darkness, landing on a figure emerging from the shadows.

Marco.

He moved with the easy grace of a predator, his dark jeans and black jacket blending into the night. The faint silver light caught the sharp planes of his face—dangerously handsome, yet hardened, a man who had been shaped by loss and betrayal. His eyes, dark and piercing, locked onto hers, unreadable yet intense enough to pin her in place.

"You came," he said softly, his voice carrying through the stillness like a low growl.

"You knew I would," Bella replied, her tone steady even as her pulse hammered in her ears.

He stepped closer, his hands visible at his sides, empty but still commanding. "Just me. Just like I promised."

"That doesn't make you less dangerous," she shot back, her gaze unwavering.

A faint smile tugged at the corner of his mouth,

humorless but genuine in its way. "And yet, here you are."

She squared her shoulders, lifting her chin in defiance. "I'm here for answers. For Sam."

The name hit him like a bullet. His smile vanished, replaced by something darker, something more haunted. "Sam was a casualty in a war he didn't even know he was fighting."

"You killed him," Bella spat, her voice trembling with rage. "Don't you dare twist this into some noble cause. You took him from me. I'll never forgive you for that."

Marco's expression hardened, his gaze sharpening into something cold and dangerous. "You think I wanted him dead?" He stepped closer, his voice low, menacing. "You think I had a choice? Dusker Corporation put a target on his back the moment he got too close. If I hadn't acted, they would've come for you next. Is that what you want to hear, Bella? That I killed him to protect you?"

Her hand moved before she even realized it, the sting in her palm satisfying as she slapped him across the face. Marco didn't flinch, didn't even blink. He merely stared at her, his cheek reddening under the moonlight.

"Don't you dare," she hissed, her voice shaking. "Don't you dare make this about me."

The tension snapped like a coiled spring. Marco moved first, a blur of motion as he grabbed her wrist. Bella didn't hesitate. She twisted her arm free with a sharp Krav Maga move, stepping into his space and delivering a brutal elbow strike to his ribs.

He grunted, stumbling back a step, but his smile returned—sharp, dangerous, impressed. "Agency-issued Krav Maga," he said, catching his breath. "Nice touch."

"Shut up," Bella snapped, lunging at him again.

This time, Marco was ready. He sidestepped her attack, his arm snaking around her waist as he spun her into the stone wall. She twisted, her knee snapping up to strike his thigh. He blocked it with ease, his hand catching her wrist as she aimed another punch at his face.

"You're good," he murmured, his breath hot against her ear as he subdued her with maddening precision. "But I know you, Bella. I know every move you'll make before you do."

She struggled against his grip, her fury giving her strength. "You don't know me," she bit out, her voice venomous.

His hold tightened, not enough to hurt, but enough to remind her who was in control. "Don't I?" he countered, his tone low and intimate. "I know you're here because you don't trust anyone else to finish this. I know you hate me almost as much as you hate yourself for wondering if I'm right. And I know…" His voice softened, almost a whisper. "That you still feel it. That pull. That fire."

Her breath hitched, the truth of his words cutting deeper than she wanted to admit.

He licked her neck, slowly and deliberately.

She shivered, but it wasn't entirely from disgust.

Marco's body pressed against hers, a reminder of his power and the effect she still had on him. "I know you're not immune to this," he said, his voice husky and his breath warm against her skin.

Bella's stomach tightened, a traitorous part of her responding to his touch, to his words. She felt his hard on against her ass, and the thought flashed in her mind: He wants me.

Marco's hands slid down her arms, a possessive gesture. "I know your body is remembering what it feels like when I fuck you," he growled.

She hated how her core flooded with heat. Hated how she could feel her panties soaking. Hated that her nipples were hardening beneath her shirt.

"Fuck you," she snarled, twisting her head to glare at him.

He chuckled and nipped her ear. "Not tonight, Bella."

His hold was firm, his body warm and solid against her back. Bella could feel the tension rising between them, a taut, palpable energy that threatened to shatter her resolve. She swallowed, her pulse quickening as he ran his fingers down her hips.

"Let me go," she said, hating the tremor in her voice.

Marco chuckled. "You can pretend all you want that you don't want this, but I know you do. I can feel it." His hand slipped beneath her shirt, his palm hot against her bare stomach. "Tell me I'm wrong, Bella. Tell me you don't want my cock buried deep inside you, and I'll let you walk away.

It was a dare, an invitation to prove him wrong. But as he slid his hand lower, his fingers brushing the waistband of her jeans, she felt herself faltering. Her body betrayed her, desire sparking in her core, a needy ache she couldn't ignore.

"I..."

"Say it, Bella," Marco murmured, his voice a seductive purr. "Tell me you don't want me, and this is over. No strings attached."

Bella's mind raced, the words on the tip of her tongue. It would be easy, so easy, to push him away, to deny him, to walk away with her dignity intact.

But her body refused.

As his hand dipped lower, sliding past the barrier of her jeans and panties to the slick folds of her wetness, she found herself unable to speak. Instead, a soft, needy moan escaped her lips, her hips arching into his touch.

Marco chuckled, his breath hot against her neck. "That's what I thought."

His fingers slid deeper, stroking her clit with a maddening rhythm. Bella's knees trembled, her body melting into his touch. She couldn't stop him, couldn't deny the desire coursing through her veins.

"Tell me you want me, Bella," he growled, his teeth grazing her earlobe. "Say it, and I'll give you what you need."

She bit her lip, her resistance crumbling. "I want you," she gasped, the words a confession as much as an admission.

"Good girl," he murmured, his approval sending a shiver of pleasure down her spine.

His fingers continued their torturous rhythm, her clit swelling beneath his touch. She felt herself getting wetter, her body responding to his skillful strokes.

"Tell me you want my cock," he ordered, his voice low and commanding.

"I want your cock," she whispered, her eyes closing as she surrendered to her need.

Marco pulled her closer, his cock grinding against her ass, hard and thick. "What else do you want, Bella?"

She could feel the pressure building inside her, a tight coil of desire ready to snap. "I want you to…" she breathed, her voice barely audible.

"I'm sorry, Bella," he said, his tone teasing. "I didn't quite catch that."

"Let me go," she demanded, her voice weaker now, her resolve cracking under the weight of his gaze.

He released her, stepping back but keeping his eyes on hers. "I don't want to fight you, Bella. But you need to know—this war isn't black and white. If you keep chasing me, you'll see things you can't unsee. Are you ready for that?"

Bella's chest heaved as she fought to steady herself, her mind racing with questions she didn't want answers to. The man in front of her was a criminal, a killer. But in his eyes, she saw something she couldn't ignore—a fractured soul fighting battles no one else dared to face.

And that terrified her more than anything else.

The air between them felt thin, heavy with words neither wanted to say but couldn't avoid. Bella kept her distance, her muscles taut, every nerve on edge as she glared at Marco. The moonlight carved sharp planes across his face, highlighting the hardness in his jaw, the shadows under his eyes.

"I want answers, Marco," she demanded, her voice sharper than the cold night air. "No more riddles, no more games. Why did you kill Marcus Kane?"

The mention of Kane's name was a trigger. Bella saw it in the way Marco's mouth tightened, his shoulders squaring. His ever-present smirk faded into something harder, something carved from pain and grim determination.

"Kane wasn't a victim," he said finally, his voice low but laced with venom. "He was a puppet. A face Dusker Corporation used to keep their hands clean. He wasn't just complicit—he was their architect."

His words hung in the air, unsettling and unrelenting. Bella's stomach churned, but she kept her expression steely.

"His Advanced-System wasn't about protection," Marco continued. "It was about control. Do you have any idea how many lives he destroyed in the name of 'progress'? You think you're stopping criminals, Bella, but all you're doing is protecting the ones pulling the strings."

Her hands clenched into fists. "By killing him, you became the very thing you claim to fight against," she shot back, her voice rising. "You don't get to play God, Marco."

He took a step closer, closing the space between them until she could see the flicker of frustration in his dark eyes. "You think I wanted this? You think I woke up one day and decided to become an assassin? I tried everything—legal channels, the press, whistleblowers—but they silenced everyone. Kane's death wasn't a choice, Bella. It was the only way to stop him."

The bitterness in his voice, the unfiltered rage, left Bella momentarily stunned. But she rallied, her own anger rising to meet his.

"You don't get to decide who lives and dies," she spat. "That's not justice. That's murder."

"Justice?" he echoed, the word twisted into something cold and jagged on his tongue. He let out a bitter laugh, one that scraped against her already raw nerves. "You want to talk about justice? Tell me, Bella, what does that even mean in a system like this? You arrest people like me because it's easier than going after the real criminals. The ones sitting behind their desks, signing orders with clean hands. You're a pawn."

The accusation hit her like a slap, and for a moment, her voice caught in her throat. She stared at him, the weight of his words sinking in.

"That's not true," she said finally, but the crack in her voice betrayed her uncertainty.

Marco moved closer, his tone softening as he leaned in. "Isn't it? You've seen the files, Bella. You've seen what Dusker Corporation is capable of. How many lives they've ruined, how deep their influence runs. You think your badge makes you a hero, but all it does is tie your hands. The moment you try to pull the strings, you'll find yourself at the end of one."

The sting of tears burned behind her eyes, but she blinked them away. "If you'd just trusted me, Marco," she said, her voice breaking. "If you'd come in—surrendered willingly—we could've fought them together."

He let out a breath, something between a sigh and a bitter chuckle. "You still don't get it, do you? The second I step into their custody, I disappear. And if you push too hard, Bella, so will you."

Her heart clenched. She stepped back, shaking her head as if trying to physically push away the weight of his words.

"You have a capture-or-kill order on your head," she said suddenly, her voice hardening. "Do you know that? Lawson will have you dead before you take another step out of this country."

Marco's lips twitched into something that wasn't quite a smile. "Of course I know. But thanks for confirming it."

"Then surrender!" she snapped. "Turn yourself in, give me something to work with, and maybe—just maybe—you won't end up in a body bag."

"And work for someone like Lawson?" Marco's

voice sharpened, his eyes narrowing. "The man who's ready to put a bullet in you the second you become inconvenient?"

Her breath caught, and for the first time, Bella hesitated. The accusation cut too deep, too close to a truth she hadn't dared to face.

"He recruited you right out of college, didn't he?" Marco pressed, his voice almost gentle now, a scalpel slicing through her defenses. "Told you he saw potential. That you were special. And you believed him."

A memory surged, vivid and unrelenting: Bella, barely twenty-two, sitting on the edge of the fountain at her college campus. Lawson had appeared out of nowhere, his tailored suit immaculate, his smile disarming.

"You've got the instincts," he'd said, handing her a folder with her name on it. "You could make a real difference, Bella. The Bureau needs agents like you."

She had been wide-eyed, eager, desperate to matter. She'd trusted him, followed him into the Bureau without a second thought.

Now, the thought of Lawson betraying her—of him orchestrating the same kind of deceit Marco was describing—felt like a knife twisting in her chest.

"You're lying," she whispered, but even to her own ears, the words sounded hollow.

Marco tilted his head, his gaze softening as he watched the conflict play out across her face. "Am I?"

The silence between them was suffocating, the

weight of their shared past and uncertain future pressing down on her chest. Bella wanted to lash out, to demand that Marco stop playing these games, but the truth was far more terrifying than his accusations.

It wasn't just her faith in Lawson unraveling. It was her faith in herself.

"Was any of it real?" she asked, her voice trembling despite her best efforts. "Us?"

Her fingers curled into fists at her sides, nails biting into her palms, but she didn't flinch. She didn't dare show the fissures in her armor. Not to him. Not now.

She hated herself for asking, for giving him even an inch of the vulnerability she was barely holding together. "Answer me."

Marco's expression shifted, a flicker of something raw crossing his face. Regret? Pain? Guilt? She couldn't tell. It was gone as quickly as it came.

"It started as part of the plan," he said quietly, his tone weighted with an honesty that made her stomach twist. "Getting close to you was supposed to be a means to an end."

The words were like a knife to her chest, sharp and deliberate. Bella sucked in a breath, her throat tightening as she forced herself to keep her composure.

"But it became more than that," he added, his voice softening, the intensity in his eyes pinning her in place.

She let out a sharp, bitter laugh, a sound that felt foreign even to her own ears. "More lies," she said, the accusation slicing between them.

"No." The word snapped out of him, sharp and unyielding. He stepped forward, his presence looming, and the faint scent of leather and salt—Marco's scent—hit her like a memory she'd tried to bury. "Not a lie. I cared about you, Bella. I love you. I still do. But caring about you didn't change what I had to do."

His voice cracked on the last word, and for a moment, the walls Bella had carefully constructed felt as fragile as glass.

Her heart ached, a deep, raw throb that made her want to believe him, to fall into the comfort of his arms, even if it meant drowning in his chaos. But she couldn't.

"I can't keep chasing you, Marco," she said, the weight of her exhaustion bleeding into her voice. "You need to stop this before it's too late."

His lips pressed into a thin line, his jaw tightening as he closed the space between them. She could feel the heat radiating off him, the tension vibrating in the air.

"And what happens when you catch me?" His voice was a low rasp, almost a whisper, but it carried more weight than any shout could. "You lock me away? Hand me over to the people who want me dead?"

His hand hovered near hers, close enough that her skin tingled at the proximity.

"You're not chasing me, Bella," he continued, his words cutting like shards of glass. "You're chasing answers to questions you're too afraid to ask."

Her breath hitched. She hated how his words struck home, how he could still read her like a book despite everything.

And then, without warning, Marco leaned in.

It wasn't a soft, tentative kiss. It was desperate, raw, and all-consuming. His lips crashed against hers, igniting something wild and uncontrollable. Bella's mind screamed at her to pull away, to shove him back and remember who he was—what he'd done. But her body betrayed her, melting into him for one agonizing second that stretched into forever.

When he pulled back, his hands lingered on her arms, his forehead resting against hers. She could feel his breath, warm and uneven, against her skin.

"Walk away, Bella," he murmured, his voice rough with emotion. "Or come with me. But you can't stay in between."

She froze, her heart pounding so loud she was sure he could hear it.

He stepped back, his gaze locked on hers for a moment longer, before turning and walking toward the exit. The sound of his boots echoed in the hollow space, each step pulling him further away.

Bella's hand twitched toward her pocket, where her cuffs rested, cold and ready. Her instincts screamed at her to stop him, to do her job. But her feet stayed rooted in place, her mind spinning with every word he'd said.

She stood there, motionless, as Marco disappeared

into the shadows. The clang of the heavy metal door shutting behind him reverberated through the room, a final punctuation to their confrontation.

And she was left alone, the silence pressing down on her harder than ever.

CHAPTER 12: THE EXTRADITION ATTEMPT

T he high-speed train sliced through the Italian countryside like a blade, its sleek, silver body reflecting the muted afternoon sunlight. Through the windows, the sprawling hills rolled by in a blur of emeralds and ochres, dotted with bursts of crimson poppies and the occasional silhouette of a stone villa perched on a ridge. The rhythmic hum of the train against the tracks filled the cabin, a white noise that did little to soothe Bella's nerves.

Inside, the train was an understated world of luxury—plush leather seats, gleaming chrome fixtures, and the faint, bittersweet aroma of freshly brewed espresso curling from the dining car. Bella sat across from Luca in one of the private compartments, her fingers clenching the edge of the table between them. The steady tap of her boot against the polished floor betrayed the storm brewing within her.

Her dark jeans and soft gray sweater were chosen with precision—neutral, unassuming, meant to help her blend into the crowd. But the tension radiating off her was impossible to mask. She was a live wire, her thoughts looping endlessly back to Marco's parting words and the kiss she still felt on her lips, a phantom sensation that both angered and haunted her.

Luca's sharp gaze cut through her reverie. He leaned back, one arm draped over the back of his seat, his well-worn blazer rumpled but his demeanor anything but. His jaw ticked, the only sign of his barely contained frustration.

"You've been quiet," he said, breaking the silence. "Something tells me it's not just pre-mission jitters."

Bella's eyes flicked to him, then back to the aisle outside their compartment. She hesitated, weighing her words, before finally speaking. "I went to see him."

Luca's posture stiffened. "You what?"

"I met him," she said, her voice barely above a whisper. "Alone. Yesterday."

He sat forward, his expression a volatile mix of relief and anger. "You went to Marco by yourself?" he hissed, keeping his voice low but razor-sharp.

"I just wanted to talk to him," she said defensively. "To ask him to surrender."

"And you thought that would work?" Luca's laugh was humorless, his voice tight. "What the hell were you thinking, Bella? Do you have any idea how dangerous that was?"

"I thought I could stop him," she admitted, her tone hollow.

"No," Luca said, leaning closer. "You thought you could save him. There's a difference."

His words hit harder than she expected, the truth of them settling like a weight in her chest.

"He's playing you," Luca continued, his frustration bleeding into every word. "Every move he makes, every word he says—it's all part of his game. You know that."

"Maybe," she said, her voice softer now. "But what if it's not?"

Luca sighed, running a hand through his hair. "If you're not careful, this is going to destroy you."

Bella's gaze drifted to the window, watching the countryside whip past, a blur that mirrored the chaos in her mind. "It might already be too late," she murmured.

Her admission hung between them like a fragile thread, threatening to snap under the weight of the moment.

Luca shifted in his seat, his jaw tight. "Can I count on you, Bella?" he asked, his voice quieter now but no less intense.

She didn't answer, her silence speaking louder than any words could.

Frustrated, Luca grabbed her wrist and pulled her to her feet. Before she could protest, he guided her out of the compartment and down the narrow aisle, his grip firm but not harsh.

"Where are we going?" she demanded, but Luca didn't answer. He opened the door to the cramped lavatory at the end of the car, ushering her inside before locking the door behind them.

The space was claustrophobic, the air heavy with the faint scent of antiseptic. Bella leaned against the small sink, her arms crossed defensively as Luca stood inches away, his presence overwhelming in the tight quarters.

"You don't get to shut me out," he said, his voice low but fierce. "Not when we're this close. I need to know if I can trust you to do your job, Bella. Can I?"

Her eyes darted to the floor, unable to meet his. "It's not that simple, Luca."

"Yes, it is," he countered, his hand bracing against the wall beside her. "You either stand with me, or you let your feelings for him ruin everything we've worked for."

His words stung, and she hated the way they forced her to confront the truth she'd been avoiding.

"I don't..." she started, but her voice faltered.

Luca's hand moved to her chin, tilting her face up so she had no choice but to meet his gaze. "This isn't just about you, Bella," he said, his tone softening. "This is bigger than both of us."

The intensity in his eyes made her breath hitch. He was close now, the heat of his body radiating against hers in the confined space. For a moment, the world outside the tiny lavatory faded, leaving only the two of them and the charged air between them.

Then, without warning, Luca closed the distance. His lips brushed hers, tentative at first, testing, before deepening into something more certain, more consuming.

Bella's pulse raced, her hands gripping the edge of the sink as she kissed him back, a mix of desperation and confusion fueling the moment. But as quickly as it started, she pulled away, her chest heaving.

"This doesn't change anything," she said, her voice trembling.

"Maybe not," Luca said, his gaze searching hers. "But at least now I know you're still here."

The train jolted slightly, pulling them back to the present. Luca stepped back, giving her space, but the tension between them remained, thick and unresolved.

Bella exhaled shakily, pushing past him to unlock the door. She needed air, space—anything to clear her head. But as she stepped back into the aisle, she couldn't shake the feeling that the choices she made in the next few hours would change everything.

∞

The train's metallic hum vibrated through Bella's core as she stood in the narrow aisle, her body taut with anticipation. Outside, the once-picturesque countryside was now cloaked in the steel gray of an approaching storm. The light drizzle streaked the windows, distorting the view, as if the world outside was just as fractured as her thoughts. The muted luxury of the train—the polished brass railings, the whisper-soft carpet underfoot—did little to ease the knot of tension coiled in her chest.

The lead had been solid: Marco was here, somewhere in the train, traveling to Milan to meet a high-ranking member of his network. Intercepting him now was their last chance to pull the thread before his web became too tangled to unravel.

Bella scanned the compartments as discreetly as possible, her keen eyes trained to pick apart the smallest details: a passenger's hand trembling as they lifted their coffee cup, a man shifting nervously in his seat, a glance held too long in her direction. Every movement, every nuance, was another piece of a puzzle she couldn't afford to get wrong.

Next to her, Luca was a study in controlled focus. His gaze, sharp and calculating, swept the train with the efficiency of someone who had played this game too many times before. She could feel the heat of his presence beside her, grounding her even as her nerves buzzed like live wires.

Then, Luca's low murmur broke the silence between them. "Third car. Window seat. Gray jacket. That's him."

Bella followed the subtle tilt of his head, her eyes locking on the man he'd identified. Marco.

There he was, sitting with his back to the window, one leg crossed casually over the other. A dog-eared paperback rested in his hand, the corners of his mouth lifted ever so slightly in a faint smile. He looked, for all intents and purposes, like any other passenger enjoying a quiet afternoon on the train. But Bella saw it—the rigidity in his jaw, the faint flicker of his eyes as they scanned the passing aisle. He knew. He always knew.

Her pulse kicked up, pounding like a drumbeat in her ears. She clenched her fists, her nails digging into her palms as she whispered, "We move now."

Luca's hand shot out, firm and steady, his fingers wrapping around her forearm. "Not yet," he said, his voice low and edged with steel.

Her head snapped toward him, her eyes flashing with frustration. "He's right there, Luca. We can't let him slip away again."

"And if he's not alone?" Luca's voice was calm, but the tension in his grip betrayed him. "What if there's a tail or backup we don't see? You know he doesn't travel without a safety net."

Bella bit down on the retort bubbling in her throat. She hated when he was right, hated even more that she hadn't thought it through. Marco was like a cornered wolf—calm on the surface, but ready to strike the moment someone got too close.

"Do we ever know for sure?" she muttered, her voice tight.

Luca's eyes softened, just barely, as he released her arm. "We're not losing him, Bella. But we do this smart. We need to flush him out, isolate him."

Her lips pressed into a thin line, but she nodded. Every second felt like an eternity, her muscles coiled with the urge to act.

Luca's hand hovered near his waist, where his weapon was concealed beneath his jacket. "I'll circle around and watch for backup. You stay here and keep an eye on him."

"No," she said, the word sharper than intended. "I'm not staying behind, Luca. Not this time."

He sighed, his jaw tightening as his eyes searched hers. "Fine. But stay close. If this goes south, I need to know you've got my six."

The quiet intensity of his words hit her harder than expected, the unspoken weight of what he was really asking lingering between them.

She met his gaze, her voice steady. "I always do."

He held her stare for a moment longer before nodding. "Let's move."

The two of them began their approach, weaving through the aisle with the practiced ease of predators stalking their prey. The narrowness of the train cars amplified every sound—the murmur of voices, the occasional clink of a glass, the rhythmic rattle of the tracks. Each step brought them closer, the space between them and Marco shrinking like a noose tightening around his neck.

As they neared the third car, Bella's heart thundered in her chest. She kept her face impassive, her hands relaxed at her sides, even as her mind raced through every possible scenario.

Then, Marco's eyes flicked up, meeting hers through the glass door separating the compartments.

For a split second, time seemed to freeze.

His expression didn't change, but she saw it—the flash of recognition, the faint smirk tugging at his lips, as though he'd been expecting her all along.

Bella's breath caught, her hand instinctively moving toward her concealed weapon. But before she could reach the door, Marco stood, dropping the paperback onto the seat.

"Damn it," Luca growled under his breath. "He's moving."

Bella surged forward, the game now fully in motion. The train car seemed to close in around her, the walls pressing tighter as she followed Marco's retreating figure. The passengers blurred into shadows, their voices dull hums beneath the pounding in her ears.

Marco glanced over his shoulder, his smirk deepening as he stepped into the next car.

"Split up!" Luca barked, peeling off to circle around through the opposite door.

Bella nodded, her focus narrowing to a razor-sharp point. This was it—the moment they'd been waiting for. But as she pushed through the door into the next car, she couldn't shake the feeling that Marco wasn't running.

He was leading her.

∞

The air in the cabin felt charged, thick with the weight of tension and the faint, metallic tang of impending violence. Luca took point, his body moving with precision born from years of experience, while Bella followed close behind, her hand hovering near her holstered weapon. Every fiber of her being was taut, her senses heightened, the muffled rhythm of the train's wheels against the tracks a hollow drumbeat in the background.

Luca's gloved hand slid the cabin door open with a soft hiss, and Marco's head lifted from the worn paperback in his hands. His dark eyes gleamed with the kind of self-assuredness that had always made Bella's skin crawl.

"Bella," he said smoothly, his lips curving into a knowing smile that danced dangerously close to mockery. "Right on time."

Her heart hammered in her chest, but her hand was steady as she drew her gun and leveled it at his chest. "Hands where I can see them, Marco. No games."

He didn't flinch. If anything, the faint flicker of amusement in his expression deepened. With deliberate care, he set the book on the small table beside him, the gesture so nonchalant it bordered on insolent.

"If I wanted games, cara mia, I wouldn't have chosen a train."

Luca stepped inside, his movements deliberate as he drew his own weapon and closed the door behind him with a final, decisive click. His voice was ice, sharp and unyielding. "Stand up. Now."

Marco's gaze flicked to Luca, then back to Bella. He moved slowly, deliberately, his hands raised just enough to appear compliant without ever conceding his control of the situation.

"You're only catching me because I want you to," Marco murmured, his voice a quiet taunt, his gaze flickering to the corridor outside the cabin as though daring them to look.

Bella's jaw tightened. She wanted nothing more than to knock that smug grin off his face, but she held her ground. "You're out of moves, Marco."

"Am I?" he whispered, his voice silk over steel.

And then all hell broke loose.

The first shot shattered the glass window of the cabin, the sound deafening in the confined space. Bella ducked instinctively, the sharp spray of glass cutting across her cheek as chaos erupted. The train lurched slightly, as though even it felt the shock of the violence now spiraling out of control.

Two figures burst into the cabin, their weapons drawn, scarves obscuring their faces. They moved like shadows, swift and calculated. Bella barely had time to process their presence before Luca's gun roared to life, the echo bouncing off the narrow walls.

His shot struck one of the attackers, grazing his shoulder and sending him crashing into the cabin wall with a muffled grunt. Bella turned her focus to the second assailant, who was already lunging toward her, a blade glinting in his hand.

She dodged the first swipe, the cold rush of air

slicing past her face. Her training kicked in, her movements fluid and instinctive as she countered. She lashed out with her boot, the hard leather connecting with the attacker's shin. He stumbled, and she followed up with a sharp jab to his throat, her knuckles biting into the soft flesh beneath his jaw.

"Marco!" she shouted, her voice raw with adrenaline as she twisted to see him.

But Marco hadn't moved. He stood near the shattered window, his expression unreadable, his dark eyes fixed on her like a predator watching prey. The chaos around him seemed to barely register, as though he was content to let the storm rage while he remained in its calm center.

The fight spilled into the corridor, the narrow space amplifying every sound—the rapid crack of gunfire, the metallic clang of weapons hitting walls, the panicked screams of passengers scrambling to get out of the way.

Bella's pulse thundered in her ears as she chased one of the attackers down the corridor. Her gun was raised, her finger steady on the trigger, but she didn't fire. Instead, she lunged, tackling the man to the ground with a force that rattled her bones. The impact knocked the air from his lungs, and she wasted no time pinning his arm behind his back, twisting until he cried out in pain.

Behind her, Luca was locked in a brutal struggle with the other assailant. Blood darkened the sleeve of his jacket, seeping from the wound on his side, but he didn't falter. His movements were precise, calculated, every punch and counterstrike aimed to disable.

With a final, desperate move, Luca slammed the man's head into the wall. The dull thud was followed by a heavy silence as the assailant crumpled to the floor, unconscious.

By the time the backup team swarmed the train, the fight had devolved into a grim aftermath of sweat, blood, and shattered glass. The assailants were on their knees in the corridor, restrained with zip ties, their weapons confiscated and lying in a grim pile at Luca's feet. Passengers huddled at the far end of the car, their faces pale with shock, whispering in a dozen languages as uniformed officers moved in to secure the area.

And yet Marco sat serenely in his cabin, a man utterly unbothered by the chaos he had orchestrated. His hands were cuffed in front of him, the silver metal gleaming under the harsh fluorescent lights. His posture was relaxed, his legs crossed as though he were waiting for a maître d' instead of a police escort.

Bella stood over him, her chest heaving, her fingers still trembling with the aftershocks of adrenaline. Her gun remained clutched in her hand, the barrel angled slightly downward, but the weight of its presence was impossible to ignore.

"You still think this is a game?" she spat, her voice low but seething with rage.

Marco tilted his head, a faint smirk ghosting across his lips. His dark eyes—eyes she used to know too well—met hers with unnerving calm. "No, amore."

His voice was a quiet drawl, each syllable deliberate. "I think this is the beginning of the end."

The words were a challenge, a taunt wrapped in honey, and Bella felt her grip tighten on the gun. Her mind raced through the possibilities, each more insidious than the last. The fight, the attackers, the timing of it all—it was too perfect, too orchestrated.

"Bella," Luca's voice cut through the fog of her thoughts, firm but measured.

His hand came down on her arm, grounding her, reminding her that the moment wasn't hers alone to carry. She turned to him, catching the faint wince as he shifted his weight, blood seeping through the hastily applied bandage on his side. His face was pale, his jaw tight, but his eyes held hers with unwavering steadiness.

"He's in custody," Luca said, his voice brooking no argument. "We've got him. Don't let him pull you into whatever game he's playing."

Bella's jaw tightened, but she nodded, lowering her weapon. Her shoulders ached with tension she couldn't quite shake, and the questions buzzing in her mind grew louder with every second she spent staring at Marco's infuriatingly composed face.

Marco let out a low chuckle, the sound like gravel against glass. "You should listen to him, cara mia. Luca always did have a better sense of control than you."

Her fist clenched at her side, the temptation to wipe the smugness from his face almost overwhelming. "Shut up, Marco," she bit out, her voice laced with venom.

He leaned back against the seat, his cuffed hands resting on his lap. "As you wish," he said softly, though the gleam in his eyes suggested he'd already said enough.

The train's rhythmic clatter on the tracks filled the silence, a jarring reminder of their relentless forward motion. Each passing mile brought them closer to Milan, but the destination offered no comfort. If anything, it felt like a countdown to something darker.

Bella turned away from Marco, stepping into the corridor where Luca leaned against the wall, one hand pressed to his side. She lowered her voice, keeping the words between them. "This isn't right. The timing, the attack—it's too convenient. He wanted this."

Luca exhaled sharply, the breath catching slightly as he straightened. "I know," he admitted, his voice grim. "But right now, we have him in cuffs and two of his men in custody. That's something."

"Is it?" Bella's gaze flicked back to the cabin, where Marco sat like a king awaiting his court. "What if this is part of his plan? What if..."

"Then we figure it out," Luca interrupted, his tone gentle but firm. "But you don't let him get inside your head. Not again."

The words stung more than she wanted to admit, but she nodded, swallowing the knot of doubt in her throat. "You're right," she said finally, though the unease coiled in her gut refused to loosen its hold.

They fell into silence as the train sped onward, the

fluorescent lights casting harsh shadows that flickered with every bend and shift of the track. The air in the car felt heavier now, the weight of unspoken truths and unanswered questions pressing down on them.

Bella leaned against the window, her reflection a ghostly silhouette in the glass. Behind her, Marco's voice murmured something to one of the officers, his tone calm, almost conversational. She forced herself not to turn around, not to let him draw her back into the vortex of his manipulation.

But as the lights of Milan began to glitter on the horizon, she couldn't shake the feeling that they weren't heading toward resolution but toward the next act in Marco's carefully constructed play.

And this time, she wasn't sure who the real players were—or who would end up being the pawn.

CHAPTER 13: THE TRIAL BEGINS

T he federal courthouse in downtown Manhattan towered above the bustling streets like a somber sentinel, its granite facade and imposing columns exuding an air of indomitable authority. Beneath its shadow, the city churned with frenetic energy, a stark contrast to the grave proceedings unfolding inside.

The press swarmed like vultures, their cameras flashing in bursts that mirrored lightning strikes, their questions slicing through the cold January air with surgical precision.

"Detective Rossi! Will Marco DeLuca face the death penalty?"

"Were you complicit in his crimes during your relationship?"

"Do you regret loving him?"

"Do you still love him?"

The last question hit like a sucker punch, making Bella falter for the briefest of moments. Her breath caught, but she recovered, forcing her steps to remain steady. She pulled her coat tighter around her frame, as if the wool fabric could shield her from their probing stares and venomous insinuations. She didn't dare lift her gaze until the courthouse doors loomed ahead, their weighty presence promising a reprieve from the chaos.

She shoved through the doors, their cold brass handles biting against her palms. The heavy thunk of the doors closing behind her silenced the reporters' cacophony, leaving only the sterile hum of the courthouse's fluorescent lights.

The air inside was thick, almost oppressive, carrying a mix of stale coffee, tension, and the faint metallic tang of the security scanners. People filled every corner of the lobby: journalists scrawling furiously into notepads, attorneys dressed in severe black suits muttering to clients, and spectators jostling to catch a glimpse of the infamous Marco DeLuca.

Bella pressed on, her heels clicking against the marble floor in a deliberate rhythm that betrayed none of the turmoil roiling beneath her composed exterior. Every step brought her closer to the witness room and further away from the woman she had once been—the woman Marco had once held in his hands like a prized possession.

Inside the small witness room, Bella sank into one

of the uncomfortable wooden chairs, her fingers curling tightly around the edge of the table. The room was unremarkable, save for the stale air and the droning hum of the overhead light. A stack of case files sat untouched in front of her, the neatly printed names and dates blurring together.

She stared at her hands, noting the faint tremor in her fingers. She'd testified in court more times than she could count—each one high-stakes, each one demanding the same unflinching confidence. But this was different. This wasn't just a case. It wasn't just about Marcus Kane or the victims Marco had left in his wake.

This was about him.

"Detective Rossi."

The voice came from the doorway, startling her out of her spiraling thoughts. She looked up to see Lawson standing there, his broad shoulders filling the frame. He looked tired, shadows pooling beneath his eyes, his suit slightly rumpled—a far cry from the meticulous agent she'd once known.

"Lawson," she said, her voice sharper than she intended. She straightened in her chair, her hands slipping beneath the table to hide their tremor.

He hesitated, his hand gripping the doorframe like he wasn't sure whether to step in or leave. "You okay?"

She nodded, her movements mechanical. "I'm fine."

For a moment, he just stood there, the silence between them thick and heavy. It wasn't like him to linger. In the months since her return, he'd made a point of keeping his distance. She barely saw him at the precinct, and when she did, their interactions were clipped and impersonal, like he was trying to avoid any acknowledgment of their shared past.

"You barely looked at me when I came back," Bella said, the words tumbling out before she could stop them. Her tone was steadier now, but her gaze locked on his, daring him to deny it. "Why?"

Lawson shifted uncomfortably, his jaw tightening. "It's not the time for this, Bella."

"When is the time?" she pressed, her voice rising just enough to cut through the tension in the room.

He exhaled sharply, running a hand through his hair. "You really want to do this here? Now? Fine." His blue eyes met hers, and there was something raw and unguarded in his expression. "I kept my distance because watching you with him, even now, makes me wonder how much of you I'll ever get back. And it kills me that I can't tell if you're testifying against Marco because you want justice—or because you're trying to prove to yourself that you're not still in love with him."

His words hit like a freight train, each one sinking deep into places she didn't want to admit were still tender. She opened her mouth to respond, but the sound of a sharp knock at the door interrupted them.

"Detective Rossi," a young court officer said, sticking his head in. "They're ready for you."

Bella stood, smoothing her coat with trembling fingers. She turned back to Lawson, her jaw set, her eyes hard. "I'm here for justice. That's all you need to know."

With that, she stepped past him, her head high, and walked toward the courtroom.

∞

The courtroom was a hive of tension, its every corner vibrating with a mix of morbid curiosity and restrained hostility. Marble walls reflected the sterile glow of fluorescent lights, casting a cold, unforgiving sheen over the room. Even the air seemed stifled, thick with sweat and whispers. The gallery was packed—spectators shifting uncomfortably in creaky wooden seats, their voices weaving an electric undercurrent of speculation.

Bella Rossi sat on the witness stand, the weight of a hundred pairs of eyes pressing down on her. She could feel the collective scrutiny—journalists scribbling in notebooks, Marco's devout supporters glaring daggers, and victims' families silently pleading for justice.

Across the room, Marco DeLuca sat in chilling composure. His tailored navy suit clung to him like a second skin, his silk tie a precise shade of muted gray. Not a hair was out of place. He leaned back in his chair, fingers laced loosely on the polished mahogany table, his lips curving into a faint, knowing smirk. Marco didn't look like a man on trial for murder; he looked like a king surveying his subjects.

And Bella couldn't ignore the way her pulse skipped when his eyes met hers, his gaze sharp enough to pierce through her armor.

The prosecutor, Valerie Kerrigan, was everything the room demanded of her—sharp, no-nonsense, and radiating command. Her presence carved through the heavy tension as she strode toward Bella, her stilettos echoing like a metronome of inevitability.

"Detective Rossi," she began, her voice clear and steady, "you've testified in numerous cases throughout your career. But this one—this one is personal, isn't it?"

Bella drew in a slow breath. Her hands gripped the edges of the stand, knuckles white, but her voice didn't waver. "Yes. It is."

Valerie nodded, pacing with the deliberation of a predator circling its prey. "Let's start at the beginning. Can you describe how you came to know the defendant, Marco DeLuca?"

Bella felt the weight of Marco's stare but kept her gaze firmly on the prosecutor. "We met at a charity auction," she said evenly. "He approached me, introduced himself as an art dealer. He was charming, intelligent, and seemed genuinely interested in the work I did as a detective. It seemed... genuine."

"And this relationship progressed romantically?" Valerie pressed.

"Yes." The single word left her lips like a confession.

"At any point during the early stages of your relationship, did you suspect Marco DeLuca was involved in organized crime?"

Bella shook her head. "No. He presented himself as legitimate. He had an art gallery, employees, and a seemingly spotless record. I had no reason to believe otherwise."

Valerie stopped pacing and turned to face Bella fully, her voice gaining an edge. "And yet, Marco DeLuca is now accused of orchestrating the assassination of Marcus Kane—a high-profile witness in a federal investigation. When did you first begin to suspect his involvement?"

The courtroom seemed to constrict, every creak of a chair or cough swallowed by the charged silence.

Bella straightened in her seat, her voice unwavering as she recounted the facts. "It started at the gala. I noticed Marco disappear right around the time of the shooting. At first, I thought nothing of it. But when I returned to the precinct, there was footage. Surveillance caught him leaving the scene minutes before the hit. His face was unmistakable on the screen at FBI headquarters. That's when I knew."

Her words were precise, clipped, but they carried a weight she couldn't mask. Every detail felt like reliving a betrayal, a knife twisting deeper with each syllable. She could feel the heat of Marco's gaze on her, unrelenting, like he was silently challenging every word she spoke.

Valerie Kerrigan tilted her head, her expression softening just enough to feel disarming. "And how did that moment affect you, Detective Rossi? Personally, I mean. Learning the man you were involved with wasn't who he claimed to be."

Bella's chest tightened. She hated the question, hated the sympathy lurking beneath it. "It was devastating," she admitted, her voice barely above a whisper. "But my job was to see the case through. Personal feelings couldn't get in the way of justice."

Valerie let the silence hang for a beat before stepping back. "No further questions, Your Honor."

Bella exhaled, her shoulders relaxing by a fraction. But the reprieve was short-lived.

"Mr. Trask?" Judge Barlow prompted, turning to Marco's defense attorney.

Nathan Trask rose from his seat with the smooth confidence of a man who knew the game and had no intention of losing. His salt-and-pepper hair and tailored suit lent him an air of sophistication, but there was something serpentine in the way he moved, in the way his eyes gleamed with calculated intent.

He approached the stand with an almost predatory grace, his voice calm, bordering on friendly. "Detective Rossi," he began, the faintest smile tugging at his lips, "thank you for your testimony. Truly."

Bella didn't respond, her posture stiffening as he loomed closer.

"You said Marco DeLuca presented himself as legitimate," Trask continued, his tone conversational. "He charmed you, made you believe he was an honest man. That must have been difficult to reconcile when you saw that surveillance footage."

"It was," Bella replied tersely, her guard rising.

Trask nodded sympathetically, but there was something in his eyes that made Bella's stomach twist. "And yet, despite this so-called betrayal, you continued to work the case. You remained impartial?"

"Yes," Bella said firmly, though her grip on the stand tightened.

"Impartial," Trask repeated, his voice almost mocking. He stepped closer, lowering his voice just enough to draw everyone in. "Tell me, Detective Rossi—did impartiality drive you to his bed in the weeks leading up to his arrest?"

The room seemed to implode with whispers, a wave of shock rippling through the gallery. Bella's heart slammed against her ribcage, her face heating with a mix of anger and humiliation.

"Objection!" Valerie snapped, her voice sharp. "Relevance, Your Honor."

Trask raised his hands in mock surrender. "I'm simply establishing the nature of their relationship, Your Honor."

Judge Barlow's gavel struck the bench. "Sustained. Move on, Mr. Trask."

Trask smirked, the damage already done. Bella's jaw clenched as she met his gaze, refusing to let him see the cracks forming beneath her composed exterior. But as Trask shifted to his next line of questioning, Bella couldn't shake the feeling that Marco's defense had already planted a seed of doubt in the courtroom—and perhaps, in her own mind.

∞

Nathan Trask moved like a panther in a designer suit, each step deliberate, his polished leather shoes tapping softly against the marble floor. He oozed confidence, his reputation as a courtroom predator shimmering like an oil slick across the tense atmosphere. Bella could feel the weight of his attention, his every movement designed to pull her apart piece by piece in front of the watchful courtroom.

"Detective Rossi," Trask continued, his voice smooth as whiskey but with an undercurrent of steel, "would you describe yourself as a dedicated officer of the law?"

"Yes," Bella replied, her tone clipped, her hands folded tightly in her lap.

"And in your dedication," Trask continued, circling her like a shark, "would you say you've always maintained objectivity in your cases?"

"Yes." The word came out sharper this time, but Bella knew where this was headed.

Trask nodded as though he expected her response, his expression serene, but his eyes gleamed with predatory intent. "And yet," he said, his voice softening like a trapdoor opening, "you were in a romantic relationship with my client. A man you claim you didn't suspect of any wrongdoing. Doesn't that suggest a certain… lack of objectivity?"

Bella's spine straightened as she leaned forward, her jaw tightening. "I didn't know what he was involved in at the time," she said evenly, though the words burned on their way out.

Trask tilted his head, feigning curiosity. "But you were close to him, weren't you?" He stopped pacing and turned to face her directly. "Close enough to miss the signs. Close enough to let your emotions blind you to the truth. And now, Detective," he added, his voice hardening, "you expect this court to believe you've suddenly regained your objectivity?"

Her grip on the witness stand tightened. "I'm here to present the facts," Bella snapped, her composure showing its first crack.

"The facts as you see them," Trask countered, stepping closer. His tone was still calm, but it had an edge sharp enough to draw blood. "But isn't it true, Detective, that your personal history with Marco DeLuca compromises your credibility? That your judgment, both then and now, is colored by your feelings for him?"

Bella opened her mouth, but her throat constricted. The courtroom seemed to tilt, the air thick with anticipation. Every breath was a struggle, every eye a reminder of her exposure.

"Answer the question, Detective," Trask said, his voice razor-sharp now.

"No," she said finally, her voice trembling but determined. "My judgment isn't compromised. My job is to pursue justice, no matter how personal the case."

Trask's lips curved into a thin, predatory smile. It wasn't triumph—it was pity. The kind designed to make a person question themselves. "Justice," he repeated, rolling the word over his tongue as if it tasted bitter. "Is that what this is about? Or is this about a woman scorned, trying to make sense of a betrayal?"

The words hit like a punch to the gut, but Bella held her ground. She met his gaze with defiance, her breathing shallow but steady.

Then Trask's smile sharpened, his voice dropping an octave, intimate and cutting. "Detective Rossi, did you know that Marco DeLuca was planning to leave you?"

The room went still. Even the creak of a shifting chair seemed sacrilegious in the oppressive silence. Bella blinked, caught off guard by the question.

"What?" she managed, the word barely audible.

Trask seized the moment, stepping closer to the stand. "He was going to end things, Detective. That's why he disappeared during the gala that night. He wasn't just vanishing into the shadows to commit a crime—he was walking away from you."

The floor seemed to drop out from under her. Bella's composure, already frayed, unraveled completely. Her pulse roared in her ears as the implications sunk in, as the whispers in the gallery swelled like a tide.

"That's not..." Bella started, her voice cracking. She gripped the edge of the stand as though it were the only thing keeping her upright.

"Isn't it true," Trask pressed, his voice a cruel scalpel, "that you suspected Marco's affections were waning? That he'd been growing distant? And now you're here, painting him as a villain because you can't accept that he walked away first?"

"Objection!" Valerie Kerrigan shot to her feet, her voice slicing through the tension. "Badgering the witness!"

"Withdrawn," Trask said smoothly, stepping back, but the damage was done. The gallery buzzed like a hive on the verge of swarming.

Judge Barlow's gavel slammed down, his voice cutting through the chaos. "Recess. We'll resume in thirty minutes."

The moment the gavel struck, Bella bolted from the stand, her heels clicking in rapid succession as she pushed through the side door of the courtroom. The hallway was cool and dim, but it offered no reprieve. She leaned against the wall, her breaths coming in shallow gasps, her chest tight with a mixture of anger and humiliation.

The door creaked open behind her, and Kerrigan appeared, her expression taut with concern.

"Bella," she said softly, stepping closer. "Don't let him get to you. That's what he wants."

Bella nodded, though her throat was too tight to respond. Her mind was a storm, Trask's words echoing like thunder. She closed her eyes, her composure hanging by a thread.

And through it all, one thought pulsed in her mind like a wound she couldn't stop probing—what if Trask was right?

∞

It was after recess that Marco DeLuca's legal team began their final gambit. A low hum seemed to vibrate through the room, as though everyone present could sense that the ground beneath them was shifting.

Nathan Trask strode to the center of the courtroom with the precision of a seasoned predator. His tailored suit gleamed under the fluorescent lights, his every movement deliberate, like a magician about to reveal his greatest trick. He held up a thin stack of documents, the edges crisp and dangerous as a blade.

"These," Trask announced, his voice slicing through the din, "are internal files from Dusker Corporation, obtained through means my client would describe as 'necessary.'" He paused, letting the weight of his words settle like fog over the gallery. "These documents show how Dusker Corporation weaponized Advanced-System to suppress dissent, destroy reputations, and rig elections."

The courtroom erupted into chaos. Gasps mingled with whispered exclamations, and the gallery surged as reporters leaned forward in their seats, already scribbling down headlines. Bella, seated at the edge of the room, felt her chest tighten.

Projected onto the courtroom screen were damning emails, spreadsheets, and system logs. Each one painted a chilling picture of corporate greed and unchecked power. Bella's stomach churned as she scanned the evidence. It was worse than she'd imagined.

The defense had their angle, and they played it

masterfully. Trask turned to the jury, his voice a mixture of outrage and gravitas. "My client isn't a criminal. He's a whistleblower. A man pushed to the edge by an organization too powerful to confront directly. His actions weren't murder; they were justice in the absence of any other recourse."

Bella's gaze flickered to Marco. He sat at the defense table, his hands clasped loosely in front of him. His expression was maddeningly calm, but his eyes burned with a quiet ferocity. He wasn't just defending himself—he was reconstructing his image, reshaping himself into a martyr.

Her throat tightened as conflicting emotions clawed at her chest. She had loved that man once. Trusted him. And now? Now he was a stranger—a stranger whose every move was a calculated effort to manipulate those around him, herself included.

The prosecutor tried valiantly to steer the focus back to the murder of Marcus Kane, but the defense had planted a seed of doubt. The jury's shifting expressions betrayed their unease. Trask's strategy was working.

When the court recessed for the day, Bella slipped out into the hallway, where the tension between her and Lawson finally reached its breaking point.

"You shouldn't have gone up there," Lawson said, his voice low and sharp as they stood beneath the flickering glow of a buzzing overhead light. The hallway was narrow, the walls yellowed with age, and the faint hum of the courthouse machinery made the space feel claustrophobic.

Bella spun to face him, her frustration bubbling to the surface. "I didn't have a choice," she shot back, her tone edged with defiance. "I'm the one who brought Marco in. My testimony matters."

"Not if it costs you everything," Lawson snapped, stepping closer. His expression was hard, but his tone carried something raw, something almost vulnerable.

Bella crossed her arms tightly over her chest, her eyes narrowing. "You think I don't know that? Every second I'm up there, I'm reliving every mistake I made with him. But this isn't about me, Lawson. It's about doing what's right."

"And what's right," Lawson said, his voice rising just enough to make her flinch, "is putting him behind bars—not letting him twist this into some kind of righteous crusade."

Bella's jaw tightened as she turned away, the tension coiling tighter in her chest. She stared out the narrow courthouse window, the city beyond a blur of gray rain and muted lights. "You think I'm blind to what he's doing? I see it, Lawson. I see all of it. But that doesn't erase what he's done. It doesn't make it right."

Lawson sighed, his tone softening just enough to twist the knife. "I just don't want to see you get hurt again, Bella."

She froze, his words hitting her like a blow she hadn't braced for. Slowly, she turned back to him, her voice low and measured, laced with a bitterness that cut through the thick air. "Really? Then maybe you shouldn't have tried to kill me too."

Lawson's face flickered with something she couldn't quite name—guilt? Regret? For a moment, he seemed to reach for a response, but the silence between them was louder than anything he could have said.

Bella walked away, her heels clicking against the cold tile. Her mind raced with too many thoughts, her body thrumming with adrenaline she couldn't burn off. As she pushed through the heavy courthouse doors into the damp night air, she wondered if this wasn't just about justice anymore.

Maybe, just maybe, she was chasing something else—redemption for mistakes she couldn't undo, for love that had blinded her, for trust she had given too freely. And deep down, she feared that no matter how hard she ran, she'd never catch it.

Inside, Lawson stood in the empty hallway, his hands shoved into his pockets, his face a mask of unreadable tension. But in his eyes, something raw lingered—a truth he wasn't ready to admit.

⸻ ❖ ⸻

CHAPTER 14: A JURY DIVIDED

The courthouse loomed ahead, its gray stone facade etched with rain streaks that glinted like tears under the morning light. Outside, the crowd churned like a restless sea, their chants rising and crashing in waves. Protesters lined the steps, some hoisting signs with bold slogans like "Justice for DeLuca" and "Expose the Real Killers". Others held placards condemning him as a murderer, their voices swallowed by the roar of his supporters.

Bella Rossi tightened her grip on her bag, her knuckles whitening. The din of chants clawed at her nerves, a cacophony of anger and desperation that followed her every step. Reporters jostled for position, cameras flashing in quick bursts, their lenses like unblinking eyes recording her every move.

"Agent Rossi!" one of them shouted. "Do you regret your relationship with Marco DeLuca?"

Another voice cut through the noise: "Did you sleep with him to cover for the FBI's corruption?"

Bella pushed forward, the heat of the crowd pressing in around her. A woman lunged into her path, thrusting a sign into her face. The words "FBI: Corrupt and Complicit" were scrawled in red, the ink smeared like fresh blood. Bella flinched, her pulse quickening.

A familiar figure appeared at her side, a wall of muscle and quiet authority. Luca. His broad shoulders and steely gaze parted the crowd like a blade. "Keep moving," he growled, his hand brushing lightly against her back, guiding her through the chaos.

The courthouse doors closed behind them with a heavy thud, muffling the storm outside. But the reprieve was short-lived. Inside, the tension was just as palpable, humming in the polished floors and the whispered conversations of legal teams and journalists. The air smelled of disinfectant and stale coffee, a sharp contrast to the rain-soaked streets outside.

Bella ducked into an empty conference room, the sterile space offering a fragile illusion of solitude. She dropped her bag onto the table and pressed her hands against the cool surface, her breath coming in shallow bursts.

"They're eating it up out there," she said, her voice tight, each word edged with exhaustion. "Marco's turned this into a circus."

Luca leaned against the doorframe, his arms crossed over his chest. His presence filled the room, solid and unyielding. "He's not doing it alone," he said, his tone clipped but not unkind. "His defense team is playing the media like a violin—scandal, corruption, a martyr to rally around. And you..." He hesitated, his eyes narrowing. "You're their perfect target."

The words landed like a punch to the gut. Bella's jaw tightened, but she didn't respond. What could she say? He wasn't wrong.

The headlines had been relentless.

"FBI Detective Slept with the Killer She Now Testifies Against."

"Did the FBI Engineer a Scapegoat to Hide Corporate Corruption?"

"From Lover to Enemy: Bella Rossi's Tangled Pursuit of Marco DeLuca."

Every detail of her personal life had been dragged into the spotlight, dissected and distorted until she barely recognized herself. Pictures of her and Marco— smiling at a charity gala, walking hand in hand down a Manhattan street—were splashed across screens and newspapers. The contrast was brutal when paired with images of him in handcuffs, his jaw set in defiance.

At first, she'd stopped reading the articles. But the whispers were harder to ignore. In the courthouse hallways, among her colleagues, even in the guarded exchanges with Luca, the questions hung in the air like smoke.

Had she let her emotions cloud her judgment? Had Marco played her from the start?

Bella straightened, forcing herself to meet Luca's gaze. "You think I don't know how this looks?" she said, her voice sharper than she intended. "Every headline, every whisper—I hear it all. But that doesn't change the fact that Marco killed Marcus Kane. No matter what his defense team spins, that's the truth."

Luca's eyes softened, just a fraction. "I'm not questioning the facts, Bella. But public opinion can bury the truth. You know that better than anyone."

She exhaled slowly, the tension in her shoulders refusing to ease. "It doesn't matter. I'm not here to win a popularity contest. I'm here to do my job."

"Even if it costs you everything?" he asked, his voice low, almost a whisper.

Her stomach tightened, but she didn't waver. "If that's what it takes."

Luca's expression darkened, a flicker of something unspoken passing through his eyes. He pushed off the doorframe and crossed the room, his presence a storm cloud that loomed too close.

"Bella," he said, his tone softer now, but no less intense. "You're good at this—better than most. But you're not invincible. Don't let him destroy you, too."

She looked away, her gaze falling to the rain-speckled window. The city beyond was a blur of gray and shadows, a mirror of the chaos inside her. "He won't," she said, more to herself than to him.

But as the words left her lips, a hollow ache settled in her chest. Because for the first time, she wasn't sure she believed them.

∞

The courtroom was a pressure cooker, its atmosphere thick and suffocating. The heavy oak paneling seemed to close in with every passing minute, trapping the restless tension that hung in the air. Bella sat at the far end of the gallery, her posture rigid, her hands clasped so tightly in her lap that her nails bit into her palms. The jury had been deliberating for three excruciating days, each hour stretching like a taut wire threatening to snap.

At the defense table, Marco DeLuca sat with a composure that bordered on arrogance. His tailored charcoal suit clung to him perfectly, the crisp white shirt beneath it as unwrinkled as his serene expression. His dark eyes scanned the courtroom with detached amusement, landing on Bella for just a moment too long. The flicker of emotion in his gaze sent an uninvited shiver down her spine.

It wasn't triumph. It wasn't remorse. It was something in between, a calculated mixture of acknowledgment and challenge.

The prosecutor, Kerrigan, leaned in, her voice a low murmur that was barely audible over the anxious whispers in the room. "The jury's deadlocked," she said, her tone edged with frustration. "I can feel it. The Dusker Corporation leaks—this case isn't about Marcus Kane anymore. It's about corporate conspiracy, the damn media frenzy, and Marco's ability to charm anyone with a pulse."

Bella's jaw tightened. "It's bigger for him. Smaller for Marcus."

Kerrigan's lips pressed into a thin line. "Juries hate gray areas. They want clear heroes and villains. And Marco's team has painted him as anything but the villain."

The words sank into Bella's chest like stones, weighing her down as the jury filed back into the room. Their faces were tired, their expressions unreadable. She watched the foreman's every move, her pulse hammering in her ears as he handed the folded note to the bailiff, who passed it to the judge.

The silence was electric, the anticipation unbearable.

"Your Honor," the foreman began, his voice steady but strained. "We are unable to reach a unanimous verdict."

The words dropped into the courtroom like a grenade. The reaction was instantaneous. Gasps erupted from the gallery, a cacophony of cheers and shouts following in their wake. Bella felt the room tilt around her, the floor dissolving beneath her feet.

A mistrial.

The word rang in her ears, louder than the chaos erupting around her.

At the defense table, Marco stood, shaking his attorney's hand with an air of detached confidence. His supporters in the gallery exploded into applause, their voices spilling into the hallways beyond. Bella sat frozen, the weight of her failure crushing her. Months of painstaking work—endless hours of piecing together evidence, the risks she'd taken, the sacrifices she'd made—all of it unraveled in a single breath.

Marco DeLuca, unconvicted, unbroken, was free to go.

As he turned toward the gallery, his eyes found hers again. Even amid the pandemonium, his gaze was steady, sharp, and unwavering. It wasn't the gaze of a man relieved to escape justice. It was the gaze of a man who knew he'd won a round but not the war.

Bella forced herself to her feet, her knees trembling beneath her. The courtroom faded into a blur of angry voices and blurred faces as she followed the tide of bodies spilling into the hall.

Outside, the courthouse steps were a frenzy of noise and motion. Marco emerged to the roar of the crowd, his name chanted like a battle cry. Reporters swarmed him, microphones jabbing like weapons, their questions drowned out by the jubilant cheers of his supporters.

Bella lingered in the shadows of the entryway, her pulse erratic. She watched as he descended the steps, his posture loose but deliberate, as if every movement had been rehearsed for maximum effect.

Then, just as the crowd swallowed him, he turned. His dark eyes locked onto hers through the chaos, cutting through the noise and the bodies like a knife.

Her breath caught. There was no smirk on his face, no sign of gloating. Instead, his expression was unnervingly calm, the barest flicker of intensity in his gaze. It wasn't an invitation. It was a dare.

"Bella."

Luca's voice jolted her back to the present. He stood behind her, his jaw set, his broad shoulders tense. The controlled anger in his eyes mirrored the storm brewing inside her.

"We need to go," he said, his voice low and clipped.

She nodded, her feet moving automatically even as her mind remained trapped in the silent conversation she'd just shared with Marco.

Out on the courthouse steps, the rain began to fall, soft at first, then harder, until the pavement gleamed like black glass beneath the storm. Bella's breath fogged in the cold air as she followed Luca to the car, her thoughts spinning like a relentless current.

She couldn't shake the feeling that this wasn't the end. Marco DeLuca hadn't just escaped justice—he'd set the stage for a game far more dangerous than the one they'd already played.

And she wasn't sure she had the strength to face it.

CHAPTER 15: MARCO'S OFFER

Bella's apartment felt smaller tonight, its walls pressing inward with each passing second. The hum of the city outside seeped in through the thin windows—horns blaring, voices rising, the distant thrum of music from a bar somewhere down the block. Manhattan never slept, and tonight, neither could she.

The glow of her phone lit up her face as she scrolled through headline after headline, each one more infuriating than the last. "Marco DeLuca: The People's Hero or a Killer Set Free?" The photos were the same—his perfect smile, his calm demeanor, his eyes that seemed to hold secrets just out of reach. He looked untouchable, as if the courtroom had been a stage and he'd been the leading man.

Her phone buzzed in her hand, Luca's name flashing across the screen. She ignored the call.

A text followed immediately after: "Don't do anything reckless."

Her lips twisted into a bitter smile. Reckless? She'd played it safe, followed the rules, and where had it gotten her? A mistrial. A man like Marco DeLuca walking free.

She tossed the phone onto the coffee table and stood, pacing the room. Her gaze caught on the window, the distant lights of the city drawing her in. There was a pull, a magnetic force that wouldn't let her stay put.

Her mind wandered back to another night, years ago, when she and Marco had climbed the fire escape to the rooftop of their building. It had been their secret hideaway, a place above the chaos where they could be alone. She'd thought it was romantic back then, the way the city stretched out before them, glittering and alive. Now, the memory felt like a cruel joke.

The rooftop had been a sanctuary once. Tonight, it was something else entirely.

The chill bit at her skin as Bella stepped onto the gravel-covered roof. The air was sharp, carrying the faint scent of winter and the metallic tang of the city. The skyline loomed before her, skyscrapers piercing the inky sky, their windows glowing like stars. Below, the Hudson River glistened, its surface fractured by the reflection of the city lights.

Marco stood at the edge, his silhouette stark against the glow of Manhattan. He was motionless, his hands tucked casually into the pockets of his coat. The faintest hint of a smile played at the corner of his mouth, as if he'd been expecting her.

A small table sat beside him, elegant and out of place on the gritty rooftop. An opened bottle of wine and two glasses caught the moonlight, glinting like a temptation she didn't want.

"Bella," he said, his voice smooth and low, cutting through the silence. He didn't turn. He didn't need to. "I knew you'd come."

Her boots crunched against the gravel as she stepped closer, stopping just far enough away to keep the space between them. "Don't flatter yourself," she said, her voice tight and cold.

Now he turned, his face illuminated by the silver light of the moon. His features were as arresting as ever—sharp cheekbones, a strong jaw, and those eyes that had once seen straight through her. But there was something harder in his expression now, a darkness that hadn't been there before.

He gestured to the table, his movements deliberate. "Join me for a drink?"

She scoffed, crossing her arms. "You think a glass of wine is going to erase everything you've done?"

"No," he admitted, his voice steady as he poured the wine. The crimson liquid swirled in the glass, catching the light. "But it might make this conversation easier."

She stayed where she was, her muscles taut, her pulse racing. Every instinct screamed at her to leave, but she couldn't. Not yet.

"Why are you here, Marco?" she demanded. "What do you want?"

He stepped closer, his movements slow and deliberate, like a predator approaching its prey. "I want to talk," he said softly.

When he reached for her hand, she didn't move. His fingers brushed against hers, warm and firm, but the sensation left her cold. Once, his touch had ignited something in her—a spark, a thrill, a promise. Now, it was just empty.

She pulled her hand away, her gaze locking onto his. "Don't."

His smile faltered, just for a moment. "Bella, we were good together once. You can't deny that."

"We were a lie," she shot back, her voice sharp. "Just like everything else about you."

For a moment, something flickered in his eyes— regret, maybe, or something darker. Then it was gone, replaced by the mask he wore so effortlessly.

"You want the truth?" he asked, his voice dropping lower. "You're not going to find it in a courtroom. You know that as well as I do."

She took a step closer, her eyes narrowing. "And where will I find it?"

He smiled again, but this time it didn't reach his eyes. "Right where you left it."

The words hung in the air, heavy and suffocating.

Bella's fists clenched at her sides, her nails biting into her palms. She wanted to scream, to hit him, to make him feel even a fraction of the pain he'd caused.

But she did none of those things.

Marco handed her the glass, his fingers brushing hers just long enough to make it intentional. Bella felt the heat of his touch, but she masked the ripple of unease it sent through her. The wine was deep and rich, its garnet hue catching the moonlight, but she didn't lift it to her lips. Instead, she studied him, the man she once thought she knew.

There he stood, leaning against the low wall of the rooftop, the city lights behind him casting his face into sharp relief. He looked every inch the man who had fooled the system—a dangerous mix of charm, conviction, and quiet menace.

"Say what you came to say, Marco," she said, her voice brittle with anger. "Go on, rub it in my face. Tell me how you got away with it."

His lips curved into a faint smile, one that didn't reach his eyes. "This isn't about gloating, Bella. It's about truth." He swirled his glass absently, the wine catching the light. "The justice system is broken. You know it as well as I do. It's not designed to deliver justice—it's designed to protect the powerful. People like me? We're the scapegoats, the villains they use to distract the public while corporations like Dusker Corporation run the real game."

Her eyes narrowed, her voice a sharp blade cutting through the night. "You mean corporations you kill people for."

His jaw tightened, the slight tick betraying his calm façade, but he didn't bite. "Kane wasn't innocent.

None of them are. You saw the files, Bella. Dusker Corporation isn't just corrupt—it's a machine, a cancer eating away at everything. They don't just destroy lives; they erase them. And if you stay within the system, you'll never be able to stop them."

She shook her head, her grip tightening around the stem of the glass. The pressure grounded her, kept her from saying something reckless. "Spare me the monologue. You think you're some kind of vigilante? A modern-day Robin Hood? You're not. You're a killer, Marco. And you don't get to pretend otherwise just because you think your victims deserved it."

His laugh was soft, almost bitter. He stepped closer, his movements deliberate, as if closing the gap between them would help him break through her defenses. "And yet here you are," he murmured, his voice low, dangerous. "Listening to me. If I were just some monster, you wouldn't be here. But you know, deep down, that I'm right."

"Don't flatter yourself," she snapped, but her voice lacked the bite she'd intended.

Marco leaned in, his eyes locking onto hers, the intensity in them suffocating. "You're afraid," he said, almost gently. "Not of me, but of what they'll do to you. To people like you. How long, Bella? How long before Dusker Corporation decides you're in the way? Before they twist the truth and turn the system against you?"

His words burrowed under her skin, festering. She hated that he could read her so easily, that he could find the cracks she worked so hard to conceal.

"You don't know anything about me," she said, her voice a low growl.

"I know enough." He set his glass down on the table, stepping even closer. The heat of his presence enveloped her, and she felt the old, familiar tension creep up her spine—the kind that used to thrill her, but now only made her wary. He reached out, his hand brushing against her hair, tucking a loose strand behind her ear.

"Don't," she said, her voice tight, her body rigid.

His smile faltered, but he didn't move away. "We were good together once, Bella. You can't deny that."

"Whatever we had died the moment I learned who you really are." She took a step back, creating space between them. The cold air filled the void, sharp and unforgiving.

"Maybe," he said softly. "But you're still here. That means something."

"It means I want answers," she shot back, her voice rising. "Not whatever this is." She gestured between them, her frustration boiling over.

His expression darkened, the charm slipping away to reveal something harder, more raw. "You'll never get the answers you're looking for if you keep playing by their rules," he said, his voice like gravel. "You think your badge protects you? It's a leash, Bella. And you're letting them pull it tighter every day."

Her hand tightened around the glass, the urge to throw it at him nearly overwhelming. Instead, she set it down on the table with a sharp clink.

"You're delusional if you think I'd ever join you," she said, each word deliberate, cutting.

"Am I?" His tone softened, almost pleading now. "You've seen the files. You know what they're capable of. We could dismantle them, piece by piece. Together."

She shook her head, a bitter laugh escaping her lips. "Together? You're a liar and a murderer, Marco. Whatever fight you think you're waging, it's not justice. It's vengeance."

For a moment, his mask slipped, and she saw it—a flicker of vulnerability, a shadow of the man she once believed in. But it was gone as quickly as it came, replaced by the hardened resolve of someone who believed his own lies.

"You can't outrun the truth, Bella," he said, his voice low, his gaze piercing. "Not forever."

"Stop," Bella said, her voice breaking like glass under pressure. "You don't know me, Marco. You don't know what I stand for."

The city hummed behind him, a cacophony of distant car horns and laughter muffled by the altitude. The rooftop was suffocating, the walls closing in, though it was open air. It smelled faintly of tar, smoke, and the bitter tang of wine that clung to her hand.

Marco smiled faintly, his gaze sharp enough to cut. "I know you better than you think." He took a measured step closer, his tone so calm it grated against her nerves. "I know you've spent your entire career fighting for a justice you're starting to doubt exists. I know you've felt the weight of the system you serve, how it crushes everything it touches—how it's crushing you. And I know," his voice dipped lower, velvet and venom, "you've thought about what it would feel like to burn it all down."

Her chest tightened as if the words had wrapped themselves around her lungs. They were too close to the truth she hadn't dared to acknowledge, even to herself.

"This isn't about justice for you," she said, her voice trembling with anger. "It's about revenge."

Marco tilted his head, his expression unreadable. "Maybe it started that way," he admitted. His voice softened, threading through the cold air like a dangerous lullaby. "But it's more than that now. This is about balance, Bella. About giving people a fighting chance against the ones who think they own the world."

She stared at him, the wineglass trembling in her hand. The glass felt heavier, as if the weight of this conversation had seeped into it. Every instinct screamed at her to put a bullet in him, to end this twisted game. But a small, insidious voice whispered a question she hated herself for entertaining.

Was he wrong?

Marco stepped closer, his movements deliberate, the predator testing how close he could get before his prey bolted. "You've seen the files. You've seen the bodies they leave behind. You're too smart to pretend this is black and white. Don't tell me you haven't thought about what it would feel like to actually make a difference, to stop spinning your wheels and really change something."

"Stop it," she hissed, but her voice lacked its usual authority.

His smile returned, faint and knowing. "You wouldn't be here if you didn't already feel it, Bella. That itch. That ache. The system isn't just broken—it's eating you alive."

She took a step back, desperate for space, but he followed, a shadow matching her movements. Then, before she could stop him, he reached out, cupping her cheek with a touch so gentle it made her blood boil.

"Don't," she said through clenched teeth.

But he didn't listen. His thumb brushed against her skin, and then he leaned in, his lips brushing hers with calculated softness.

The kiss landed like a dead weight. She didn't feel anything—not the rush of adrenaline, not the flicker of the old chemistry that had once existed between them. Nothing but cold, empty detachment.

She shoved him back with a force that surprised even herself. Her hand flew to her face, wiping at her lips as if scrubbing away a stain.

"Don't ever do that again," she spat.

Marco stepped back, his expression unreadable, but she caught the faintest flicker of disappointment before it vanished behind his mask. "I had to try," he said softly, as if that excused it.

"Try what? Manipulating me into this delusional crusade of yours?" She set the wineglass down on the table with a sharp clink, her fingers trembling despite her iron will. "You think I'd turn my back on everything I've fought for? That I'd ever..."

"I think you'll come to that conclusion on your own," he interrupted, his voice maddeningly calm. "You're too smart not to."

She glared at him, her hand hovering near her pocket where her cuffs sat cold and ready. She could end this here, now. Drag him back in, let the justice system he despised chew him up and spit him out.

But she hesitated.

Marco noticed. Of course, he noticed. He always noticed.

He leaned in one last time, his voice dropping to a whisper. "You can arrest me if you want, Bella. But it won't stop what's coming."

Her jaw clenched, the weight of his words pressing against her like a vise.

Before she could respond, Marco stepped back, retreating toward the edge of the rooftop. His footsteps were maddeningly soft, like a ghost fading into the night.

He paused at the edge, turning to face her. The wind ruffled his hair, but his gaze stayed steady, unyielding. "Think about it," he said. "We could do so much more together than you ever could as their puppet."

And then, with the ease of someone who'd

mastered disappearing acts, he was gone.

Bella stood frozen, the cold wind whipping around her, stinging her cheeks. Her pulse thundered in her ears, her mind a storm of conflicting emotions. The line between right and wrong, between justice and revenge, had never felt so blurred.

She picked up the wineglass, staring at the deep red liquid swirling inside. For a moment, she considered hurling it off the rooftop, watching it shatter into a thousand pieces below. But instead, she set it down carefully, her hands trembling.

The city stretched out before her, glittering and unyielding, a thousand lives continuing obliviously below. Bella's world felt smaller, darker.

And for the first time in her career, she wasn't sure what side she was on anymore.

∞

Bella's apartment felt like a cage. Every creak of the floorboards beneath her feet, every faint hum of the fridge in the corner, set her nerves on edge. The city outside her window buzzed with life, but inside, it was as if the world had slowed, compressing into a singular moment of suffocating stillness.

She clutched her phone with a trembling hand, her thumb hovering over Luca's number. Her mind replayed the rooftop encounter with Marco, his piercing gaze, his chilling words, and that hollow kiss that had left her cold in every way that mattered.

When the call connected, her voice came out

barely above a whisper. "Luca."

"Bella? What's wrong?" His voice was steady, a lifeline in the chaos swirling around her.

"He was here," she said, forcing the words out before they dissolved into panic. "Marco. He found me."

There was a pause, just long enough to make her wonder if the line had gone dead, before Luca's tone sharpened. "I'm on my way. Don't move."

She hung up and sank onto the couch, her head in her hands. The shadows of the room seemed to lengthen, creeping toward her like specters. She told herself it was just her imagination, that Marco wasn't lurking in the corners. But the doubt gnawed at her, insidious and unrelenting.

When Luca arrived, he didn't knock. He had a key—an arrangement born out of practicality during a previous case but one that now felt like an unspoken promise. He stepped inside, his presence immediately filling the room with a calm she hadn't realized she needed.

"Bella," he said, crossing the room in long strides. His dark eyes scanned her face, then the apartment, assessing, calculating. "Are you okay? Did he hurt you?"

She shook her head, but the tremor in her hands betrayed her. "No. But he…he's planning something, Luca. I can feel it. He's always one step ahead, and I…"

"Hey." He crouched in front of her, his hands firm but gentle on her knees. "We'll stop him.

Whatever he's planning, we'll stop it."

She nodded, the knot in her throat making speech impossible.

Luca straightened, his posture brimming with quiet determination. "There's something I need to tell you. I've been digging into Dusker Corporation, trying to figure out why Marco's so obsessed with them. It's not just about revenge, Bella. There's a server farm—hidden, off the grid. I think Marco's planning one last act against them. If we can find him there, catch him in the act..."

"We'll have the evidence we need," she finished, her voice steadier now.

Luca nodded. "Psychopaths like Marco don't stop until they're forced to. This could be our chance to end this madness for good."

The room fell silent except for the muffled sounds of traffic outside. Bella stared at Luca, his face illuminated by the dim light of the overhead lamp. His jaw was set, his eyes unwavering, and for a moment, the weight of his conviction pressed against her chest, making it hard to breathe.

"Luca," she said softly, her voice trembling with an emotion she couldn't quite name.

He turned back to her, his expression softening. "What is it?"

She didn't answer. Instead, she closed the distance between them, her lips capturing his in a kiss that was as sudden as it was desperate. Unlike the hollow emptiness she'd felt with Marco, this kiss ignited something deep inside her—a warmth that spread through her veins, chasing away the cold that had gripped her since the rooftop.

Luca froze for a fraction of a second before responding, his hands sliding up to cup her face. The kiss deepened, the world outside the apartment fading into nothingness. For the first time in what felt like forever, Bella felt grounded, tethered to something real, something good.

When they finally pulled apart, both breathing heavily, Luca rested his forehead against hers. "Bella…"

"I'm sorry," she whispered, her cheeks flushing.

"Don't be," he said, his voice rough with emotion. "Just…tell me you're okay."

She managed a shaky smile. "I will be. As long as we stop him."

He nodded, his thumb brushing against her cheek. "We will."

The moment hung between them, charged and fragile, before Luca stepped back, his professional demeanor sliding back into place.

"I'll start coordinating with the team," he said, his tone brisk. "We'll need a warrant and a tactical plan. If Marco's targeting that server farm, we have to be ready for anything."

Bella nodded, her mind already shifting into gear. The fear was still there, lurking in the corners of her mind, but it was tempered now by something stronger. Determination.

As Luca moved to make the call, Bella glanced out the window. The city lights stretched endlessly before her, a reminder of the lives at stake if they failed.

She wouldn't let Marco win. Not this time.

CHAPTER 16: THE FINAL SHOWDOWN

The warehouse loomed like a hulking specter on the outskirts of the city, its silhouette sharp against the bruised sky. Clouds hung low and heavy, promising rain but withholding it for now. The air was electric with tension, a storm both in nature and within the hearts of those waiting to act. Bella sat in the passenger seat of an unmarked SUV, her fingers drumming an uneven rhythm against her knee. The vehicle's cabin was filled with the faint smell of old coffee and worn leather, the only sounds the muted crackle of the radio and the occasional groan of the seats as someone shifted uncomfortably.

"Still nothing," Luca muttered, lowering the binoculars he'd been using to scope the warehouse from a distance. The light from the dashboard cast sharp shadows across his face, highlighting the hard set of his jaw.

Bella stole a glance at him, noting the tension in his shoulders, the way his hands flexed around the steering wheel. He looked like a man holding himself together with sheer will, and for some reason, that unsettled her more than the mission ahead.

The van they occupied was a mobile command center of sorts, its cramped interior filled with surveillance monitors, communication equipment, and gear stowed neatly in reinforced racks. Despite the hum of technology, the space felt oppressively small, like the walls were closing in around them.

"How long are we supposed to sit here?" Bella asked, breaking the silence.

"As long as it takes," Luca replied without looking at her, his tone clipped.

She leaned back against the seat, staring out the window at the warehouse. The structure was a monument to decay—rusted beams, shattered windows, and an air of abandonment that screamed danger. Yet, somewhere inside that crumbling facade was Marco, plotting his final act of destruction.

The radio crackled to life, and Lawson's voice came through, sharp and authoritative. "Team Alpha, hold positions. Surveillance confirms movement inside the warehouse. Stand by for further instructions."

Luca exhaled sharply, his eyes flicking to Bella. "This is it."

She nodded, her throat tightening. Her fingers itched for action, but the waiting was necessary.

Critical.

They spent the next hour in tense surveillance, the van's interior growing warmer as their collective anxiety filled the space. The team outside reported minimal movement—a shadow flitting past a broken window, the distant sound of heavy machinery starting up inside. Marco was in there. They knew it.

Finally, the green light came.

"Gear up," Luca said, his voice low but steady.

Bella nodded, reaching for her vest and slipping it on with practiced ease. She checked her weapon, the cold, familiar weight grounding her. As she loaded her magazine, she caught Luca watching her, his expression unreadable.

She hesitated, her pulse quickening. She needed to say it before they stepped into the unknown.

"Luca," she began, her voice barely above a whisper.

"Yeah?" He was strapping on his holster, his attention now fully on her.

"The kiss," she said, forcing herself to meet his gaze. "It was a mistake."

For a moment, he didn't respond, his dark eyes searching hers. Then, he gave a small nod, his expression hardening. "Understood."

His tone was neutral, professional even, but she saw the flicker of something else beneath the surface. Hurt? Disappointment? She couldn't dwell on it now, not when their lives depended on clarity and focus.

"You sure about this?" he asked after a beat, his

voice softer now, his concern evident.

She tightened the straps of her vest, forcing the words past the lump in her throat. "I don't see another choice."

"There's always a choice," Luca said, his jaw tightening. "Just make sure this one doesn't cost us more than we can pay."

Before she could respond, the radio crackled again.

"Team Alpha, you're a go. Move in."

Bella and Luca shared a final glance, the weight of unspoken words hanging between them.

"This time, we end it," Bella said, more to herself than anyone else.

Luca's gaze lingered for a moment longer before he opened the door, the cool night air rushing in like a slap to the face. The rest of the team was already moving, their silhouettes darting through the shadows toward the warehouse.

The world outside was eerily quiet, the kind of silence that made every sound—every footstep, every whispered command—feel amplified. The team approached the warehouse with precision, their movements choreographed to perfection.

As they reached the entrance, Bella felt a flicker of doubt. Not about the mission, but about everything else. About Marco. About Luca. About herself.

But there was no time for second-guessing.

Luca glanced back at her, his expression calm, resolute. "Ready?"

She nodded, tightening her grip on her weapon. "Let's do this."

The FBI team fanned out across the perimeter, their movements silent and precise, melting into the shadows of the moonless night. Bella's heart pounded against her ribcage as she watched them advance, her eyes locked on the grimy, broken windows of the warehouse. Shadows flickered inside like ghosts in the dim light. Marco was in there. She could feel it—a presence that made her skin prickle with both dread and resolve.

The wind howled through the skeletal trees lining the industrial lot, rattling loose pieces of corrugated metal clinging to the warehouse's façade. Bella pulled her jacket tighter, as if the extra layer could shield her from the storm brewing both outside and within.

Lawson appeared beside her, his face carved in lines of grim determination. His tactical gear seemed to amplify his already imposing presence, but it was the weight of his words that made Bella's stomach knot.

"Surveillance suggests about a dozen operatives inside, armed and moving equipment," he said, his tone clipped. "This isn't just a sabotage mission. They're staging something bigger—coordinated, systematic."

Bella swallowed hard. "And Marco?"

Lawson's jaw tightened. "He's here. Server room on the second floor. Surveillance confirms he's coordinating the operation himself."

Her grip on her weapon tightened. "Then let's

take him down."

Lawson's gaze turned sharp. "We'll go in hard and fast. But you..." he pointed at her, his voice firm—"you stay behind. No distractions. No heroics. This is bigger than personal vendettas, Bella."

Her nostrils flared. "He's not just another suspect. You know what he's capable of. You need me in there."

"I need you alive," Lawson snapped, stepping closer, his voice low but commanding. "We have a plan, and it doesn't include you running into a situation half-cocked and getting yourself or someone else killed."

She clenched her jaw, resisting the urge to argue further. He wasn't wrong, but that didn't make it any easier to swallow.

"You have Luca," Lawson continued, softening slightly. "He knows how to handle this. Trust him to take point."

Her eyes flicked to Luca, who stood a few feet away, his face partially illuminated by the glow of a tactical screen in the van. Their eyes met, and for a moment, the world shrank to just the two of them. She saw the same determination in his gaze, the same fear lurking beneath the surface.

"Fine," she bit out, her voice tight. "I'll stand down."

Lawson nodded, satisfied, and moved to brief the rest of the team. Bella turned to Luca, who stepped closer, his expression unreadable.

"Bella…"

"Don't," she cut him off, her voice low. "I don't need a lecture."

"I wasn't going to give you one," he said evenly. "Just… be smart about this."

She didn't reply, but her silence said enough.

The raid erupted in a symphony of pure chaos.

The FBI team stormed the warehouse, their shouts mingling with the deafening roar of gunfire. Bella remained near the van as ordered, every fiber of her being screaming at her to move, to fight, to do something. The sharp staccato of bullets echoed through the night, accompanied by the acrid tang of smoke and the metallic bite of adrenaline that hung in the air like a suffocating fog.

"Left!" Luca's voice cut through the chaos, his sharp command followed by the explosive crack of his weapon.

Bella's hands trembled as she gripped the edge of the van's open door, her breathing shallow. She could see the team moving inside, their figures darting between shadows. And then she saw it—a flash of movement on the second floor, a figure she recognized instantly.

Marco.

The sight of him was like a jolt of electricity, igniting a fire in her chest that burned hotter than fear. Her body moved before her mind could catch up, her feet carrying her toward the warehouse.

"Bella!" Lawson's voice shouted behind her, but

she didn't stop. She couldn't.

Inside the warehouse was filled with industrial equipment and stacked pallets, the air thick with dust and the acrid scent of oil. Bella pressed forward, her heart hammering as she weaved through the chaos, her weapon at the ready. The firefight raged around her, but it was distant now, muffled by the singular focus driving her forward.

She reached the stairs leading to the second floor, her boots clanging against the metal as she ascended. The narrow staircase felt like it was closing in around her, the sound of her own breathing deafening in her ears.

At the top, she paused, her back pressed against the wall. The door to the server room was slightly ajar, faint light spilling out into the dim corridor. The hum of machinery filled the air, the racks of servers casting long, ominous shadows under the flickering fluorescent lights. She could hear voices—Marco's unmistakable tone, calm and calculated, giving orders like a general on the battlefield.

Bella's fingers tightened around her weapon as she inched closer, her pulse racing. This was it. The moment everything came down to.

She pushed the door open, stepping inside.

And there he was.

Marco stood at the far end of the room, his back to them as he worked at a terminal. The glow of the screen bathed him in cold light, his posture relaxed despite the mayhem raging just beyond the walls.

"Marco!" Bella shouted, her gun trained on him.

Marco turned, his eyes meeting hers, and for a moment, the world seemed to stop.

"Well, well," he drawled, a slow smile spreading across his face. "Look who couldn't stay away."

He faced her, his expression calm, almost resigned. "Amore," he said, his voice a quiet echo of their last meeting. "You always find me."

Bella raised her weapon, her hands steady despite the storm raging inside her.

"This ends now," she said, her voice cold and resolute.

Marco chuckled, the sound low and menacing. "Oh, Bella. It's only just beginning."

"Step away from the terminal," Bella commanded, her voice slicing through the tense stillness like a blade. Her gun was steady, but her pulse pounded like a war drum in her chest.

Marco turned slowly, his hands raised in a gesture of mock surrender. His lips curled into a faint, maddening smile, one that twisted the dim light of the server room into something sinister.

"Do you even know what you're stopping?" he asked, his voice smooth, calculated—a man who had nothing to lose and everything to prove.

"You've crossed too many lines," Bella said, her gun unwavering, though the weight of its aim seemed heavier tonight. "Whatever justification you think you have, it ends now."

He stepped closer, his hands still raised but no less

dangerous. The air between them grew charged, thick with unspoken tension and the scent of burnt electronics. "It doesn't end, Bella. Not while Dusker Corporation exists. You've seen the files. You know what they're capable of. If I walk away now, they win. And you know it."

Her grip tightened, her knuckles whitening against the gun's cold steel. Her mind was a storm of conflicting emotions, the sharp edges of duty and morality colliding with something more personal, more dangerous.

"This isn't the way to fight them," she said, her voice edged with both determination and doubt.

"Isn't it?" His voice rose, cutting through the hum of the servers and the distant gunfire. "What's your way, Bella? Another trial where their lawyers bury the truth under piles of red tape? Another mistrial where they twist the narrative until they're the victims and people like me are painted as monsters? I can end it. Right here, right now."

He gestured toward the terminal, where a progress bar blinked ominously on the screen. 83%.

"I'm uploading everything," he said, his voice taking on a fervent edge. "The world will know what Dusker Corporation has done—what they've destroyed. It's the only way."

"You're no savior," she spat, her voice trembling with barely contained fury. "You're a killer."

His gaze was steady, unflinching. "I'm both," he admitted. "But stop pretending you don't understand.

You do, Bella. You've always understood. You want justice, no matter the cost. That's why you're here. That's why you're not running away."

The words hit her like a physical blow, and for a brief, terrifying moment, she wondered if he was right.

Before she could respond, Marco moved.

The sharp beep of a device pierced the air, followed by a deafening explosion. The room seemed to implode, the force knocking Bella off her feet. Smoke poured into the space, acrid and suffocating, burning her lungs as she coughed and stumbled to her knees.

"Marco!" she shouted, her voice hoarse, but the word was swallowed by the chaos.

Through the smoke, she saw his silhouette, dark and ghostlike, disappearing into the shadows. She raised her gun and fired, the shots cracking like thunder in the confined space. But her aim was thrown off by the confusion and the swirling haze, and Marco slipped away, as elusive as ever.

The terminal, once the linchpin of their operation, was now a charred ruin. Sparks flickered from exposed wires, and the screen was shattered, its glow extinguished.

"Bella!"

Luca's voice cut through the haze, desperate and raw. He stumbled into the room, blood streaking his temple, his breathing labored but otherwise intact. His eyes found her immediately, scanning for injuries.

"Are you okay?" he asked, his voice tight with

concern.

She nodded, though her breath came in ragged gasps. "He's gone. Again." The words tasted bitter, like failure.

Luca's gaze fell to the wreckage, his expression darkening as he took in the destroyed terminal, the shattered servers, the smoldering fragments of evidence. "What the hell did he leave us?"

Bella stepped closer to the wreckage, her boots crunching over shards of glass and twisted metal. The acrid smell of melted circuits filled her nose, and her heart sank as she surveyed the damage.

Only fragments remained—charred bits of code, scattered pieces of a puzzle she couldn't yet solve.

She swallowed the lump in her throat, her voice barely above a whisper. "Not enough."

The weight of her words settled between them, heavy and suffocating. Luca reached out, his hand brushing hers in a moment of unspoken solidarity. For all their battles, all their betrayals, they were still in this together.

But as Bella stared at the ruins of their last chance to bring Marco to justice, she couldn't shake the feeling that they were losing the war.

∞

The FBI field office buzzed with low voices and the rhythmic clatter of keyboards, but the usual urgency was muted, swallowed by a collective sense of defeat. The air reeked of stale coffee and burnt adrenaline, the kind of oppressive atmosphere that settled after a mission gone sideways.

Lawson stood at the head of the briefing room, his jaw locked tight, the veins in his temples pulsing with restrained frustration. His tone was clipped as he debriefed the team, each word laced with a simmering anger that didn't need to be shouted to be felt.

"We're back at square one," he said, his gaze scanning the room like a hawk assessing its prey. "Marco slipped through our fingers, and now we've got a few corrupted files and a smoldering wreck of a server room to show for it. That's not good enough. We don't get to lose—not on this."

Bella sat at the far end of the room, isolated from the huddle of agents who whispered amongst themselves. Her shoulders were slumped, her gaze fixed on the fragmented files displayed on her laptop. The recovered data was a chaotic jumble of broken code and corrupted images, offering only tantalizing glimpses of Dusker Corporation's sinister operations. It wasn't enough.

And the worst part? Marco knew it.

"Gupta," Lawson barked, turning his attention to her. The room fell silent.

She straightened in her seat, her heart sinking as his cold gaze pinned her in place.

"A word. Now."

The eyes of her colleagues followed her as she rose and crossed the room, every step heavy with dread. Lawson motioned her into his office, the blinds drawn tight to shut out prying eyes. The door clicked shut behind her, sealing them in a space that suddenly felt claustrophobic, the air too thick to breathe.

Lawson leaned against his desk, arms crossed. "What the hell were you thinking?"

Bella met his gaze, her voice quiet but steady. "I was thinking Marco was about to destroy the only chance we had of stopping him."

"And in the process, you disobeyed a direct order, jeopardized the team, and compromised the mission," he snapped. "We don't work like that, Bella. This isn't some rogue vigilante operation. We're the FBI. We follow protocols for a reason."

She didn't argue. What would be the point? The weight of her actions pressed down on her, heavy and unrelenting. She'd made her choice in that server room, and now she had to live with it.

Lawson exhaled sharply, running a hand through his graying hair. "I don't have a choice here. You're suspended, effective immediately."

Bella felt the words hit like a punch to the gut, but she didn't flinch. Instead, she reached for her badge and gun, her movements deliberate and measured. She placed them on his desk with a quiet finality that made her heart ache.

"I understand," she said simply.

The door burst open, and Luca stepped inside, his face flushed with anger. "Wait a second," he said, his voice sharp. "You can't do this. Bella was the only reason we got anything at all. If she hadn't disobeyed..."

"Enough," Lawson cut him off, his voice firm. "This isn't up for debate, Rossi. She crossed a line, and there are consequences for that."

"She saved lives," Luca shot back, his tone heated.

"And endangered others," Lawson countered, his voice rising. "She broke the chain of command. End of story."

Bella placed a hand on Luca's arm, stopping him before he could say more. "It's fine," she said softly, her voice laced with resignation.

"No, it's not," Luca argued, turning to her. His dark eyes searched hers, looking for some flicker of fight.

But Bella was tired. Tired of fighting, of losing, of feeling like every step forward came with two steps back. "It's done, Luca," she said, her voice firm but not unkind.

She stepped past him, her movements slow, deliberate. The weight of her badge was gone, but the heaviness in her chest lingered. She paused at the door, glancing back at Lawson. "I still want him stopped," she said quietly.

Lawson's expression softened, just a fraction. "So do I," he admitted.

Bella nodded once, then walked out, her footsteps echoing down the corridor like the closing of a chapter she wasn't ready to end.

Luca caught up with her in the parking lot, the cool night air a sharp contrast to the suffocating tension inside.

"You didn't have to do that," he said, his voice tight with frustration.

She turned to him, her eyes tired but resolute. "Yes, I did."

Luca took a step closer, his gaze searching hers. "You're not alone in this, Bella. You don't have to carry it all on your own."

Her lips curved into a faint, bittersweet smile. "I appreciate that. But Marco's my responsibility. I'm the one who let him get close, and I'm the one who has to bring him down."

She turned away before he could respond, her heart heavy with the knowledge that she might not have the strength to see it through.

The night stretched out before her, dark and uncertain, but she couldn't stop now. Marco was still out there, and no matter what it took, she would find him.

CHAPTER 17: BELLA'S BREAKING POINT

Bella's apartment had become her prison. The once-cozy space now felt suffocating, the walls closing in like silent witnesses to her unraveling. The hum of New York City filtered faintly through the grime-streaked windows—honking cars, distant sirens—but even the city's cacophony couldn't drown out the relentless storm in her mind.

The kitchen table was buried beneath a clutter of papers, files, and her laptop, its screen dimmed to save power as if even the machine had given up on her. A single lamp cast a sickly yellow glow over the scene, illuminating the scattered breadcrumbs of a case she could no longer claim as hers.

Bella leaned forward, elbows on the table, her head cradled in her hands. Her eyes burned from staring at the same documents for hours, the words bleeding together until they became indecipherable hieroglyphs. Population Control. Whistleblower Elimination. Dusker Corporation Internal Memos. Each phrase carried the weight of a thousand unanswered questions.

Marco's voice haunted her, as vivid as if he were standing in the room.

"You're just like me, Bella. You want justice, no matter the cost."

She gritted her teeth, shaking her head as if to dislodge the memory. "I'm nothing like you," she muttered, but her words lacked conviction. The truth was far more complicated, far more damning.

Days passed, though Bella couldn't be sure how many. Time had become elastic, stretching and snapping in disorienting intervals. Mornings bled into afternoons, afternoons into sleepless nights. The sun rose and set behind her drawn curtains, and still, she stayed locked in her apartment, consumed by the puzzle before her.

The calendar on the wall remained unchanged, mocking her with its static certainty. Somewhere, people were going to work, meeting friends for drinks, falling in love. Bella had lost track of all of it.

She flipped open her battered notebook, pages crammed with hastily scribbled notes. Dates, names, locations—all the breadcrumbs she'd gathered while chasing Marco. At the center of it all was a single line, underlined twice in angry slashes:

"The real killers are the ones you work for."

Her fingers brushed the words as if touching them might make them disappear. They didn't.

How had it come to this? Marco was the criminal. The liar. The manipulator who'd used her trust as a weapon. And yet... the deeper she delved into Dusker Corporation's operations, the harder it became to ignore the venomous truth in his accusations.

She reached for a fragment of a recovered file, one of the few salvaged from the wreckage of the server farm. The document was incomplete, corrupted in parts, but the word Specter appeared repeatedly, its implications chilling. Bella pieced together enough to form a picture: Specter was an initiative designed to monitor dissenters globally. Not just monitor—neutralize.

Her stomach twisted as the full scope of it hit her. This wasn't just corruption. This was tyranny.

Her phone buzzed on the edge of the table, dragging her back to the present. A message from Luca.

"We need to talk. I'm on my way."

She stared at the text, her thumb hovering over the screen. She wasn't sure whether to be relieved or terrified.

∞

The bathroom mirror was streaked with condensation, its surface foggy from the too-hot shower she'd just forced herself to endure. Bella stood at the sink, a towel wrapped around her body, water dripping from her dark hair and pooling on the tiles beneath her feet.

She looked at her reflection, almost startled by what she saw. Her skin was pale, her eyes ringed with shadows that told the story of too many sleepless nights. The exhaustion etched into her features made her seem older, a stranger she barely recognized.

She reached for her razor, hesitating for a moment before applying it to her leg. The motion was mechanical, her mind drifting as she worked. Why am I doing this? The question echoed in her thoughts, sharp and unrelenting.

For Luca? The thought startled her, and she almost nicked her skin.

The idea of him seeing her like this—raw, broken—made something in her chest tighten. She hated the vulnerability it exposed, the reminder that she still cared about how he saw her. But maybe, just maybe, it wasn't about Luca at all.

Maybe it was for herself. A small, desperate act of reclaiming control when everything else had spiraled into chaos.

She finished quickly, wrapping herself in a robe and stepping back into the main room. The air smelled faintly of her shampoo, a rare comfort in the suffocating space. Her phone buzzed again, signaling Luca's arrival downstairs.

Bella glanced toward the door, her pulse quickening. She wasn't ready to see him. But she also knew she couldn't keep running from him—or from herself.

The knock came, sharp and deliberate, cutting through the oppressive silence of Bella's apartment. She hesitated for a moment before pulling the door open. Luca stood there, leaning casually against the frame, but the fatigue etched into his features betrayed the nonchalance. His tie was loosened, his shirt wrinkled from a long day, and his storm-gray eyes fixed on her with a look that was equal parts concern and frustration.

"You eating? Sleeping?" he asked, stepping inside without waiting for an invitation. His gaze swept over the chaos of papers, files, and takeout containers scattered across the room.

"Thanks for the wellness check, Mom," she retorted, shutting the door with a little more force than necessary.

He didn't take the bait, didn't even crack a smile. Instead, he reached for a file on the table, flipping through it with practiced efficiency. "You've been at this nonstop since the raid."

"Because I'm the only one who seems to care," she snapped, crossing the room in three angry strides to snatch the file from his hands.

"That's not true," he said, his voice calm but with an undercurrent of steel. His jaw tightened, the faint tick in his cheek betraying his restraint. "We all care, Bella. But burning yourself out isn't going to solve this."

Her laugh was sharp, brittle. "So, what, I should

sit back and let the system work? Like it worked for the whistleblowers Dusker Corporation silenced? Or for the people Specter targeted?" She shook her head, her grip tightening on the file until her knuckles turned white. "I can't do that, Luca. I won't."

"You're suspended," he reminded her quietly, though the weight of those words hung between them like a noose. "If Lawson finds out you're still digging…"

"He can take my badge," she shot back, her voice rising. "Hell, he already has. But he can't take this." She gestured to the mountain of evidence she'd pieced together, the fragile thread of a truth she was determined to unravel. "This is all I have left."

Luca ran a hand through his hair, his frustration bubbling just beneath the surface. He took a step closer, his presence commanding in the small space. "You're playing a dangerous game, Bella. And it's going to get you killed."

"Maybe," she admitted, her voice softer now, almost a whisper. She looked up at him, her eyes glassy with unshed tears. "But at least I'll die doing something that matters."

For a moment, the room fell into a charged silence. The tension between them was palpable, crackling like a live wire. Then, almost unconsciously, her hand reached out, brushing against his arm.

Luca stiffened, his gaze dropping to where her fingers rested against his sleeve. "Don't," he warned, his voice low and rough.

She ignored him, stepping closer. "You can't tell me you don't feel it," she said, her voice trembling but resolute. "You can't stand there and act like this—like we—don't mean anything."

"Bella," he said, his tone heavy with warning, but there was something else there too—something raw and unguarded.

Her hand moved up, curling around the back of his neck, her fingers brushing the short hair at his nape. "Please," she whispered, her voice breaking. "Just... make me forget. Even if it's just for a little while."

He closed his eyes, his jaw clenching as if battling some internal war. "This is a bad idea," he murmured, though his hands found her waist almost instinctively, his grip firm but hesitant.

"Maybe," she admitted, tilting her face toward his. "But it's the only thing that feels real right now."

Her lips met his, tentative at first, testing the boundaries of his resolve. For a heartbeat, he didn't move, didn't breathe. And then he broke, his restraint shattering as he pulled her closer, his mouth claiming hers with a hunger that left no room for doubt.

The kiss was desperate, consuming, a collision of need and frustration, of passion and pain. His hands tightened around her waist, drawing her flush against him as if proximity alone could silence the storm raging inside them both.

When they finally broke apart, their breaths came in ragged gasps, their foreheads resting against each other. "This doesn't solve anything," Luca said, his voice hoarse, though his hands betrayed him by staying where they were, holding her steady.

"No," Bella agreed, her voice barely above a whisper. Her fingers trailed along the line of his jaw, her touch feather-light. "But it makes it bearable."

Without another word, he kissed her again, deeper this time, as if trying to anchor her to him, to this moment.

And for now, that was enough.

∞

Bella sat on the edge of her unmade bed, the sheets tangled from a restless night—and not just because of the man standing before her. Luca stood near the window, his back to her as he buttoned his shirt, his movements quick and mechanical. The first pale rays of dawn filtered through the blinds, painting jagged slashes of light across his broad shoulders.

"This was a mistake." His voice was low, almost too quiet, but the words landed like a slap.

Bella flinched, the rawness of the statement cutting deeper than she cared to admit. She wrapped the sheet tighter around her, suddenly feeling exposed in every sense of the word. "It was just a hook-up, Luca," she said, forcing her voice to sound casual, detached. "Nothing more."

He turned, his expression unreadable, but there was a flicker of something in his eyes—regret, maybe, or something darker. "You and I both know that's not true."

She let out a bitter laugh, shaking her head. "Don't

flatter yourself. We were two people looking for a way to forget for a night. That's all this was."

Luca's jaw tightened, his hands stilling on the buttons of his cuffs. "Bella, you can lie to yourself all you want, but don't lie to me. You think this helps? That burying yourself in something meaningless makes the pain go away?"

Her eyes narrowed, anger sparking in her chest. "Don't stand there and psychoanalyze me, Luca. You're not exactly innocent here."

"I didn't say I was," he shot back, his voice sharp. "But this..." he gestured around the room, the tangled sheets, the chaos of files and notes scattered across every surface— "this isn't you solving the case. This is you chasing a ghost."

Bella froze, the words cutting deeper than she wanted to admit.

"You think I don't know that?" she snapped, her voice rising. "But Marco's not just some criminal, Luca. He's a symptom of something bigger. Dusker Corporation is rotten to the core, and we've been complicit by turning a blind eye."

"And what?" Luca stepped closer, his presence as commanding as ever. "You think teaming up with him is the answer? That's exactly what he wants, Bella—to drag you into his version of justice, to make you doubt everything you stand for."

Her laughter was bitter, humorless. "Maybe I should doubt it!" The words tore from her throat before she could stop them.

The silence that followed was suffocating. Luca stared at her, his expression darkening with something between disappointment and concern.

"You don't mean that," he said finally, his voice low but firm.

Her shoulders sagged, the fight draining out of her as quickly as it had ignited. "I don't know what I mean anymore," she admitted, her voice cracking. She pushed a hand through her hair, staring at the floor as if it might hold the answers she was desperate for. "Every lead we follow, every piece of evidence we uncover—it just proves him right. How do I keep fighting for a system that's this broken?"

Luca's expression softened, though his frustration was still palpable. He crouched down in front of her, his hands resting on his knees as he met her gaze. "By remembering who you are," he said gently, but there was an edge to his tone. "You don't get to be judge, jury, and executioner, Bella. That's what makes you different from him."

She looked at him, her chest tight with conflicting emotions. "And what if it's not enough? What if I can't stop this? What if I've already crossed the line?"

His hand reached out, hesitating for a moment before brushing against hers. The touch was brief, but it grounded her in a way she hadn't felt in weeks. "You haven't crossed it yet," he said, his voice steady. "But if you keep going down this road, you will. And once you do, there's no coming back."

For a moment, she let the weight of his words

settle over her. She hated that he was right, hated that he could see through her defenses with such ease. But most of all, she hated that she didn't know if she cared anymore.

Luca rose to his feet, his movements deliberate as he grabbed his jacket from the back of a chair. "Take some time, Bella," he said, his tone firm but not unkind. "Figure out what you want—what you're willing to sacrifice to get it. But don't do this alone."

She didn't respond as he headed for the door, his footsteps echoing in the stillness of the apartment.

"Luca," she called just as his hand reached the doorknob.

He paused, glancing over his shoulder.

"Thank you," she said softly, her voice barely above a whisper.

His expression was unreadable, but he nodded once before stepping out and closing the door behind him.

The silence that followed was deafening, the weight of his words and the choices she faced pressing down on her like a physical force. Bella sank back onto the bed, her gaze drifting to the scattered files on the table.

She didn't know what the future held, but one thing was certain: she wasn't ready to give up—not yet.

Bella sank onto the floor, her head in her hands. Luca's words echoed in her mind, but they couldn't drown out the louder voice—the one that sounded like Marco, whispering that she was fighting for the wrong side.

Her gaze drifted to the files on the table. One page caught her eye, a list of coordinates tied to Dusker Corporation's covert operations. Her pulse quickened as she traced the entries with her finger.

She wasn't done. Not yet.

As the city buzzed outside, Bella reached for her laptop, diving back into the data. She told herself it was about justice, about exposing the truth. But deep down, she couldn't ignore the nagging thought that maybe, just maybe, she was searching for him, too.

And that terrified her more than anything else.

CHAPTER 18: PUBLIC SENTIMENT SHIFTS

The streets of New York throbbed with unrest, the electric tension thick enough to choke on. From her vantage point on the corner of Fifth Avenue, Bella watched as the river of protesters swelled, spilling into intersections, drowning out the honks of impatient taxis. Their voices roared, unrelenting, crashing against the high-rise buildings like waves against a cliff.

"Justice for the silenced!"

"Expose the corporate killers!"

"Marco DeLuca: The People's Hero!"

That last chant sent a chill coursing through Bella's veins. She shoved her hands deeper into her coat pockets, her breath misting in front of her. It wasn't just the frigid January wind clawing at her skin—it was the unease coiling in her gut.

Banners rose above the crowd like jagged teeth. Marco's face was everywhere, transformed into a saintly figure by bold graphic strokes. His sharp jawline, piercing eyes, and wry smirk stared back at her from every angle. The people had crowned their hero, whether or not he deserved the title.

But it was the other images that cut deeper: grainy screenshots from the leaked Dusker Corporation footage. Emaciated children huddled in corners, eyes sunken and desperate. Burned-out villages reduced to skeletal frames of ash and soot. Families torn apart, their anguish frozen in time, their lives collateral damage in a corporate machine's insatiable hunger for control.

The protesters screamed for justice. Bella wondered if they even knew what that meant anymore.

She turned away, her jaw tight. Today wasn't about the crowd, the chants, or the sick churn of her conscience. It was about survival. She had an appointment at FBI headquarters—her disciplinary review. The words hung over her like a guillotine, her career dangling by a fraying thread.

Do or die, Bella. Do or die.

The cold corridors of the FBI's Manhattan headquarters hummed with quiet intensity. The glossy floors reflected the fluorescent lights overhead, creating an endless mirage of white and chrome. Bella's heels clicked sharply against the tiles as she made her way through the bullpen, her pulse thrumming with every step.

The air inside the building was just as charged as the streets outside. Agents huddled in small clusters, their voices low, their expressions grim. Every screen in the room was tuned to the same footage, the same headlines, the same damning evidence that had gone viral overnight.

Bella stopped in front of a wall-mounted television, unable to tear her eyes away from the broadcast. A newscaster, her lips pressed into a severe line, narrated over the now-infamous clips.

"These images, allegedly released by Marco DeLuca's network, reveal the shocking extent of Dusker Corporation's unethical experiments. Documents indicate Advanced-System technologies were weaponized to exploit vulnerable populations, destabilize governments, and eliminate dissidents under the guise of corporate interests."

The screen cut to footage of Advanced-System drones patrolling desolate villages, their sleek frames gleaming in the sunlight like vultures circling their prey. Another clip showed an abandoned laboratory, its sterile walls stained with evidence of human suffering. Emaciated figures shuffled through the frame, their hollow eyes staring into the camera as if pleading for rescue.

Bella's stomach churned. She tried to swallow the bile rising in her throat, but it lingered, bitter and corrosive.

"It's disgusting."

She startled at the voice behind her and turned to

see Luca standing there, his arms crossed, his expression a mask of barely contained anger.

"They're eating it up," he said, nodding toward the screen. "Marco's not just a whistleblower anymore. He's a damn revolution."

Bella's lips pressed into a thin line as she tore her gaze away from the television. "Because he's showing them something real. Something we failed to uncover. Or worse, something we ignored."

"That doesn't make him a hero," Luca said sharply. His eyes bore into hers, a storm brewing in their dark depths. "He's still a killer, Bella. Don't forget that."

Her silence lingered too long. The weight of it grew heavier by the second, until Luca's frustration spilled over.

"Don't tell me you're buying into this," he said, his voice low but laced with disbelief.

She hesitated, her eyes darting back to the screen. "I'm not saying he's right. I'm saying…" She trailed off, her voice faltering.

"You're saying what?" Luca pressed, stepping closer. "That we should ignore the bodies he left behind because the footage makes us uncomfortable? That his version of justice is justified because we screwed up?"

"I don't know!" The words burst out of her, raw and unguarded. She closed her eyes, taking a shuddering breath before continuing, quieter this time. "I don't know what to think anymore, Luca. Every lead we follow, every piece of evidence we uncover, just proves him right. And if he's right, then…"

"Then what?" he interrupted, his voice softening.

Her throat tightened, and she shook her head. "Then what the hell have we been fighting for?"

Luca's expression shifted, the hard edges of his frustration giving way to something more vulnerable. But he didn't reach for her, didn't offer the comfort she wasn't sure she deserved.

After a long pause, he spoke again, his tone measured. "I'm leaving."

Bella blinked, startled. "What?"

"I'm going back to Italy," he said, the words landing like a blow. "Interpol's jurisdiction over this case is done. They've made it clear Marco's the FBI's mess now. I've got nothing left to do here."

"You're leaving?" she repeated, her voice barely above a whisper.

His gaze held hers, unflinching. "In a couple of days, yeah."

The silence between them stretched, heavy and suffocating. Bella wanted to say something, to argue, to beg him to stay—but the words wouldn't come.

Luca stepped back, his hands sliding into his pockets. "You'll figure it out, Bella. You always do."

And with that, he turned and walked away, leaving her standing there, the television blaring behind her, the weight of the world pressing down on her shoulders.

∞

Hours later, Bella sat alone in a room that had become her own trial. The walls of the FBI's interrogation room seemed to close in on Bella, the air weighted with unspoken accusations. The faint hum of the overhead light was a constant irritant, its harsh glow slicing through the dim room. She sat at the steel table, her hands clasped in front of her, every muscle in her body taut. The only sound was the occasional shuffle of paper or the faint hiss of the laptop replaying that footage.

It was a room meant to unnerve, to strip its occupant of pretense. And it worked.

Across the table, Lawson sat like a stone gargoyle, his expression unreadable, his fingers drumming a slow, deliberate rhythm on the arm of his chair. To his right were two high-ranking agents Bella recognized from D.C., their sharp suits and sharper eyes giving nothing away. They had barely spoken since she was escorted into the room.

Behind them, the observation mirror loomed. She could feel the weight of unseen eyes pressing against her back, dissecting her every move, every flicker of expression.

"This isn't just about you, Rossi," Lawson said finally, his voice a low growl that carried across the table like a warning. "This is about trust. About whether the FBI can count on one of its own."

Bella didn't flinch. Instead, she met his gaze head-on, her voice steady but threaded with an undercurrent of defiance. "And it's about whether the FBI is willing to do what it takes to win this war."

Lawson leaned back, his chair creaking. He gestured toward the laptop screen where Marco DeLuca's revolution played on an endless loop. The grainy footage of emaciated victims, the slick propaganda of Marco's face superimposed over his words: Justice is not a privilege. It is a weapon.

"You see that?" Lawson's voice was sharp, cutting. "That's what you're defending? A man who's turned the world against us, who's made himself a messiah to the mob?"

"I'm not defending him," Bella shot back, her tone heated. "I'm saying we've been playing catch-up this whole time. Marco's five steps ahead of us because he's willing to go where we won't. He's exploiting every weakness we've let fester. And we keep playing by the rules like they still matter."

The older agent from D.C., a man with graying temples and a polished veneer of authority, leaned forward. "And what are you suggesting, Agent Rossi? That we throw the rulebook out the window and start taking cues from a fugitive? You've already crossed lines..."

"Because I had to!" Bella snapped, her voice rising. "If I hadn't, we wouldn't even have the scraps of evidence we do now. We've been reacting to him instead of outmaneuvering him. That has to change."

Lawson exchanged a glance with the other agents, his jaw tightening. "And how exactly do you propose we do that? Because from where I'm sitting, you've got a suspension hanging over your head, Rossi. You're not exactly in a position to dictate strategy."

Bella took a breath, steadying herself. Her heart pounded against her ribs, but she forced the adrenaline into something useful. "You want Marco? I'll get him for you."

A bitter laugh escaped Lawson's lips. "Oh, you'll get him? That easy, huh? Just like that?"

She ignored his sarcasm and pushed forward, her voice quieter now, but no less intense. "Let me go undercover. Let me join him. I'll play the role he's been trying to cast me in from the start. He already sees me as someone who understands his cause—someone like him. I'll use that. I'll infiltrate his network, earn his trust, and bring him down from the inside."

The room fell silent, the weight of her words settling over them like a shroud.

"You're out of your damn mind," Lawson said after a moment, leaning forward, his hands braced on the table. "You think we're going to let you waltz off into the arms of a known killer and hope you come back with intel? You'd be a liability, Rossi. Not an asset."

Bella's gaze didn't waver. "You think I haven't thought about that? You think I don't know the risks? But what's the alternative? We keep chasing him until he burns the whole system down? Or worse—until he wins?"

The agent with the gray temples spoke again, his voice measured. "Even if we entertained this...

suggestion, how do we know you won't end up sympathizing with him? That you won't turn completely?"

Bella felt the jab, but she didn't let it show. "Because I know what Marco is," she said, her voice hard. "He's not a savior. He's a manipulator. A killer. I can understand his grievances without condoning his methods. And I'll use that understanding to dismantle his operation."

Lawson's eyes narrowed, suspicion flickering across his face. "You're awfully confident for someone on the edge of a career-ending suspension. What makes you think we'd even give you this chance?"

"Because you don't have a better option," Bella said bluntly. "You've tried chasing him, outsmarting him, cutting off his resources. Nothing's worked. You need someone on the inside. Someone he already trusts—at least enough to let their guard down."

Another tense silence filled the room. Bella could feel the battle lines being drawn, the unspoken debate taking place in the glances exchanged between the agents.

Finally, Lawson spoke, his voice low and dangerous. "You're betting your career on this, Rossi. Hell, you're betting your life. You screw this up, and there won't be a safety net waiting to catch you."

Bella straightened in her chair, her gaze unwavering. "I don't need a safety net. I just need a shot."

The agents stared at her, the weight of their

scrutiny pressing down like a vice. For a moment, the only sound was the faint hum of the overhead light and the muted crackle of the footage still looping on the laptop.

Finally, Lawson pushed himself to his feet. He glanced at the others, then back at Bella. "We'll discuss it."

With that, he turned and strode out of the room, the others following close behind. The door clicked shut behind them, leaving Bella alone once more.

She exhaled slowly, her hands trembling as she rested them on the table. The buzz of the light seemed louder now, the shadows deeper.

This was her gamble. Her Hail Mary. And as the silence closed in, she couldn't shake the memory of Marco's voice, smooth and taunting, whispering in her ear:

"You're just like me, Bella. You want justice, no matter the cost."

CHAPTER 19: A WORLD TURNED UPSIDE DOWN

The Dusker Corporation headquarters towered over the Manhattan skyline, its gleaming facade of mirrored glass throwing back the crimson hues of the dying sun. The building exuded an air of invincibility, a fortress of technology and arrogance. From her perch on a nearby rooftop, Bella Rossi felt the weight of the moment settle into her chest like a stone.

The chill wind bit through her jacket, but it wasn't enough to distract her from the growing knot of tension in her gut. She crouched low behind a rusted ventilation unit, the metal cold beneath her gloved hand. Below, the streets buzzed with the usual chaos of Manhattan—taxis honking, pedestrians rushing, the muffled chatter of a city that never stopped. Yet tonight, it felt different. The air was electric, charged with the promise of something she couldn't quite name but couldn't ignore.

Agent Park stood behind her, his posture rigid, a dark silhouette against the hazy backdrop of the city. He didn't need to speak for her to feel his disdain. It clung to him like a second skin, palpable in the way he moved, the way he avoided looking directly at her. Park had never been subtle in his dislike of her, and tonight was no exception.

"Do you really think he's going to show?" Park's voice cut through the silence, low and edged with skepticism.

Bella didn't turn. She kept her eyes on the building's main entrance, scanning the flow of employees leaving for the day, their faces blurred behind the reflective glass doors. "Marco doesn't bluff," she replied, her voice measured, tight. "If he's planning something, he'll be here."

Park scoffed, the sound grating against her already frayed nerves. "Right. Because you're such an expert on him."

She shot him a sharp look over her shoulder. "I've spent months studying his moves. Don't mistake your lack of insight for mine."

"Months," Park echoed, stepping closer, his shadow falling over her. "And yet here we are. You're suspended, the case is in shambles, and Marco's running circles around us. Tell me, Rossi, what part of this is a victory?"

Bella turned to face him fully, rising from her crouch. Her blood simmered beneath her skin, her restraint unraveling. "You think I don't know what's at stake here? You think I don't feel the weight of every single failure? Don't you dare stand there and lecture me about what I've sacrificed."

Park's jaw tightened, his dark eyes boring into hers. "I think you've lost perspective. This isn't about you proving something to yourself—or to Marco. This is about stopping him before more lives are destroyed. And frankly, I'm not sure you're capable of doing that anymore."

The words hit like a slap, but Bella refused to flinch. Instead, she stepped closer, closing the space between them. "If you think you can do better, Park, then by all means, take the lead. But don't stand here and question my commitment. I've put everything on the line for this case, including my career. What have you risked? Your reputation?"

Park's lips pressed into a thin line, the tension between them thick enough to cut. For a moment, the only sound was the distant wail of a siren, the city's heartbeat pulsing around them.

Finally, he exhaled sharply, his shoulders relaxing just enough to show a crack in his armor. "Just don't screw this up," he said, his voice quieter, but no less cutting. "Because if you do, it won't just be your career that goes down in flames."

Bella turned away, her gaze returning to the gleaming fortress of Dusker Corporation. Park's words echoed in her mind, each one a barb that dug deeper than she cared to admit. But she couldn't afford to dwell on them. Not now. Not when Marco was out there, somewhere, waiting for her next move.

The wind picked up, carrying with it the faint scent of rain. Bella tightened her grip on the binoculars, her knuckles white beneath the leather of her gloves. She thought of Marco's voice, smooth and infuriatingly confident, whispering in her mind. You're just like me, Bella. You want justice, no matter the cost.

She inhaled deeply, her breath shaky. No, Marco, she thought. I'm nothing like you.

∞

The first sign of Marco's play wasn't the sharp burst of an explosion or the chaos of a raid—it was the silence. A strange, heavy pause that swallowed the usual buzz of Manhattan's crowded streets. Then came the flicker, subtle at first, as the towering digital screens of Dusker Corporation's headquarters began to waver. The bright, confident corporate logo—a beacon of technological progress—disappeared, swallowed by static.

Bella felt her pulse quicken, her instincts screaming danger. The air seemed to thicken around her as if the city itself held its breath.

"What the hell…" Park's muttered curse was low, but it carried, his tone laced with the kind of tension that made her stomach coil.

Before either of them could react further, the

static cleared, replaced by a face that loomed over Manhattan like a god descending to earth.

Marco.

Bella's breath snagged in her throat.

His image filled the screens, larger than life, every detail amplified—the sharp cut of his jawline, the faint shadow of stubble, the unsettling calm in his storm-gray eyes. He wasn't just speaking to the masses below; he was commanding them.

"Good evening." His voice rolled out smooth as silk, yet weighted with authority. He didn't shout. He didn't need to. Each word carried a gravitational pull, drawing the crowd beneath the screens into a stunned silence.

"Allow me to introduce myself to those who know me only through whispers and headlines. My name is Marco DeLuca, and I am not a criminal."

Beside her, Park stiffened, his shoulders rigid, his hands clenched into fists. Bella couldn't tear her gaze away.

"I am a whistleblower," Marco continued, his calm delivery betraying the fire in his eyes. "And tonight, I bring you the truth."

The static crackled again, and the screen shifted, now displaying a series of documents, charts, and photos—evidence of something far darker than corporate greed. Dusker Corporation's sins laid bare. There were blurred-out images of faces, files marked with redacted text, financial transactions scrawled across the screen in dizzying amounts.

The crowd erupted in murmurs—shock, disbelief, anger. Phones were raised, recording the broadcast, the weight of Marco's accusations already spreading beyond Manhattan like wildfire.

"Dusker Corporation," Marco said, his tone sharpening, "is not the benevolent guardian of innovation it claims to be. It is a machine built on lies, fueled by exploitation, and designed to destroy lives for profit. The executives of this corporation have silenced dissenters, manipulated elections, and sacrificed your privacy on the altar of their greed."

Bella's stomach churned as the truth hit her, each word driving nails into her resolve. The documents flashing across the screen weren't just accusations; they were a map to the corruption she had been too blind—or too afraid—to see.

"Damn it," Park growled, breaking her spiraling thoughts. "He's patching into the global network. This isn't just local."

"Turn it off," Bella whispered, her voice taut with a mixture of desperation and dread.

Park gave her a sharp look, as if she'd just suggested stopping a hurricane with an umbrella. "We can't. Not unless we shut down half the damn grid. He planned this too well."

Her mind raced, but there was no way out, no way to stop the poison Marco was dripping into the veins of the city.

"And why," Marco asked, his voice deepening with righteous fury, "do those meant to protect you—

your government, your law enforcement—turn a blind eye? Because dismantling the systems that profit from your suffering is inconvenient. Because it's easier to chase men like me."

The image of Marco shifted, his piercing gaze locking on the camera as if he could see her. As if he knew she was watching.

"And they know this," he said, his tone softening to something almost intimate. "Bella Rossi knows it."

The sound of her name was a gunshot in the night. Bella's breath hitched, her heart stuttering as a flush of heat crawled up her neck. Around her, the rooftop seemed to shrink, the air suddenly too thin.

Park's head snapped toward her, his expression an unreadable storm.

"He called you out," he said, his voice laced with accusation.

Bella tore her gaze from the screen, her pulse hammering in her ears. "I didn't ask for this," she said, her voice shaking.

"No," Park snapped, his glare cutting. "But you let him in, didn't you? Into your head. Into this case."

Before she could answer, Marco's voice rose again, drawing their attention back to the screen.

"But here's the truth," Marco said, his image replaced by more damning evidence—hidden bank accounts, whistleblowers who had vanished, elections swayed by manipulated Advanced-System data. "The corruption runs deep. And if you want to stop it, you have to start by questioning the very institutions you trust."

Bella felt a wave of nausea. His words weren't just cutting at Dusker Corporation—they were cutting at her. At the foundations of everything she'd spent her life believing in.

Park's voice broke through her haze. "He's not a hero, Bella. Don't let him fool you."

She turned to him, her eyes haunted. "What if he's both?"

Park's silence spoke volumes, but his jaw clenched, his frustration tangible. As the broadcast continued to unravel secrets that could topple giants, Bella stood frozen in place, caught between the man she'd sworn to stop and the truths she could no longer deny.

And deep down, she couldn't shake the feeling that Marco wasn't just exposing the world's lies.

He was exposing hers too.

On the screen, Marco's face softened, a faint smile tugging at the corners of his mouth.

"This is only the beginning," he said. "The truth is out there now. What you choose to do with it is up to you."

The feed cut to black, leaving the crowd below in stunned silence.

Bella stared at the darkened screen, her pulse racing. She'd expected a violent move from Marco, something dramatic and destructive. Instead, he'd done what no one else could—he'd made the world listen.

Park spoke again, his voice tight with frustration. "This doesn't change what he's done. He's still a fugitive, and he's still dangerous."

Bella didn't respond. Because in that moment, she wasn't sure who the real danger was anymore—Marco, or the system he was fighting against.

As the crowd began to disperse, Bella's phone buzzed with a new message.

"You see it now, don't you? – M"

She stared at the screen, her chest tightening.

For the first time, she wasn't sure if she wanted to bring him in—or hear him out.

CHAPTER 20: THE SEDUCTION OF DARKNESS

The abandoned pier loomed ahead like a scene ripped from a noir film, its rotting boards slick with rain and decay. The air was thick with the salt of the harbor, mingling with the faint tang of oil and the stench of seaweed rotting beneath the pilings. The dim glow of the city skyline behind her only deepened the shadows, turning the long stretch of wooden planks into a tunnel of blackness.

Bella Rossi approached with deliberate caution, her flashlight slicing through the gloom in tight, measured arcs. Every step brought a creak beneath her boots, a haunting, groaning protest that echoed into the surrounding emptiness. The weight of Marco's message pressed on her shoulders like a noose—Come alone. No weapons. Just the truth. She hadn't honored the last condition. Her Glock rested snugly against her hip, hidden but reassuring.

The wind tore through her jacket, icy fingers biting through her layers. She shivered, but not from the cold. A tight coil of apprehension wound in her chest, sharpening her senses. At the far end of the pier, a single figure emerged from the shadows. Marco DeLuca leaned against a weathered crate, his face partially lit by the orange glow of a cigarette dangling from his lips. He was waiting, as if the night were his domain and she'd simply stepped into it.

"You're late," Marco said, his voice carrying easily over the sound of waves slapping against the pilings. He exhaled a thin ribbon of smoke, the glowing tip of his cigarette flaring briefly before he flicked it into the water.

"Traffic," Bella replied, her tone sharp and controlled, though her pulse hammered in her ears.

Marco's mouth curled into a faint smile as his eyes skimmed over her, assessing. "And yet you came. I knew you would."

She stopped a few feet away, carefully maintaining the space between them. The pier seemed narrower with him there, the darkness pressing closer. Her hand hovered near her hip, close enough to her holster to give her an advantage if this went south.

"You left me little choice," she said, her words clipped.

Marco stepped forward slightly, not enough to close the gap but enough to make the air feel heavier.

"Did I? Or are you here because you've been thinking about what I said?"

"What exactly would that be?" she asked coolly, though her voice lacked its usual bite.

"Everything." He gestured to the skyline behind her, his movements almost lazy. "Dusker Corporation. Kane. The system you're killing yourself to protect. Me."

Bella bristled. The tension between them was an unbearable tug-of-war—logic demanding she stay detached, instinct urging her to get closer, find the cracks in his armor. She knew if she let herself be too cooperative, too agreeable, Marco would see through her intentions. And yet... his words had carved into her with surgical precision.

Her hand moved in a blur, drawing her gun and leveling it squarely at his chest. "Don't flatter yourself."

If she'd expected him to flinch, she was disappointed. Marco's smile only deepened, tinged with something wistful and dangerous. His hands stayed in his pockets, his posture relaxed. "It doesn't scare me when you pull that trigger finger," he murmured. "You're too good to shoot without reason. And you know I'm not it."

"Keep testing me," she snapped, though the tremor in her voice betrayed her.

"I'm not your enemy, Bella," he said softly, his voice threaded with something more than arrogance. "But I'm also not here to lie to you. You're suffocating under the weight of a cause that isn't worth it. You think I don't see it? The late nights, the sacrifices, the way they grind you down until there's nothing left. And for what? To keep people like Kane untouchable?"

Her pulse stuttered at the mention of Kane, and Marco caught it. His gaze softened, and for a moment, his expression shifted to something almost vulnerable.

"Every case you've worked for them, every lead you've chased—it's cost you more than you'd ever admit," he continued, his tone low, as if it were just the two of them in the world. "And I'm not the villain here. But you don't want to see that, because it's easier to paint me as the bad guy than to look at the real picture."

Her arm faltered for half a second, but she quickly steadied it. The weight of the gun felt heavier now, her fingers aching from the tension.

"You don't know me," she said, her voice harsher than intended.

"I know you better than you think," Marco countered, stepping closer, his boots making no sound against the damp wood. He was now close enough for her to see the flicker of pain in his eyes, buried beneath layers of charm and confidence. "You're not a machine, Bella. You can't keep doing this. It'll destroy you."

She hated that he sounded like he cared. Hated the way his words stirred something deep inside her— anger, guilt, the nagging feeling that he might be right. But more than anything, she hated the small part of her that wanted to lower her weapon.

"Stay where you are," she ordered, her voice like steel.

Marco halted, his hands slowly leaving his pockets in a gesture of compliance. "I'm not here to hurt you," he said simply. "But I can't stand by and watch you hurt yourself anymore, either. You think the truth is black and white, but it's not. It's messy. And you're in the thick of it now, whether you want to be or not."

She swallowed hard, the cold metal of the gun biting into her palm. His words lingered in the air like smoke, their weight pressing down on her. The darkness around them felt alive, a silent witness to the battle raging between them.

"You don't get to decide what I believe in," she said, her voice trembling slightly.

Marco held her gaze, unflinching. "No, but you do."

The silence that followed was deafening, broken only by the crash of the waves against the pier. Bella stood frozen, her gun trained on him, her mind a storm of conflict. Marco's words echoed in her head, relentless and unyielding.

Somewhere deep inside, a truth she wasn't ready to face began to surface.

The briny tang of the harbor thickened as the waves below whispered secrets to the night. Bella's breaths were shallow, measured, her chest rising and falling with deliberate precision as Marco edged closer, his presence oppressive yet intoxicating. His every move was calculated, designed to disarm her—not just the Glock she clutched with trembling hands, but her resolve.

"You have a choice," Marco said, his tone low, resonant. Each word seemed to slice through the humid air. "Keep playing the agency's game, clinging to a fantasy that your justice system does anything but protect its own. Or..." He took another deliberate step forward, the worn planks groaning beneath his boots. "Step into the gray. Fight fire with fire. Together, we could incinerate Dusker Corporation, expose their rot, and watch it burn to ash."

The idea was poison wrapped in honey, and yet it seeped under her skin, tempting her in ways she couldn't admit. Her arm remained raised, the barrel of the gun unwavering, but her conviction faltered.

"You think becoming what they are makes you better?" Bella's voice cracked, a harsh whisper against the crashing waves.

Marco smirked, though it wasn't amusement that curled his lips. It was something darker. "Not better," he said. "More effective. The difference is, I don't hide behind a badge or promises I can't keep. I'm honest about what I am. And I know you, Bella. Deep down, you know this is the only way."

She swallowed hard, her grip tightening on the gun. His words struck a raw nerve, and the truth she refused to face unraveled in the spaces between them. Her gaze flicked to his face, searching for weakness, for something she could exploit—but there was only steel and certainty.

Her silence didn't deter him. Marco stepped closer, now barely a foot away, his voice dropping to a near whisper. "You're tired, Bella. Tired of burying the lies, watching criminals walk free while you're left to sweep up the carnage. You deserve better than that life. We both do."

She bit down on her lower lip, the salty air stinging her dry throat. "And what, Marco? What do I deserve? To be dragged into your world and become like you?"

"Not like me," he said, leaning in just enough for his words to wrap around her like smoke. "Better than me. Smarter. Stronger." His eyes narrowed, and for a fleeting second, something vulnerable flickered in his gaze. "I didn't come here to recruit you. I came here because I can't do this without you. And if you're honest, you can't do it without me either."

Her heart lurched in her chest as she absorbed his words. She hated how they resonated, how they fed a dark, unspoken part of her that longed for freedom from the chains of bureaucracy. It was the very part of her that made her agree to the double-agent mission to begin with—a need to shatter the lies she'd been fed, even if it meant creating new ones.

Bella let out a slow, measured breath and lowered the gun, her movements deliberate but calculated. She couldn't let Marco think she was anything less than conflicted, torn between duty and a longing for something real. Her fingers slackened on the weapon, allowing him to step closer, his hand brushing hers as he disarmed her.

"Maybe you're right," she said, her voice quiet and raw, infused with just the right amount of doubt. "Maybe I'm done pretending to be something I'm not. Maybe it's time I leave the agency behind... for good."

Marco studied her, his eyes searching her face as though dissecting every word. The tension between them was suffocating, a living thing that wound tighter with every passing second. "You'd give it all up?" he asked, skepticism threading his tone.

"I already have," she lied, keeping her expression unreadable. "They used me, Marco. The system used me. I'm tired of being their pawn, their cleanup crew."

The admission wasn't entirely false, and that was what made it dangerous. Marco stepped closer still, his voice dropping to a conspiratorial whisper. "Then let's burn it all down, Bella. Together."

Her pulse thundered in her ears as he extended a hand, palm open, the invitation a symbol of everything she was risking.

She hesitated, long enough to make it convincing, before slipping her hand into his. His fingers closed around hers with a strength that promised loyalty—but also dominance.

"What now?" she asked, her voice barely above a whisper.

"Now," he said, his lips curling into a dangerous smile, "we stop pretending."

Bella's stomach twisted, and she forced a faint smile, concealing the turmoil brewing within. The darkness around them seemed to close in as Marco led her back along the pier. The water lapped hungrily at the pilings below, the sound a reminder of the depths she'd plunged into.

The agency had warned her this mission would be the ultimate test of her loyalty. What they hadn't told her was how much of herself she'd have to betray in the process.

∞

The pier's shadows stretched long and jagged beneath the moonlight, swallowing Marco and Bella as they vanished into the night. From a vantage point across the harbor, Agent Park watched the scene unfold through the lens of his scope, his breath slow, deliberate, synchronized with the faint hum of static in his earpiece.

"Package is in," Park murmured, his voice low, calm, professional. His finger hovered just above the trigger of his sniper rifle, though he knew tonight wasn't the night for action. Not yet. "Rossi made the handoff. She's fully embedded now."

There was a pause, filled only by the faint crackle of the comms.

"Stay on her," came the reply. Lawson's voice, clipped and terse, crackled through the line. Despite his authoritative tone, Park detected the undercurrent of worry—something Lawson rarely let show. "We can't afford another misstep. Keep me updated on her position."

"Understood," Park said, shifting slightly in his

crouched position, the scope following the faint silhouettes of Bella and Marco as they disappeared down a side street.

Back in the FBI's Washington headquarters, Lawson sat in his dimly lit office, his eyes fixed on the television screen mounted on the wall. The Director of the FBI stood at a podium, delivering a statement to a throng of reporters. The words were carefully measured, as though each one had been weighed and approved by a team of public relations experts.

Lawson's jaw tightened as he watched. The Director was a master at saying nothing while making it sound like everything. Promises of justice. Assurances of progress. Carefully sidestepping the glaring truth: the Marco DeLuca case had spiraled into a labyrinth of lies, betrayals, and dead ends.

And now, their best shot at unraveling the mess lay in the hands of Bella Rossi—a woman Lawson had once doubted, dismissed, even considered untrustworthy.

He leaned back in his chair, the weight of his failure pressing down on him like an iron vice. He had underestimated her. When she'd volunteered for the mission, he'd been skeptical, convinced her judgment was clouded by personal ties to DeLuca. But now, as he replayed the reports in his mind—the intelligence she'd fed them, the risks she'd taken to infiltrate DeLuca's inner circle—he realized he'd been wrong.

If anyone could end this nightmare, it was her.

He ran a hand through his graying hair, the leather

of his chair creaking as he turned away from the TV. The room was suffocating, the air thick with the scent of stale coffee and failure. He stared at the stack of files on his desk, each one representing another loose thread in the DeLuca case. Every lead had gone cold. Every attempt to corner the fugitive had ended in disaster.

But Bella… Bella was different.

"Damn it," he muttered under his breath, his fists clenching. He should've trusted her from the start. Maybe then the case wouldn't have spiraled into the chaos it had become.

A knock at the door startled him, and he turned to see his assistant, Margaret, standing hesitantly in the doorway.

"Sir," she said softly, her face pale, "the Director will be expecting your briefing in an hour."

Lawson nodded, dismissing her with a curt wave. As she closed the door behind her, he leaned forward, his elbows on the desk, and buried his face in his hands.

This was it. The final play. If Bella could deliver DeLuca, Lawson's name would be etched into the history books. He'd be the one to clean up this disaster, the one to salvage the agency's reputation. The Director's chair would finally be his—it had always been his rightful place, hadn't it?

But at what cost?

Lawson glanced back at the television screen. The Director was wrapping up his statement, the flash of cameras illuminating the smug satisfaction on his face.

Lawson clenched his jaw.

No one deserved that promotion more than him. Not after the sleepless nights, the sacrifices, the backbreaking effort he'd poured into this case. He'd earned it.

But as his gaze shifted to the photograph on his desk—a candid shot of Bella, taken during a team briefing months ago—his resolve faltered. Her face, determined yet haunted, stared back at him.

He had a sinking feeling that when the dust settled, and Bella finally took down DeLuca, it wouldn't be his name the world remembered. It would be hers.

Somewhere, far from the gleaming halls of FBI headquarters, Bella walked beside Marco through the twisting alleys of the city. The air was heavy with the stench of saltwater and gasoline, the faint glow of distant streetlights casting eerie shadows on the damp brick walls.

Her heart thundered in her chest as Marco spoke, his words a mix of calculated charm and dangerous conviction. She forced herself to nod, to mirror his intensity, all the while cataloging every detail—the cadence of his voice, the subtle tension in his posture, the glint of steel at his waistband.

She was in.

But as the darkness closed in around them, Bella couldn't shake the gnawing doubt in her gut. Marco was smart, sharper than anyone she'd ever faced. One wrong move, one crack in her façade, and everything would unravel.

And when that happened, there would be no one to save her.

CHAPTER 21: A NEW BEGINNING

The Amalfi Coast stretched like a painted masterpiece beneath a sky streaked with amber and crimson. Jagged cliffs jutted out over the glittering Mediterranean, the waves crashing below in a soothing rhythm that belied the storm inside Bella's chest. The salty tang of the sea wafted through the open car windows, but it wasn't enough to dissolve the tension knotted in her shoulders.

Marco was silent as he navigated the snaking cliffside roads with ease, his grip on the steering wheel firm but relaxed. His presence next to her was a contradiction—warm and familiar, yet steeped in danger. He was a man who could smile as he ordered a hit, charm as he planned his next betrayal.

"You've been quiet," he said finally, his voice low,

his Italian accent curling around each word like smoke.

Bella didn't turn to look at him. Her gaze was fixed on the horizon, the sun melting into the sea in a fiery blaze. "Just thinking."

"About?"

"About what comes next," she admitted.

His lips quirked in a wry smile. "What comes next," he said, glancing at her, "depends entirely on us. On you."

She swallowed, her throat dry despite the humid coastal air. The duality of her role pressed down on her—betray him, and she'd save countless lives but destroy her soul in the process. Fall too deeply into this world, and there might be no coming back.

The safehouse was hidden deep in a grove of ancient olive trees, their gnarled branches arching like silent sentinels over the narrow dirt road. When the villa came into view, Bella's breath caught, but not for its beauty. It was the kind of place that could easily become a tomb.

The stone façade, weathered and unassuming, betrayed nothing of what lay within. The shutters hung slightly askew, and ivy crawled up the sides, giving it the appearance of abandonment. But as Marco pushed open the heavy wooden door, the truth came into sharp focus.

The air inside was thick with the hum of activity. Keyboards clattered, monitors glowed with maps and encrypted code, and conversations—hushed and clipped—filled the space. The faint smell of stale coffee and dust mingled with the tang of freshly printed paper.

Bella's senses sharpened as she stepped inside, scanning the room in a practiced sweep. Shelves were crammed with binders, surveillance equipment, and encrypted drives. A corkboard on one wall was crowded with pinned photographs, red string connecting faces and places.

Her entrance didn't go unnoticed. The operatives stopped, their eyes narrowing as they sized her up. Suspicion radiated from every corner of the room like an electric charge.

Marco's voice cut through the silence. "Everyone," he said, his tone laced with authority. "This is Bella."

A murmur rippled through the room, followed by silence so thick it felt as though the air had been sucked out.

The first to speak was a tall woman with tightly braided hair and eyes like shards of obsidian. Her gaze raked over Bella with cold precision, each word she spoke carrying a sharp edge. "The FBI agent," she said, her lips curling into something between a sneer and a snarl.

"Former FBI," Marco corrected, his voice taking on a harder edge. He turned to Bella, his expression unreadable. "She's with us now."

The woman folded her arms across her chest, her muscles taut beneath the black fabric of her shirt. "And we're just supposed to take your word for it?"

Marco's response was swift, his voice low and sharp enough to slice through the tension. "You'll trust her because I trust her."

For a moment, the room hung in uneasy silence. Then the woman turned away with a small, derisive snort.

Bella felt the weight of their scrutiny as Marco introduced her to the team. These were hardened operatives—cyber specialists, intelligence gatherers, field agents—all united by their loyalty to Marco and the cause he claimed to champion. And she, despite all her skills, was the outsider.

She met their stares with a calm she didn't entirely feel, reminding herself of her training. If she showed even a crack in her armor, they'd devour her.

Later, the safehouse was quieter, the operatives dispersed to their respective corners. Bella found herself alone with Marco in the dimly lit living room, the air between them heavy with unspoken words.

"You've made an impression," Marco said, his voice teasing but undercut with something darker.

She turned to him, forcing a small smile. "Not all good impressions, I'm guessing."

His lips curved into a slow grin as he stepped closer, his presence intoxicatingly warm. "They'll come around," he said, his voice dipping into a register that sent shivers down her spine. "They'll see what I see."

"And what's that?" she asked, her voice steady despite the hammering of her pulse.

He reached out, brushing a strand of hair from her

face. The gesture was deceptively tender, a predator feigning softness. "A woman who's more dangerous than she looks."

She met his gaze, her heart pounding as she leaned in. This was the role she had to play—the seductress, the confidante, the woman he believed he could trust.

"Dangerous," she murmured, her lips inches from his, "but loyal. To you."

As their breaths mingled, and the space between them disappeared, Bella fought to bury the turmoil in her heart. She'd play her part, but every touch, every word, felt like a knife's edge, cutting deeper into the fragile line between duty and betrayal.

That night, when the villa was quiet and the others had gone to bed, Bella sat by the open window in her room, her journal balanced on her knees.

The pages were filled with fragments—half-finished thoughts, questions she didn't know how to answer.

Am I doing the right thing?

Is justice worth it if it's delivered this way?

Or am I just doing this because of him?

She stared at the last line, her pen hovering above the page. She wanted to believe she was here for the right reasons—that she was fighting for something greater than herself. But a part of her, a part she couldn't ignore, whispered that she'd been drawn here by more than ideology.

It was Marco. His conviction. His charm. The way he made her feel seen, even when he infuriated her.

The soft knock at her door pulled her from her thoughts.

"Come in," she said, setting the journal aside.

Marco stepped inside, his presence filling the room. He leaned against the doorframe, his arms crossed.

"Couldn't sleep?" he asked.

She shook her head, her fingers brushing the edge of the journal. "Too much on my mind."

He studied her for a moment, his gaze lingering. "You're doing better than you think, Bella."

She let out a bitter laugh. "Is that supposed to be reassuring?"

"It's supposed to remind you that you're stronger than you realize," he said, his voice softening. "You've always been stronger than you realize."

For a moment, neither of them spoke, the silence stretching into something charged and unspoken. Then, with a faint smile, Marco pushed off the doorframe.

"Get some rest," he said, his tone gentle. "Tomorrow, we get back to work."

As the door closed behind him, Bella let out a shaky breath.

The path she'd chosen was dark and uncertain, but for the first time in her life, she wasn't walking it alone.

Whether that was a blessing or a curse, she couldn't yet say.

∞

The days that followed blurred into a haze of sweat, exhaustion, and relentless instruction. Marco left no room for mistakes, no mercy for weakness. For Bella, it was a crash course in the art of operating outside the lines of law and morality.

By day, she mastered the fine line between invisibility and manipulation. Marco stood close as she forged identities, guiding her hands as she aligned stamps and signatures with meticulous precision. The passports and documents she produced looked as real as the ones that had once landed on her FBI desk. Each creation came with an uncomfortable realization—she was getting good at this.

"You've spent your career playing by someone else's rules," Marco said one afternoon as they stood at the makeshift shooting range behind the villa. The air was heavy with the smell of gunpowder, the sun hot on her back. "But rules won't save you out here. Only results will."

His voice, steady and unyielding, hit her harder than the recoil of the pistol she gripped. He wasn't wrong. The badge she'd once carried had been her armor, but now it felt like a relic of a life she could no longer claim.

In the evenings, the villa became their battleground. The olive grove at the property's edge was eerily quiet, the scent of earth and aged wood clinging to the air as Marco pushed her through hand-to-hand combat drills.

"Again," he commanded, circling her like a

predator.

Bella clenched her fists, sweat trickling down her temple. "I'm exhausted."

"You think exhaustion matters in a fight?" Marco countered, his voice a low growl. "When it's your life— or someone else's—on the line, there's no room for excuses."

His tone grated on her nerves, but it was his nearness that unsettled her. Every correction he made—a shift of her elbow, a repositioning of her stance—came with the heat of his touch. He lingered just a second too long, his fingertips brushing her skin like the whisper of a storm.

"You're holding back," Marco said, his dark eyes boring into hers as they circled each other.

"I'm not," Bella snapped, swiping her forearm across her damp brow.

"You are," he said, stepping closer, his voice dropping into a tone that made her heart skip. "You're afraid of what it means to let go. To truly fight. For something. For someone."

The tension between them coiled tighter, the air charged with more than just physical exertion. Her pulse hammered in her ears, but she refused to look away.

"Show me," he challenged.

Bella moved before she could second-guess herself. She feinted left, drawing him off balance, then pivoted sharply. Her elbow jabbed into his ribs, and she swept his legs out from under him. The world tilted as he hit the mat, a soft grunt escaping his lips.

Before he could react, she was on top of him, pinning him down with her forearm against his chest. Her knees straddled his waist, locking him in place. The element of surprise was hers, and for a moment, she let herself feel the thrill of it.

Marco's expression shifted—shock melted into amusement, and then into something deeper, something darker. His chest rose and fell beneath her arm, his breathing steady despite the position he was in.

"Well done," he murmured, his voice rough, the faintest hint of a smile tugging at his lips.

"I didn't hold back this time," Bella said, her own voice barely above a whisper.

"No," he agreed, his eyes locked on hers. "You didn't."

The world around them seemed to fall away, the only sound the faint rustling of the olive trees outside. Marco's hands rested lightly on her thighs, his touch setting her nerves on fire.

"You should get up," he said, though his tone betrayed no urgency.

"Should I?" she replied, her heart pounding in her chest.

The corner of his mouth lifted in a smirk. "Unless you want me to turn the tables."

Bella hesitated, her grip loosening just enough for him to roll them. In a fluid motion, Marco shifted their weight, reversing their positions until she found herself beneath him. His body was a solid, unyielding wall above hers, his hands braced on either side of her head.

Their faces were inches apart, and the space between them buzzed with unspoken words, with a pull that neither could deny.

"This is why you can't hold back," Marco murmured, his voice low and rough. "Because if you do…" He leaned closer, his breath warm against her cheek. "Someone will always take advantage of it."

Bella swallowed hard, the intensity of his gaze rooting her in place. "I'll remember that."

For a heartbeat, neither moved. The line between them blurred further, the weight of their choices pressing down like the humid night air. Then Marco pushed off her and stood, offering a hand to pull her up.

As Bella took it, she couldn't help but notice the way his fingers lingered against hers, a silent reminder of the charged moment they'd just shared.

"Tomorrow, we'll see if you can surprise me again," Marco said, his tone lighter but his eyes still smoldering.

"Don't count on it," Bella replied, though her lips curved into a small smile.

She walked away, her pulse still racing, her mind spinning. She'd bested him this time, but she wasn't sure if she'd won—or lost—something far greater.

CHAPTER 22: THE FIRST MISSION

The grand ballroom of the Hôtel des Arts was a gilded cage, dazzling in its excess but suffocating in its intimacy. Crystal chandeliers, suspended like floating galaxies, bathed the room in an ethereal glow that softened the sharp edges of power and wealth. The air was thick with a heady mix of roses, musk, and the sharp tang of secrets disguised as champagne bubbles. Each polished surface—the marble floors, the mirrored walls—reflected not just the wealth of its occupants but their carefully curated lies.

Bella stood poised at the entrance, her arm looped through Marco's, her smile a delicate mask of elegance. She wore a midnight-blue gown that clung to her like a second skin, the thigh-high slit teasing just enough to draw glances. A diamond necklace—on loan, like everything else in this charade—rested coolly against her collarbone, catching the light with every turn of her head. She looked every bit the part of a wealthy debutante, yet beneath the glamor, every muscle in her body was wound tight.

Her heart pounded against her ribcage as she took in the room, her gaze flitting from the string quartet in the corner to the armed guards stationed with unnerving subtlety along the edges of the ballroom. She felt the weight of scrutiny even if no one was openly watching her.

"You're doing fine," Marco murmured, leaning closer than necessary. His warm breath tickled her ear, his voice a velvet thread that seemed to tie her to the moment.

Her fingers tightened against his arm in reflex. "If by 'fine' you mean pretending not to notice that half the room is armed to the teeth, then sure. I'm thriving."

Marco chuckled softly, the sound low and intimate, like a private joke only they shared. To anyone watching, it was the laugh of a man enamored with the woman on his arm. To Bella, it was infuriating.

"Relax," he said, his tone easy, yet layered with authority. "The trick is to look like you belong. Wealth doesn't question itself, cara mia. Neither should you."

She forced herself to breathe, the movement making her gown shift against her skin, a tactile reminder of the role she was playing. Bella had played parts before—undercover assignments that blurred the lines between identity and illusion—but this one cut too close. Marco's team already doubted her loyalty, and she couldn't afford a single misstep. Not when the stakes were this high.

The room suddenly felt smaller, the press of bodies and laughter closing in on her. Bella tilted her chin up, forcing her discomfort into submission.

"Eyes front," Marco murmured. His hand rested lightly on the small of her back, guiding her deeper into the room. The gesture looked natural, protective even, but Bella knew better. Marco was always in control, always calculating.

Their target stood near the grand staircase at the far end of the ballroom. Claude Vautrin was a man who wore his sins openly, wrapped in the sheen of tailored suits and practiced charm. His ruddy face glistened under the lights, his laughter booming over the polite murmurs of the crowd. He was the kind of man who thrived on excess, his every gesture a declaration of invulnerability.

"He's had too much to drink already," Marco observed, his voice low and calm. "The guards are close but not paying enough attention. Perfect."

Bella spotted the staircase he'd mentioned, leading to the private quarters above. Her pulse quickened. The plan was simple on paper: Marco would slip upstairs to retrieve incriminating evidence while she distracted the guards. Simple. Yet nothing about this night felt simple.

"What's my role?" she asked, her voice steady despite the nerves coiling in her gut.

Marco turned to her, his dark eyes meeting hers with an intensity that made her stomach twist. "Distraction," he said, his lips curving into a faint smile. "When the time comes, make sure their eyes are on you, not me."

Bella raised a brow, her own lips tugging into a smirk. "That's vague."

"It's deliberate," he replied, the teasing edge to his voice softening the tension. His gaze lingered on her for a moment longer than necessary, a flicker of something unreadable passing between them.

Her pulse skipped, though not from attraction. She wasn't sure what she felt for Marco—admiration for his skill, irritation at his arrogance, or something darker, something she didn't want to name. But she knew one thing: she didn't trust him. Not entirely.

"Just make it convincing," Marco added, his tone softer now. "You're good at that."

Bella bit back a retort, forcing her focus back to the task at hand. "And what if I don't feel like being convincing tonight?" she asked, her voice laced with mock sweetness.

His smile widened, a predator's grin. "Then fake it."

She shot him a glare, but he was already leading her through the crowd, his hand steady on her back.

The scent of roses thickened as they neared Vautrin, the opulence of the evening now tinged with something cloying, almost nauseating. Bella's grip on Marco's arm tightened, her resolve hardening.

Whatever moral lines she'd crossed to get here, whatever doubts clawed at the edges of her conscience, none of it mattered now. She would do what needed to be done.

As Marco pulled her closer, leaning down to whisper something else in her ear, Bella caught a glimpse of Vautrin turning their way. His gaze lingered for a fraction of a second too long.

"Game on," she murmured under her breath, her smile never faltering.

The ballroom's dazzling opulence felt like a trap closing in on Bella with every passing second. The chandeliers, dripping with crystals, threw shards of golden light across the polished marble floors, and the air buzzed with laughter and clinking glasses. But beneath the glamour lay an undercurrent of danger, sharp and undeniable. Bella's spine tingled as she noticed a shift in the energy of the room.

"Marco," she murmured under her breath, her lips barely moving. She didn't dare glance directly at him as they navigated the crowd. "There's more security than we expected."

Marco lifted a champagne flute, tilting it casually to his lips. The flicker of a muscle in his jaw betrayed his concern, but his voice remained maddeningly calm. "I've noticed. We adapt."

Adapt. Easy for him to say. Bella's palms were slick against the beaded clutch she carried, her pulse hammering in her ears. She wove through the throng of guests, her midnight-blue gown trailing behind her like liquid moonlight. The diamonds at her throat sparkled with deceptive innocence. She looked every bit the part of a woman who belonged in such a gilded cage—but felt anything but.

The staircase loomed ahead, flanked by a pair of guards whose broad shoulders and unyielding stances made it clear no one was going upstairs without permission—or a damn good distraction.

Taking a deep breath, Bella stepped into their line of sight, her hips swaying with a confidence she didn't feel. As she approached, the taller of the two guards moved to block her path, his face a mask of polite suspicion.

"Madame, this area is restricted," he said in French, his tone clipped and final.

Bella tilted her head, letting her lips curve into a slow, inviting smile. Her voice, low and honeyed, carried just enough suggestion to crack his resolve. "Restricted? Surely you can make an exception. A woman does need her privacy."

The guard's eyes flickered, just for a moment, betraying his hesitation. She took a step closer, brushing her fingers lightly against the sleeve of his uniform. "I promise I won't be long," she murmured, her tone teetering on the edge of innocence and sin.

Behind her, Marco melted into the shadows, his movements as fluid and untraceable as smoke. Bella didn't dare look back.

The guard swallowed hard, his professionalism wavering under the weight of her stare. She felt a flicker of guilt—this was a game she didn't particularly enjoy playing—but pushed it aside. Lives were at stake.

Upstairs, the air was colder, heavier, as if the walls themselves held their breath. The private quarters were stark compared to the ballroom below. Dim lighting cast long shadows across a corridor lined with heavy wooden doors. The faint scent of cigar smoke lingered in the air, mingling with the sterile tang of expensive cleaning products.

Marco moved ahead of her, his footsteps soundless on the plush carpet. He paused outside a door, pressing his ear against the polished wood. Bella stood back, her heart in her throat as he withdrew a silenced pistol from beneath his jacket.

Inside, Claude Vautrin was hunched over a desk, his bulk illuminated by the glow of a single desk lamp. Papers spilled across the surface—financial ledgers, contracts, names. Bella's stomach churned at the thought of what those documents might reveal.

Marco didn't hesitate. The soft hiss of the silenced weapon was almost anticlimactic. Vautrin's body jerked once before slumping forward, his forehead hitting the desk with a dull thud.

Bella entered the room as the metallic tang of blood began to taint the air. Her breath hitched at the sight of the tycoon's lifeless form. She had seen death before, but this was different—colder, more calculated.

"Is it done?" she asked, forcing her voice to remain steady.

Marco turned to her, his dark eyes unreadable in

the dim light. "It's done. We move now."

The escape was a blur of narrow service corridors and silent urgency. Bella's heels clicked against the tiled floor, each sound magnified in the oppressive silence. Every corner they turned felt like a gamble, every shadow a potential threat.

By the time they slipped out into the crisp Parisian night, Bella's lungs burned from the effort of holding her breath. She leaned against the cool stone wall of the alley, her chest heaving as she tried to ground herself.

Marco stood beside her, his composure infuriatingly intact. He adjusted the cuffs of his jacket, glancing at her with an expression that was half amusement, half admiration. "Not bad for your first mission," he said.

Bella shot him a look, her pulse still racing. "Not bad? I just flirted my way past a guard and helped you assassinate a man. Excuse me if I don't hand myself a gold star."

His lips quirked in a faint smile, but there was something darker in his gaze, something she couldn't quite name. "You proved you can handle yourself under pressure. That's more than most can say."

She straightened, her breath finally evening out. "And the team?"

"They'll see this as a success," Marco said, his voice low. He stepped closer, his presence unsettlingly magnetic. "But you don't care about them, do you? You care what I think."

Bella's heart stuttered, but she forced herself to meet his gaze. "What you think doesn't matter," she said coolly, even as her pulse betrayed her. "I'm here to do a job. Nothing more."

Marco's smile widened, and for a moment, she thought he might kiss her. But then he stepped back, his expression unreadable once more.

"Good," he said simply. "Because caring makes you vulnerable. And vulnerable gets you killed."

As they disappeared into the Parisian streets, Bella couldn't shake the feeling that she had crossed an invisible line—one she could never uncross.

∞

The safehouse in Paris was tucked away in the shadow of an unassuming building in the Marais. It was the kind of place that would be forgotten even as you passed it—a faceless door framed by crumbling brick, its chipped paint a testament to years of indifference. Inside, the air was heavy with silence, interrupted only by the occasional murmur of the city below. The space was dim, lit by a single overhead bulb that cast long shadows on the scuffed parquet floors.

Bella stood at the window, her reflection ghostlike against the backdrop of the Parisian night. Beyond the glass, the city glittered, its beauty untainted by the blood spilled just hours earlier. She pressed her fingertips to the cool pane, as if the touch could steady her, could pull her back from the edge of the dark precipice she now teetered on.

Behind her, Marco moved with unhurried efficiency, his every motion deliberate. She heard the faint clink of glass as he poured wine, the sound jarring in its domesticity.

"You handled yourself well tonight," he said, his voice low and calm as he approached. He handed her a glass of red wine, its rich color deepening in the faint light.

She accepted it, though her grip felt tenuous, like she might shatter the delicate stem with the weight of her thoughts. "It was easier than I thought it would be," she murmured, her voice barely audible over the pounding of her heart.

Marco leaned against the edge of the small dining table, studying her with an intensity that made her pulse jump. "Easier to distract a guard? Or easier to help me take a life?"

Her eyes snapped to his, her breath catching at the question. The glass in her hand felt heavier now, as if it carried the weight of her guilt. "Both," she admitted, her voice breaking slightly on the word.

He inclined his head, acknowledging her honesty, though his expression remained inscrutable. "Does that bother you?"

Bella exhaled slowly, the words tangling in her throat before she finally forced them out. "Yes. And no."

He pushed off the table, closing the space between them with a predator's grace. She felt his presence before he spoke, the heat of him pressing against her even though they weren't touching. "That's the line, Bella," he said softly, his voice like a blade sheathed in silk. "The one you've just crossed. It's not about whether it bothers you—it's about whether you can live with it."

Her gaze dropped to the wine in her hand, the liquid swirling like blood in the dim light. "And can you?"

His laugh was soft, almost bitter. "I stopped asking myself that question a long time ago."

She looked up then, meeting his eyes. For the first time, she saw something beyond his polished exterior. There was a flicker of weariness there, a glimpse of the man beneath the operative—a man who carried the weight of every decision, every life taken, whether he admitted it or not.

"And yet, you keep going," she said, her voice laced with something she couldn't quite name. Admiration? Pity?

"I don't have a choice," Marco said simply, his tone devoid of self-pity. "But you do."

The weight of his words settled between them, heavy and unyielding. Bella's grip on the glass tightened as she turned back to the window, the reflection of the city's lights dancing in her eyes. "I used to think justice was black and white," she said quietly. "But tonight, I realized it's just shades of gray."

Marco stepped closer, his fingers brushing her shoulder. The touch was light, almost hesitant, but it sent a ripple of awareness through her that she couldn't ignore. "Welcome to the real world," he said, his breath warm against her ear.

She turned to face him, her pulse racing. "And in your world, Marco? Do you ever stop to wonder if there's another way?"

His eyes searched hers, dark and unreadable. For a moment, the distance between them seemed to shrink, the tension thick enough to drown in. "Not anymore," he admitted. "But maybe I should."

Her breath hitched as his hand slid from her shoulder to her waist, the heat of his touch searing through the thin fabric of her dress. The glass of wine dangled precariously from her fingertips, forgotten as she felt the pull of him, the magnetic force that had been there from the start.

"Marco..." she began, her voice a warning, a plea.

"Bella," he countered, his voice rougher now, laced with something raw and unguarded. "You're not just crossing lines—you're erasing them."

She didn't know who moved first, but suddenly his mouth was on hers, the kiss a collision of desperation and need. It was messy, consuming, a tangle of tongues and gasps that left her breathless. The wineglass slipped from her hand, shattering on the floor, but she barely noticed.

When they finally broke apart, her chest was heaving, her lips swollen. Marco's hands stayed on her waist, anchoring her as her world tilted.

"I don't know if I can live with it," she whispered, her voice trembling.

His gaze softened, just enough to reveal a flicker of vulnerability. "Then let me teach you how," he said.

The promise in his words was both terrifying and tantalizing, and as Bella met his gaze, she realized there was no turning back. She had crossed the line, and Marco was waiting on the other side, ready to show her what came next.

Her breath hitched as she felt his hand slide down her thigh, tracing the slit of her dress until he found the hem. His fingers grazed her skin, and the world outside the safehouse, the blood-soaked ballroom, the ghosts of her past, all seemed to fall away, leaving only the two of them, tangled in a dance of desire and uncertainty.

When his lips met hers again, Bella gave herself over to the darkness, letting him lead her deeper into the unknown.

She knew that she wanted him, and the knowledge was both terrifying and exhilarating. He was a criminal, a killer, and yet, when he looked at her, she felt like the only thing worth protecting in his world.

His hands were gentle, but firm, and she could feel the barely controlled desire radiating off of him. The intensity of his focus was intoxicating, and she couldn't help but respond to him, wanting nothing more than to lose herself in his touch again.

And when he kissed her, it was like fire and ice, burning and soothing all at once.

As his lips trailed down her neck, Bella knew that this was a line she would never be able to uncross, and yet, as his hands found her hips and pulled her closer, she found that she didn't want to.

"I love you," Marco whispered, his voice a low growl in her ear. "I have since the moment I first saw you."

Bella couldn't speak, couldn't breathe, as the words sank in. She had never heard him sound so vulnerable, so open, and she knew that this was a part of him that no one else got to see.

"I love you too," she managed, her voice hoarse. "More than you'll ever know."

She felt his lips curl into a smile against her neck, and then he was kissing her again, his hands roaming over her body. The passion between them was almost overwhelming, and Bella knew that she had never felt anything like this before.

"You're mine," Marco said, his voice barely above a whisper. "And I will do whatever it takes to protect you."

His words should have scared her, but instead, they made her feel safe. She knew that he would do anything for her, and that was a feeling she had never experienced before.

He pulled her towards him, his hands cupping her ass, and she moaned as his lips met hers. The kiss was deep and passionate, and Bella knew that she was falling harder for him than ever before.

She straddled him on the couch as she unbuckled his pants. Her heart raced as she slid them off and saw the growing bulge in his boxers.

She ran her hands over his toned abs, savoring the

way his muscles clenched under her touch. She could feel his desire, his need, and it made her ache for him.

His hands found the zipper on her dress and tugged it down, the fabric pooling around her waist. He leaned forward, his lips brushing against her bare skin as he removed the straps of her dress and tossed them aside.

His breath was hot against her skin as his hands explored her body, caressing her breasts, teasing her nipples. Bella gasped as he cupped her breasts and gently squeezed them.

"Fuck, you're perfect," he growled, his voice sending shivers down her spine.

She reached behind her and unclasped her bra, letting it fall to the floor. Marco's eyes widened as he took in the sight of her breasts, and he groaned as he palmed them.

Bella closed her eyes as she leaned into his touch, enjoying the sensation of his hands on her body. He squeezed her breasts, his thumbs teasing her nipples, and she let out a moan. But she was hungry for him, she lowered herself into his lap.

He grunted as his cock slid between her folds, and she could feel his desire, his need. She ground against him, savoring the feeling of his hardness pressed against her.

"Fuck, you're so wet," he groaned, his voice strained. "I need to be inside you."

"Then take me," Bella breathed, her voice barely above a whisper.

He wasted no time, grabbing her hips and guiding her onto his cock. She cried out as she sank down on him, her eyes rolling back in pleasure. He was thick and hard inside her, and she savored the feeling of being filled by him.

His hands tightened on her hips as he guided her movements, thrusting up into her. Bella gasped and moaned as she rode him, her body aching for release. She could feel his pleasure, his need, and it fueled her own desire.

He leaned forward and captured her lips in a kiss, his tongue teasing hers. She tasted the wine on his lips, the sweetness mingling with his own masculine taste.

Bella's body shuddered as she reached her peak, her orgasm washing over her. She cried out, her fingers digging into his shoulders as her body trembled. Marco held her close, his hands stroking her back as she came down from her high.

"I love you," he whispered, his voice filled with emotion. "I've never loved anyone the way I love you."

Bella rested her forehead against his, her heart pounding. She had never felt anything like this, this intense, consuming love, and she knew that she would do anything for him. And the last rational thought Bella had was that she was never going to want anyone but Marco ever again.

She had fallen too far, too fast, and the only way out was to keep falling.

At dawn, Bella lay awake beside him, listening to his breathing slow, the rhythmic cadence a sharp contrast to her own racing thoughts.

Her body ached from the night before, the physicality of it a reminder of what she had just done, the line she had just crossed.

⸺•❦•⸺

CHAPTER 23: THE BOND DEEPENS

Venice shimmered like a dream, its moonlit canals threading through shadows cast by ancient, crumbling facades. The soft lap of water against stone created a melody that seemed to echo through centuries, a reminder of the city's resilience. Gondolas glided like phantoms over the water, their gondoliers murmuring to the current, their voices carrying in faint, melodic whispers.

Bella sat perched in the gondola's seat, her fingers brushing the cool iron edge, eyes tracing the ethereal glow of lanterns reflecting off the canals. The city seemed to hold its breath, suspended between beauty and decay. Across from her, Marco leaned back, his dark silhouette sharp against the silvery water, his eyes scanning their surroundings with the cautious ease of a man who had made a career out of survival.

"It's beautiful," she murmured, her voice fragile, as if speaking too loudly would shatter the moment.

Marco tilted his head, a faint smile playing at his lips. "Venice is more than beautiful. It's a paradox. Fragile, yet it's endured for centuries. The salt, the storms, the wars... everything tried to destroy it. But it adapted. Survived."

His words curled around her, weighted with unspoken meaning. Fragile but enduring. She wondered if he saw Venice as a mirror, a reflection of the people sitting in the boat. People who'd weathered storms of their own, still afloat, but carrying the scars.

The gondolier shifted his weight, his strokes smooth and methodical as they moved further into the labyrinth of canals. Marco broke the silence, his voice taking on a softer, nostalgic tone.

"My father used to bring us here every summer. He'd drag us through galleries, museums, churches—anything with a historical plaque. Alessandro hated it, of course."

The corner of Bella's mouth quirked up. "Your brother didn't like history?"

"Oh, he liked history," Marco said with a faint chuckle. "He just liked gelato more. He'd say, 'Why look at paintings of dead people when we could be eating something alive with flavor?'"

Bella couldn't help but laugh, the sound breaking through the tension that had been brewing in her chest since their mission. But when Marco's eyes clouded, the humor evaporated, replaced by something darker.

"What was he like?" she asked, her voice soft, knowing instinctively that this was a wound rarely shared.

Marco's gaze dropped to the rippling water. "He was... unstoppable. Fearless. Alessandro could walk into a room full of strangers and walk out with a hundred friends. He made people feel seen. Like they mattered."

His voice tightened, and Bella caught the flicker of grief that shadowed his face. "He was the best of us," he continued. And then, more quietly, "I should have saved him."

The gondola slipped beneath a low stone bridge, the air feeling heavier, the light dimmer. Marco shifted forward, his elbows resting on his knees as if the weight of the memory had pulled him inward.

"You've seen the files, Bella. You know why I'm doing this. But I haven't told you everything. Not about Alessandro."

Bella leaned closer, the intimacy of the moment urging her to ask. "What happened to him, Marco?"

He hesitated, his jaw tightening. "Dusker Corporation didn't just destroy our business. They destroyed my family. My father fought them— lawsuits, petitions, anything to stop their algorithms from flooding the market with counterfeits. But it wasn't enough. The pressure broke him."

He exhaled sharply, the sound brittle in the still night. "Alessandro... he blamed himself. He thought he should've done more, even though he was just a kid.

One night, I came home, and he was gone. He left a note apologizing. For being weak. For not living up to the DeLuca name."

Bella's heart clenched, her breath catching in her throat. She could see the pain etched into Marco's face, hear it in the rawness of his voice.

"It wasn't his fault," Marco said, his voice low but filled with anger. "It was theirs. Dusker Corporation didn't just bankrupt us—they erased us. They erased him."

"I'm so sorry, Marco," Bella whispered. The words felt small, inadequate against the enormity of what he'd lost.

His gaze met hers, fierce and unflinching. "That's why I'm doing this. They think they can destroy people, ruin lives, and walk away with their profits intact. I won't let them. I can't."

The intensity in his eyes, the sheer force of his conviction, pulled Bella closer, as though gravity itself had shifted. She reached out, her hand brushing his. The touch was tentative at first, but when his fingers curled around hers, the connection sparked something deep and unspoken between them.

"I'm with you," she said, her voice steady despite the storm raging inside her.

Marco's hand tightened around hers, pulling her closer until the space between them vanished. His other hand lifted to her face, his thumb tracing the line of her jaw. The air between them thickened, charged with something electric.

"Are you sure about that?" he asked, his voice low, his breath warm against her skin.

"Yes," Bella whispered, her pulse thrumming as his lips brushed hers, tentative at first, then deeper, more insistent. The kiss was equal parts desperation and solace, a tether to something real amid the chaos.

The gondola rocked gently beneath them, the rhythm of the water lulling the city into sleep. But for Bella and Marco, the night was wide awake, and for the first time, the darkness felt less suffocating.

As the gondola emerged into the open canal, the moonlight casting a silver path ahead, Bella realized something had shifted—not just in her, but between them. They were no longer just allies or accomplices. They were something more. And as dangerous as that was, she couldn't bring herself to let it go.

Later that night, they walked along a quiet canal, the faint glow of lanterns casting soft halos on the cobblestones. The air along the quiet canal was dense with the salty tang of brine, mingling with the faint sweetness of wisteria blooming from a nearby trellis.

Bella walked beside Marco, their footsteps a rhythmic echo of the night's stillness. His hand brushed hers, a fleeting, almost accidental touch that sent a current through her veins.

She glanced at him, catching a rare vulnerability etched across his sharp features—an openness she wasn't sure he even knew he'd let slip. But just as quickly as it appeared, it vanished. His gaze darted to the shadows, his broad shoulders tensing as if he were preparing for the weight of an invisible threat. He scanned the narrow alleyways and the bridges overhead, his focus razor-sharp.

"You're always looking over your shoulder," Bella said, breaking the silence. Her voice carried a quiet curiosity, layered with a concern she couldn't quite suppress.

Marco stopped mid-stride, turning to face her. The golden light from a nearby lantern painted one side of his face, while the other seemed carved from shadow. His lips curved in a wry smile, but it didn't reach his eyes.

"When you live the life I do," he said, his voice low and edged with something raw, "you learn to anticipate the knife before it's in your back."

Bella folded her arms across her chest, her gaze steady. "Is that why you trust so few people?"

A bitter smile flickered across his face, there and gone in an instant. "Trust is a luxury I can't afford."

Her heart tightened, though she wasn't sure if it was from sympathy or frustration. "And me?" she asked, the words slipping out before she could stop them.

His expression softened, a rare warmth flickering in his dark eyes as he stepped closer. Gently, his hand reached up, brushing a loose strand of hair from her face. His fingers lingered for a moment, his touch impossibly tender.

"You're the exception, Bella. You always have been."

Her breath caught at the sincerity in his voice, but doubt coiled in her chest like a serpent. Could she trust him, a man who thrived in the shadows? Or was she just another pawn in a game so intricate she couldn't even see the board?

∞

Back at the cramped apartment they'd rented for the night, Bella sat by the single window, her knees pulled to her chest. The canal stretched out below, glinting in the pale moonlight, its surface broken only by the occasional ripple of a passing gondola. On her lap rested the journal she'd been carrying since the beginning of this dark, winding journey.

Flipping it open, she picked up her pen and wrote:

The deeper I go, the harder it is to tell where he ends and I begin. He believes in what he's doing. But do I?

She paused, her pen hovering above the page. Her mind swirled with unanswered questions, doubts she couldn't fully silence.

Or am I just following him because I can't bear to let him go?

A buzz shattered the silence, the sound sharp and intrusive in the still night. Her phone, face-down on the table, vibrated insistently. Bella's heart skipped a beat as she picked it up. The screen glowed with a number she didn't recognize. She stared at it, her instincts warring with her exhaustion.

Marco's voice cut through her hesitation. "Bella,"

he called softly from the doorway, his silhouette dark and beckoning. "Come to bed."

Her gaze lingered on the phone for a moment longer before she reached for the power button, silencing it with a firm press. Whoever it was could wait. Tonight, she was with Marco.

Setting the phone aside, she rose and crossed the room, leaving the journal behind on the windowsill. As she slipped into bed beside him, she felt the familiar pull of his arms around her, the solid reassurance of his presence. But as she pressed her cheek against his chest, the unanswered call lingered in her mind like a shadow she couldn't quite shake.

Thousands of miles away, in the fluorescent-lit conference room of a nondescript government building, Agent Lawson stared at the call log on his phone, his jaw tight with frustration.

"She missed three check-ins," he muttered, his voice clipped.

"I told you this would fucking happen," Agent Park said, crossing her arms with smug finality. "She's gone rogue. I told you from the start she was too emotionally compromised to handle this op."

Lawson shot her a sharp look, his patience fraying. "Bella's not rogue. She's in deep. And until I see proof otherwise, I'm not throwing her under the damn bus."

Park snorted, her lips twisting into a smirk. "Well, here's your proof." She tossed a file onto the table. Photographs spilled out, glossy and damning. Bella and Marco, captured on security footage, walking into the

Hôtel des Arts in Paris.

Lawson's stomach dropped as Park continued. "Claude Vautrin was assassinated in his suite that night. Witnesses put Bella and Marco at the scene hours before it went down. Tell me again how she's not involved."

His fists clenched as he studied the grainy images. Bella's face was partially obscured, but he knew it was her. "This doesn't prove anything," he said through gritted teeth.

"It proves she's in way deeper than she should be," Park countered, her tone laced with triumph. "And now, Vautrin's dead. She's either helping DeLuca—or worse, she's fallen for him. Either way, Lawson, we've lost her."

Lawson's jaw tightened, his mind racing. He refused to believe Bella was compromised. Not yet. Not until he heard it from her own lips.

"Get me everything we have on the Hôtel des Arts," he barked, his voice steely. "If she's in trouble, I'll pull her out myself."

Park arched a brow, leaning back in her chair with a satisfied smirk. "Good luck with that. Wherever Bella is, she's not coming back anytime soon."

Lawson ignored her, his focus narrowing as he dialed Bella's number again. But this time, it didn't even ring. She'd turned her phone off.

⬤◆⬤◆⬤

CHAPTER 24: THE TARGET IN BERLIN

erlin stretched beneath the velvet blanket of night, its skyline a jagged contrast of sleek, modern architecture and the stone relics of a darker history. The city hummed with an air of mystery and danger, the cold wind threading through the streets like a whispered warning.

The politician's estate stood as a bastion of excess, its stone facade illuminated by the harsh glare of floodlights. An opulent fortress, guarded by more than just wrought-iron gates and armed security. Tonight, it was alive with laughter, the clink of champagne flutes, and the murmured promises of backroom deals.

Inside, Bella blended seamlessly into the throng of Berlin's elite. Her black evening gown was an exquisite sheath of danger, hugging her lithe frame in all the right ways, the slit high enough to promise distraction but low enough to conceal the slim knife strapped to her thigh. A pair of emerald earrings dangled from her ears—each piece a custom listening device Marco had personally outfitted.

As she glided across the ballroom, the weight of their mission hung heavy in her chest. Every glance felt calculated, every smile practiced. She knew what this was—a performance. The stakes weren't just life or death tonight. They were far more personal.

"Reception is solid," Marco's deep timbre crackled in her earpiece, his voice steady despite the danger that loomed. "West wing. Second floor. Security's heavier than expected, but I've tracked their rotations. Timing is everything."

Bella sipped her champagne, her lips curving in an effortless smile as she murmured back, "Understood."

"And, Bella," Marco added, his tone dipping into something softer, something more intimate, "don't push your luck. You're no use to me dead."

"Charming," she replied, her voice tinged with humor. But his words clung to her, settling beneath the layers of professional detachment she wore like armor.

She spotted Dietrich Heller across the room, the politician's face a mask of charisma that hid the predator beneath. The puppetmaster pulling the strings of Dusker Corporation, a corporation at the epicenter of global power plays and digital manipulation. If the rumors were true, Heller wasn't just corrupt—he was ruthless.

Bella's pulse quickened as she slipped past a trio of laughing guests, her body weaving effortlessly through the crowd. She knew her target, and she knew her window.

"Stay close to the east column," Marco's voice instructed, sharp and precise. "There's a blind spot from the overhead camera. You'll have ten seconds, no more."

She glanced at her surroundings, careful not to reveal the tension simmering just beneath her polished exterior. The corridor loomed ahead, bathed in dim light, every shadow a potential threat.

"Blind spot starts in three… two… now," Marco said.

Bella moved. The marble beneath her stilettos muffled her steps, the faint click drowned out by the murmur of distant conversation. Her breathing slowed, her senses sharpening as she reached the heavy oak door of Heller's office.

"The lock's an old mechanical type," Marco said. "Takes finesse but no sweat for you."

"Glad to know you're confident," Bella muttered, her fingers working deftly to manipulate the lock.

"You don't need my confidence, Bella," Marco shot back. "You've got enough of your own. Just get it done."

The lock clicked open with a soft snick, and Bella slipped inside, closing the door silently behind her. The office was a study in excess: a sprawling mahogany desk, the gleam of polished brass fixtures, and the faint scent of cigar smoke clinging to the air.

Her hands moved quickly, retrieving the small bug from her clutch—a sleek device that Marco had engineered himself. The window for planting it was tight, the risk high, but she worked with the precision of someone used to tightroping between survival and discovery.

"Status?" Marco asked, his voice the only tether she had in the silence.

"Placing the bug now," Bella whispered, sliding open the panel beneath Heller's desk. Her pulse thundered in her ears as the seconds ticked by, her every move deliberate.

"Almost there," Marco murmured, his voice low and calm. "Breathe, Bella."

She smirked faintly, his words tugging at something deep within her. He always knew when to steady her, even when her hands were steady enough on their own.

The bug was secured, and Bella straightened, brushing invisible dust from her gown as she cast a glance around the room. Something about the silence felt heavier now, the air thick with an unnamed tension.

"Bella, move," Marco warned.

But before she could respond, her phone vibrated softly in her clutch. The screen lit up with an unknown number. For one fleeting second, doubt flickered in her chest.

"Problem?" Marco asked, sensing the pause.

"Not yet," she said, silencing the phone and slipping it back into her bag.

"Then get out of there."

As she straightened, she heard it—the faint but unmistakable sound of footsteps approaching.

"Marco," she whispered, her pulse spiking. "We've got company."

"Two guards heading your way," he said, his voice sharp. "Get out now."

She moved to the door, but the footsteps were too close. Thinking quickly, she ducked behind the desk, her breathing shallow as the door creaked open.

"Check the room," a deep voice ordered.

Bella crouched lower, her hand instinctively reaching for the small knife strapped to her thigh beneath the gown. The guards' heavy boots echoed as they entered, their flashlights cutting through the shadows.

One of them stopped near the desk, the beam of his flashlight sweeping dangerously close. Bella held her breath, her muscles coiled like a spring.

"Clear," the first guard said finally.

"Let's move," the other replied, and Bella waited until their footsteps faded before slipping out the way she'd come.

∞

Downstairs, the party continued, oblivious to the chaos unfolding above. Bella slipped into the shadows of the garden, her heels crunched against the gravel as she moved, her breath fogging in the cool night. The distant murmur of laughter and clinking glasses barely reached the secluded garden where Marco waited, shadowed by the towering hedgerow.

His face was carved with tension, his jaw locked as he slipped a silenced pistol into his jacket. The weapon gleamed faintly under the garden lights, a cold reminder of the line they were about to cross.

"Heller's in the library," he said, his voice low and clipped.

Bella nodded, her pulse quickening as she followed him down the path. The gravel seemed louder underfoot now, every crunch magnified by the weight of what was coming. She caught a glimpse of the library through its tall windows, the golden glow inside spilling onto the dark garden like a lure.

Marco moved with an assassin's precision, his strides purposeful, his movements calculated. Bella mirrored his steps, her breathing shallow.

"You don't have to do this," she murmured as they approached the door, her voice just above a whisper.

Marco stopped, his head turning just enough for her to see the icy determination in his eyes. "Yes, I do."

The words hit her like a blow. There was no hesitation in his tone, no crack for doubt to slip through. He pushed open the door, his presence filling the room before she even stepped inside.

Heller stood by the far wall, a crystal tumbler of amber liquid in hand, his back turned as he studied a painting. The warm light softened his features, almost humanizing the man Bella knew to be a ruthless manipulator.

Marco's silence drew Heller's attention. He turned, his face a mask of confusion that quickly twisted into alarm. "Who the hell are you..."

The question was cut off as Marco raised the pistol, the motion fluid and practiced.

"You can't stop this," Heller said, his voice surprisingly steady despite the weapon aimed at his chest. His gaze flicked briefly to Bella, curiosity laced with something darker. "Dusker Corporation isn't the real power. They're just the beginning."

"What do you mean?" Bella demanded, stepping forward despite the warning glare Marco shot her.

Heller smirked, his eyes locking onto hers with unnerving clarity. "You'll find out soon enough."

The gunshot cracked like thunder in the confined space, shattering the tense silence. Bella flinched as Heller crumpled to the floor, his body folding awkwardly, the drink spilling from his hand in a slow, golden arc.

The room seemed to hold its breath in the aftermath. Bella stared at the lifeless form on the polished floor, Heller's cryptic warning clinging to the air like the faint tang of gunpowder.

Her chest tightened, her vision tunneling as the weight of the act bore down on her. She had known what this mission entailed. She had prepared herself for it. And yet, standing there, the moral lines she thought she'd blurred now seemed as sharp as the jagged shards of glass on the floor.

Her voice came out hoarse. "Was this the only way?"

Marco turned to her, his expression as unreadable as ever. "You knew what we were here to do."

She swallowed hard, the lump in her throat refusing to budge. "But knowing and doing aren't the same."

"Don't fall apart on me now," Marco said sharply, stepping closer. His eyes searched hers, not for weakness, but for signs of defiance. "If you're questioning this, tell me now. I need to know if you're all in, Bella."

She met his gaze, forcing herself to remain calm despite the roiling storm inside. "I'm here, aren't I?"

He studied her for a beat longer, his jaw tightening before he turned away. "Good. Let's move."

The drive back to the safehouse was suffocatingly quiet. Bella stared out the car window, her reflection faint against the backdrop of Berlin's twinkling lights. The city passed in a blur, but her mind was fixed on Heller's final words.

Dusker Corporation isn't the real power.

The phrase looped in her mind like a haunting melody, each repetition fueling her unease.

"You're quiet," Marco said, his voice breaking the silence. His tone was neutral, but Bella heard the undercurrent of irritation.

She didn't look at him. "He said we don't know

what we're really up against."

Marco's hands tightened on the wheel, the leather creaking under his grip. "Doesn't matter. Heller's gone. One less piece on their board."

"But what if we're just pawns too?" she pressed, her voice firmer now.

His jaw ticked, a muscle jumping as he cut his eyes toward her. "You're thinking too much."

"No," she said softly, meeting his gaze for the first time. "I'm thinking exactly enough."

The safehouse came into view, its nondescript exterior bathed in the glow of a flickering streetlamp. Bella let out a slow breath as they pulled into the driveway, the tension between them thick and unresolved.

Marco killed the engine and turned to her, his gaze sharp and unyielding. "If you have second thoughts, now's the time to say it."

She didn't flinch under his scrutiny. "I don't need to convince you, Marco. And I don't need to convince myself. I'm here because I chose to be."

Her calmness was like ice to the fire of his anger, dousing it before it could burn out of control. He nodded once, curtly, and stepped out of the car.

As Bella followed, her mind churned with questions. Heller's cryptic warning, Marco's guarded response, and the darkness of the path she had chosen. For the first time, she wasn't sure if they were dismantling a machine—or becoming its gears.

CHAPTER 25: A NEW IDENTITY

Vienna shimmered like a jewel beneath the gauzy veil of rain. The cobblestone streets, polished to a slick shine, mirrored the fractured amber glow of gaslit streetlamps. Every uneven step Bella took echoed faintly against the ornate baroque facades, standing tall and indifferent, their grandeur whispering of secrets older than the city itself. She tightened the oversized scarf around her neck, a shield against the damp chill, but it offered little comfort.

Her reflection in a bakery window stopped her mid-stride. She stared at the woman looking back at her. The Bella Rossi she had known—tailored suits, sleek ponytails, a badge tucked into her waistband— was gone. The woman before her wore dark denim that fit her like a second skin, a black leather jacket she didn't remember choosing, and a cascade of honey-toned waves that softened her features in a way she barely recognized.

For a moment, she thought she saw the ghost of herself staring back. But ghosts didn't breathe, didn't feel the quickening beat of their hearts, didn't carry the weight of choices that couldn't be undone.

She pulled away from the window and continued through Stephansplatz, the crowds bustling around her as if she didn't exist. That anonymity was both liberating and suffocating.

The flat Marco had chosen was nondescript, tucked between two unmarked buildings on a narrow alley where the rainwater pooled in inky rivulets. Inside, the air was close, thickened by the scent of coffee and the faint musk of damp leather. The dining table, the room's only piece of furniture that looked remotely cared for, was strewn with the tools of reinvention: passports, counterfeit IDs, burner phones, and crisp stacks of euro notes that gleamed under the dim light of the single bulb overhead.

Marco stood at the table, sleeves rolled up to his elbows, his hands working methodically as he arranged the papers. Each movement was deliberate, precise, the calm efficiency of a man who had done this countless times before. His jaw was tight, a shadow of stubble darkening his face, but his eyes burned with focus—a sharp contrast to Bella's restless energy as she leaned against the wall.

"You're picking this up faster than I expected."

Marco's voice cut through the silence, low and rough. He glanced at the forged passport Bella had prepared earlier, nodding once in approval. "Most people fumble with their backstories for weeks. You've got yours down in days."

Bella picked up the passport he'd referenced, turning it over in her hands. The name "Elena Koslov" gleamed in embossed gold against the navy-blue cover. The pages inside told a story that wasn't hers: a Russian national born in Odessa, fluent in four languages, with an affinity for art and a penchant for blending into the background.

"It feels strange," Bella murmured, her voice barely above a whisper. She ran her thumb along the edge of the paper, tracing the lines of her new name. "Like I'm erasing myself."

Marco looked up from his work, his expression softening. "You're not erasing yourself." He moved closer, his presence commanding the small space between them. "You're evolving. Bella Rossi was tied to rules and bureaucracy—a system that failed you. Elena Koslov isn't. She's whoever she needs to be. She's free."

Bella's eyes darted to his, searching for something in their dark depths. Truth? Reassurance? She wasn't sure. "And what happens," she asked quietly, "when I forget her too? When Bella Rossi disappears completely?"

Marco's lips curved into a faint, almost imperceptible smile. He reached for her hand, his touch warm but firm. "Then you'll finally be free."

The words hung in the air between them, heavy and intoxicating.

Bella wanted to believe him, to lose herself in the promise of freedom he painted so vividly. But there was a weight in her chest that wouldn't budge, a quiet voice in the back of her mind reminding her of all she'd sacrificed to get here.

Marco leaned in, his hand brushing the curve of her cheek, his gaze flickering between her eyes and her lips. When he kissed her, it was deliberate—slow and sure, as though he were daring her to push him away. Bella didn't move. Her lips responded instinctively, but her eyes remained open, locked on his face.

She studied the sharp lines of his jaw, the faint furrow of his brow, the tension that never fully left his expression, even in this moment of intimacy.

He was testing her—she knew that much. Testing her loyalty, her resolve, her willingness to shed the last fragments of the woman she had been.

When he finally pulled back, she met his gaze with an unreadable expression. Calm, measured, and unyielding.

"Elena Koslov doesn't need to be free," she said, her voice steady. "She needs to survive."

Something shifted in Marco's eyes, a flicker of satisfaction tempered by caution. He nodded, stepping back, the space between them suddenly too vast and too close all at once.

"Then you're ready," he said simply, turning back

to the table.

But as Bella stood there, clutching the passport to her chest, she wondered if survival was enough—or if she'd just traded one cage for another.

∞

The café was a hole-in-the-wall, tucked in the shadows of Vienna's labyrinthine streets. Its windows were fogged from the rain outside, the interior dimly lit by flickering candles and an old chandelier that hung precariously overhead. The scent of espresso mingled with something metallic and faintly sour, as though the room itself had absorbed decades of whispered secrets and tense negotiations.

Bella sat in a corner booth, her back to the wall, her eyes scanning the room. The group had gathered here under Marco's orders, though the cramped space and the charged atmosphere made her feel like a caged animal.

Nico was the first to speak, his voice as sharp as the angles of his wiry frame. He lounged in his chair as if the world existed solely for his amusement, his dark eyes glittering with mischief—or malice. His perpetual smirk was the kind that made you want to wipe it off his face, though Bella knew better than to let it show.

"You've been playing house with Marco, huh?" Nico drawled, his fingers drumming an idle rhythm on the table. "Bet he's told you all kinds of things. But has he told you the whole truth?"

Bella tilted her head, her expression calm but her pulse quickening. "If you have something to say, Nico, just say it. I don't have time for games."

Nico chuckled, low and condescending, before sliding a battered folder across the table. The papers inside fanned out slightly, revealing black-and-white photographs and handwritten notes. "Take a look," he said. "Consider it an educational moment."

Bella hesitated, her fingers hovering over the folder before she flipped it open. Her stomach tightened as she took in the contents: photos of smoldering ruins, shadowy figures exchanging briefcases in poorly lit alleys, and pages of notes detailing operations that reeked of brutality and betrayal. Each detail was painstakingly crafted to implicate Marco, painting him as a man without limits, without conscience.

Nico leaned forward, the candlelight catching the gleam in his eyes. "He's good at what he does. Too good, if you ask me. So, Elena," he said, his tone almost mocking as he used her alias, "how's it feel to work for a ghost with blood on his hands?"

Bella's chest tightened, but she forced herself to remain calm. She studied the notes with a meticulous eye, her training as an investigator kicking in. Something wasn't right. The details were too convenient, the handwriting inconsistent, the photos poorly edited. It wasn't just sloppy—it was insulting.

She closed the folder with deliberate precision, letting it snap shut with a finality that echoed in the silence. When she met Nico's gaze, her expression was as sharp as a blade.

"These aren't Marco's," she said evenly, her voice steady despite the adrenaline surging through her veins. "This is a bad forgery. The timestamps don't match, and the handwriting's been doctored. If you wanted to shake my confidence, you should've tried harder."

The café went still. Conversations at nearby tables died as if the room itself was holding its breath.

Nico's smirk faltered, replaced by a flicker of something that could have been respect—or perhaps irritation. He leaned back in his chair, crossing his arms. "Well, aren't you clever?" he said, though the edge in his voice betrayed him.

Marco, seated across the table, had been silent until now. He leaned forward, his presence commanding as he rested his elbows on the table, his dark eyes locked on Nico. "She's right," Marco said, his voice cold enough to chill the air. "And I don't appreciate games, Nico. Not when we have real work to do."

Nico raised his hands in mock surrender, though the tightness in his jaw betrayed his discomfort. "Just making sure your protégé's got what it takes," he said, his gaze flicking back to Bella. "Looks like she does."

Bella didn't flinch under his scrutiny. Instead, she leaned back in her seat, her expression cool and unreadable. But inside, her thoughts churned. The test had been obvious, but the implications lingered. Loyalty here wasn't just a necessity—it was currency.

As the tension in the room eased, Marco's attention shifted to Bella. His gaze softened, but only slightly. "There's a package you need to pick up," he said, his tone low but firm. "Nico will give you the details."

Bella nodded, her mind already cataloging the information she would need to prepare. As Nico leaned in to relay the specifics, she felt the weight of Marco's gaze on her. It wasn't just a test of loyalty—it was a test of trust, of endurance, of her ability to navigate a world where every move was scrutinized, every decision dissected.

As the meeting ended and the group began to disperse, Bella lingered for a moment, her fingers brushing the edge of the now-closed folder. She glanced at Marco, who was watching her with an intensity that felt like both a promise and a warning.

"You passed," he said quietly, his voice just for her.

Bella looked at him, her expression guarded but her resolve unshaken. "Let's hope that's enough," she replied.

Marco's lips curved into a faint, knowing smile. "It will be," he said. But as they stepped into the rainy streets, Bella couldn't shake the feeling that in this world, passing the test was only the beginning.

∞

Later that night, Bella stood on the balcony of the flat, the rain having given way to a cool, starless sky. Bella stood on the narrow balcony of Marco's flat, overlooking a city that never seemed to sleep. Lights flickered like restless spirits in the buildings below, and the faint hum of distant traffic wove through the air. The balcony itself felt like an island, high above the chaos but tethered to it, the cold metal railing biting against her palm as she gripped it.

In her other hand, she held a glass of deep red wine, the rim stained faintly with the imprint of her lips. The wine tasted sharp, tangy, and wholly unlike the smooth cabernets she used to drink at FBI banquets. Somehow, she preferred it that way now. The old Bella—Agent Bella Rossi—had been polished and predictable, a cog in a well-oiled machine. Standing here, though, under a sky that had long since swallowed the stars, she realized she didn't miss that life.

The memories of her FBI days flickered unbidden—Lawson's measured voice cutting through tense mission briefings, Luca's steady presence by her side during stakeouts. They had been her compass, her sense of home. But now, those memories felt distant, like a dream fading at dawn.

She turned to her reflection in the sliding glass door, her own face a shadowy outline against the night. The name Marco had given her floated to her lips, unbidden.

"Elena Koslov," she murmured, tasting the words as though they belonged to someone else.

But the woman staring back wasn't a stranger. She was someone sharper, someone freer. Someone alive in a way Bella Rossi had never been.

Behind her, the faint shuffle of footsteps broke the quiet. She didn't turn; she knew who it was before Marco's reflection appeared in the glass. His presence filled the small space with an almost palpable energy, his charisma raw and inescapable. He moved like a predator that had no need to hunt—his confidence drew people to him, willingly.

"You handled Nico well today," Marco said, leaning against the railing beside her. His voice was low and smooth, a dangerous blend of warmth and calculation.

Bella tilted her head, her tone clipped. "I didn't need his approval."

Marco chuckled, a sound that curled around her like smoke. "No, but you earned it anyway. Nico doesn't trust easily."

"Neither do I," she shot back, her eyes fixed on the city below.

A glint of amusement flickered in Marco's gaze, but there was something softer in his expression tonight. He studied her as though trying to decipher a puzzle. "Good," he said finally. "Trust is dangerous. You've learned that already."

The silence that followed was taut, not uncomfortable but heavy, like a storm waiting to break.

"You're not just following me anymore," Marco said, his voice quieter now, almost intimate. "You're becoming my equal."

Bella turned to face him, the intensity of his words striking deeper than she cared to admit. Her chest tightened as she held his gaze, dark and unreadable. "Is that what you want, Marco? An equal?"

For a moment, he didn't respond, his eyes searching hers. Then he leaned closer, the faint scent of his cologne—a mix of cedar and something darker—coiling around her. "What I want," he said slowly, deliberately, "is someone who sees the world the way I do. Someone who knows what it takes to change it. I think you've become that person."

The air between them crackled, electric with unspoken tension. Her breath caught as the pull she'd fought to ignore all this time grew impossible to deny. Marco wasn't just dangerous; he was intoxicating. And that terrified her.

Setting her wineglass on the railing, Bella stepped closer, the movement deliberate, her pulse racing as she tilted her chin to meet his gaze. "Then don't underestimate me, Marco," she said, her voice steady despite the rush of adrenaline. "I'm not here to follow. I'm here to lead."

A slow smile spread across his face, filled with admiration and something far more personal. "I wouldn't dream of it," he murmured.

His hand lifted, hesitating for only a fraction of a second before brushing a strand of hair away from her face. The touch was light, almost reverent, but it sent a shiver down her spine. Her breathing quickened as his fingers lingered, tracing the line of her jaw with deliberate care.

"Bella," he said softly, her real name slipping from

his lips like a confession.

Her heart hammered in her chest as his thumb grazed her cheek, and for the first time in what felt like forever, she let herself feel—desire, longing, and the dangerous thrill of surrender.

Then, without warning, she stepped back, her movements sudden and resolute. Reaching into her jacket pocket, she pulled out her phone—the last tether to the life she'd left behind. With a flick of her wrist, she sent it sailing over the railing. It disappeared into the shadows below, the faint sound of it shattering on the pavement carrying up to them.

Marco's eyes narrowed, but a smirk tugged at the corner of his mouth. "That's one way to cut ties," he said.

She turned to him, her voice calm but laced with steel. "There's no going back now."

As the weight of her decision settled over her, Marco stepped closer, his hand resting lightly on her waist. "You were never going back," he said, his voice a low promise. "You just needed to admit it."

The night deepened around them, the city below a restless sea of light and shadow. Bella didn't know where this path would take her, but for the first time, she felt powerful. Dangerous. Whole.

And as Marco's lips brushed hers, igniting something fierce and undeniable, she knew one thing for certain: the woman she was becoming would never look back.

CHAPTER 26: THE MONACO JOB

Monte Carlo was a city of excess—gleaming sports cars that purred like jungle cats, mansions perched like gods over the sea, and streets that sparkled under the Mediterranean moonlight as if paved with crushed diamonds. The Hôtel de Paris sat at its heart like a crown jewel, casting long, opulent shadows across the square. Tonight, its grand ballroom was a den of decadence, brimming with power players who thrived on deals inked in secrets and sins.

Inside, the room shimmered with wealth. Crystal chandeliers threw fractured light across walls gilded with gold trim, and mirrors reflected the glittering crowd, amplifying their arrogance. The scent of wealth hung heavy in the air—a mix of imported perfume, aged cognac, and the quiet, insidious undercurrent of fear.

Bella adjusted her bracelet—a replica so perfect that only a jeweler would catch the lie—and slipped further into the crowd. Her emerald gown clung to her curves like a second skin, its thigh-high slit revealing just enough to command attention without relinquishing power. Her stiletto heels clicked against the polished marble floor in a rhythm that matched her heartbeat, steady despite the storm swirling beneath her calm exterior.

She smiled, not warmly but with the precise calculation of someone who had learned how to weaponize charm. A small tilt of her head, a glance over her shoulder, and the wolves began to circle. These men, so accustomed to dominance, didn't realize they were the prey.

Across the room, Marco leaned against the bar, his tailored black tuxedo exuding effortless sophistication. He had discarded the bow tie, leaving the top buttons of his shirt undone, and a faint five o'clock shadow framed his jaw. He was the kind of man who belonged in a place like this, who could pass as a billionaire or a hitman depending on the company he kept. His dark eyes tracked Bella like a hawk, and when her gaze met his, a flicker of heat passed between them.

"See anyone worth killing yet?" Bella murmured into the mic embedded in her bracelet, the words low enough to be lost in the din of champagne-fueled conversation.

Marco's reply crackled in her ear, smooth and unhurried. "Not yet. But you never know—the night's young, cara mia."

Her lips quirked into a small smile, though she didn't break stride. "You'd better be careful. I hear Monaco has a strict no-corpse policy."

"They also have excellent housekeepers," Marco shot back, his tone laced with amusement.

Bella bit back a laugh, scanning the room as the auctioneer took the stage. The first item was announced: an advanced Advanced-System algorithm capable of bypassing military-grade encryption. It was a piece of digital weaponry disguised as innovation, and the polite applause from the crowd made her stomach churn. These people, dressed to the nines, weren't bidding for art or antiquities; they were buying power, control, chaos.

Her gaze landed on a man standing near the edge of the crowd. He was balding, his suit tailored to hide the soft swell of his stomach, but his eyes were sharp, predatory. Bella sidled closer, her smile disarming, her movements graceful.

"That's quite the prize," she said lightly, as though commenting on a painting at a gallery.

The man glanced at her, his gaze dipping to the neckline of her dress before flicking back up. He smiled, a thin, condescending curve of his lips. "Not for long," he said, his voice dripping with smug confidence. "I intend to win it."

Bella tilted her head, letting her fingers trail lightly over his sleeve, a gesture as intimate as it was dismissive. "Then I guess you'll have to outbid me."

His laugh was loud and grating, the sound of a man who believed himself untouchable. Bella's smile sharpened, though she kept her expression playful. He was exactly the kind of man she loved to destroy.

"Bella," Marco's voice buzzed in her ear, low and commanding. "Don't get too cozy. We're not here to make friends."

Her lips curved, though this time it was for him. "Relax, tesoro. I'm just being polite."

"You? Polite?" Marco's laugh was soft, almost inaudible beneath the hum of the room. "Now I know you're up to something."

She stepped away from the bidder, her gaze flicking toward a set of doors marked Private. They were guarded, but the guards weren't paying attention to the auction. That would be their first mistake.

"I'm heading to restricted access," Bella murmured.

"Of course you are," Marco replied, the teasing edge in his tone replaced by something darker. "Be careful."

"Worried about me?" she asked, glancing over her shoulder to catch his reaction.

Marco smirked, his gaze meeting hers across the room. "Always. You're terrible at following orders."

She turned away, the corner of her mouth twitching. "And you're terrible at giving them."

As she moved toward the doors, her heart picked up speed, though her face betrayed none of it. She could feel Marco's gaze on her, protective and possessive all at once. It was both a comfort and a warning.

"Try not to get jealous," she whispered into the mic.

"Try not to get killed," he shot back, his voice softer this time.

But as Bella slipped past the guards and into the darkened corridor beyond, she felt the weight of the mission settle on her shoulders. This wasn't just about stealing data or sabotaging a deal. It was about survival—hers, Marco's, and maybe even the world's.

The tycoon's private yacht loomed in the marina like a floating palace, its sleek white hull gleaming beneath the starlit Monaco sky. Strung lights lined its decks, spilling golden reflections onto the dark, rippling water below. Even in a city saturated with opulence, the yacht stood out—a brazen monument to greed and unchecked power.

Marco moved through its shadowed corridors like a phantom, his every step deliberate and silent. The hum of distant laughter and clinking glasses on the upper deck gave him a cover of ambient noise as he worked. He crouched in the engine room, the air thick with the metallic tang of fuel and machine oil.

"Three charges set," he murmured into the mic hidden in his cufflink, his voice steady and low. "Bella, what's your status?"

Miles away—or so it felt—Bella stepped deeper into the restricted section of the hotel, her pulse thundering in her ears. The transition from the ballroom's gilded grandeur to this sterile, high-tech underbelly was jarring. The hum of servers filled the cool, glass-lined corridor, accompanied by the faint, almost imperceptible buzz of fluorescent lights.

She swiped her forged access card again, the scanner beeping its approval. As the final door hissed open, her breath caught.

The room was a high-tech nerve center, its walls lined with floor-to-ceiling screens. Holographic schematics of Advanced-System weaponry floated in midair, their soft blue light casting ghostly shadows. Names and data scrolled across the displays—names she recognized. Not just buyers, but power players tied to destabilization efforts across the globe.

Her chest tightened as she scanned the room. "Marco," she whispered, her voice barely audible. "This isn't just an auction. It's a nexus. They're building an entire network—using Dusker Corporation's tech to target global infrastructure. This isn't about money; this is war."

There was a pause, a beat of silence that stretched taut over the line. Then Marco's voice came through, clipped and grim. "Get what you can and get out. We'll take the whole damn thing down another day."

Bella slid a flash drive from her clutch, its matte black casing cool against her trembling fingers. She slotted it into the nearest terminal, her hands flying across the keyboard. The data transfer bar crawled across the screen, every percentage gained feeling like a lifetime.

"Come on, come on," she muttered under her breath.

"Hurry up," Marco urged, his tone sharper now.

"I'm going as fast as I can," she snapped, her voice low but tight with frustration.

Behind her, the faint click of a door lock sent a chill skittering down her spine. She froze, every muscle coiled, then turned slowly. A guard stood in the doorway, his gaze narrowing as it landed on her.

"Hey! Who the hell are you?" he barked, his hand already moving toward the gun holstered at his hip.

Bella didn't hesitate. In one fluid motion, she slammed the terminal's lid shut, yanked the flash drive free, and bolted for the far side of the room. The guard shouted, the heavy thud of his boots echoing as he gave chase.

"Marco," she hissed into the mic, "I've got company."

His reply was immediate, edged with steel. "I'm on my way. Stall them."

She ducked behind a row of server racks, her heart hammering as the guard's shadow loomed closer. Spotting a fire extinguisher mounted on the wall, she grabbed it, hefting the weight in her hands.

The moment he rounded the corner, she swung. The extinguisher connected with a sickening thud, and the guard crumpled to the floor, groaning.

"That's one way to stall," Marco's voice drawled in her ear.

"Not the time for jokes," she bit back, already

sprinting toward the exit.

As she burst through the final door, Marco appeared at the end of the corridor, his expression tight but composed. Another guard rounded the corner behind her, gun drawn. Marco's arm shot up, the silenced pistol in his hand spitting two precise shots. The guard dropped without a sound.

"Subtle," Bella muttered as she reached him.

"You're welcome." He grabbed her arm, pulling her into step beside him. "Now let's get the hell out of here."

The pair slipped through the hotel's labyrinthine back hallways, emerging into the cool night air near the marina. They didn't stop moving, their pace quick and efficient as they made their way to the stolen speedboat waiting at the docks.

The roar of the explosion came moments after they hit open water. The yacht erupted in a fiery inferno, a brilliant orange plume tearing through the night sky. Bella turned, the heat of the blast prickling her skin even at this distance. The acrid scent of burning fuel and scorched metal filled her nose.

Marco handled the boat with practiced ease, the choppy waves no match for his steady hands. Beside him, Bella gripped the edge of her seat, her adrenaline still spiking.

She turned to him, her eyes flashing with a mix of anger and admiration. "You didn't have to blow the whole damn thing up."

He glanced at her, the corner of his mouth lifting

in a cocky half-smile. "A little theater never hurts."

She shook her head, her frustration tempered by a grudging sense of awe. "You're insane, you know that?"

"Maybe," he replied, his tone casual. "But you're still here, cara."

Bella didn't respond, though the faint smile that tugged at her lips said enough. As the glow of the burning yacht faded into the distance, the weight of what they'd uncovered settled between them—a silent reminder of the stakes they were up against.

For now, though, they had survived. And in their world, survival was its own kind of victory.

∞

The safehouse was a cramped, nondescript flat on the edge of Monte Carlo, wedged between aging stone buildings with sagging shutters and narrow balconies. The faint smell of seawater drifted in through the cracked window, mingling with the sharp tang of gun oil and sweat that clung to the room. A single dim bulb overhead cast long shadows, painting everything in muted tones of gray and gold.

Bella sat on the edge of the bed, her posture stiff, hands clasped so tightly her knuckles turned white. The adrenaline that had carried her through the mission was gone, leaving behind a hollowness that gnawed at her insides.

Marco stood by the makeshift bar in the corner, pouring two glasses of whiskey. His movements were slow, methodical, his usual grace tinged with a tension that betrayed his carefully maintained composure. He crossed the room and handed her a glass, his fingers brushing hers in a moment so fleeting it felt accidental. But Bella knew better.

"What's on your mind?" His voice was low, almost a growl, the kind that demanded answers but offered no comfort.

She took a sip of the whiskey, the liquid burning its way down her throat and settling like fire in her chest. "The people at that auction," she said finally, her voice tight, "they weren't just buyers. They were architects. Puppeteers pulling the strings on chaos. And we…we let most of them walk away."

Marco's jaw tightened, the muscle there ticking like a detonator counting down. He set his glass on the nearby table with a sharp clink. "We can't take them all down at once. Tonight wasn't about justice. It was about sending a message."

Bella's frustration boiled over, her voice rising as she set her own glass on the nightstand. "And what message was that? That we're no better than they are? That we fight corruption with destruction? What's the line, Marco? Because tonight, I didn't see one."

Marco's eyes darkened, his calm facade splintering as he turned to face her fully. There was something in his expression that made her stomach tighten—a flash of raw anger, of something darker and more dangerous than she'd ever seen from him before.

His voice, when it came, was low and sharp,

cutting through the tension like a blade. "Don't lose sight of why we're doing this, Bella. Every move we make weakens them. Every target we take out sends ripples through their network. This isn't about morality. It's about survival."

The words hit her like a physical blow, and for the first time, she saw him not as her partner, her anchor in the chaos, but as something far more volatile. His manic energy seemed to fill the small room, a storm barely contained beneath his skin.

Her heart raced, not with fear but with a cold, disquieting unease. She couldn't show it—wouldn't. Not to him.

"And what if we're wrong?" she demanded, her voice trembling despite her best efforts. "What if all we're doing is feeding the same cycle of violence they thrive on? How does this end, Marco? With us standing on a pile of ashes, claiming victory?"

His expression softened, but not in a way that reassured her. The steel in his gaze remained, tempered now by something closer to desperation. "You've seen what they've done, Bella. You've felt it. Don't let doubt cloud your vision. Doubt is how they win."

She stood, crossing the room to face him, the space between them charged with unspoken tension. "I want to believe that," she said, her voice barely above a whisper. "But every day, it gets harder. Every choice we make feels like one step closer to becoming the thing we're trying to destroy."

Marco stepped closer, his presence consuming the

air around her. He reached out, his hand brushing hers, and the gentleness of the gesture felt at odds with the man who had just detonated a yacht without a second thought.

"Then let me carry it for you," he said, his voice soft now, the storm momentarily subsided.

Bella looked up at him, her chest tight with the weight of everything unsaid. In Marco's world, there was no room for hesitation, no space for second-guessing. But as she stared into his eyes—eyes that burned with conviction and something else she couldn't quite name—she couldn't shake the gnawing doubt that had taken root in her soul.

The silence stretched between them, heavy and suffocating, until finally, she broke it. "You're right. I've seen what they've done. And I hate them for it." Her voice faltered, her own vulnerability slipping through. "But sometimes, I hate us too."

The admission hung in the air like a live wire, sparking with tension. Marco didn't reply, but the flicker of something—regret, guilt, or maybe understanding—passed over his face before it disappeared behind the mask he wore so well.

Bella turned away, the weight of their shared crusade pressing down on her like an anchor. And for the first time, she wondered if they'd already crossed a line they could never come back from.

CHAPTER 27: CRACKS IN THE FOUNDATION

The FBI office was unnaturally cold—too brightly lit and too suffocatingly silent. The walls were lined with bulletin boards covered in maps, photographs, and red string connecting faces to places. It was the kind of room where decisions were made not with the heart, but with the cold, calculated precision of justice, no matter how bitter it tasted.

Lawson stood in the center of the room, his shoulders squared as if bracing for impact. The phone in his hand felt heavier than it should have, a weight that seemed to tether him to the floor. Sweat beaded at the back of his neck, hidden beneath the crisp collar of his suit. The air smelled faintly of stale coffee and printer ink, but it might as well have been blood and betrayal.

He stared at the desk in front of him, where a grainy photograph of Bella Rossi lay beneath a single spotlight. Her image was defiant, frozen in time, her eyes staring back at him like an accusation.

"Agent Lawson," came a voice from behind him, sharp and impatient. It was his superior, Director Madden, her expression carved from stone. "We don't have all night. Either you make the call, or I'll find someone who will."

Lawson's jaw tightened. Bella had been more than just a colleague. She'd been his partner, his confidant. Hell, she'd been the person he trusted most when the lines blurred, and the job became too much. But now? Now she was a fugitive. A rogue agent working alongside Marco DeLuca, the man who'd eluded justice for years and left a trail of destruction in his wake.

His thumb hovered over the phone's keypad. He could feel Madden's eyes drilling into him, waiting for him to crumble under the weight of his hesitation.

"They've crossed every line we've drawn," Madden said, her tone cold and clinical. "The yacht explosion, the stolen intel—she's working with DeLuca, Lawson. She's not one of us anymore."

Lawson slammed the phone onto the desk, his frustration spilling over. "You think I don't know that?" His voice echoed in the room, raw and unguarded. He turned to face her, his expression a storm of anger and despair. "You think I don't know what this means? For her, for us? For everything we've built?"

"She made her choice," Madden said, unflinching. "And now you have to make yours."

His gaze fell back to Bella's photograph. He saw her as she used to be—sharp-witted, relentless, someone who could outthink and outmaneuver anyone in the room. But he also saw the cracks, the moments when she questioned the cost of their work. The doubt that had taken root in her long before it became a chasm.

"Damn it, Bella," he muttered under his breath, his voice breaking on her name.

Lawson picked up the phone again, dialing the secure line with mechanical precision. Each beep of the keypad felt like a nail in her coffin, and his heart hammered against his ribs as he waited for the call to connect.

"This is Agent Lawson," he said, his voice colder than he thought possible. "Effective immediately, Agent Bella Rossi is to be reclassified as a rogue operative and added to the international most-wanted list. Her accomplice, Marco DeLuca, is already listed, but I want their profiles linked. She's working with him now. Treat them as a unit. Armed and extremely dangerous."

The words felt foreign in his mouth, as though someone else was speaking through him. He kept his tone steady, professional, but inside, he was unraveling.

"Understood, Agent Lawson. Confirmation received," the voice on the other end replied.

The line disconnected, and the silence that followed was deafening.

Madden crossed her arms, her expression unreadable. "You did the right thing."

Lawson turned to her, his eyes blazing with something close to fury. "Did I? Because it sure as hell doesn't feel like it."

She didn't respond, and he didn't wait for her to. He stormed out of the room, his footsteps echoing in the empty hallway.

In the privacy of his car, he let out a shuddering breath and gripped the steering wheel until his knuckles turned white. He wanted to believe Madden was right, that he'd done the right thing. But as he stared out at the dark city skyline, he couldn't shake the feeling that he'd just betrayed the one person who had never betrayed him.

And somewhere out there, Bella was running—her face now plastered across databases and bulletin boards, her name whispered in circles she'd once hunted.

He didn't know if she'd ever forgive him.

Hell, he wasn't sure he'd ever forgive himself.

∞

The city of Zurich wore its secrets like a second skin. Beneath the polished veneer of its financial district lay shadows thick with deceit. Rain slicked the cobblestones outside, the city's pulse muffled by the whisper of tires on wet streets and the muted glow of streetlamps fighting through the fog. The air smelled faintly of damp stone and tension.

Bella Rossi moved like a ghost through the opulence, her footsteps nearly silent against the gleaming marble of the lobby floor. Her trench coat hung heavily on her shoulders, her scarf hiding the rigidity in her jaw. Every inch of her was a study in control, but her pulse hammered a frantic rhythm beneath her skin.

Marco's voice was low and sure in her earpiece, a lifeline tethering her to focus.

"Room 314. Minimal security, but keep your eyes open."

She allowed herself a small smile, the faintest flicker of humor in an otherwise grim mission. "Relax, Marco. You'll live longer."

The elevator doors slid open with a muted chime, and Bella stepped into the dimly lit corridor. The office was exactly as she'd expected—sterile, functional, and reeking of corporate anonymity. Gray walls absorbed the sparse light, while the hum of the computer terminal filled the silence like a heartbeat.

She moved quickly, her fingers dancing over the keyboard as the decryption drive began siphoning information from Dusker Corporation's hidden account. Streams of data scrolled across the screen, evidence of the corporation's labyrinthine operations, each file more damning than the last.

She was so focused she almost missed the faint creak of the door behind her. Almost.

"Step away from the terminal."

The voice was smooth, too calm for the weight of the situation, and it sent a chill down Bella's spine. She turned, her movements slow and deliberate, to find Nico leaning against the doorframe, a Glock trained on her chest.

His smirk was infuriating, a mask of confidence tinged with condescension. "You've got a bad habit of poking your nose where it doesn't belong."

Bella's mind raced, every instinct firing at once. "And you've got a habit of showing up at the wrong time. Care to explain?"

"Why bother?" he said, stepping into the room with the relaxed arrogance of someone who thought he had all the power. "You're not walking out of here, Bella. Not with that data. Not at all."

She studied him, her gaze flickering to the faint sheen of sweat on his forehead, the tightness around his mouth. He was nervous. Beneath the bravado, Nico wasn't as certain of his dominance as he wanted her to believe.

"It was you," she said, piecing it together even as she spoke. "The bad intel. The ambush in Prague. You've been selling us out this entire time."

"Smart girl." His tone was mocking, but there was no denying the admiration in his eyes. "But it's too late for smarts now."

Nico moved suddenly, and Bella reacted on instinct. She dove behind the desk as the first shot rang out, the bullet embedding itself in the wall where her head had been a second earlier.

The confined space turned the confrontation into a brutal dance. Papers scattered as the desk overturned, and the air filled with the acrid tang of gunpowder and the sound of grunts and heavy breaths. Nico was stronger, his grip like a vise when he caught her wrist, but Bella had speed and training on her side.

She twisted, using his momentum against him to break free and send him stumbling. Her eyes locked onto the gun that had skidded across the floor. She lunged for it, her heart hammering as she felt the cold metal beneath her fingers.

"Don't move!" she shouted, leveling the weapon at him. Her voice shook, but her grip didn't.

Nico froze, his chest heaving as he stared at her with a mixture of contempt and something darker. "You won't do it," he said, his voice low and taunting. "You don't have it in you."

But when he lunged, she didn't hesitate.

The shot echoed like thunder, and time seemed to slow. Nico staggered, his hand flying to the crimson stain spreading across his chest. His eyes widened in shock, and he sank to his knees before collapsing onto the floor.

Bella stood over him, the gun still raised, her breath coming in short, uneven gasps. The room smelled of blood and spent adrenaline, the copper tang clinging to the back of her throat.

By the time Marco arrived, Bella was still in the same spot, her hands shaking as she stared at Nico's lifeless form.

"Bella!" Marco's voice crackled in her ear, sharp with alarm. "What the hell just happened?"

She lowered the gun slowly, her hand trembling as the reality of what she'd done began to sink in. "Nico," she said, her voice hollow. "He was a double agent. He was going to kill me."

Silence hung heavy between them for a moment before Marco spoke again, his tone grim. "Finish the job. We'll deal with the rest later."

She nodded, even though he couldn't see her, and turned back to the terminal. But as her fingers resumed their work, her mind replayed the moment over and over, Nico's taunt ringing in her ears.

You don't have it in you.

He'd been wrong.

And that terrified her more than anything.

Marco surveyed the scene with a calm detachment, stepping over the body as he moved toward her. "Are you hurt?"

She shook her head, unable to meet his gaze. "I didn't want to... but he—he didn't leave me a choice."

Marco placed a hand on her shoulder, his grip firm but not unkind. "You did what needed to be done. Guilt has no place in this world, Bella. Nico made his choice. You made yours."

His words were meant to comfort, but they didn't. If anything, they deepened the chasm opening inside her.

"How can you be so calm?" she asked, her voice

breaking.

Marco's expression softened, but there was a hardness behind his eyes. "Because this is the life we chose. Regret is a luxury we can't afford."

Later, back at the safehouse, the city's cold, damp embrace clung to Bella like a second skin as they slipped back inside. The small flat was tucked into the corner of a narrow street, its walls as thin as its furniture was threadbare. Shadows danced erratically across the room as a streetlamp flickered outside, casting the space in an almost suffocating half-light. The air reeked faintly of mildew, the scent curling into her nostrils and mingling with the metallic tang of blood she couldn't seem to forget.

Bella perched on the edge of the sagging bed, her hands wrapped around a chipped porcelain mug. The tea inside had gone cold, but she didn't notice. Her thoughts were louder than the silence in the room, a cacophony of regret, fear, and self-recrimination that refused to settle.

Marco stood in the doorway, arms crossed over his chest. He filled the room with his presence, an imposing figure dressed in black, his tailored coat draped over the chair. His expression was unreadable, his dark eyes fixed on her like he was trying to solve a puzzle.

"You're blaming yourself," he said, his voice low and steady, the words slicing through the tension.

She lifted her gaze to him, her eyes rimmed red

but dry. "Of course I am," she said sharply, her tone carrying a jagged edge. "I killed someone, Marco. Doesn't that mean anything to you?"

He didn't flinch, didn't move. "It means everything," he replied evenly. "It means you saved our lives tonight."

Bella let out a brittle laugh, setting the mug down with a forceful clink. "That's what you're telling yourself? That we're heroes in this mess? Because it doesn't feel like that to me. It feels like murder."

Marco's jaw ticked, a faint pulse of tension rippling beneath his calm exterior. He stepped closer, his boots muffled against the thin carpet. "Nico was a traitor," he said. "I've had my doubts about him for weeks. His intel was sloppy, his timing always off. But tonight proved it. He wasn't just a liability—he was a threat. You saw it yourself."

Her stomach twisted. She had seen it. Nico's smirk, the gun raised with cold precision, the way he'd dismissed her as if her death was a foregone conclusion. And yet...

"I didn't want to kill him," she murmured, her voice trembling. "I didn't want this."

Marco knelt in front of her, his hands bracing on either side of her knees. His eyes softened, but the steel in them remained. "I know," he said quietly. "But this is the life we chose. And guilt? Regret? They have no place here. You did what needed to be done. Don't let this break you."

She stared at him, her breath catching as his words

settled over her like a shroud. "How can you be so calm about this?"

His lips pressed into a thin line. "Because I've made peace with what it takes to survive. Regret is a luxury we can't afford, Bella."

She pulled away, standing abruptly and pacing the small room. The walls seemed to close in on her, the shadows pressing tighter. "That's just it, Marco. If we lose the ability to question what we're doing, we're no better than the people we're fighting against."

His patience frayed visibly, his voice sharpening. "You think I don't question it? Every damn day, I question it. But I don't let it paralyze me. You can't afford to, either."

The air between them crackled, charged with more than anger. It was the weight of everything unspoken—her doubts, his frustrations, the dangerous thread that tethered them to each other.

After a tense silence, Marco exhaled and turned toward the door. But before he stepped out, he stopped and looked back at her. "For what it's worth, Bella... I trust you. More than anyone."

His words lingered, wrapping around her like a fragile promise.

Hours later, when the city outside had gone silent, Bella found Marco in the darkened living room, his silhouette outlined by the faint glow of a streetlamp. He didn't turn as she approached, his posture rigid, his hands shoved into his pockets.

"I've seen too much to believe in happy endings,"

he said softly, his voice carrying an edge of vulnerability she'd never heard before. "But with you... I want to believe. I need to believe."

Her heart twisted painfully at the rawness in his tone. She reached out, her fingers brushing his arm. "Marco..."

He turned then, his eyes locking onto hers with an intensity that stole her breath. "Promise me," he said, his voice barely above a whisper. "Promise me you'll stay with me, no matter how dark this gets. I can't... I can't do this without you, Bella."

Her throat tightened as she saw the man beneath the armor—the one who had been battered and bruised by this life as much as she had. Slowly, she nodded. "I promise."

The tension between them shifted, a magnetic pull drawing them closer. When Marco leaned in, his lips brushing hers, it wasn't the fiery passion she'd come to expect from him. It was slow, tentative—achingly tender.

In that moment, the lines between right and wrong blurred completely, leaving only the fragile truth that they were in this together, for better or worse.

CHAPTER 28: THE ULTIMATE TARGET

The mansion stood like a dark monolith on the edge of Prague, its silhouette stark against the ink-black sky. The glow from a waxing moon barely penetrated the thick mist clinging to the surrounding forest, creating a suffocating sense of isolation. The estate exuded power and secrecy—a fortress for a man whose sins had stained continents.

Bella crouched low in the underbrush, her breath condensing into fleeting wisps that dissolved into the cold night air. Her pulse drummed steadily in her ears, her gaze fixed on the shifting patterns of red laser grids projected across the estate's perimeter. In her hand, a handheld signal jammer hummed faintly, its vibrations seeping into her bones. Beside her, Marco was unnervingly still, his sharp features set in a mask of unshakable focus.

"The east side," Bella whispered, the words barely audible over the distant rustle of leaves. "Twenty seconds. Camera loops start..." she glanced at her wrist timer, "—now."

Marco didn't reply. He didn't need to. His movements were fluid as he surged forward, his body a shadow merging with the darkness. Bella followed, her heart pounding in unison with her footsteps. The air tasted metallic, tinged with anticipation and the earthy dampness of the forest floor.

They darted across the manicured lawn, every step deliberate. The mansion loomed larger with every second, its façade a cold blend of Gothic grandeur and modern impenetrability. Inside those walls, the target waited—unaware that death was creeping closer.

At the service entrance, Bella dropped to her knees, her fingers deftly working over the keypad. Her hacking module blinked green as it overrode the encrypted system, bypassing layers of digital security with a soft beep. The door clicked open, and a burst of warm, stale air greeted them.

Marco held the door ajar, his hand grazing the small of her back as she slipped inside. "Stay close," he murmured, his voice a deep vibration that sent a shiver through her already-tense body.

The interior was stifling, every inch of the mansion reeking of old money and unchecked power. The walls were adorned with heavy tapestries and priceless art that seemed to mock them with their gaudy excess. Crystal chandeliers cast fractured light across the marble floors, the luxury at odds with the ugliness of what they knew this place concealed.

Bella scanned the hallway, her trained eyes catching the subtle gleam of a hidden camera lens. "Blind spot's there," she whispered, nodding to a stretch of shadow between two grotesquely oversized vases.

"Upstairs," Marco replied, his tone low and sure. "Second door on the left. That's where he'll be."

They slipped through the corridor like ghosts, their steps muffled against the thick Persian rugs. Bella's every sense was heightened—the faint hum of electricity in the walls, the distant murmur of guards on their rounds, the tang of fear she couldn't quite suppress.

They reached the staircase just as two guards rounded the far corner. Marco's hand shot out, gripping her arm and pulling her into the recess of a doorway. His breath was warm against her temple as they pressed together, waiting.

The guards passed so close she could see the scuff marks on their boots, hear the faint static of their radios. Her pulse thrummed in her throat, her entire body wired to fight or flee. But Marco didn't move, his stillness a command. When the guards disappeared down another hall, he released her, his fingers lingering a second too long on her arm.

"Focus," he said quietly, though the heat in his

gaze suggested he wasn't just reminding her.

Bella's lips parted to respond, but she swallowed the words and nodded instead. They had no time for distractions—not tonight.

The staircase creaked beneath their weight as they ascended, every sound amplified in the oppressive silence. At the top, Bella pressed her ear to the second door on the left, her breath shallow as she listened for movement.

"Clear," she mouthed, stepping aside for Marco.

He didn't hesitate, his gloved hand gripping the doorknob as he pushed the door open. The room beyond was opulent, its decadence almost blinding. A massive bed dominated the space, its canopy draped in rich velvet. The air was heavy with the scent of expensive cologne and cigar smoke, clinging to the walls like a taunt.

The man in the bed stirred, his features barely illuminated by the faint glow of a laptop screen on the bedside table. Marco moved first, a predatory grace in every step as he approached the sleeping figure. Bella hung back, her breath catching in her throat as she watched him.

This wasn't just a mission to him. There was something personal in the way he moved, a silent rage simmering beneath his composed exterior. She'd seen him like this before—controlled but deadly, his emotions hidden behind a mask of professionalism.

Her grip tightened on the silenced pistol at her side. "Marco," she whispered, her voice barely audible.

He didn't turn, his attention fixed on the target. "He's one of Dusker Corporation's cronies," he said, his tone cold and detached. "You know what that means."

Bella hesitated, her mind racing. He hadn't told her everything—she knew that now. The anonymous client, the real reason for this mission. It was all shrouded in a layer of secrecy she wasn't sure she could penetrate.

And yet, standing there in the suffocating stillness of the room, she couldn't deny the dark thrill that coursed through her. She loved him—God help her, she did. And in that moment, she realized he loved that about her. She was his, caught in a web of trust and lies, too far gone to escape now.

"Such a good girl," he murmured, almost to himself, as he glanced over his shoulder. "Always right where I need you."

Bella's stomach tightened, a sick mix of pride and dread.

And as Marco turned back to the target, she wondered if she'd ever truly understand the man she'd chosen to follow—or if she'd already lost herself trying.

The room exuded opulence and power, but there was a sinister undercurrent beneath the polished mahogany and velvet drapes. It wasn't just a study; it was a shrine to control. Ornate bookshelves groaned under the weight of legal tomes and global histories— symbols of the knowledge their target had wielded as a weapon. The fire in the hearth crackled with a malevolence of its own, its flickering light casting long, twisting shadows across the room.

Bella felt the weight of the air, dense with cigar smoke and arrogance. Her skin prickled with unease, a visceral warning that every corner of this place held secrets that could kill. Marco, however, moved like a predator, his steps soundless against the thick Persian rug.

Behind the imposing desk, the man they'd been sent to eliminate lounged in a high-backed leather chair, a crystal tumbler of scotch balanced in his hand. The politician's expression shifted when he saw Marco step from the shadows—first surprise, then anger, and finally fear. It was always fear in the end.

"You're making a mistake," the politician growled, his voice low and dangerous, though it quavered under the bravado. "Do you know who I am?"

Marco's voice was cold, his silencer leveled and steady. "Do you know how many lives you've destroyed?"

The politician's eyes darted to a hidden panic button beneath his desk. Bella caught the motion before Marco did, her voice slicing through the tension. "Don't even think about it."

Her gloved hand was already on her weapon, her aim steady as the man froze mid-reach. She could feel the adrenaline clawing at her insides, but outwardly she was a picture of steel.

"You don't have to do this," the man said again,

but the desperation had seeped into his tone.

"You don't have to do a lot of things," Marco replied coolly, his finger tightening on the trigger.

The shot was muffled, a sharp hiss in the silence, and the man crumpled forward. His scotch spilled, mingling with the crimson that began to spread across the polished wood of the desk. Marco lowered his weapon, his expression unreadable as he turned to Bella.

"Secure the scene," he said briskly, already moving to ensure their exit was clean.

Bella swallowed the lump rising in her throat and forced herself to focus. There was no time for guilt— not now. She moved to the desk, her hands methodically rifling through drawers and folders. She'd learned over time to compartmentalize her emotions, to separate her discomfort from the mission. But when her fingers closed over a folder embossed with a familiar, ominous symbol, her stomach dropped.

She flipped it open, scanning the pages with a growing sense of dread. It was all there—names, dates, transactions. The pieces of a puzzle she hadn't even realized they'd been assembling. And then, on the final page, she found it: a ledger linking their target to Marco's anonymous client.

"Marco," she called, her voice tight and trembling.

He was beside her in an instant, his movements smooth as he took the folder from her hands. Bella studied his face as he read, watched the subtle tightening of his jaw, the flicker of something dangerous in his eyes.

"This doesn't change anything," he said finally, snapping the folder shut and slipping it into his bag.

Her voice rose, sharper than she intended. "It changes everything! We're working for someone tied to this man. Don't you see what that means?"

He turned to her, his expression unreadable, though his voice was low and even. "It means we keep going. We don't ask questions, Bella. We do the job."

"And what happens when the job makes us no better than the people we're fighting?" she shot back, her frustration boiling over.

His gaze darkened, and for a moment, she thought she saw a flash of vulnerability behind the mask. "You think I don't ask myself that every damn day? But this is how we win—one piece at a time. Sometimes we don't get to choose which devils we work with to destroy the others."

The weight of his words settled between them, an invisible barrier that felt impossible to cross. Bella stared at him, her mind a whirl of doubts and questions. She'd always trusted Marco, but now that trust felt like it was hanging by a thread.

Their escape was a dance of precision and adrenaline. Bella's pulse hammered in her ears as they retraced their path, her eyes constantly scanning for movement. Twice they had to melt into the shadows as guards passed by, their footsteps heavy with authority.

By the time they reached the edge of the forest,

the mansion was behind them, a glowing monument to corruption and secrets. The faint wail of approaching sirens carried on the wind, spurring them into the waiting vehicle.

The drive to their safehouse was steeped in silence, thick and suffocating. Marco's hands gripped the wheel tightly, his knuckles white in the dim glow of the dashboard. Bella stared out the window, the dark landscape rushing past, her thoughts tangled and heavy.

When she finally spoke, her voice was quiet but resolute. "If we're just shifting power from one monster to another, then what are we really doing here, Marco?"

He didn't answer immediately, his gaze fixed on the road ahead. When he finally spoke, his voice was laced with something she couldn't quite identify—regret, maybe. "We're surviving. And sometimes, Bella, that has to be enough."

The words hung in the air between them, a fragile truce in a war neither of them fully understood. But as the safehouse came into view, Bella couldn't shake the feeling that the lines between right and wrong had blurred beyond recognition.

∞

The road stretched out before them, a ribbon of shadows lit only by the thin beams of their headlights. The forest outside was a blur of blackened trees, their skeletal branches clawing at the night sky. Inside the car, the air was stifling, heavy with the weight of unspoken words and simmering tension.

Bella stared out the passenger window, her reflection ghostly against the glass. The engine's low hum was the only sound, a maddening monotony that gave her mind too much room to spiral. Finally, she couldn't hold it in any longer.

"You knew," she said, her voice cutting through the silence like a scalpel.

Marco didn't flinch, his hands steady on the wheel, but his jaw tightened just enough for her to notice.

"You knew our client was connected to him, didn't you?" she pressed, her voice trembling with both anger and disbelief.

His silence was confirmation enough.

"Answer me, Marco," she demanded, her tone sharper now, fueled by the betrayal she felt clawing at her chest.

"It doesn't matter," he said finally, his voice flat, devoid of the warmth she once thought was buried somewhere beneath his hardened exterior. "What matters is the mission. We can't afford to get distracted by questions that lead nowhere."

"Nowhere?" she repeated, incredulous. Her fingers curled into fists on her lap. "How can you justify that? How can you keep pretending this is about justice when it's starting to look like it's about power?"

He exhaled sharply, a sound that was part frustration, part resignation. His eyes flicked to her for a brief second before returning to the road. "And what would you have me do? Turn down every lead that doesn't come with a clean moral stamp? We're fighting a war, Bella. Wars aren't won with idealism."

The words hit her like a slap. She'd heard him justify their actions before, but this was different. This was colder, emptier.

Her voice softened, cracking under the weight of her doubt. "Maybe not. But I need to know that what we're doing is worth the cost."

For the first time, his grip on the wheel faltered, his fingers flexing as if her words had struck a nerve. When he spoke again, his tone was quieter, almost pained. "It is," he said, his gaze fixed on the road ahead as though he couldn't bear to look at her. "You'll see that, Bella. Eventually, you'll see."

She wanted to believe him. God, she wanted to believe him. But the cracks in his resolve were showing, and for the first time, she wasn't sure if they were fighting for the same thing.

When they finally reached the safehouse, the tension between them was a living, breathing thing. The cabin was cloaked in darkness, its silhouette barely visible against the backdrop of towering pines. Marco killed the engine, and for a moment, neither of them moved.

Bella stepped out first, the cold night air biting at her skin and forcing her to pull her jacket tighter around herself. She could hear the crunch of Marco's boots behind her as he followed, his presence as imposing as ever.

Inside, the safehouse was stark and functional, its dim lighting casting long shadows across the bare walls. The hum of the generator was a faint background noise, a reminder of their isolation. Bella lingered in the center of the room, her arms crossed over her chest as Marco set down his bag and began unloading their gear with the same methodical precision he always did.

Finally, she broke the silence. "How long have you known?"

He didn't look at her as he answered. "Long enough."

His casual tone sent a fresh wave of anger coursing through her. "And you didn't think I deserved to know?"

He turned to face her then, his expression hard, but his eyes… his eyes betrayed him. There was something there—regret, maybe even guilt.

"What would you have done if I told you?" he asked quietly. "Would you have walked away? Because that's not an option, Bella. Not for either of us."

Her breath caught, the weight of his words settling heavily in her chest. "You don't get to decide that for me," she said, her voice barely above a whisper.

He took a step closer, the space between them shrinking, the air crackling with unspoken tension. "I didn't decide it for you. You did. The moment you chose this life, you made that choice. We don't get to pick and choose who we work with. We take the opportunities we're given and we use them to get closer to the endgame."

She shook her head, her voice breaking. "And what if the endgame isn't what we thought it was? What if we're just pawns in someone else's game?"

His hand twitched at his side, as if he wanted to reach for her but stopped himself. "Then we adapt. We survive. That's the only way we win."

She held his gaze, searching for something—anything—that would reassure her. But all she saw was a man who had buried his doubts so deeply they'd turned into conviction.

Without another word, he turned and walked toward the adjoining room, leaving her standing there in the dim light, the shadows closing in around her.

Bella sank onto the edge of the worn couch, her head in her hands. She'd always known this life would demand sacrifices, but she wasn't sure how much more she could give without losing herself entirely.

And as the wind howled outside, rattling the thin windows of the safehouse, she realized that the man she'd once trusted with her life might just be the person who would destroy it.

CHAPTER 29: DOUBTS AND DECISIONS

The villa sat on the edge of a cliff, its pale stone walls gilded by the amber glow of a setting sun. The Italian Riviera stretched out below, the Mediterranean's restless waves glinting like shards of broken glass. It was a place that should have been a refuge, a sanctuary where secrets couldn't penetrate. Instead, it felt suffocating, as though the villa itself conspired to trap Bella in the web of lies she'd begun to unravel.

She paced the terrace, her heels clicking against the polished tiles. The air smelled of salt and citrus, a deceptive sweetness that contrasted with the storm brewing in her chest. Marco stood in the doorway behind her, the light from inside the villa casting his shadow long across the terrace. He didn't move, but

Bella felt his presence like a weight pressing against her back.

"You've been quiet since Prague," he said, his voice low, almost too calm.

Bella stopped abruptly, gripping the wrought-iron railing until her knuckles whitened. Below, the waves crashed against jagged rocks, their fury a mirror to her own. She didn't turn to face him.

"I've had a lot to think about," she said, her voice tight.

Marco stepped onto the terrace, the soft scuff of his boots on the stone floor setting her nerves on edge. His movements were deliberate, controlled, like a predator stalking prey. "About what?"

Finally, she turned, her eyes locking onto his. The sunset behind her turned the edges of her figure to fire, but her expression was ice. "About who we've become," she said, the words sharp and unforgiving.

His brows furrowed, a faint crease forming between them. "What does that mean?"

She took a step closer, her jaw set, her emotions bubbling dangerously close to the surface. "It means I'm starting to wonder if we're even on the same side anymore."

Marco's head tilted slightly, his expression a careful mask of neutrality. But Bella could see the cracks—his clenched fists, the subtle tic in his jaw. "That's a hell of a statement," he said.

"Is it?" she shot back. "Prague wasn't just a mission, Marco. It was a wake-up call. That client of yours..."

"Ours," he interrupted, his voice cutting through hers like a blade. His dark eyes narrowed, daring her to challenge him.

Her laugh was brittle, edged with disbelief. "Don't," she snapped. "Don't pretend I'm complicit in this. You knew. You knew they were tied to Heller, and you didn't say a damn word."

Marco's calm shattered like glass. He closed the distance between them in two swift strides, his presence suddenly overwhelming. "And what would you have done if I told you, Bella? Walked away? Blown the mission?" His voice was low, dangerous, each word laced with the fury he fought to contain. "We're not playing a clean game here. We're dismantling a system that's been rotting from the inside out for decades. You don't do that without getting your hands dirty."

"Dirty?" she repeated, her voice rising as her frustration boiled over. She stepped back, needing the space to breathe, to think. "We're drowning in blood, Marco. And it's not just theirs—it's ours, too. Do you even see that anymore? Or are you too far gone to care?"

His jaw tightened, the muscles in his neck flexing as he struggled for control. For a moment, the only sound was the relentless crash of the waves below, each one echoing the tension between them.

"You think I've lost sight of the mission," he said finally, his voice quieter now, but no less sharp.

Bella met his gaze, her eyes shimmering with the weight of her conviction. "I think you've stopped asking questions," she said. "And I can't follow someone who doesn't question what we're doing. Someone who doesn't question themselves."

Her words hung in the air like smoke, thick and suffocating. Marco's expression was unreadable, his body as still as stone. But in his eyes, she saw something—regret, fear, or maybe just the remnants of the man she'd once trusted with her life.

He stepped back, retreating into the shadows of the villa. "You don't have to follow me," he said, his voice colder now, detached. "But if you're staying, you'd better decide whether you're in this fight or not. Because we can't afford hesitation, Bella. Not now."

And with that, he disappeared into the villa, leaving her alone on the terrace. The sea breeze wrapped around her like a shroud, carrying the scent of salt and the faintest hint of flowers.

Bella turned back to the horizon, her grip tightening on the railing as she stared out at the endless expanse of water. The sun dipped below the edge of the world, casting the villa in shadow, and for the first time, Bella wondered if they'd ever been fighting for the same thing—or if she'd been chasing a mirage all along.

∞

The study felt colder than the rest of the villa, as though the warmth of the Mediterranean couldn't quite penetrate its walls. The scent of leather-bound books and polished wood hung heavy in the air, a deceptive reminder of order and permanence. Outside, the sea whispered against the cliffs, the rhythm unnerving in its constancy. Bella barely noticed.

She closed the study door behind her with a soft click, the sound swallowed by the hush of the room. Marco's steady breathing from down the hall echoed in her mind, a rhythmic reminder of the man she now had reason to doubt.

The desk lamp cast an anemic circle of light, its glow stark against the darkness pressing in from the corners. She slipped into the chair, her fingers grazing the cool metal of Marco's laptop. The machine felt heavier than it should have, as though it carried the weight of the secrets she suspected it held.

Her hands trembled as she typed in the password, the sequence etched into her memory from months of stolen glances over his shoulder. For a moment, she hesitated, her breath catching in her throat. This wasn't just about curiosity—it was betrayal.

But she pressed enter anyway.

The screen illuminated her face, casting shadows across her sharp features. The desktop was meticulously organized, folders labeled with innocuous names like "Operations" and "Financials." Each one felt like a locked door, and she was a thief with no map.

Her pulse quickened as she opened the first folder. It contained dossiers—profiles of their targets, complete with photos, schedules, and grim notations about their "neutralization." Bella's stomach turned, but she forced herself to keep scrolling.

As she delved deeper, the patterns began to emerge, stark and undeniable. These weren't just corrupt politicians or dangerous operatives. Some of them were pawns, small-time players who held little real power. Yet their deaths had shifted fortunes, paved the way for promotions, and cleared paths for figures she didn't recognize—figures tied to a shadowy network of names that meant nothing to her but clearly meant everything to someone else.

One file in particular stopped her cold. A woman in her late forties, smiling in her headshot, her eyes kind but sharp. Dr. Eliza Hartwell. Bella recognized her from the Prague mission. The dossier painted her as a pharmaceutical executive profiting from corrupt drug trials, but buried in the correspondence was something else entirely: emails between Hartwell and a whistleblower.

The whistleblower had been silenced, Bella realized, just weeks before their team had been sent after Hartwell. The so-called "evidence" against Hartwell had been planted, and the real purpose of the mission was clear: Hartwell's research had threatened someone's billion-dollar empire.

Bella leaned back in the chair, her breath shallow. The edges of the room seemed to close in, the walls pressing tighter with every revelation.

They weren't dismantling a broken system. They were fortifying it for someone else.

The realization hit her like a punch to the gut. Marco hadn't just known—he'd orchestrated it. His carefully worded justifications, his fiery speeches about justice and revolution—they were all lies.

The weight of it all crushed down on her chest as she stared at the laptop screen, the cold glow illuminating the tears threatening to spill from her eyes.

"Bella?"

The sound of Marco's voice shattered the silence, low and laced with sleep. She froze, her heart pounding so loudly she was sure he could hear it.

"What are you doing?"

He stood in the doorway, his frame backlit by the faint light from the hall. His hair was mussed, his jaw shadowed with stubble, but his eyes were sharp, calculating. The warmth she usually found there was gone, replaced with something cold.

"I couldn't sleep," she said, her voice surprisingly steady despite the storm raging inside her. "Thought I'd catch up on some reports."

His gaze flicked to the laptop, then back to her. "At three in the morning?"

She forced a smile, closing the laptop slowly. "Couldn't shake the adrenaline from Prague."

He stepped closer, the air between them tightening with tension. "Adrenaline doesn't keep you up," he said softly. "Guilt does."

Bella's breath hitched, but she held his gaze. "Maybe you should ask yourself what's keeping you up, Marco."

For a moment, the room was silent except for the distant crash of the waves. Marco's eyes searched hers, and she saw a flicker of something—doubt, regret, or maybe just the realization that she wasn't the woman he thought she was anymore.

"I hope you know what you're doing," he said finally, his voice low, almost a whisper. Then he turned and walked away, leaving her alone with the weight of what she'd uncovered.

As the door clicked shut behind him, Bella exhaled shakily. Her fingers grazed the laptop once more before she closed it, locking the secrets back inside.

She didn't know what her next move was, but one thing was certain—she could no longer trust Marco. And if she wasn't careful, she might not live long enough to regret it.

Bella stepped back into the bedroom, the soft click of the door punctuating the tension that had been hanging in the air for hours. Marco sat on the edge of the bed, his posture rigid, his dark eyes searching her as if she held the answers to every question they'd ever asked each other. His jaw was tight, a storm brewing behind his usually composed exterior.

"I thought you'd left," Marco's voice was rough, like gravel scraping against skin. The faintest tremor in his words betrayed the vulnerability he fought so hard to conceal.

Bella paused at the threshold, the weight of the moment sinking in her chest. The coldness of the hardwood floor beneath her bare feet felt like a cruel reminder of the chasm that had grown between them. She swallowed, fighting the tightness in her throat. "I couldn't sleep," she murmured, her voice a fragile whisper, betraying more than just her insomnia.

He rose to his feet in one swift movement, his presence overwhelming. Marco closed the distance between them with an urgency that made her breath catch. His hands, large and steady, landed on her shoulders, gripping her as though she might slip through his fingers. He looked at her with a raw intensity, the walls he'd carefully constructed crumbling in front of her eyes. "Talk to me, Bella. Whatever's going on, we can fix it."

Bella felt the pull of his sincerity, the strength that had always been a part of him, but there was something else there too—something darker, something more dangerous. She searched his eyes, seeing the man she had once trusted with her life, the one who had challenged her, fought beside her, and whispered promises of a future together. But beneath the surface, there were cracks—deep, jagged fissures that she wasn't sure she could ignore any longer.

"I'm scared," she confessed, the words tumbling out before she could stop them. Her voice cracked, barely a whisper. "Not of the missions, or the danger. But of what we're becoming."

Marco's grip on her tightened, and his voice dropped to a near-whisper, raw with emotion. "You think I don't feel the same?" His hands slid down to her arms, the heat of his touch searing into her skin.

"Every time I send you into the line of fire, Bella, I think about what I'd do if I lost you. And every time you doubt me, I think about how close I am to losing you anyway."

Her breath hitched, and a tear slipped from her eye before she could stop it. She wiped it away angrily, but the truth of it hit her like a sledgehammer. She wanted so desperately to believe him, to believe in the future they'd planned, in the safety of his arms. But the files. The evidence. The things she'd seen, the things she hadn't been able to unsee.

"Then give me a reason to stay," she whispered, her voice breaking. She reached up, her hands trembling as they cupped his face. "Tell me we're not just pawns in someone else's game."

His eyes softened, and for a moment, the hardness, the ruthless edge that had defined him over the past few days, seemed to fade. His thumb brushed away the remaining tear on her cheek, his touch gentle. "You're not a pawn, Bella. You're my partner. My equal. Everything I've done, I've done for us—for the world we're trying to fix."

She wanted to believe him. She wanted to let herself be swept up in his conviction, to drown her doubts in the heat of his kiss. But something deep inside her was screaming, a warning she couldn't ignore.

She's slipping away.

The thought came unbidden, a cold truth she couldn't shake. The walls between them were closing in, but it wasn't the mission that was driving them apart. It was the man standing before her.

Marco's lips crashed against hers before she could voice another word. It was desperate, heated—his kiss pulling her in like gravity. She responded with equal fervor, her hands threading through his hair, her body pressing against him as though she were drowning and he was the only lifeline she had left. But even as the passion surged between them, even as her heart raced with the fire of his touch, the doubt lingered.

When they finally broke apart, her chest rose and fell, breathless and unsettled. His hands remained on her, grounding her, but the weight of the moment was suffocating. She couldn't ignore it anymore.

Bella stared past him, her eyes focused on the window. Through the pane, she could see the reflection of their figures—tangled together, but separate in a way that felt like a cruel irony. Outside, the night was still, a stark contrast to the storm inside her. The city sounds below were muffled by the thick walls, but the tension in the room was deafening.

Is our love enough to hold us together? The thought spiraled in her mind, like a broken record repeating over and over. She wanted to believe it. She wanted to believe that they could weather the storm— that the bond they shared was unbreakable. But as the moonlight filtered through the curtains, casting long shadows across the room, Bella wondered if their love was the very thing pulling them apart.

Because in this world we've created, she thought

bitterly, love is a luxury. And it's one we might not be able to afford.

She closed her eyes for a moment, taking a deep breath as Marco's arms tightened around her. His warmth was the only thing anchoring her to the present, but even that was beginning to feel like a trap.

CHAPTER 30: INTO THE SHADOWS

The night hummed with a tension that seemed to seep through the streets, wrapping the city in a shroud of uneasy anticipation. The European skyline glittered under a blanket of stars, but below, the air was thick with the heavy pulse of the metropolis—cars speeding along the rain-slicked streets, the hum of distant conversations spilling out of cafés. Yet, amidst the noise, there was only silence between Bella and Marco.

They moved through the crowd like shadows, their bodies slipping between pedestrians with practiced ease. Marco's presence was an anchor at her side, the warmth of him a reminder of everything that had brought them to this moment. Her heartbeat quickened, the familiar rush of adrenaline filling her veins, mixing with the excitement of the final mission that loomed before them.

"We've crossed the line one too many times, Bella," Marco's voice was low, his tone laced with a rare seriousness. "This is the last one. After this, we're done. No more running. No more games."

Bella's eyes flickered to his, the flicker of their past—their triumphs and their betrayals—reflected in his gaze. The city stretched out before them, a labyrinth of possibility, but it was the gleaming tower that held their focus. The tech billionaire's empire, towering above them like a monolith to greed, was their target. A symbol of everything they'd fought against. And this mission... it wasn't just the end of the road. It was the end of everything that had come before.

She tightened her grip on the bag at her side, the weight of the tools inside comforting in its familiarity. "We've been in deeper than this," she replied, her voice a cool mask, but her heart was another story. "It's just one more. One last job, and then we walk away. You, me... no more shadows."

Marco's jaw tightened as he looked at her, his face softening for a split second before it hardened again. "You think it's that simple?" His voice dropped, his eyes flicking over the crowd, scanning the faces that passed by. "I can't lose you, Bella. Not like this. Not when we've come this far."

Bella felt a sharp pang in her chest at his words, but she pushed it away. This was what they were, what they'd chosen. The world they'd built together was one of shadows and half-truths, and it was all they had left. "We're too far gone for goodbyes, Marco," she said quietly, the weight of it sinking in as they reached the base of the towering structure. "No turning back."

The skyscraper loomed before them, sleek and imperious. A technological fortress, wrapped in glass and steel, rising against the night like a defiant statement of power. At its pinnacle was their target— the billionaire who'd funded Dusker Corporation's most dangerous projects, the mastermind behind the chaos that threatened to tear the world apart.

Bella's pulse quickened. This was it. The last mission. No more. No more doubts. She glanced at Marco again, catching the flicker of fear buried deep beneath his steely resolve.

"Northwest entrance," Marco's voice was steady through the earpiece, but there was a crack in it that Bella could hear, like a thread holding him together. "Two guards out front, four in the lobby. Cameras synced to the Advanced-System. You've got thirty seconds to bypass them before the loop resets."

"Piece of cake," Bella replied, her fingers already moving to adjust her equipment. The tools were an extension of herself now—every piece vital, every step calculated.

Marco's voice was sharp, a hint of frustration seeping through. "Don't get cocky."

Bella's lips thinned. "I'm not. You need to stop treating me like a rookie, Marco." But she bit back the rest of her words, unwilling to let their bickering derail the mission. The tension between them had been building for days now. Their arguments, the cracks in their relationship—each one adding weight to the burden they carried. The mission, the target, the stakes... it was all leading them to this single, pivotal moment.

She squared her shoulders, pushing the doubts aside. She had one job: get inside. Once they were in, the clock would start ticking. Every move would have to be perfect.

The guards at the northwest entrance barely glanced at her as she walked past. Her heart was steady, but her mind raced as she slipped into a side corridor. The cool air of the building wrapped around her like a shroud, the sharp scent of metal and glass mingling with the faintest trace of something artificial—slick, polished, controlled.

At the access panel, her fingers flew over the keypad, entering the sequence without hesitation. The lock clicked open, and she stepped inside, disappearing into the belly of the beast.

The hallway gleamed under harsh fluorescent lights, sterile and uninviting. The Advanced-System hummed faintly, a low thrum that was the heartbeat of the building. It knew everything, saw everything. Bella's pulse quickened, but she kept her breathing steady, hands calm as she reached for the disruptor device Marco had designed. A small, sleek tool capable of scrambling the building's security feeds for a brief window—a window that would give them the precious seconds they needed to bypass the cameras and reach the elevator.

"Loop starting now," Marco's voice crackled in her ear. "Twenty-eight seconds."

The countdown echoed in her head as her hands worked with practiced precision. The disruptor beeped quietly, a reminder that the clock was ticking. Each second felt like an eternity, but Bella's training kicked in, her body moving with the fluidity of a machine built for this very moment.

"Done," she whispered into the silence, slipping the device back into her bag with a quiet sense of satisfaction.

"Good," Marco's voice was steady now, the tension of their earlier exchange melting into something more focused. "Head to the elevator. I'll meet you on the thirty-fourth floor."

As she moved toward the elevator, a strange sense of finality washed over her. There was no more running from the truth. No more pretending. The man she loved—and feared—was standing by her side, but for how much longer? The walls were closing in. This was it. The final countdown. She didn't know if they'd make it out alive, or if this would be the mission that broke them.

But she couldn't stop now. She couldn't go back.

And as the elevator doors closed behind her, her thoughts were consumed by the chilling reality of what they were about to do—and the man she was about to destroy.

∞

Wagner's office was a cathedral of excess—chrome, glass, and shadow. The sprawling walls were lined with abstract sculptures, oil paintings that probably cost more than entire neighborhoods, and rare wood furniture polished to an unnatural gleam. The floor-to-ceiling windows presented a panoramic view of the city that made Bella feel small, as if the entire skyline was watching her, judging her.

He sat at his desk like a king in his throne, fingers dancing across a holographic screen that glowed with the data of his empire. He didn't look up, even when the door slid open with a sound too faint to be called a creak but loud enough for Bella's pulse to leap.

"Mr. Wagner," Marco's voice cut through the air, low and commanding.

Wagner didn't flinch—he simply froze, then looked up, eyes narrowing as he took in the sight of Marco's weapon, sleek and deadly. Fear flickered in his eyes for only a heartbeat, and then the practiced calm of a man who had never feared death settled into his features.

"How many times have I heard this before?" Wagner's voice was smooth, like honey, but with a bitter aftertaste. "How many people have tried to kill me? Do you know? It never works out the way they think it will."

Marco's grip tightened on the gun. "This time, it will." His voice was cold as ice, but the edge in his tone was unmistakable.

Bella stood beside Marco, her fingers resting lightly on the cold metal of her own weapon. But her hand felt like it belonged to someone else. Marco's presence was a furnace beside her, the heat of his resolve scorching her skin. But her own heart—a traitor—was hesitating, pulling her in another direction, towards something else, something she couldn't quite define.

Wagner leaned back in his chair, the soft creak of leather filling the space between them. "You won't change anything by killing me. Someone else will rise. You'll keep killing, keep chasing shadows, and nothing will ever really change."

His words weren't empty. Bella felt their weight settle over her like a heavy fog. He was right, wasn't he? The cycle wouldn't stop. It had never stopped.

Marco's voice snapped her from her reverie. "Bella, do it." His command was sharp, desperate even. He had never sounded so cold, so certain.

Bella felt the metallic tang of fear on her tongue, and for the briefest of moments, her finger tightened around the grip of her gun. The impulse was there, raw, dangerous. But then doubt crept in, insidious, like a poison that she couldn't quite expel.

"This isn't justice," Bella said, the words leaving her throat before she even realized she'd spoken them. Her voice was rough, a mixture of frustration and something far darker. "It's vengeance."

Marco's eyes flared, the fire in them burning

hotter. "This man funded Dusker Corporation, Bella. He's the reason so many innocent lives were destroyed. You think leaving him alive is justice?" His voice rose, jagged with emotion.

Bella met his gaze, the two of them locked in a silent battle, each understanding the stakes in a way that no one else could. But she felt the weight of his words, the truth buried deep in them, and still, something inside her rebelled.

"Killing him won't bring them back, Marco," she said quietly, her heart squeezing. "It won't change anything. We're just feeding the cycle."

Marco's expression darkened, his knuckles turning white around the gun. "This is the only way, Bella." His jaw was clenched so tight she could hear the muscles grinding beneath his skin.

Bella's breath caught as she stepped between Marco and Wagner, the space between them narrowing until it was suffocating, like being trapped inside a vacuum. The air was thick with tension—dangerous, like a storm waiting to break.

"I can't do it," she whispered, barely audible.

Marco's jaw worked, his gaze piercing, flickering between her and Wagner. There was a moment of hesitation, an almost imperceptible shudder in the space between them. And then, with an effort that seemed to physically cost him, he lowered the gun. His breath was ragged, the anger in his eyes replaced with something deeper, darker. Something Bella couldn't place.

"You're making a mistake," he said, the words a venomous hiss, but there was something in his voice that made her heart ache. It wasn't anger anymore. It was regret, disappointment.

"Maybe," Bella replied softly, her voice trembling under the weight of the decision. "But I have to live with it."

She turned to Wagner then, her eyes hardening as she stared him down. "The authorities will deal with you. If they don't, I'll make sure you never forget this moment."

Wagner's smirk faltered just slightly, his composure slipping for the first time. He leaned forward, the hint of a challenge in his gaze, but the laughter had died from his voice.

"You think you're saving anyone?" he asked, his tone sharp with derision.

Bella's fingers twitched on the gun, but she didn't raise it. She simply stepped away from the ledge, her eyes never leaving his. She had made her choice. She had drawn the line in the sand, and she wasn't about to cross it.

"We'll see," she said, her voice low and controlled.

The silence that followed was thick, heavy, suffocating. Bella felt Marco's eyes burning into the side of her head, but she didn't flinch.

Wagner stared at them, his face unreadable, but Bella could feel the fury radiating off him. He knew this was far from over, and so did she.

But for now, it was done.

Marco didn't speak. His silence was deafening, suffused with unspoken words.

She wasn't sure if she had done the right thing. All she knew was that she couldn't be the one to kill this man. Not like this.

And for the first time in a long time, Bella wondered if the shadows they were chasing would ever truly let them go.

The room felt suffocating, like a pressure cooker about to explode. Marco's rage crackled in the air like static, raw and unrestrained, as he stood just inches from her, the gun still gripped tightly in his hand.

"You've crossed the line, Bella," Marco's voice was low, deadly. He didn't raise his weapon again, but his fury was evident in every rigid muscle of his body. "You betrayed me. After everything we've been through, you turn your back on me?"

Bella's pulse hammered in her ears, the heat of Marco's anger making the room feel like it was closing in, but it wasn't just the fury she felt—there was something darker, something that tasted of betrayal, too. She had never been more uncertain in her life, but she refused to back down.

"Marco, I didn't…" She tried to find the words, but they stuck in her throat. "I couldn't kill him. Not like this."

Marco's gaze flicked to her, and in that instant, she saw the familiar darkness—a deep well of emotion, one she had once believed she could understand. The weight of their shared past was there, between them, but so were the new, jagged edges of their fractured relationship.

"Do you think you can just walk away from this?" Marco's voice dropped to a soft growl. "Do you think there's a way out?"

Bella's grip tightened on her weapon, but her finger hovered over the trigger, her entire body trembling with indecision. She could hear Marco's breathing, shallow and fast, as if his pulse were a ticking clock counting down to a moment she wasn't sure she was ready for.

"I love you, Bella," Marco said suddenly, his voice raw and vulnerable, the words slipping from his lips as if he was trying to claw his way back into her heart. "I always have. And I always will. Don't you see? We're meant to do this together. You and me—this world, this life, this chaos... we make it ours. We can't just walk away from it."

His words hit her like a storm, pulling her into the undertow of everything they had been. Her thoughts raced, but in the midst of it, something in her chest cracked, leaving her exposed, raw. She had always believed in him, in them. But now... she wasn't so sure.

As Marco took a slow, deliberate step toward her, his hand brushing the edge of his coat, Bella's breath hitched. He was reaching for something—the knife—hidden beneath his jacket. The gleam of steel reflected the harsh light of the room, and in that instant, Bella knew what he intended.

"No," she whispered, a shudder of disbelief running through her. "Marco—don't..."

But it was too late.

In a split second, he made the motion to grab it, and Bella's instincts screamed at her. Without thinking, she pivoted, the weight of the weapon in her hands pushing her into action. Her heart thundered as she aimed it at Marco, her finger tense on the trigger, the cold metal of the gun now in perfect alignment with his chest.

The world seemed to slow down, and for a brief moment, Bella was suspended in time. Every decision, every misstep, flashing before her eyes. She wasn't sure if she could do this. She wasn't sure if she should do this.

Her vision blurred with the tears that pricked the corners of her eyes. "I… I can't do it, Marco. I can't. Not like this. I can't…"

Marco's face twisted, caught between defiance and a vulnerability she hadn't seen before. His hand had barely grasped the handle of the blade when—

A sharp crack of gunfire shattered the tension.

Bella's body jerked in shock, the sound ringing in her ears, before she realized what had happened. Marco staggered back, his hand flying to his side, blood seeping through his fingers. He let out a strangled gasp, his face pale, eyes wide with the shock of the sudden betrayal.

Wagner had pulled the trigger.

Before Bella could react, Wagner moved with

lethal precision, his pistol trained on her. The barrel of the gun gleamed in the low light, steady and cold.

"Step away from him," Wagner commanded, his voice devoid of emotion. "Don't make this worse."

Bella's hands shook as she lowered her gun, the sudden numbness in her limbs making it hard to breathe. She looked at Marco, at the blood spreading across his shirt, and something inside her shattered.

"I saved your life," Bella said, her voice barely a whisper, but the words carried weight. "I did. You wouldn't be standing here if I hadn't stepped in. If I hadn't..."

Wagner's gaze flickered between Bella and Marco, but the gun never wavered from her face. "I don't need your salvation," he spat. "You get out of here. Before I change my mind."

Bella's breath hitched as the air between them thickened. She had saved Wagner's life, but the exchange had cost her something far more precious— Marco. And she knew, deep down, that this was far from over. She couldn't leave him like this, not after everything they'd been through.

But the tension in Wagner's eyes told her the truth she'd already realized—she had no choice but to walk away.

With a final glance at Marco, who was crumpling to the ground, Bella nodded slowly. The door to Wagner's office loomed ahead, and she moved towards it, each step feeling like the last thread of her resolve slipping away.

She wasn't sure where she was going, or what she was doing. But as the door clicked shut behind her, she understood one thing: the story wasn't finished yet.

And neither was she.

EPILOGUE: THE SHADOWED PATH

The café was a pocket of quiet amidst the restless energy of Paris, its dim light casting warm hues on weathered wooden tables and chipped porcelain cups. Faint jazz played from a vintage radio perched precariously on a high shelf, its notes winding through the air like smoke. The air was infused with the sharp tang of espresso and the buttery richness of croissants, a combination that clung to Bella's senses as she sat in the corner booth. Her position was deliberate—back to the wall, facing the room. Old habits died hard.

On the battered oak table before her, a tablet glowed faintly, illuminating the headline that had demanded her attention: Tech Billionaire Arrested in Global Corruption Scandal.

Her finger hovered over the screen as she scrolled,

absorbing every detail with quiet intensity. Bank records, encrypted communications, witness testimonies—it was all there, an unyielding chain of evidence that had torn apart an empire.

The files she'd left behind had been the spark.

She let out a measured breath, her chest rising and falling as a flicker of relief threaded through her. Not victory—she wasn't foolish enough to think it was ever that simple—but a step closer to the justice she sought. It was enough, for now.

She lifted her coffee cup, its chipped rim brushing her lips, and took a sip. The bitter warmth grounded her, yet her thoughts strayed into a colder place. Marco.

Weeks had passed since Prague—since the mission had crumbled under the weight of betrayal and choices they couldn't take back. She had vanished after that final, fateful night.

No texts. No cryptic notes scrawled in his neat handwriting and left in her path. No sudden, shadowed appearances.

Because Marco was gone for good.

Her chest tightened as the thought solidified. Dead or merely gone, it hardly mattered. His absence cut the same. Bella stared into the dark liquid swirling in her cup, the memories swirling even darker.

Marco had been a contradiction—a storm of vengeance cloaked in charm, capable of both violence and tenderness. He had been her partner, her lover, her mirror. And she had broken that fragile bond when she hesitated, when she had chosen to let mercy temper justice.

Her fingers grazed the edge of the tablet. She replayed the moments that had defined them: Marco's fervent monologues about dismantling the powerful, his rare, unguarded laughter, the electric charge in the air whenever they were near each other.

She didn't regret him.

But she couldn't regret leaving him, either.

The scrape of footsteps broke her reverie, and the waiter appeared, clearing away her empty cup with a perfunctory nod. He left behind a folded receipt on the edge of the table.

Bella's gaze caught on it as she reached for her coat. The neat handwriting on the back of the receipt stopped her cold.

The shadows are yours now.

Her pulse surged, the café's warmth turning stifling. She scanned the room, her eyes darting from one face to the next. The barista wiping down the counter, the elderly couple near the window, the student hunched over a textbook. None of them were him.

But she felt it—a presence, unseen but undeniable.

The faintest breath of cold air seeped through the cracks of the café's old windowpanes, curling around her neck like a ghost's whisper.

For a fleeting moment, she could imagine Marco watching from the periphery, his gaze a blend of challenge and unspoken goodbye.

But she knew better.

Marco didn't linger.

Sliding the receipt into her pocket, Bella rose, her movements slow and deliberate as she draped her scarf around her neck. The café's cozy cocoon unraveled the moment she stepped outside, the sharp winter air stealing her breath and replacing it with crisp clarity.

The streets of Paris were alive—tourists with maps clutched in gloved hands, locals bustling with purpose, the metallic clang of bicycle bells cutting through bursts of laughter. Bella melded into the crowd with practiced ease, her steps steady and unhurried.

The receipt burned in her pocket, its words echoing in her mind.

The shadows are yours now.

She let the corners of her lips tilt upward, a bittersweet smile pulling at her features. The shadows had always been hers. Marco had only taught her how to wield them.

As the crowd thickened, she disappeared into its ebb and flow, her figure blending seamlessly into the city's pulse. And for the first time, she felt untethered—not to Marco, not to her past, not even to the shadows that had once threatened to swallow her whole.

Her voice, soft yet resolute, whispered through her thoughts, a mantra she carried with her as she vanished into the chaos of the city.

"The shadows will always call to me. But now, I choose

when to answer."
And just like that, she was gone.

THE END

ABOUT THE AUTHOR

Kathy Winslower is a gifted storyteller with a passion for weaving tales of love, resilience, and triumph. With her captivating narratives and richly drawn characters, she takes readers on unforgettable journeys that explore the depths of human emotions and the power of love to transform lives.

Born with an insatiable curiosity and a love for words, Kathy began her writing journey at a young age, filling countless notebooks with her imaginative stories. As she grew older, her passion for storytelling only deepened, leading her to pursue a career as a novelist.

Drawing inspiration from her own experiences and the world around her, Kathy's writing is characterized by its heartfelt authenticity and emotional depth. She skillfully delves into the complexities of relationships, capturing the raw and tender moments that shape her characters' lives.

When she's not immersed in her writing, Kathy can be found exploring nature, seeking inspiration from the beauty of the world around her. She believes that every moment holds the potential for a story, and it is her mission to capture those moments and share them with her reader.